This book is dedicated to my wonderful wife, Yvonne,
who always believes in and supports me.

THE JOURNEY CONTINUES

BOOK 2 OF THE SHAMRA

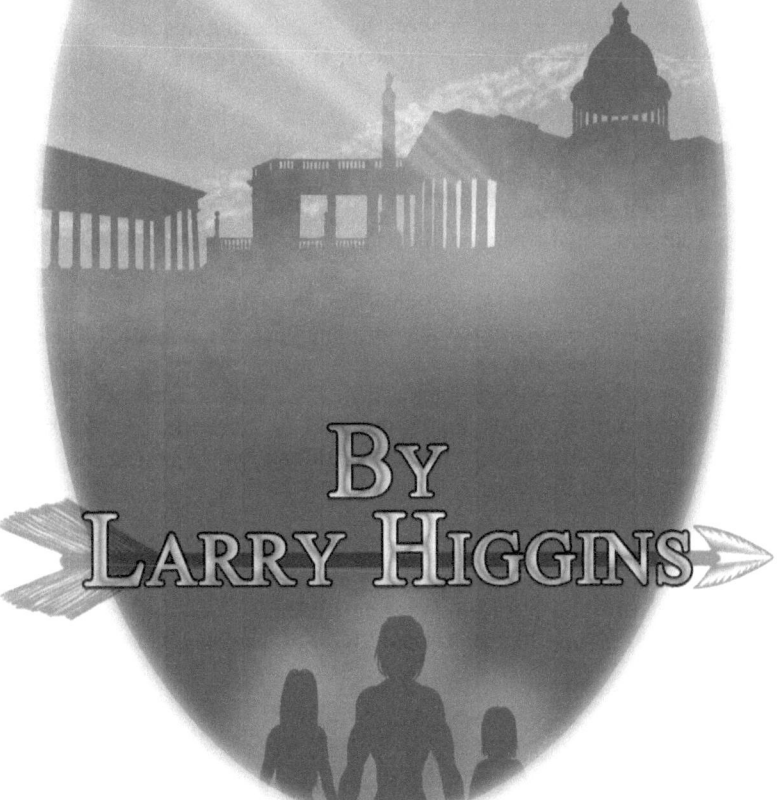

BY
LARRY HIGGINS

Published by True Beginnings Publishing.
Copyright by Larry Higgins, 2017.

Edited, Formatted, and all artwork by True Beginnings Publishing.
This Work is Copyright Protected under US Copyright Law.

ISBN-13: 978-1947082984
ISBN-10: 1947082981

Ordering Information:
To order additional copies of this book, please visit Amazon.

The Journey Continues, Book 2 of The Shamra.
© Larry Higgins.
First Printing 2017.
Printed in the United States of America.

Table of Contents

Epilogue - Infinitim

Chapter 1
Lasapulis

Darkness. And pain. So very little light and the pain was excruciating.

"I must pray through this," thought Togorasom. He actually winced and shed tears at the spiritual pressure he was encountering. He knew he was in the presence of demonic spirits, but he had not been able to cast them out. "If my people are to go into this dark place, I must make a way for them."

For three days and nights, he had sat in his chamber and prayed, eating and sleeping little. Finally, in desperation at the lack of power he was experiencing, he had taken a horse and moved his 'temple' to a little tent on the road near the border of Lasapulis. Here, for two more days, he had still made no progress in his battle against the spiritual forces surrounding the area. Terrible things awaited this kingdom's future if the Rasomites were unable to deliver their message there. The destruction of Lasapulis was imminent.

"Oh! My God!" he yelled out for the hundredth time in desperation. "At least allow me to see the wickedness I am battling against. I battle an unknown enemy with unsharpened weapons. Give me my sword and show me my foe, but don't leave me in the battlefield alone."

He sat quietly for a moment and wiped his tears on his sleeve.

"Then, I suppose," he said, getting up and moving out of his tent, "if I cannot wage war in a spiritual place, I must go and encounter them face to face and battle them in the world."

"Everything is nearly ready, your Highness. Every chariot has been prepared, the horses are exercised and groomed, every weapon has been cleaned and sharpened. The army has been given one day and tomorrow shall be well rested and prepared to go."

King Lasapulis gritted his teeth and forced a breath of air through his mouth. He closed his eyes tightly and yawned. Opening his eyes again, he looked upon his Head of Court and, after they had stared into each other's eyes for a moment, the King spoke.

"Eamo, I am very tired. It is hard for me to even think straight. We have endured all the suffering of preparation these last few days. I almost believe the prelude to war is more taxing than the battle itself. You have stood beside me well, better than any, and I am thankful for this. When the slaughter is over, you shall be richly rewarded."

"Hee hee," chuckled the old man. "Sire, I have served you well all these years in court as I served your father in the field and your grandfather as a lowly cupbearer. All I desire is a quiet place to wait and die."

Eamo leaned his slight frame against the side of the King's throne with no apology. His collar-length whitened hair was damp, what little hair was left, as he had just doused his head with cold water to keep alert just a bit longer. He no longer wore the brightly-colored garments of a man of war. He no longer required it, as these were merely the show of attention needed to gather a measure of respect. He wore a simple white tunic, and his gold chain amulet depicting his duty. He had already earned everyone's respect.

The King leaned back on his immense chair and, therefore, his head was closer to his old friend and aide.

"You talk of death and, so soon, so many shall die and there are no alternatives. If we do not go to war, we shall be overrun from two sides."

Since youth, the King had constantly prepared for or engaged in battle. Not yet thirty, he preferred to dress sparsely to show his rippling muscular frame. His black hair was cropped close and held securely with a bright red headband. On his feet were elaborate leather sandals with laces trailing up and down his bulky legs.

"I agree, Lord. Though, I would so prefer to live in peace. I suppose, not yet. After your victory, there shall be a measure of peace, no doubt."

"Have the prophets retired?" asked the King of his astrologers.

"They have conferred all the day, Lord. The elders are resting as they have reached some agreement. Martin and his young flock are about."

"Why him?" asked the King gloomily. "He is a crackpot. A charlatan."

"Beware, sire, as he commands spirits we know little of. If he is angered…"

"If he is angered, I shall have him thrown into the canal to cool off. Show him in."

Eamo hobbled out of the room, as one leg was lame, to go in search of the astrologers. Lasapulis leaned against the back of his throne and closed his eyes. He was securely asleep when he was suddenly startled by the entrance of a great din of noise.

The courtroom was instantly filled with naked dancing women and minstrels with tambourines and rattles. Following closely behind this racket was Martin and three other young astrologers. The music lasted for only a few moments as the King roared, "Get those skinny wenches out of here and send these court fools to a tavern where their stupid merry-making will be better accepted."

Eamo entered lastly. "I told them, your Majesty. I said you were weary and needed only a few words of confidence."

Martin, arms crossed in front of him, stepped forward. He was quite dashing in his brightly-colored outfit that looked to the King as more of a silken quilt a clown would wear than something a spiritual leader would be seen in. Though still a young man, he was adept if not at commanding spiritual forces, at least at commanding attention.

"Your most excellent Highness, Lord of all. Great King Lasapulis the third…"

"Stow it and talk to me," asked the King.

"Here is the meaning behind these things, oh most excellent of kings." Lasapulis rolled his eyes skyward. "I am dressed to celebrate your victory. The white in my outfit is the purity of character which you possess. The black is to demonstrate your great power and leadership as you trample the enemy underfoot. The red is their blood. The blue is the sign of everlasting peace and joy, which you shall be the author of. I come prepared to dance and sing the conquest the stars have given you. It is confirmed, Lord. The spirits of your predecessors have confirmed the truth revealed in the stars of an awesome victory over our enemies. Soon, we shall be dancing in their courts, Lord."

"My heart says we shall be dancing at the end of a pole. Each of Marsa and Lusack have us outnumbered three to one. How, one who has never seen war, do you suppose we shall even harm them?"

"Ah, this is where the spirits themselves shall destroy the enemies in their hearts and give you the victory. Your majesty, you are correct, I do not know war. That is your territory to command. I command the spirits."

Eamo came forward. "You have just told us the spirits have confirmed the victory. Did you command them to do this?"

"That's enough," said the King. "I had hoped, foolishly, that you would give me some word or action that would encourage me..."

Martin interrupted him as he fell to one knee. "Your Majesty. This is what I desire. I have already told you the spirits of the dead and the stars in heaven have given you victory. Is there any greater?"

"Yes," came the voice of a young child no one had seen enter.

The King bolted to his feet. "Who are you, infiltrator, and how did you get in here?"

The boy addressed himself to the astrologer. "The God who owns the spirits of the dead and who created the very stars in the sky is greater."

"What God is this?" Martin shot back. "Who commands the spirits or stars, but those appointed over them?"

"You would have no power at all, except that God granted it to you," said Togorasom.

"No one anywhere grants me anything. I assumed power myself through my own knowledge."

"Thank you for not blaming God for your foolishness. He is disgraced."

"I will not stand for this," yelled Martin as he hurled himself at the boy.

"See that you do not touch him, Martin! I like his cockiness. Young boy, come here," beckoned the King.

The astrologer stood back as Togorasom went before the King. Stopping a few paces before him, the boy knelt and then proned himself in front of the throne. Lasapulis was shocked and delighted.

"Arise, young man."

"Sir, I serve no man and I worship no man, only God. However, I do honor this position He felt you were worthy of serving in."

"I accept the honor you bestow upon me and am curious at this humility before your gods."

"No gods, sir, but one God almighty. He is maker of Heaven and earth and all things living and dead. It is God who controls all things."

"You are a mere babe," snapped Martin from behind as Togorasom stood up. "What do you know of such things?"

Ignoring him, he looked the King in the face. "Your Majesty, unless you deny all this," he waved at the astrologers who were now huddled together, "and seek peace and seek God, you shall die within a year."

Everyone gasped. The King covered his face with his hands and the room was silent for several seconds, which seemed like hours. He looked up and slowly raised himself to his feet.

"Eamo," he said quietly to his aide, "the astrologers have said I shall be victorious. Inside of me, my heart is wrenched between the fear of another battle and the necessity of protecting the kingdom. Now, this child has given me one year to live. If I die performing my duty, as my father and grandfather, then so be it. I leave for the front immediately. There are things I must do if we are to win."

Martin was filled with glee and began dancing in circles and clapping his hands. His friends also expressed great delight. Togorasom, now ignored, stood off to the side and shook his head. Lasapulis slowly walked out of the courtroom followed by all, except the boy, now nearly forgotten.

It was bad enough to travel in the night to the plains where the battle would take place, but now it had begun to rain.

The King had placed his entire army on quarters the day prior to the battle. He would not disturb that ruling because of his decision to leave a day early. Once arriving at the front line, he would inspect the border guards and then rest as he awaited the troops.

His heart was heavy with the fear of this battle. It was greater than that frightening elation he had felt at other battles. He was afraid of death and capitulation in spite of the prophecies of victory that had been announced. He was weary of war. His kingdom was torn apart with all sorts of beliefs, none were of much value. They all spoke of spirits and gods. Everyone had a prophecy.

But who was this grey-skinned boy? He also offered a prophecy, but he spoke of some very strange things. And he spoke with such authority.

"Eamo," said Togorasom, "what hour is it?"

"It is just after midnight."

"I can see a great spiritual fire burning in the sky over the city. Eamo, Satan wants this place eagerly. His servants, the King's people, are working diligently to create his kingdom and they don't even know it. The evil one will gobble them up."

"What do you see in the future?"

"The future is in the hands of King Lasapulis. He can either create peace and good will or he can turn this city into a desert."

"What must be done?"

"If I tell you, will you believe?"

"I will believe as much as I am able," replied Eamo.

"Today, King Lasapulis shall die."

"Oh no!" Eamo bolted to his feet. "How can this be? Earlier, you told him he had one year."

"What were my words? I told him he would die, not in a year, but within a year."

Eamo fell to his knees. "Then, we are lost. If the King dies, the kingdom will fall apart. We will be overrun by our enemies, if you are correct. What must be done?"

"The King must repent and he must obey God."

"It's not the King's fault," sighed Eamo. "He is a good man. The people are foolish and disrespectful."

"If the King cannot command his own people, how is he good? He must repent."

"But he has done nothing wrong," said Eamo angrily.

"His kingdom is about to be overrun by two armies he already has treaties with, satanic forces are holding their power over him, his own astrologers have turned him into a laughingstock and his army is asleep, but you tell me he has done nothing wrong. Some say you are the wisest man in all of Lasapulis, so how can you be such a fool?"

"I cannot believe I am up at this ungodly hour arguing with a mere child."

"Eamo, believe me, this is a very godly hour."

"All of these things you have mentioned are not the King's responsibility…"

"Then what," shouted the boy as he leapt up, "is the King's responsibility? Who is in charge here? Has this King abdicated all of his responsibility and gone to fight a war alone?"

"The army shall follow him tomorrow."

"To their deaths. And that will be his legacy. He will be remembered as the king who led his people to their deaths. And you shall be a slave to a king you don't even know."

"I would never be a slave. I would take my own life first."

"And this is to be your legacy?"

"What," asked Eamo as he sat down, "must be done?"

"As I said, the King must repent and obey God."

There came the sound of galloping hooves near the tent. King Lasapulis was startled from his sleep and lay, half-awake on his cot, knowing he would soon be disturbed by the messenger. He could hear the voices outside in the rain, but was unable to distinguish what was said. He wondered if it always rained the night before an important battle.

"Your majesty!" He was startled awake again. "There is an urgent message from Eamo." The guard stood in the light of the candle. He was dripping wet and attempted with great difficulty to stop shaking and stuttering due to the cold. Another man came from behind him and fell to one knee.

"I am sorry to disturb your sleep, sir. There is a message from Eamo."

The King sat up and pulled the blanket up around him. "What is the message?"

"The Head of Court requires your immediate presence in your court."

"Man," he said angrily, "it is a two hour ride back to Lasapulis and I have no more but come from there an hour ago. What does he want?"

"I do not know, sir. However, I have never seen him shed such tears and carry on so."

"I do not know what could have brought this about. Everyone! Out! I need a few moments alone." The tent was instantly cleared out and it was silent but for the sound of the rain beating against the tent.

He sat against the side of the tent and wondered what could have driven Eamo to call him home with such urgency. He wondered if he even had the strength to respond. He fell back to sleep. He slept but for a few moments and woke up with a start, knowing he must return home immediately.

"Saddle my horse!" he yelled from the doorway. "I must return home."

A few minutes later, Lasapulis reemerged from his tent, tightening the belt of his overcoat.

"Your majesty," spoke his officer, stepping forward. "It is, of course, your decision. However, I feel it would be very unwise to return home at this time. The Marsian troops shall be here before nightfall again and our troops will be here in the morning, only a very few hours away. They need your leadership. We can wage war, but it is your very presence that will create the desire to win."

"Are you calling me a deserter?" the King snapped back at him.

The officer fell to his knees. "Never would I denounce a leader as yourself. As I said, it is your decision. I never meant to imply anything like fear or desertion."

"Therefore, I depart at the call of Eamo. He would not call me if it were foolish."

"Then, I beg you, sir. What would you have us do?"

"Delay. The Marsian troops will not attack until we are prepared, as they know they have the upper hand. Chiam would not waste an opportunity to disgrace me in combat against him. I leave everything else in your capable hands until the staff officers arrive from Lasapulis." Looking about, he called out, "Where is my escort?"

In response, two horses appeared from behind the tents and stopped next to the King and his officer. The rider on one horse led the other. Lasapulis quickly mounted and, with no further comment, they departed.

Often on the evening before a contest or an expected battle, many of the women came together in what had once been a stadium for winter sports. They would first feed and entertain their men and, finally, pack overnight essentials and move out of the house with the rest of the household. This would allow their warrior complete silence and rest and the opportunity to prepare for the following day.

Daedena, sister of King Lasapulis and wife of Madaro, a high ranking officer, also spent these evenings out of the house though they had no children to disturb her husband's slumber. Daedena was unable to bear children. She spent these nights with the other women to show them her disregard for rank. However, her true reason was to be able to assist in caring for their children.

It was not possible to get any true sleep at the stadium due to the racket of the wailing children and uneasy mothers. They looked forward to the following day when there would be no men present to care for and they could relax in their own homes.

Daedena had finally found a place to relax with a crying child nestled in her arms. She had crept away to a small room apart from the main room, occupied by only one other woman and a nursing baby. Once the baby she held had settled down and she had propped up several pillows around it, she covered herself with a blanket and lay down.

She hated Madaro. It was not enough that the man's entire life was consumed with battlefields. Her home had become a battlefield. He constantly insulted her and nagged at her. His names for her due to her barrenness drove her into deep depression. There was no one to turn to. She trusted no one. If only she could talk to someone who cared.

"You can talk to God Almighty. He understands," came a whisper near her.

She snapped to a sitting position. It was dark, but she could identify the shape of a young woman kneeling at her feet. The woman was scantily clad, but Daedena could make out no clear features as the only light was the torch in the hallway behind the woman.

"What did you say?" asked Daedena.

"I said you can trust God. It is possible to pour out your heart to him and, perhaps, he shall hear your requests."

"What requests?"

"That you may have children and your husband will love you. As a matter of fact, God is already answering your prayers."

Daedena was startled by the strange woman's forwardness.

Too tired to move, she lay there gazing at this person, hoping to discern who she could be.

"You do not know me, but we have been sent here to minister," said Crazon. "Follow me!" She arose and walked out of the room.

Daedena looked across the room in the darkness to where the other woman lay with her child. The other woman obediently held her baby to her chest and followed Crazon.

When Daedena had left the great chamber, there had been some measure of solemnity. However, upon returning, all had changed. A crowd was gathering on one end of the room where several strange-looking women were organizing some sort of speech. Many women, some of Lasapulis and some of the strangers, were proceeding about the room lighting the torches. In the new light, Daedena could more easily distinguish these strange women. They looked like female warriors, however, none of them bore any weapons. She had never seen anyone like these people before. Everything about them amazed her; their dress, their skin-tone, their authority.

Then, the woman Daedena had followed began speaking. "Women of Lasapulis! Listen to these words and save your lives. I know you do not know who we are or why we are here. We are here to teach you a lesson from our own experience. We are of the remnant of the great nation of the Rasomites." A ripple of understanding went through the room. Their reputation had preceded them. "Once, we were a mighty and proud nation. Our kingdom spread across the mountains and plains and seasides. But, we battled spiritual enemies with weapons made of metal and wood and, alas, have been reduced to but a remnant of what we were. There are not many, besides us. All of our husbands are dead because they went to war against impossible odds and forgot to let God lead them. We have no real home. Our cities were destroyed. Many of our children were sacrificed to evil gods of fire."

Several of the women at this point began weeping and some cried out.

"I know," Crazon said more quietly with tears in her eyes. "Evil followers of these same pitiless gods have begun their disgusting deeds in your own homes. Do you love your children and your men? I know you do! Then it's up to you to save their lives and their souls. Or, one day, you will be even as us or our slain relatives. You will be childless and alone. But, God has granted us the grace to begin again. Do you want to begin again, yourselves?"

One part of Daedena hated her husband. He was selfish, brutal and unloving. However, her compassionate side loved him with abandon. "Yes! I want to begin again!" she yelled out. "What must we do?" She forced herself to the front after handing the baby to its mother.

When she reached Crazon, the Rasomite woman took the lady's hand. "Are you truly ready to change? To renounce your own sins and mistakes and, then, to obey God?"

"I believe we have no hope against the armies of Marsa led by Chiam and Lusack led by Amelian. I believe, unless something changes what appears to be inevitable, in a few days, we shall all be destroyed. I will do anything."

"Then," replied Crazon, "it is up to we women to stop this war. Even capitulation is greater than death, but if you all trust God, you will not see capitulation, but victory."

Daedena wiped her tears away and turned to the women. "Women of Lasapulis. Sisters. We must turn the tide and not allow this butchery to go on any longer. Unless you are fools, I want you to follow my lead and renounce the spiritual lies you have filled your lives with. Let us be ministered to by these women. We know they speak the truth, for many of us have heard the rumors and gossip concerning these people. Now, they have come to save us."

Suddenly, a commotion broke out near the back of the crowd and one woman seemed to lose control of herself. First, she spun around several times and fell. After arising, she ran a few paces across the room and flung herself into a large stone column. She backed off, blood streaming from her forehead, and prepared to ram herself once again. She was restrained by many of her neighbors, but the woman began biting and kicking to free herself. Then, one of the Rasomite women arrived on the scene.

"Many of you restrain her!" said Ambacudadi.

"She is a witch," one of the other women said.

"She is possessed." She placed the palms of her hands on the woman's forehead. "In the name of the almighty God, I command you to come out of her and seek her no more! My Lord, fill her with your spirit."

The woman released a painful screech, and her entire body

began quivering. In a few seconds, she fell to the floor and lay still.

One of the women spoke up. "Is she still alive?"

As though in response, the woman opened her eyes and quietly looked about and, then, began crying. Ambacudadi explained to her that the demon no longer owned her but, now, she was filled with the spirit of God.

Suddenly, another incident took place. "I know why you have come to us," yelled a woman, pointing her finger at Crazon. "You would destroy us and take the little we have left." Her face was horribly disfigured and, when she spoke, it was with an ugly, rasping voice.

Crazon approached her. "Are you also filled with an ugly spirit? In the name of God…"

The woman cut her off and fell back, pointing her finger at her. "Don't you try using that God stuff on me. I'm just fine."

"Then," replied Crazon, looking on her as though she herself had been possessed, "since you won't come out of her, I command that you be shut up for a time so that we are able to minister in this place."

The woman opened her mouth. Her face took on an appearance of horror as she tried to speak, but could only release gurglings and silent babblings.

"Women," she said to everyone, "we have little time as, within two hours, the sun will be rising and your men shall be preparing for battle. You must minister to each other's needs, and we shall roam among you to help you. God has placed his hold on this building and Satan shall have no power here."

If anyone had been roaming the streets at this early hour and gone near the stadium, they would have trembled at the noise emanating from within. Women cried out and fainted from the release of so many burdens. These neighbors knew full well what the needs were for each other and worked quickly to strengthen themselves for the next task.

"Eamo!" King Lasapulis called out as he walked through the courtyard entering the palace. Two guards appeared in the doorway. "Go get the Head of Court!" he yelled out at them as he passed. He entered the throne room. Togorasom entered from another door.

"Your Majesty. I anticipated your return."

"You!" snapped the King. "Where is Eamo?"

"Resting comfortably. He was very weary, so I allowed that he would get some sleep."

"Who do you think you are?" the King demanded. "What right do you have coming in here and acting like an impudent child? I could have you…"

"Why have you disobeyed God?"

"Huh?"

The boy glared at the man. "Why have you allowed that Satan should have a foothold in this place?"

"What are you talking about?"

"Why do you allow the children of Lasapulis to feed the evil flames of death and allow your very servants to treat you like a laughing stock?"

"Where are my guards?" he demanded, nervously looking around.

"Your guards are performing their duty of keeping people out of this place. But, they have neglected their duty of keeping the evil one away from you."

Lasapulis looked around for an object to strike the boy with. Finding nothing, he approached him with one arm raised. As he swung, the boy spoke. "It is said of one who strikes a Rasomite, he shall die. Would you like to challenge that prophecy?"

The King stopped. He stood with his mouth hanging open in awe. His angry appearance changed suddenly to a peaceful expression. "That's it. I should have known. Now, I don't know what to do."

"Would you like to subdue your enemies?"

"I would like peace at any cost," he responded thoughtfully. "But, I fear, it cannot be obtained."

"It is a difficult thing to obtain peace by waging war."

"But, I don't know what else to do." He shook his head in confusion. "I feel my choices are enslavement or death. I am so very tired, I cannot even think properly."

"Sit in your throne and I will show you how to subdue your enemies."

Togorasom led the King to his seat. The moment he was seated, he fell asleep.

"Your Majesty," called Eamo from across the room. "Oh, my God. I fear the worst." He hurried across the room and shook the King by the shoulders. Lasapulis started to slump over as his friend nervously watched him and held him. The King groggily came around.

"Eamo, my good servant. What is wrong? You look so afraid."

He lowered his head in shame and mumbled. "I was afraid you had died." He looked up at the King's questioning expression.

"Why would I die? I feel so…so rested and so at peace. What time is it?"

"The sun is up, barely. Where is…where is…" Eamo looked about the room.

"The boy? A most interesting situation. I must have slept for hours, but it does not seem as I slept at all. It was as though I were awake and asleep at once. Do you understand?"

"I'm sorry, I do not, your Majesty."

The King thought for a moment. "The boy led me to this seat, and I know I must have fallen into sleep but…we still conversed. The things he told me…Oh…And I feel so refreshed. Are you certain the sun has only just come up? I feel as though I have slept for hours."

"What did he tell you as you slept, sire?"

"I can't say I enjoyed it at all at first but…On the one hand, I feel my mind is as clear as ever and, on the other hand, I feel as though I am under a powerful elixir."

"Did he speak of his God?"

"Oh, yes. He told me the truth about his God and he told me of the lies which have permeated this once-noble city. He told me who I can trust and who to be wary of and, he told me who must die."

"What must be done, your Majesty?"

"Prepare for Chiam of Marsa to enter the city with his troops."

"Your Majesty," he said in alarm. "Will there be time?"

"I am already prepared."

"But the army?" queried Eamo. "I should forewarn them."

"Let them rest. I can handle this. Praise God!"

Madaro stirred in his sleep, rolling over and burying his face in the pillows. Then, he realized there was a commotion in the street beneath his room. He sat up and stretched and yawned. After a few moments, he stood up and walked to the shutter, opening it slowly. It was just becoming light. He had never seen such an amount of activity in the streets so early in the day. He opened the window and called out to a man as he ran past

"You there! What is this confusion so early in the streets?"

The man looked up and called back. "There has been a very strange turn of events, Master. It seems that Chiam is marching on the city and King Lasapulis, who earlier left for the plains, has returned to await Chiam's arrival."

Madaro slammed the window shut. He wondered if this battle would be fought in the streets of Lasapulis, perhaps on his very doorstep. He quickly pulled on his clothing and armor. He then reached for his sword. It was not at his bedside. He looked on the floor behind the bed. He cursed himself as he ran down the stairs to his den that he should be so stupid as to leave it anywhere but at his side. He looked over the mantle to where his dueling swords should have been. The pair of swords were missing. He distinctly remembered leaving his long-bladed knife in its sheath on his belt hanging from a chair. It was gone. Had some enemy come before Chiam and stripped him of his weaponry? He imagined the whole army being defenseless and then realized how absurd that idea was. No enemy could be so efficient as to disarm an entire city in its slumber. He was taken as a victim of a very cruel joke. Then, he heard a noise in the front room and proceeded to investigate instantly.

It was merely his wife, Daedena. She sat in a rocker, moving slowly back and forth. The look on her face was peaceful enough, but tears began to form as she spoke.

"Good morning, husband. Did you rest well?"

"Wife!" he snapped. "Have you perpetrated this ridiculous joke? Give me my sword?"

"I cannot, Madaro. I have taken your swords, knives, clubs and all and thrown them into the canal."

He was shocked. For a moment, he could not believe his ears.

"I do not want you to die," she said.

Then he came at her, grabbing her shoulders and pulling her from the chair. He drew his fist back and was prepared to release a blow to her face.

"Madaro! Don't! Please, listen to me." He waited. "I love you. Why must you always fight?" Then, struggling with her new faith, she added, "I'm going to have a baby." She burst into tears and clutched Madaro, resting her head on his shoulder. He could think of no other way to respond, so he held her.

The ladies had worked quickly in the pre-dawn and moved through their homes, ridding them of as many objects of war as they could lay their hands on. They also woke their neighbors and, through the power of Daedena's name and the grace of God, had acted upon the household of every officer who held a title and the bulk of the entire army. The realization in every house did not go so smoothly as that of Madaro. There were some very angry men. Wisely, most of the women had retreated back to the stadium to wait out their husband's wrath.

When Chiam entered the city a few hours later, there was no one who could make a defense. Mostly, the families stood by the sides of the road and hailed him and his men with greetings. Once entering the city and receiving the unexpected welcome, Chiam and his staff stopped and consulted. He issued an order for his army to retreat to beyond the city borders, whereas he and his staff rode on with a contingent of about forty men.

King Chiam was nearly old enough to be King Lasapulis' father. He also considerably outweighed his favorite enemy. He had seen war all of his life. To him, war was a game; a gruesome game, but just a game.

In his game, Lasapulis was merely a player. Chiam made the rules. He had thoroughly expected to meet Lasapulis' army that morning on the plain, roughed them up soundly, and driven them home for the winter after extracting some type of tribute. When he arrived and found no enemy, he at first believed Lasapulis had withdrawn from fear and, therefore, decided to hound him at his doorstep. He had never seen a trick like the one he felt was being played on him today. However, he allowed Lasapulis to make the moves for a time.

Even before Chiam arrived at the palace, another messenger arrived. "Your Majesty," he called out in great haste as he was hurriedly ushered in. "We are in deep despair. A second army approaches." This messenger had nearly ran into the one announcing the defenselessness of the city. "Amelian and his hordes have been sighted approaching the perimeters. Whatever are we to do?"

The King looked at the charcoal-grey boy standing alongside him and smiled. "Then our plan is working out. How pleased I am."

"Your Highness," said the messenger, "I do not understand."

"It is not necessary you understand. You have delivered your message. You may depart."

Another announcement was made that King Chiam was within sight of the palace and directions were given that he should be fed and entertained.

"I have never seen the King behave this way," one man whispered. "Can he not tell that the end is near?"

"I do not understand," agreed another. "We are about to be clawed to death by two invading armies and he serves breakfast to our enemy."

"Hmph!" shrugged the other. "Amelian shall be here for lunch."

"What does he mean to do?"

As though in answer, the King arose, strode across the room, paused and began speaking as he wandered about.

"Good folk of Lasapulis, it is well time we learn how to live in peace with our neighbors. What do you think? Are we able to destroy an army three times our size today and another tomorrow? What foolishness. These people are our friends and neighbors and we should seek to live in peace with them."

"Your Majesty," one of his advisors said, stepping forward. "We are under attack by two great armies. Militarily, we are weak and, economically, we are suffering. How can you suggest we should live in peace?"

The King walked back to his throne, picked up his sword which lay alongside, and handed it to the man. "Now, brave soul, you are armed. Go to battle."

The man stood still, letting the sword hang limply at his side.

He glanced back and forth nervously. "Your Majesty, you have made your point. I am too weak to defeat the enemy."

The King turned and proceeded back to his seat, when suddenly a great noise arose outside of the courtroom and Martin pranced in.

"What is the meaning of this?" Martin demanded.

All were silent for a moment, until Togorasom spoke up. "Let me remind you, your Majesty, yesterday this one sent you to your death."

"You little ninny!" bellowed Martin. "I have a mind to have you whipped. All night, I have been dealing in spiritual realms. I have conjured up great armies of spiritual forces. I have soaked the very walls of this city in the blood of departed souls. You!" he pointed at the King, "You must immediately lead the army out of here to meet Chiam in battle or this good city will come under attack."

King Lasapulis took a deep breath, shook his head and looked at the advisor he had just conversed with. He looked back at the astrologer. "Martin," he said quietly. "Go to Hell." He looked back at his advisor and, as the King began shaking from anger, ordered him, "Kill him!"

"Yes, your majesty," was the response.

"No!" screamed the astrologer out of fear. He turned to flee, but the way was barred by onlookers. The great sword crashed into his skull and killed him instantly. There was silence in the hall.

The assailant looked plaintively at the King. "I have never killed a man, sire."

"Then," said the King compassionately, "you are still innocent of killing a man, as this one was a demon." He arose from his seat and, to everyone's surprise, embraced the man who stood sobbing until the corpse could be removed. As he walked back to his seat, he turned back to the small crowd before him. "Today is a new day. We have won the war."

"Your Majesty!" spoke up one of his advisors. The King nodded for him to continue. "Lasapulis is surrounded on two sides by armies considerably outnumbering ourselves. How is it you can say we have won the war?"

King Lasapulis turned and walked a few steps toward his throne and then looked back at the man. He laughed. "That wasn't the war I was referring to." He returned to his seat.

"Eamo!" he called out.

The elderly man had been alongside the throne and stood up abruptly at the sound of his name. "Yes, your Majesty."

"Clear the court! I need time to speak to you and the boy."

The banqueting room of King Lasapulis was busy with activity that morning. When the servants were told of their King's peaceful intentions and their need to feed Chiam, a tremendous feast was prepared. Chiam still had not seen King Lasapulis, but was told of his peaceful intentions and admired him for it.

He was prepared for peace. His ancestors had engaged in war for as long as they had history. There had been thousands of Marsian men lost in battle during that time. But never once had there been a lasting peace. He longed for a day away from battle. He had proudly sired six beautiful boys and several girls. All but one of the boys had been lost to war or assassins. Two of his young girls had even been killed due to war. Whenever he closed his eyes, he saw bloodshed. Whenever he dreamed, he saw war. He was sick at the thought of going through it one more time. In all the years of battle and the great loss, his prosperity and borders remained about the same. It all seemed so purposeless. He was prepared for peace, regardless of the consequences. He was tired of the game.

The spy ducked behind a rock when he heard the sound of horses. He knew, however, he had been seen.

"You there," called out the leader of the sentinels. "Come out of there and make yourself known."

The beggarly-looking man slowly stood up and, head hanging, limped forward.

"Who are you?" demanded the rider who had called him, "and state your purpose quickly!"

"I...I am merely a poor farmer who tries to scratch out an existence in the fields."

"I see," said the man, stroking his beard. "Tell me, what charge would you assess for two barrels of oats to feed our horses?"

"Oats?" asked the man, bewildered. "I...I don't know."

"You are not a farmer; you are a liar! Slay him!" he called to an archer astride the horse next to him.

19

"No...no...I am a spy for your King. Please," he fell to his knees, "you must protect me."

"How can I believe you," he said, looking the beggar up and down. "You look as though you had crawled out from under a rock. Prove who you are."

Slowly, the spy reached into his shirt and pulled out a gold medallion with Amelian's seal on it.

After a moment of considering, the leader spoke up again. "And from where did you steal this?"

The man stood up indigently. "I am under the employ of your leader, Amelian. I am debtor only to him and not to the likes of you. I insist I be conveyed to his Majesty, immediately."

"If you have any information, it can be passed on to me. I will see he hears it in due time."

"The news I have is urgent, and I report only to the King. Give me a horse and I will travel alone."

"If you want to see Amelian, you must get past me first," he said as he swung from his horse. He handed the reins to another rider and stated. "I'll have me a little fun." He laughed as he approached the spy.

"You waste my time!" yelled the spy, taking a swing at him and missing.

The sentinel almost casually swung his right arm and slammed his fist against the spy's face, knocking him over and bringing a round of laughter from his comrades.

"You are quite a fighter, beggar. Let me teach you a few moves." He struck the toe of his boot into the ground and filled the man's eyes and open mouth with dust.

The spy vainly attempted to clear his vision. As he stood up, the sentinel kicked him in the shoulder and sent him reeling with pain to the ground.

"Okay," the spy said, lifting his hand. "I've had enough. However, I still must deliver my message."

"I have already explained to you that if you have a word, simply tell me and I shall pass it on." He punched him square in the jaw and prepared to let him feel the toe of his boot in his groin. Suddenly, he saw a flash before him and was unable to move his foot. He had been pinned to the ground by an arrow, which had pierced his boot, but not shed any blood. He looked up and saw five women perched upon the rocks with bows drawn. He prepared to react.

"Stay completely calm," called out Zoana, "or you shall all die."

Struggling to release the earth's grasp on his foot, he spoke up. "There be eight of us and only five of you. You are at a disadvantage."

"You, great fool, are pinned to the ground. Therefore, there are seven of you. If you had been more observant, you would notice we are all aimed at you. I order you to drop your weapons."

He nodded his head and the bows, arrows, and knives slowly began falling to the ground.

"Get off your horses!"

After the men had dismounted, Zoana, her compatriots, and the spy mounted up and took off towards Amelian's main phalanx.

"I am totally in your debt," explained the spy. "What is your name?"

"I am called Zoana. And you?"

"Badaa," he answered. "At least, on this trip. I am a spy and have many names."

The front lines of the rabble called an army, of the nonexistent nation of Lusack, were actually a considerable distance away. Amelian's 'nation' was no more than a collection of vagabonds, barbarians and thieves.

At the slow trot the Rasomites and their companion moved along at, it was another thirty minutes before they sighted anyone else. They rode mostly in silence, but their minds, especially that of Badaa, were filled with thoughts. He bore allegiance only to himself. His past and nationality changed according to his needs. His trade included not only spy, but also terrorist and assassin. He could have easily overcome the sentinel and got his own way with the others.

"How will we handle this situation?" he asked as they approached the horsemen. "I am not used to traveling in a company."

"I shall handle this," Zoana stated. She raised one hand simultaneously as a greeting to those approaching and as a sign to halt.

"You are riding upon a stolen horse, woman," called the sentinel when he was within distance. "What is your business?"

"This gentleman," she motioned to Badaa, "is an agent of King

Amelian of Lusack. We are escorting him to his Majesty with important information concerning Lasapulis. Will you help us?"

"I need some sort of proof?" he demanded.

Immediately, Badaa withdrew the medallion.

"That is sufficient," he nodded. "However, you must surrender your weapons."

"I am no fool," said Zoana. "I shall make but one demand on you. If you will not aid us in reaching your King then, at least, get out of the way."

One of the others laughed. "Lovely and with spirit, as well."

He never saw the woman riding behind Zoana string, draw, and fire an arrow, as she moved so quickly. The shaft seemed to appear in one of the pouches hanging from the horse.

"No more banter!" stated Zoana. "You cannot afford the price. Which way to the King."

Suddenly, the leader to whom Zoana spoke, had a complete change of countenance. He first apologized for acting in such an arrogant manner. He then carefully directed that they should proceed straight beyond their present position for another fifteen minutes. They would arrive at the main body of the army. He removed from his neck another medallion, similar to the one Badaa wore, and tossed it to Zoana.

"Wear this," he said, "and tell them, 'the sun is red'. That is the code. Also, say that Ambulan, the sentinel, has given you passage."

"Thank you," she responded as she placed the chain over her neck.

"Idiots," said Badaa to Zoana after they had rode on a bit. "That is the same foolish code they used in their last campaign."

"Then," asked Zoana, "what do you suppose if they had changed it and Ambulan was lying?"

He stared at her nervously. "We would be falling into a trap. What can we do?"

"Do not fear, there is no danger. Watch and stay near," Zoana replied. "And remain silent. I have no need for their foolish codes."

Before they could see Amelian's army, they could hear the dull roar of the movement of horses and men and the clatter of weaponry. As they approached the front line, the women held their heads high. However, Badaa slunk down on the horse as though that would make him less obvious. As they passed the first line of troops, the soldiers gazed at them dumbly. However, they were mostly ignored. As they moved along, some of those on horseback waved or nodded greetings at them, which were mostly ignored by the women. Badaa studied the stern look of Zoana's features as they passed line after line of troops headed in the opposite direction. No one made any attempt to stop them or even mounted an objection.

"What is going on?" he asked quietly.

Zoana placed her forefinger to her lips to indicate he should remain silent. "The Spirit of God has gone on before us to make a safe passage." He was still terrified of being stopped and was awed by the authoritative way Zoana led them through. Before he realized it, they came to a halt before a team of rather brilliantly-dressed steeds. Badaa suddenly realized he was in the presence of Amelian and flung himself off of his horse to the ground in a kneeling position.

"Your Majesty," Zoana explained, pointing to the spy, "I deliver your servant." She looked down at the quivering Badaa. "Tell your King the truth of what is happening in Lasapulis."

Amelian was not a King, at all, except he claimed to be. His choice of weapons was anything that would kill. His hair and beard were long and dirty. The chopped-up fur pieces he used for clothing made him look like the uncivilized barbarian he was. His only weapon was a hand-ax. However, those in his attendance carried every imaginable type of fighting device.

Badaa had carefully constructed his story in his mind, long ago, in order to baffle Amelian into an unprovoked attack in which he hoped to profit. Now, he could not remember what he had intended to say.

"Speak up, man!" ordered one of Amelian's aides. "The King tires of watching you grovel."

The spy looked up at the heavily-armored men poised above him, and his heart filled with terror as he continued to search for the right words. He sat on the ground with his mouth hanging open stupidly.

"I am afraid," Zoana interjected, "that your servant has been very rudely treated by some of your own people, and this has left him in some shock." She looked at Badaa. "Do you want me to explain?"

"No! No!" he insisted as he saw any hope of receiving a prize drifting away. "I can speak on my own." He stood up, took a deep breath, and proceeded. "Early this morning, Chiam arrived in

Lasapulis with his forces. It appears King Lasapulis will begin making overtures of peace or an alliance with him. He has, at least, exhibited no movement of war against him. Lasapulis' army has been disarmed. Let me also say that there are even stranger things than this going on in the city."

"Such as..." asked Amelian, leaning forward in his saddle.

"He has slain one of his astrologers and has taken as an advisor and, I mock you not, a young boy scarcely old enough to dress himself in the morning."

"But what does all this mean," asked Amelian, shaking his head in confusion.

"I do not know, sire, except that it represents a very great change in the thinking of these people."

"And what," Amelian stopped as he reasoned at the wisdom of his next question. "What do you advise?"

"One more thing, Highness. I believe King Lasapulis also desires you to be a guest in his city."

"A guest? Ha ha," he laughed. "I would rather level the city."

"Sire," noted one of those alongside him, "consider the strategy of attacking with the troops of Marsa engaged in treaty. They would outnumber us five to one. It would not be an easy victory."

Amelian stroked his beard. "Hmm," he thought aloud. "What should be done?" He looked at Badaa and said, "you have done well. Go and take your ease while I consider this." He looked at Zoana. "And who are these?"

"We are but servants, sir. Will we be of any further use to you?"

"Ah, then you are for hire?" He seemed interested.

"No, sir. We work for no man."

"Then, you work for yourselves?'

"No, sir. We do not serve ourselves."

He glanced around nervously at his men. "I do not understand. If you are not for hire and you work for no man and you do not serve yourselves, who is your master?"

"You are correct. We serve none of these. We serve one you do not know, even God."

"And who is this God?"

"If you would take the time, I am quite free to tell you of my God."

"Is your god of flesh or did you create your god with your own hands?"

"Can a god of flesh or of clay create the stars in the sky or cause the earth to shake free from its foundation?"

"If your god can create stars, he must be very powerful."

"My God created the very womb that bore you."

"I am a man of war. To me, the life of a horse is of the same value as that of a man. I am not a kind man, either. I have been called brawler, barbarian and animal. I'd as soon crush a man's skull and take his wife as to swat at a bug. But if your god is powerful, I must know of him. Will you teach me?"

"My God is not a plaything!" she snapped angrily. "Today, when you are routed from Lasapulis, perhaps you shall be more open minded."

Amelian nearly choked as he began a hideous laugh. "Go!" he finally screamed, "and tell Lasapulis I shall feed him to the dogs." He pointed his finger at Zoana. "When it is done, your skinny body will please whomever I decide to give it to."

Zoana pulled at the horse's mane, and she and her compatriots turned to go.

"Wait!" yelled Badaa as he clamored back onto his horse. "I'm going with you."

King Lasapulis sat in a small conference room with Eamo and Togorasom on either side. Both sat with eyes closed, one in prayer, one seeking rest. Lasapulis relaxed. In spite of the swirl of events and changes transpiring, he felt extremely confident. Confident, except when he allowed his mind to wander. Togorasom had filled his mind with the words to say and it all made great sense. However, when he began to recall the battle he had nearly faced or the anger which could, and certainly would, rise from Martin's death or the logic of listening to a child's advice, he began to feel nervous. However, he continued to follow through on Togorasom's advice. He wanted to let God use him. He wanted to do what he knew to be right. If he failed, he would lose everything but would still have no less than if he had taken another course of action. If he succeeded, he would gain everything.

There was a movement at the door and Chiam entered the room with a smile on his face. A few paces behind him was a young man, though only slightly younger than Lasapulis himself. The young man's blond hair was cropped off shaggily about halfway down his ears and above his collar in back. The ruddy appearance of his face showed he spent great amounts of time outside. He was clad in light, ornamental chain mail which was formed like a tunic and fell to just above his knees. His eyes quickly darted about the room as he absorbed his surroundings before taking a seat next to his father and opposite Lasapulis. Lasapulis knew this to be Chiam's sole surviving son, Pasca.

There were a few moments of quiet as the five gazed back and forth at each other. Chiam broke the silence.

"I have always felt the best way to start a good day was with a hearty breakfast. Don't you agree, Pasca?" He smiled at his son.

Pasca sat up straight and glared at his enemies. "A man needs good food to maintain his strength to be able to fight," he said coldly.

"And," continued Chiam, "it puts his mind at ease to allow him to grasp his surroundings with comprehension and not have to worry about a grumbling stomach. I don't believe we have met, son." He smiled at Togorasom.

The boy briefly introduced himself and went on. "In the midst of the sea, there were two great waves, which began to beat ferociously at each other. Until, alas, neither of the waves existed anymore. Near the shore erupted another great wave, and it beat against the rocks. Then came another and another and they continued to beat against the rocks until the rocks finally gave way and then there was a great peace upon the water."

"Then," asked Chiam of him, "are we coming ashore?"

"That is my prayer," interjected Lasapulis.

Pasca placed his hand on his father's sleeve and growled. "Outside of my door is the grave of one of my brothers. Throughout the Kingdom of Marsa are the tombstones of those slain in battle. I will never rest until they are avenged."

"And, allow me to ask," Lasapulis said to Chiam, "how are your wife and your lovely daughters?"

"I suppose they are fine."

Lasapulis nodded. "That is good. I have never been able to enjoy a home life or know the treasure of children as this fast-paced life has never allowed me to marry."

"You are breaking my heart!" snapped Pasca.

Chiam glared at his son. "Do you know how strongly I care for you? Can you not see you have an opportunity here to save your children's lives?"

"I have no children," he said sheepishly.

"Then allow me to negotiate the lives of my grandchildren," he said sternly.

"It is our hope," spoke up Eamo, "that we may negotiate our way to peace. What grandeur history would heap on the man who salvaged peace from the jaws of war."

Lasapulis smiled as his own words were spoken by his old friend.

"Our people want revenge!" yelled Pasca.

"Would your mother trade your life to avenge those of your dead brothers and sisters?" his father asked.

"I can see I am off by myself. Go forth then, Father, get your peace. I'll not stop you." Pasca sat back in his chair and stared off into a corner of the room.

After a few moments of quiet, Lasapulis spoke up. "I can appreciate the anger and sadness in your son's heart. I truly can for, you know, we also have not been free of the ravages of war here. Many lay buried. Our kingdom has also been stripped. The eyes of our women are empty as they contemplate seeing their brave men go forth one more time to challenge death. And for what purpose? To go forth again to avenge the last battle? It holds no promise at all. Our women have lost a great deal. We need to offer them more. I believe we can."

"Yesterday, when I left home," replied Chiam, "and bade farewell to my wife, I spoke, as it seemed, to a dead woman. She has gone beyond grief. I don't believe she is able to cry anymore. I don't believe she expects to see her son again." Pasca glanced at Chiam briefly and looked away. "I would like to be able to love my unborn grandchildren. Do you know," gazing toward the ceiling wonderingly, "there was once a beautiful garden that completely surrounded the palace. It's gone now. All weeds and debris. It should be so lovely to restore the garden and the walks."

"I would like to visit it when it is complete," said Lasapulis.

"Oh, you most assuredly shall," was the response. "What then is our agreement?"

"That we shall be as one. That whatever person raises his hand against either of us, the other shall speedily come to his rescue."

Lasapulis waited to let this sink in. "That we begin building each other up economically by making fair trade amongst us. Also, the people of Marsa and those of Lasapulis may freely live among each other."

"This is a very great plan," Chiam said, stroking his beard. "What do you have to offer as a pledge that these things will be?"

"That you shall leave a portion of the Marsian troops here to defend us and we shall also send a contingent with you as good faith we are together."

Chiam smiled and replied. "It seems, however, your army has a problem. It is quite toothless since the women took over."

"We shall overcome that. Silly women. We must fish these weapons out of the canals and clean them up a bit. Do you agree?"

Pasca turned about and caught Lasapulis' eye. "And what will be my position in this great plan of yours? I vowed I would not return home until this city was mine."

"Then," said Lasapulis, "if your father agrees, I want you to fulfill your vow. I propose you be the chief of the contingent which remains here until other arrangements can be made."

"I agree," replied Chiam, "but, this lad of mine can be a hot head. What can you offer to give him peace in his heart?"

"Peace in one's heart," said Togorasom, "is not granted by one's physical surroundings, but is a gift from God. If men seek God in their lives, they will be less concerned with running the lives of other men."

"What is God?" Pasca asked the boy. "And how can I know God?"

"If you stay here, you will know God," laughed Eamo. "For He shall find you."

There came a rap at the door and a messenger entered. "I apologize for this interruption, your Majesty, however an urgent situation has arisen."

"Speak on," said Lasapulis.

"That rogue, Amelian, has entered the city with his army in force and they are headed this way."

"Then," said Pasca with a smile, "I have a duty to do. I must defend my city." Before anyone could stop him, he was gone.

"What," asked Lasapulis quickly as he arose and prepared to leave, "has Amelian requested?"

"He has not slowed down to make any request, but is

overtaking the entire city by force. Sir," he said more quietly, "I don't need to remind you we have no defense."

"You have your allies," responded Chiam. "You have our full assistance. But there is little time. Before I could leave the city and return with a force, I am afraid Lusack would be very entrenched. Nonetheless, we shall do what we can."

The room quickly emptied out, leaving Togorasom alone. The young boy closed his eyes and leaned back in the chair saying aloud, "Father, why do they always forget you and me?" He began to pray.

Upon departing, Eamo and the two monarchs immediately noticed it was uncomfortably quiet in the streets. "Where has my son, Pasca, and the entourage gone?" Chiam asked of an unarmed guard left to watch the doors.

"Sire, he has taken them to meet Amelian."

"That is insane!" he shouted, whirling around and facing Lasapulis. "What can forty men do against so many? Why, they shall easily be outnumbered a hundred to one. They have no chance."

"Then you must return with your forces, and we shall try to hold them down," said Lasapulis as he signaled for horses.

"Yes, of course you are correct," he replied reluctantly.

In a few moments, the three had departed in opposite directions. Chiam promised to retain his army. Old Eamo and Lasapulis went in an attempt to raise the remnant of his own army. Lasapulis headed toward the center of town and raised an alarm of the danger of the invaders. Eamo was instructed to circle the palace on his horse and notify the palace guard, should they not have been informed. He disobeyed.

When Eamo arrived at the scene of the battle, he could see immediately who was gaining the upper hand. The unarmed citizens and troops of Lasapulis and the handful of battle-hardy, well-equipped officers who had accompanied Pasca were utilizing every tactic to contain the swarm which was overtaking the city.

Eamo easily penetrated to the front lines where the officers and Lusack were most heavily engaged. The old man had to hold his hand over his face to prevent his breathing the foul air. It smelled and even tasted of blood. Every man who arose to do battle was instantly pummeled to the ground. The only advantage offered to Pasca and his group was their superior position of being on horseback. Despite this advantage, it also made them better targets.

There was not a defender of the city who was under attack against fewer than ten of his competitors. It seemed hopeless. Eventually, Eamo was able to get alongside Pasca.

"Aye! Old friend!" Pasca yelled between sword thrusts at those around him. "This is no place for you..." His foot hit the chest of a charging soldier who fell and was trampled by the horse's hooves. "Best to return home!"

"I shall die before I see my home besieged!" Eamo called out. Unfortunately, the old statesman was not armed, at all.

It was becoming nearly impossible to contain the horses amid the foray and to keep their footing among the bodies which in some places were three deep.

Despite Eamo's age, he was still strong enough to engage one of Amelian's ruffians, and his sharp eye quickly found a weapon he could use in the form of a Lasapulian sword. Instantly, the old soldier felt thirty years younger. When the attack came, he was prepared. The barrel-chested lance-bearer of Lusack had expected no contest when he saw the old man wielding a sword. Eamo brought the sole of his boot down so hard upon the tip of the lance as it approached him, the man dropped the lance. He hesitated for a moment from the surprise of the old one's strength before he stooped to regain his lance. It was a moment long enough for Eamo's steed to step forward, bringing him close enough to the assailant that the tip of his sword was able to slash the man's neck. He stumbled backward and was lost in the dance of the horse's hooves.

Eamo and Pasca made a good team. Standing side-by-side upon their horses with their backs toward each other, it was impossible for a sword or lance to reach them. The battle was cut short, however, when Eamo felt Pasca first slump against him and then roll from his horse.

The old man instantly dismounted and straddled himself over the younger man. Grasping the shaft of the arrow in one hand, a short tug removed the deadly stinger. As if moved by an unknown force, he glanced upward to a balcony a few paces away through the angry melee and his eyes fell upon Amelian himself. The barbarian's ugly expression of laughter and his grasp upon the bow allowed Eamo to know from where the shaft had flown. Eamo had thrown down his sword when he dismounted and now sat unarmed, but for the broken arrow. He cast the arrow down and, standing to his feet, picked up the only weapon he could find, a cobblestone. Still, his body moved not under his control as energy flowed through his muscles. He launched his missile and Amelian realized, too late, how well-aimed it had been. The rock struck him in the side of his head.

Amelian tumbled to the ground and buried his head in his arms as he tried to subdue the pain.

Eamo still stood over Pasca, stunned that his wild aim had been so accurate. He was not able to consider this for long as he suddenly felt an excruciating pain in his throwing arm. Instinctively, he grabbed at the pain and realized he too had been hit with an arrow. Suddenly, the archers of Lusack let loose. Several of the shafts passed by, but one struck him in the chest, and that was all he felt. Before he hit the ground, his body was riddled with arrows.

Amelian raised himself to his feet, and his eyes beheld a horror. King Chiam's troops of Marsa on horseback were filling the streets. They had not yet reached his position. However, a giant cloud of dust spewed from behind Chiam, who was in the lead. Amelian could not discern the number of troops, but the clattering of the hooves and the dust told him of masses. With only seconds to react, he quickly called a retreat. Amelian's men caught sight of the defending army after he had. There was utter panic. They knew they would be no match for Chiam's superior skill and weaponry. For Amelian's men on foot, it was probably hopeless. They ran.

Even before Chiam could reach the battle line, the enemy was fleeing in terror. Each man desired to save his own life and cared little for how many of his comrades needed to be slain to get them out of his path. They began slaughtering their own men in their desperate charge out of the city.

Amelian was offered the backside of a horse with another rider and was able to escape. Still, he was baffled as to how the Marsian troops had been able to respond so quickly.

When Chiam saw his enemies flee, he brought his horse to a halt and watched them turn and run. He too was baffled, as he traveled alone. The Lord had deceived the barbarian troops of Lusack into seeing an army that was not actually there. It was only then he realized the devastation that had been brought upon his guard, led by Pasca, and the handful of locals who had been able to aid him. He quickly leaped from his horse and ran to his son's side.

"Father," rasped Pasca through blood-stained lips. Chiam fell over him, too stunned to weep. Pasca's lips quivered silently as he tried to speak. "I...I am sorry I have failed."

"You have not failed, my son. You have saved and obeyed." Chiam helped Pasca to a sitting position, so he could see the last of Lusack's departure.

The effort was too great for Pasca, though he felt relieved at the outcome. "Tell mother I love her," he whispered.

"You shall tell her of your heroism," Chiam replied. The younger man's expression did not change, and it was a few moments before Chiam realized his son was dead. He was suddenly filled with grief and crushed his son to his chest.

Another horseman arrived with a contingent of local troops. Lasapulis climbed down from his mount and slowly walked toward the grief-stricken King. Then, the pang of loss struck him when he saw slain Eamo crumbled in a bloody heap a few feet away and he went and held him.

"I...I couldn't leave my son," Chiam tried to explain between sobs. "I...I didn't know what to do."

Lasapulis pulled himself away from his bloody guide. There was much racing through his mind. He wanted to speak of the relationship of honor and disobedience. He thought of the intense bravery and selflessness the two kings had arrived too late to see and the devotion between these two slain men for each other who had always been enemies. It was almost inconceivable, though, to try to think of the future. He knew these two kingdoms were now linked in mutual carnage. His body shuddered as he attempted to form a complete thought. "All...dead..." was all that came from his quivering lips.

Togorasom looked up from the quiet corner from where his prayers had been ascending as the shadow of a man covered the doorway.

"You have done well, my son. You have been faithful."

"I have only been obedient," the boy replied, shaking his head and holding up his open palms. "God has done all the work."

"He loves your faithfulness," Anam said, helping him to his feet.

"The rest of the women? I have lost track," he said nervously.

"All are safe and within the city. It's fine," Anam reassured him.

"Father?" Togorasom asked as he closed his eyes thoughtfully. He looked at Anam. "Why did they have to die?" God had already revealed to him what had happened when the others had left.

"I don't know, son. Only God can answer that. The condition of Eamo's soul?"

"I ministered to him throughout the night. He knew God."

"And what of Chiam's son, Pasca?"

"That's what bothers me, Father. I do not know. Everything happened so quickly. I...I..."

"Hush," Anam said softly as the boy began crying. "You have done everything and more than what can be expected of you."

"But," he said, holding back the tears. "I so wanted to speak to him and now it's too late."

"You have said it exactly. It's too late. Your tears are well-founded, as we normally weep for ourselves when we feel empty. You weep from the doubt of his salvation. Son, always weep from this doubt and pray to God to be tireless."

They quietly left the room together.

In many ways, Lasapulis was the hardest city yet encountered by the Rasomites to deliver. The two demons of spiritism and hatred were difficult to subdue. Despite the desire of nearly everyone to entertain peace with Marsa, there was an attitude on both sides that the other should make the more generous moves. People were not completely prepared for the diplomacy Chiam and Lasapulis had engaged in or the friendship that developed after the assault. There were occasional outbursts of anger and violence that things were not right. Fortunately, there were many who strongly desired peace. Foremost among those proponents were the women of the elite in the army of Lasapulis. They were sick of death and an unknown future.

Unfortunately, many of these same women, as well as many other citizens, were also practicing various ungodly arts. Though Satan did not run rampant in the streets, as in times past, he was still lurking in the basements and gutters.

Quickly, the God of the Rasomites had taken hold of many.

But these people were young in their faith and of very little help to the thorough cleansing required. After several weeks of ministering to the people of both kingdoms, the Rasomites seemed to be at a standstill. There were nearly as many spiritual battles being lost as there were being won. As soon as it seemed like God had snatched up one more soul, another fell back to old habits of astrology and satanism.

Every day, many of the Rasomites would gather together to discuss the situation and pray over various concerns.

"There is a power at work here that we have not yet been able to grasp," said Anam. He was sitting in a lounge chair, leaning back with his weary eyes closed. If it had been silent for a few moments, he would have fallen to sleep. "I do not understand what is going wrong."

"Are we doing everything in our power to break through?" asked Sholemazar, one of the women.

Zoana spoke up. "We are beginning to lose control. We are weary as we have been battling so hard against these forces. If something does not change very soon, we will begin to lose this battle."

"What are we doing wrong?" shouted Anam in anguish, as he sat up quickly. "I don't know what we are doing wrong."

"There are too few of us and too many of them," said Bulshadi. "We cannot do it all."

"Then, what!" called out Anam. "I would to God that a cleansing would come upon this place."

Then all sat silent for a few moments and could hear the sound drift into the room of Ernie's flute. It was a pleasant sound and created a sense of peace to their anguish. The little ones were all sleeping soundly by this hour, thanks to Ernie's tenderness. There were things to be thankful for.

"How can we teach them the love we can give them through God when they are so entangled with obedience to their own master?" asked Paluqua. "There must be a way."

Anam sat down and stroked his chin thoughtfully. "When we were in Foramen, did we have friends?"

"Well, certainly," Paluqua asserted. "There were many good people there."

"Why were they good?" he asked. "What caused them to be seen as good?"

Crazon responded. "The people of Foramen were a confused bunch and their spiritual leadership was rotten, but they had an expectancy of salvation and their city was not wholly given to demons."

"And what of Aris-Akana?" he asked.

"Sinful and dark," one woman responded.

"Was it?" Anam queried her. "Yes, I suppose it was. Was it hopeless?"

Paluqua again saw what he wanted. "The people of Aris-Akana included many who had been schooled by the Mozanas. The leadership had only been interrupted briefly by the entrance of Pholipi, who we knew as Artero having been possessed by the devil. We were able to restore much that the people knew before these times."

"Where is the temple?" Anam asked.

"What temple?" asked Zoana. "There is no temple. But there are devilish altars in people's homes and, until recently, in the very palace itself."

"You don't understand," he said. "Where is the temple of God? Where do the people go to learn of God? Where can they say, 'this is God's house'?" He was being very adamant.

"Why," said Zoana, "there really is no place. We teach in the streets or, occasionally, in the palace. There is no center."

"These people are altogether unschooled in God. They have no temple of God. Until recently, they never even heard of God. What better payment can be expected, they have not made any investment. Where are their priests and spiritual leaders?"

Crazon acknowledged that there were no spiritual leaders in the city other than themselves. "We must pray that spiritual leaders be raised up among them and there must be a center of worship."

"Exactly," said Anam.

It was very dark and there was the clammy feeling of death hanging in the air. They had gathered in a place between the real world and the world being prepared for the dead.

"She is weak, I say, I can have her."

"She is quickly becoming a leader in the church," spoke the second spirit. "I can see her growing closer to God daily. Better to drop her and move onto a willing vessel."

"I tell you she is merely going through the motions of devotion. Inside, she is still a weak and crumbling mess. Give me more time."

"How much time? What will you do?"

The first considered, then spoke, though not with confidence. "I'm not certain. A few days, perhaps."

"There is not enough of us. Too many have been sent back. We need to find new flesh that will be willing to build the kingdom." He was growing angry. "Why do you insist upon tormenting this unwilling woman when there are others?"

"I want her. If I delivered her, master would be pleased. He would send me back for a greater prize. Perhaps, the King."

"I strongly urge you to return and gather your items and move out. Let her be. If you lose her to these Rasomites, I will not be able to turn the tide alone. There will be another revival and I fear losing the whole city. If you leave her be, it may come about at a later time we can come back."

"I am afraid if I leave her now, we shall lose her entirely."

"I can see there is no reasoning with you. If you lose her, you know the price?" the second spirit spoke with an air of authority.

The first spirit nodded his head silently and was gone.

"Wife of mine," called Madaro.

"Yes, Madaro," said Daedena, appearing in the doorway. She was still dressed in her housecoat, though it was late in the morning. Her fire-red hair, draped down over her housecoat and, by her standards, it was a mess. Sleepiness still grasped at her eyelids.

However, when her husband's eyes fell upon her, they saw a woman of great beauty. He loved when her beautiful hair hung down, rather than being put up as she usually wore it. His love for her had grown daily since the arrival of these new people. He had fervently accepted their God and confessed his foolishness concerning his unloving attitude before. As he gazed at her, speechless for a moment, he also saw the woman who was bearing his child and this caused a rush of satisfaction to overcome him. How he longed to take her now into his arms and cover her angelic face with kisses. However, he closed his eyes for a moment to remember what he had meant to say. He was already late to meet the King.

"I am leaving now. Your brother awaits me, and I am already running late for this appointment, which I cannot afford. Please, later come to the palace for the ceremony. Come whenever you wish, but I will send a messenger before we begin. Will you be all right?"

"Yes, Madaro." She nodded and then stood silently.

They had already discussed this promotion which the King had on his mind. It was Lasapulis' desire to make Madaro the Head of Court due to the death of Eamo. The King had been prompted by Madaro's recent change of heart and his previous displays of heroism. He was also interested in helping his sister to mold Madaro into a family man and thus keep him at home should the future necessitate any other battles. Everyone knew Amelian had every intention to return.

Madaro stood up and, after adjusting his freshly-polished sword, embraced his wife briefly and quickly departed before his will grew too weak to stand the separation from her.

She took a deep breath and glanced about the house. After preparing a cup of tea for herself, she sat quietly in Madaro's den as she thought about her plight.

Why hadn't she arose when Madaro had, so she could have groomed herself a bit and shown him the type of woman he deserved? She could sense the improvement he was going through but was certain it was merely an act. He never would love her and, if he did, it would be merely out of a sense of duty. They were both highly favored due to their status and, of course, he would have an heir. Now, there was this appointment, this new status. He would be impossible! He would never be home due to the increased responsibility he was about to assume. She would sit around the house and grow old and ugly.

Very soon, in fact, already she felt her awkward body taking on a new and even more grotesque appearance as this baby of his began to overtake her. Why had God put her in this position? If he really loved her like these Rasomites assured her, then he would be taking better care of her. And why didn't she have any friends? Yes, occasionally she would have a visitor, but no one she could pour her heart out to. Yes, these Rasomite women had claimed to want to help, but where were they now when she needed them?

She suddenly burst into tears and lost complete control of her thoughts. After tumbling from her chair, she lay prone on the floor and wept for a great while. Finally, she regained some control over her body and forced herself to a sitting position. There were no more tears. She felt no more pain. She closed her eyes and craned her neck backwards and attempted to get control over this situation. Weakly, she opened her eyes and then she knew what she had to do. Her vision fell upon Madaro's dagger laying on the table beside the sharpening stone where he had been working. It was in her hand and she could not even remember picking it up.

She never knew the blood would run so ferociously. She passed the blade from one hand to another and attempted to perform the same ritual again, but the knife fell to the floor. Her hand was too weak to even grasp it, and it would be impossible to use it again. She wanted to go back to the easy chair, but before moving she realized her housecoat had formed a basin in her lap which was full of blood. She felt her stomach and lungs tighten inside of her and she clutched her arms around her. The floor was a mess. Her beautiful white housecoat was smeared with blood.

"I love you, Madaro," she muttered quietly. "I'll always love you." She couldn't focus her eyes anymore. The light was growing very dim. "No," she thought, "this wasn't the solution to my problem." She held her arms as tight as she could to staunch the flow of blood. It was too late. "Please, God. I was so stupid. Please God. Give me another chance." She felt her arm weakly fall into her lap. "Oh no! What have I done? My baby! Oh God. What have I done? Help me. Please, help me!"

There was a noise in the outer room and Daedena sensed a lot of activity about her.

"Oh, you precious child. Why didn't you come to me?" Daedena couldn't see clearly, however, she recognized her new friend's voice. Then, she passed out. Crazon had quickly bound the self-inflicted wound with the linen table cover, but it quickly became drenched in red. She sliced a length of cord from the curtain with her own knife and bound the wound securely. Then she began to pray.

A few minutes later, Omitu, another Rasomite woman, appeared. She instantly understood what had happened and she fell on her knees alongside Crazon and also began to raise her voice in prayer.

Omitu had been one of seven brothers and sisters. They had all been destroyed by the Atrocenes. They had been made a spectacle of as they had all been captured together. It pleased the King to have them all thrown into the fire, one each day until they had all been destroyed. She had been forced to be witness to all of this. She was the youngest of her sisters, and her life had been spared to be raised as a virgin bride for King Atrocene. A disloyal servant had aided her escape and she had spent several days alone in the forest, living in fear of recapture. Eventually, she had rejoined the Rasomites, and God had healed her of this experience as He had all her people.

After several minutes of prayer and still getting no response from Daedena, Crazon explained to Omitu she would go and bring Togorasom. "Perhaps, his prayers may be found to be those which the Lord is waiting for."

Crazon had no more than left when Madaro nonchalantly strolled into the room with a broad grin blazoned across his face. He opened his mouth to speak when his eyes fell upon the disaster that had occurred during his short absence. His hands dropped weakly to his sides as he gazed at what he thought was death. The man who had seen with his own eyes, rivers of the blood of his comrades spilled upon the battlefield, collapsed alongside the pale lady on the floor.

"Oh, my God," he moaned. "What have I done? How could I allow this to happen?" His face contorted into extreme sorrow as Omitu placed her gentle hand upon his quivering shoulder.

"Madaro," she said softly, "we have not lost her yet. The thread of life still lingers within her. You must pray. Pray that we may, through the power of the living God, restore her."

Omitu had sat beside Daedena and propped the woman's head on her lap. Acting upon her words, Madaro instantly unstrapped the belt of his sword and slung it aside. Then he gently lay his body across that of his wife's. The glistening uniform he had spent so much time preparing that morning was smeared with blood. He gazed into her pale, but still lovely, face for a moment and then softly kissed her on the lips.

"Oh, dear Lord. It will be a joyful day at your footstool when the soul of this great woman is yours. However, there are some things which aren't quite right. Whatever it takes of me, God, to make these things good for you, I will do them. But, please, don't let her go like this." He stifled his sobbing. "I know there are evil spirits that would inhabit this city and these bodies, but I will not have it and, I know, neither shall you bear it. Let us defeat this one now, Lord, and let us renew our love to you."

Daedena flinched slightly and Omitu and Madaro could see her face contort and her fingers tremble.

Madaro sat up slightly, but still over her, and screamed out. "Get out of her, you foul thing, and be confined back to your pit and, dear God, pour your life blood into her now."

Daedena's facial appearance calmed, and a smile crossed her still pale lips. Madaro moved alongside her and took her good hand in his own. She was breathing shallowly, but regularly, now. Though her hand was icy cold, Madaro could feel the life returning to it.

"You must love her very much," said Omitu.

"If I could have done it, I would have given her my own blood. I have also learned what I must tell my King for, I know now, I have a greater duty."

They were interrupted by the return of Crazon with Togorasom and Anam.

"The danger is passed," said Madaro as he stood. "At least, for my wife."

"We came as quickly as our feet would carry us," said Anam, "but what is there left we can do?"

"Continue to pray for the city of Lasapulis," he said. Then, he realized his garments were covered with blood and he attempted to wipe his blood-drenched hands on his clothes. He looked at his hands and then raised them over his head, closing his eyes. "This precious woman had to be tormented and pour out her own blood to open my eyes. Yours is the true blood, Lord. Always pour out that blood for us."

He was interrupted by the appearance of King Lasapulis.

"My sweet sister," he said as he sank to his knees. "How could this happen?"

Madaro helped Lasapulis back to his feet.

"My King," he said, facing the man within a breath's distance. "Accept my apologies. However, I shall have to withdraw my earlier vow to serve in your court. I cannot."

"I do not understand," he answered. "You are the best choice."

"Nevertheless, you shall have to find another man, for I have found my true calling. This blood-stained battle uniform shall never again caress my skin."

He perceived something from Daedena and looked down at her to see her eyes open. She still appeared very weak. Madaro knelt beside her.

"Oh, Madaro," she said softly. "Please, forgive me. I was so foolish." He opened his mouth to speak. "No," she said painfully, "I have to tell you something. It was horrible. I felt as though I were being pulled through a slimy pit. The air was thick and sickening. I could feel hands or claws pulling at me. Ripping at me. It hurt. Then, suddenly it became so very hot. It was like an inferno. I've never known it to be so awfully hot. I felt like I was being pulled through a gateway, and I didn't want to go. I could see beyond. It was all fire. Everywhere I looked forward was fire, and everywhere I looked backward was blackness, but the things that were pulling at me kept trying to drag me forward. And then, I felt someone kiss my lips. I believed for a moment I was home, but I was not. Then I opened my lips and yelled with all my power, 'Help me, God!' Suddenly, all the things released their grip on me and I could feel myself going back. The further I went, the better I began to feel. I could sense one creature trying to pull me back, but he couldn't touch me. Then, suddenly, I sensed it had fallen away and, then, I was here. I could hear all of you speaking, but I was too weak to respond. Madaro, I don't want to go back there. I don't ever want anyone to go there."

Madaro looked up at all those present. "I never finished what I was going to say. Today, I put all of the past behind me. I am now a member of a different army. One so mighty, even all of the world and of Hell cannot stand against it. Today, I am a priest. I will not rest until I know every soul on earth has been snatched away from the jaws of death. These people need one of their own to teach them what God wants. We need a temple to teach in. I suggest we may be able to convert the old stadium. As long as we have adequate space. That is my main concern. For God's house is not made of stone, but of flesh, and God's spirit is not made of men's hearts and minds, but of God's own flesh. We will be as God's arm here upon the earth, even as these Rasomites are part of God."

"Does your Majesty know that, among all of the city and the kingdom, you have control over their lives?"

Omitu had escorted Lasapulis to go back to the palace, but

they had instead gone to the stadium. He sat upon the old granite steps with his head propped upon both his hands, staring at the earth. They had left Madaro's house with he and Crazon taking turns at a vigil over his wife while she slept and regained her strength. It would be several days before she was completely restored and, during this time, she would be easy prey for spirits of either house to enter in. They would not leave her alone.

"I know I exert influence over these people, but I often feel so weak and unable to decide."

"Not only these people," she explained, "but even into Marsa and into the various independent provinces. Your name has gone out as a man who, in a flash, ended centuries of conflict. All you must do is speak the word and they will listen."

"There are so many even here in the city who are not so impressed with my new relationship with Chiam."

"Be careful that you are not looking at the fruits of the enemy as an excuse," she cautioned. "There is too much still which needs accomplishing."

"But shouldn't we look at the problem from both sides?" he asked, looking up at her.

"There are many temptations in the world laid down by the devil, but there is only one answer. God is the answer. If it is not of God, then it must be swept away, for if it is not swept away, it shall be burned on the last day."

"But I still don't know what I need to do," he said, again dropping his gaze. He looked up at her again. "I have Chiam insisting I come for a visit. I have a temple to prepare. People living in the outlying districts are calling for me. The economy and the government of the land does not even exist. And I still have one other problem which is hard for me to even discuss."

"I know you are lonely. I have wept for you for the loss of your trusted friend. His office shall be filled, but the emptiness felt by the loss of his love shall never go. We can only pray that time will diminish the pain and that someone else with a tender heart will come into your life to help you fill the void. Take pleasure in the joy that you shall see him again when the Father also calls you home."

Tears were filling the man's eyes. "I know I shall see him again, and part of my mind has accepted this but part of me is still of this world and...I feel so helpless. And now, this. I had always thought my sister was strong. My heart aches at the plight of the other people, but I still feel so helpless."

Omitu walked up the stairs to where the King sat and rested a hand upon his weary shoulder. She raised her other hand into the air and closed her eyes. "Almighty God, he from whom all life proceeds. You know more than any of us how this great man's heart has been broken due to the loss of a dear friend. We both know you have given us the Holy Ghost to be our constant companion but, Lord, we are still in the world and we sometimes need a shoulder to cry on. If it be possible for you to bring a new friend into this, your servant's life, let it be. And also, dear God, give him the fortitude and wisdom to be able to bear the burden of the station you have called him to. His heart is full of weakness and sorrow now, but so many are looking toward him for strength. Bring into his life the people who will be able to support him and put into his heart the strength he is going to need during these trying times, and put into his mind the joy that he deserves in the knowledge of your love. Thank you, dear God."

She looked down at the King and, after a moment, he looked up at her.

"Thank you," he said. "I feel better already. Sometimes, we get so hung up in the problems in our lives that we forget that there is a bigger plan of which we are all a part." She offered a hand and helped him to his feet. For a few moments, they stood there and gazed into each other's eyes. He smiled. "When I'm close to you like this, I begin to forget what my problems are, Omitu."

"Yes," she replied.

He stood and continued to stare at her. The longer he looked, the more difficult it became for him to express himself. He suddenly began laughing. "Oh, sweet woman. Here you have just asked God to grant me all this great wisdom, and now I am unable to even begin to think." As quickly as he had begun laughing, he became very grave. "Omitu, you are right. I need help, and I am no fool to let good help easily slip away. Will you help me?"

They stared at each other in silence for a moment before she answered. "I will do what I can do."

He closed his mouth and bit his upper lip as he created the nerve for the next question. "Beautiful woman of God. I am not worthy of a woman of your station. Compared to all men, I am now weak and empty. I am also selfish because I know there shall be days I will be overwhelmed by situations. I will need consoling. Will you marry me?"

"It is not my own to say. Our people have been destroyed and now we are so few. It is not possible that we nonchalantly wander away to do our own things anymore. I will go to Anam and pray that he gives me the desire of my heart, to be your wife."

"I am not aware of all your customs. I love you, and it has all happened so quickly my mind cannot contain its delight. Would it be accepted that, before you go away, I would embrace you?"

He gently took her hands in his and, leaning forward, their lips met and their arms enfolded each other.

"Dear Father, who rules Heaven and earth, thank you for taking those of little faith and leading them into labor, anyway. It would be so easy to say, 'I don't understand' and refuse to participate until our fragile human minds had gained a level of worldly knowledge. Thank you for driving me on when there is still doubt and confusion within me."

Togorasom lay back on the bedroll and looked upon the ceiling of the stadium. Even in the dull light of the evening, he could see the cold, bare granite. It pleased him that, soon, this building would come alive with the artwork and activity of the residents. After Daedena's recovery and the announcement of the King's betrothal plans, there was a great surge of support for godly things. Many had destroyed family altars and been led to salvation. There was no perfect situation on earth, though King Lasapulis vowed he would deal with those buried in their disgusting habits as he saw fit. In a few days, Chiam would be arriving with a horde of wedding guests bearing gifts. There would be a surge of witnessing and, he knew, many would be led to the Lord. Then, it would be time to move on. At the moment, it seemed, they would be moving in faith. With the exception of Omitu, they would be gathered together to drive the devil out of bounds, once again.

There was a noise near the entrance of the building, and he sat up just as Badaa and Zoana appeared.

"Ah, woman of God," said Togorasom. "I'm glad you are both here. And what brings you here?"

"Togorasom," Zoana replied, "I didn't realize you were here. We were simply out for a walk and decided to pass by here. And, say, what brings you here?"

"Tomorrow, Madaro dedicates the temple and, partly for that reason and partly because we shall be soon leaving, I made the decision to remain here."

Zoana furrowed her brow. "We are leaving so soon? There is much work that needs to be done. Does Anam know we are leaving?"

Togorasom laughed. "Wonderful woman," he said, shaking his head, "do you not know the life of a Rasomite is one of wandering and confusion? Our labor here is nearly over. There is a time when a farmer plants his crops and casts out the weeds. There is also a time when he must depart and allow the growth to happen until the harvester shall come. Will the farmer remain in his field and wander among the planting and disturb the growth? Anam always knows we are wanderers."

"Young man," spoke up Badaa, "you are wise beyond your years. I am awed by all of you people, but you amaze me the most. I know you are a prophet."

"I am flattered by the title," said Togorasom. "However, I only listen to my God and obey."

Badaa smiled. "Yes, that about defines the title of a prophet. You could teach me so much if we had the time."

"But the time goes by so quickly and the whole world needs the news. And every day, men die in their foolishness. Madaro is a good teacher and full of prayer and the Holy Spirit. You should listen to him."

"I shall, but you shall still be missed."

"It becomes late," Zoana said, looking toward the entrance, "and it becomes darker. I still have prayer with the women. I needn't ask if you will be fine."

"I'll be fine. Pray for me that it is not a cold night."

Zoana and Badaa left after the three said a short prayer for restful sleep. Togorasom lay on his side and, soon, his little eyes were closed tightly.

Chapter 2
The Calodians

Reka let the palm of his hand glide across Marissa's shimmering hair ahead of the brush. Her hair was soft and lovely to his touch, as everything about her seemed to be. When he thought about her, he often had to take a deep breath of satisfaction. So great was his love for his older sister, he would have done anything to please her. Some moments, however, were challenging as she was now entering her twelfth year, and older boys and young men had an eye on her. Reka, still only nine, was only beginning to learn about girls, and he didn't like the lessons. He saw most girls as two-faced, teasing liars capable of little more than taunting him and making his anger rise.

Between the times he was angry at older boys and younger girls, he fantasized about the great love he had for his sister. His young, handicapped mind was still not capable of creating sexual fantasies, so he turned to romance and adventure. Many times, he could see a handsome young man on horseback or lurking in the bushes awaiting an opportunity to spoil Marissa's beauty. Many men far larger and stronger than himself had fallen prey to his invisible sword or been crushed to death under the hooves of his mighty steed as he protected this flowering beauty.

"Reka?" said Marissa softly. Her voice was as beautiful as a songbird, and he clenched his teeth to quell the urgings in his young mind. She looked over her shoulder at him and smiled. "I believe mother has been calling you."

"M...mother..." he stuttered.

"Yes, silly. You know, the lady who brought us into the world?" She called out, "He's coming mother!"

Reka's hands numbly dropped to his sides, but he remained in place.

"You had best go and see what she wants, little brother, or

she'll be angry at both of us," she stated firmly.

Reka nodded, handed her the brush and shuffled out the door of the tent.

Marissa gazed at the doorway for several minutes as she wondered what to do with her little brother. The boy was little more than mute, being both hard of hearing and capable of only one-word sentences. She knew how much he loved her, and this love went beyond mere brotherly affection. While she encouraged innocent relationships between boys and herself, she was also torn apart inside because she knew how much it hurt Reka. But she didn't know what to do. Whenever a potential suitor smiled or waved to her, she could see the gloom and anger building up in Reka. They had often found him in tears when she was not around and suspected it was his jealous nature. Though their parents were stern in disciplining him when he was obviously overstepping his place, they usually felt they were wasting their time. It made no difference in his attitude.

Reka and Marissa lived with their parents in a nomadic village of about two hundred persons. Their entire lives had been one of an annual journey between the seacoast, in the north, during the summer and the desert area in the south, beyond the mountains, where they could winter. Their nationality was basically Calodian but, in spite of tribal differences, they were actually a mix of many people.

Today, as the travelers were ahead of schedule, they were remaining in place to relax before continuing their migration toward the mountains. Tomorrow, most likely, they would again be burdened down with tents and supplies as they moved on.

Marissa sat up straight on her stool as she felt the ground shake. She could not begin to imagine what was happening. Then, came a scream from outside the tent. Overcoming her fear, curiosity drove her to the doorway and outside where total confusion reigned. In a few moments, her young mind began to understand. The ugly men of Lusack were on horseback and appeared to be stampeding the village. It took her a few more moments before she realized people were dying. It was beyond her conception, as she had never seen a battle before. Now, she saw people who had worked and played and cuddled with her being hacked down by these brutal men. Inside, she screamed for this to stop, but terror forbade her to move until she saw her own mother being dragged behind a rampaging horse.

A burst of excitement propelled her across the space from where she stood and the assault, hoping to come to her mother's aid. The man released the woman just as Marissa overcame them. Her mother's arms wildly flailed about, making it impossible to assist her until the woman went limp. Marissa rolled her onto her side and saw the ax wedged into her mother's forehead.

Again, terror and confusion took over and she stumbled blindly about. None of this made any sense. It became difficult for her to even remember where she was. Then suddenly, as quickly as it began, it was over. The last of the horses stormed out of the village and jumped the embankment that bordered one side.

She would not let it be so easy for them to escape and charged after the last rider, stopping at the top of the bank. Her brother was only a few paces behind her.

"We'll get even with you, you filthy animals!" she screeched through her tears. The man on the last horse stopped the animal, released one arrow and fled. Marissa felt the stab of the shaft as it entered her heart and fell into Reka's arms, dead.

"Urrp!" belched Amelian. He again focused his attention on the man before him. "Go ahead. I'm listening." He yawned. "I said, go ahead!"

"Yes, sir. At least twenty were killed. Perhaps thirty. Very few injuries as we struck to kill," spoke the man who had just returned from the raid on the Calodian village.

"Hey, you!" hollered Amelian at another man who was headed for the wine keg.

"Yes, sir!"

"Fill mine up first." He tossed him his empty wine cup, which was immediately filled and returned. Amelian quaffed the entire contents in one chug and handed it back to the same man who again refilled and returned it. "You done yet!" he fired at the man attempting to give him the report.

"As you wish, sir!"

"As you wish, shur," he mumbled, sarcastically. "Did you get the right ones?"

"They move about a great deal. However, they appeared to be the same people we got the fish from."

"Umm. Don't matter anyway. They're all a bunch of rodents. Get lost!"

The man departed and Amelian lay back down on the ground where he had been when the war party had returned.

"Teach them a lesson," he mumbled as he passed out.

The day before, he had sent men to raid some of the nomads for supplies and among the other goods was a great deal of dried fish. The fish was consumed without their knowledge it had been rotting, and several of his men had become very ill. Despite none being certain from where the fish had originated, he had ordered an assault against the suspected providers. It mattered very little to him if the wrong people were attacked.

Such was the way Amelian made his living, raiding the nomads and small villages in the plains and mountains. He was quite careful about avoiding either Chiam or Lasapulis until this recent skirmish. It had been his belief that the city of Lasapulis would be totally defenseless with their men and Chiam's army out of the area. He had thought occupying Lasapulis would be simple. The new arrangement between the two monarchs upset Amelian considerably, as they would now probably expand their domain and be able to shove him aside. Soon, he needed to make a decision concerning where he would retreat to, realizing he was no match for this combined enemy. In the meantime, he had remained continually drunken and had begun to release his pent-up anger on the defenseless local people. They were too weak and disorganized to fight back due to their own rivalry.

He was shocked and angry as he entered the little village. Even though the Spirit had prepared him for a scene of mourning and death, his anger wanted to lash out. He knew the Shamra could be sent out for an ambush and cause a great deal of devastation in the Lusack camp. He knew God could rain down death upon them and destroy them in a moment as he had at the camp of Lusack's unknown allies, the Atrocenes, a few years ago. Despite what he knew God would allow him to do, Anam also knew what God desired and he was determined to obey.

How would this small group of nomads be turned into a mighty army? With God, he knew anything was possible.

Anam had arrived at the Calodian village the day following the assault. Eighteen people were dead. Several more had sustained crippling injuries. The wounded had been adequately tended to, however, all the bodies had been merely rolled in blankets and left in a row on one side of the village. The Calodian custom when an individual passed away during these travels was to wait until their return to one of their primary destinations for burial. During the time before arrival, the body would be prepared for internment with special oils and wrapped in a clean linen robe made especially for this purpose. Now there were too many deaths. The Calodians did not have sufficient supplies to inter them had they even attempted to. Also, it would have been almost impossible to transport all of the bodies as well as the rest of their goods. Besides all this, they were still in shock and uncertain what to do.

Many eyes looked upon Anam as he strode across the open space in the middle of the village. He had supposed, correctly, the largest tent would belong to the leader. No one halted him as he seemed so sure of himself and the people were too tired to oppose one man. There had been no sleep here the night before.

As Anam approached the tent, three men clad in goatskins arose and stood as a barrier at the doorway with their arms folded across their chests.

"I am here to speak with your leader," he informed them.

They glanced at each other. There was little difference in the appearance of these three men. All were slight in build, though they were all obviously strong men. All had the same sandy grey-streaked hair and beards. All were dearly in need of bathing. One of the men spoke.

"I am Maula. I am sorry you cannot see Lamarr as he is in mourning for his wife. Who are you?"

"I am sent by God to teach you people to throw off this yoke of oppression that these barbarians have tied you down with. My name is Anam."

The Calodians had heard the stories of the wonderful things happening between Lasapulis and Marsa. They knew the Rasomites had played a mighty part in constructing this peace and they had heard Anam's name included in the stories. The three men were momentarily awed that this man had come to this little village and, as they considered how to respond, another man emerged from the tent. He looked a great deal like the older men, but he was hardly more than a boy; only nineteen years old. He had the beginnings of a beard and was dressed also in an old goatskin. His cheeks were still moist from tears and his eyelids heavy from weeping and lack of sleep. He stared into Anam's eyes for a moment, nodded his head and retreated into the tent. Anam followed him alone.

There was little light inside the tent and it took several minutes to adjust his eyes from the brightness of the sun outside. The two men sat on straw mats which lay on the sand and did not speak for quite a while. Finally, the young man broke the silence.

"Your throat is dry from your travel across the desert. Would you like some wine?"

"I have a great deal to tell you," Anam replied. "What I have to say is very important. Yes, I would appreciate a drink."

Lamarr arose and returned with a large wooden goblet of sweet wine, which he handed to Anam with both hands. As Anam took the cup, he clasped the young leader's hands for a moment.

"I know your anger and your confusion and your sadness," he said.

"Do you really know these things?"

"All of my people but for a tiny remnant were devoured by a race more evil than these desert rats. I know all of the things that you are feeling as I have been there."

"I have always wanted a simple girl. She was so beautiful, but it seemed as there was never a need for her to preen herself. She had a lovely smile. She was as strong as an ox but the touch of her fingers was so gentle..." Lamarr began sobbing.

Anam put the goblet to one side and embraced the grief-stricken man for several minutes. Finally, Lamarr composed himself and slid back to where he had been sitting. "Last year, both of my parents were killed in a boating accident. My father had been the tribal leader for years. The people turned to me. I knew I needed to be strong but my people were faithful and stuck by me. Eulena waited on me night and day for months and I scarcely realized she existed. And then, suddenly, I returned to reality and discovered her. We were wed immediately. But now, she is gone too. Could I ask you a question?" Anam nodded. "You are a man of God. Is Eulena with my parents now? Will I see them again?"

"The Lord has said that those who have been given little shall not be expected much, but those he has chosen must obey him, for where much has been given, much will be expected. If you do as I tell you, I believe you will see your family again."

"I will do anything. I want to take Amelian and carve him up and feed him to the vultures."

"And how do you expect to do that?"

"I don't know," Lamarr answered as he lowered his gaze to the floor. "I just hate him so much."

Anam took a deep breath and prepared to deliver his message. "Tonight, you will sleep well, as will all your people."

"Last night," Lamarr responded shaking his head, "no one slept. Their grief was too strong and, I believe, we were also afraid."

"You have nothing to fear," Anam reassured him. "By now, in his drunken stupor, you are no more a memory to Amelian than the blowing of the desert sand. Now, it is time to prepare for battle."

"First, before we talk of battles and revenge, please tell me about God. I know there is a god. I know he created all things and he knows all things. But he is an unknown mystery to me. Will you tell me about him?"

Anam lowered his head and closed his eyes. "Thank you, Father, for preparing this mighty warrior's heart for being open to you. Fill this place with your power, Lord. Reveal to Lamarr how much you love and how concerned you are for him. Support him during this time of grief even as he must prepare for war. I know war is scarcely a word in the Calodian language, Father. But there comes a time when one can no longer go through life with his face cast down and live out of fear of offending his enemies." Anam raised one hand and placed it on Lamarr's shoulder. "Are you ready? Are you prepared to become a slave to God and forget your fear of man?" Lamarr nodded. Anam again closed his eyes. "He's yours now, Lord. Fill him with your holy power and reveal to him the things he must do."

Tears filled Lamarr's eyes as they had earlier. However, these were not tears of sadness and grief. These were the tears of repentance as he released himself to the unseen God, and his attitude changed from a trembling child to a man of God. Finally, he spoke to Anam.

"I have never felt like this before. I can hardly describe it. I never supposed I would feel more confident than I was when I loved Eulena. But, that was nothing. I feel like a completely different person."

"You are a different person, Lamarr. But don't be so brash as to assume you can do anything. In his time, God will lead you to do what he wants to have done."

Lamarr nodded. "I will try to do everything he asks. I know you are sent to show me. What must I do first?"

Anam chuckled. "First, you must go to sleep."

It was early morning. The sky was just beginning to show the first signs of day. There had been an unexpected frost that night, however, it was snug and warm inside the Calodian tents where the people were still deep in sleep.

Anam snapped awake. He was lying on his back on the bare floor of Lamarr's tent. He had spent most of the night in prayer and listening to God. He lay there for several minutes relaxing in the peaceful silence of the desert. It was a welcome relief from the busyness of Lasapulis. He closed his eyes and could picture the beautiful face of Paluqua and, for a moment, wished she could be lying beside him now and sharing this. However, he knew that any change he would have created on his own could have destroyed God's plan for what was to happen here. When God had told him to leave Lasapulis and come here, he had obeyed quickly. The rest of the Rasomites would eventually travel to Marsa where he would rendezvous with them in a few days after this was over.

He sensed Lamarr was awakening and glanced towards him to see the man's face. It was too dark to make out details but Anam knew the man was awake.

"Good morning, triumphant one," Anam said.

"Good morning, my friend. I have had such a night."

"Tell me."

Lamarr sat up and rolled back a small cloth which covered the entrance, immediately flooding the room with the brilliant morning sun.

"The women will soon be up," said Lamarr. "I could use a nice hot cup of ginger tea." He closed his eyes and took a deep breath. "We were on a battlefield and were, it seemed, hopelessly outnumbered. However, the enemy, Lusack, fled from us and we pursued them. Every one of them was destroyed." He paused. "I led the army and there were many people. More than I have ever seen. Will I lead an army, Anam?"

"Your army is nearly at your door. Come, let us go eat

breakfast and you'll see what I mean. Many things are about to happen."

Both men arose, left the tent and entered the chilly air outside. There was no sign of life, but as they stood there, the village activity quickly began. Within a few minutes, the fires were blazing and breakfast was prepared. Anam and Lamarr sat near the fire surrounded by several other of the men. The ginger tea was excellent. The conversation wandered among the men as they discussed incidents common to them such as boating techniques, tying knots, tanning leather. After a time, Lamarr suddenly changed the conversation and asked Anam what his dream had meant.

"Behold, your army!" Anam stood up and pointed off toward the horizon. Very soon, the Calodians began to understand as it seemed the entire landscape was coming to life. The desert was filled with people of many nationalities. They came from the seacoasts and mountains and the desert beyond the mountains. Some had been on the move for many days.

Throughout the rest of the morning, people arrived and reported in to Lamarr. Despite none of these people being warlike, they had all experienced various dreams and visions which showed them the victory over the trouble-making Amelian and, for various reasons, felt an uncontrollable urge to go to the little Calodian village of Lamarr's (most even unaware of its existence) and prepare to follow him to war. By noontime, there had gathered over a thousand persons, mostly men, under his authority awaiting directions. Anam gave Lamarr and his immediate followers orders to make the people gather around and sit down on the ground. He climbed upon the back of a horse, which had been loaned to him.

"I am not going to begin this speech explaining to you why you are here or the events that have led up to your coming. You already know these things and there are too many variations of the same theme. God himself is your captain. Lamarr of the Calodians is merely his vessel, and I am his messenger. I know many of you in your hearts do not feel godly, but God has called you to a mission and you have obeyed. Many of you are still in amazement over the miracle that has already happened, leading up to your arrival here. But I say to you, the miracle that is about to happen will be remembered among your people as a legend, forever." Anam's voice boomed across the open space amid the otherwise silent gathering. Everyone offered him the greatest respect, knowing the things he was about to say were a matter of life and death.

"You have already been obedient in a small thing. You have left your families and come to this place, not really understanding why. Now, you must be obedient in another thing. This is what God wants you to do. Tomorrow, we will all come together and worship God, but none of us shall eat. It will be a day of fasting to demonstrate to the Lord we are obedient. The following day, you will eat nothing but rice or whatever grain you are able to supply. On the third day, you will eat whatever food is your custom to eat. Each day, you will remember that God supplies everything. Tomorrow, we shall all go down to the river and bathe as we shall also do on the second and third day. During this time, you will remain sexually pure and forego any lusts of your heart. Afterwards, you will want to celebrate."

One of the men sitting on the ground near the front called out. "We have no weapons, save a few small items."

"God shall be your sword, so do not become faint-hearted."

For the rest of the day, people wandered about renewing old friendships. Gone was the hostility that had caused division among them. Many even joked about situations that previously had caused great anger. In the latter part of the evening, well-minded people began to put up their stores of food and their kegs of drink. The following day would be a day for water only.

As incredible as the gathering of this 'army of God ' seemed even to Anam, to one among them, it was only a distraction. Reka was barely aware of any of these things and sat alone in his tent most of the time, occasionally aware of the noise outside as hundreds of people went about their business. Late in the afternoon, a woman, Opur, who had been good friends with Reka's parents, entered his tent with some dinner and was not too amazed to find Reka gone. She went to Lamarr's tent to see if he were there, as Reka's father had been close to Lamarr. The Calodian leader was also gone, but one of his trusted friends was there.

"I have gone to Reka's tent with food for the boy," explained Opur, "and found no one about. I thought perhaps he would be with Lamarr."

"I feel so bad for the boy, Opur," responded the man. "He has nothing to look forward to and no one to care for him."

Opur frowned. "I am doing what I am able to do. However, it's not easy with a husband preparing for war and four children of my own."

"He's a hard boy, in his own way, to deal with."

"Yes, that he surely is. One never knows what he is thinking. He is so quiet. I know he must simply stew a great deal. And he was so devoted to his sister. I don't know what's to become of him."

"Anyway, I haven't seen him all afternoon."

"He went into his tent about the time Anam began speaking and I haven't seen him since," she said.

The man smiled. "He's probably roaming about exploring this variety of culture. For a young boy, this must be very exciting."

Opur shook her head. "You don't understand Reka very well. I don't think he has any idea what is going on. All he knows is that his sister is gone." Tears began forming in her eyes. "I feel so helpless. No one else can get through to him. Only Marissa understood him. I'm afraid his life will be so meaningless."

"Opur! Why are you crying?" Lamarr said compassionately as he and Anam appeared on the scene. She threw her arms around the young leader and tried to explain how she hurt for Reka.

Lamarr explained to Anam. "When Lusack came, they also destroyed this boy's parents and sister. All of his family. The boy is handicapped and was very close to his sister. No one knows how to communicate with him."

Anam nodded understandingly. "I will talk with the boy. May I see him?"

Opur, still in tears, explained. "This is the problem. I don't know where he has gone. He needs to eat. He won't understand not eating tomorrow, especially if he goes hungry tonight."

"Opur," Lamarr told her, "you should return to your children. They need you. We shall find the boy."

The Lusack ruffian slapped Reka's bleeding face again. The boy was tied to two poles planted in the ground about three feet apart in such a way that it was impossible for him to either lean against one of them or squat on the ground. He had been whipped several times such that his young flesh lay open. His face had been beaten so much, his eyes had swollen shut. Locks of his hair had been ripped from his head. The foolish soldier was so drunken he could not even tell the boy had lost consciousness. He was nearly dead.

"Ah, leave him be," said another soldier who had taken a few turns at him as well. "He's passed out again."

"Get water!" yelled the tormentor. There were several witnesses milling about, but none came to his assistance. The man was raging. "Get water! I'll know what he was about."

Another man commented. "Leave him be until morning. He's no harm. How will he ever answer you?"

Several others nodded in agreement.

"Ah, what's the use!" The man who had been beating Reka picked up his warm beer from where it had sat on the ground, swallowed a mouthful and spat at the boy. "I hope you die, you maggot."

Reka had been found lurking among the rocks and bushes near Amelian's tent, carrying a knife. Naturally, they had not been able to extract any information from him. Now, leaving him like a broken toy, the crowd dispersed and soon, he was alone.

It was nearly dark and it was becoming chilly as the wind began to pick up. The Lusack soldiers had posted their guards and retired for the evening. Soon, any activity had ceased except for a few dying embers of flame.

Covered by darkness, no one noticed the man steal into the Lusack camp, slice the cords on the boy's wrists and ankles and depart with the boy in his arms.

"I don't care!" yelled Lamarr. "How can you be so foolish? You've come across the desert on what would seem like a whim. You've listened to this man of God tell you what will happen. You've fasted and gone without and washed yourselves to obey him and to please God." He was standing outside his tent surrounded by several of the various leaders from the people who had followed Anam's direction for two days. "Tomorrow is the easiest day. We bathe in the morning and eat. Does this scare you? So, what is the problem? Afraid of getting wet a third time?"

One of the men spoke up. "You do not understand, Lamarr. It is not tomorrow we fear. It is the following day."

"But what of the prophecies and dreams and visions?" he asked.

"Daydreams they will seem like when I take my stick against a man on a horse with a sword."

"We have horses as well!"

"Old workhorses made for carrying a pack or tilling the earth."

"And where has this man, Anam, gone?" asked another. "Is he also afraid?"

"This man is afraid of nothing!" shouted Lamarr.

"Nevertheless," said another, "we have discussed it and most of us agree. In the morning, we are going home."

The Calodian leader could have burst into tears when he heard this. However, he said a silent prayer for strength. "You do as you wish," he said, "as for me, if need be, I shall go fight Lusack alone. But I know I shall not be alone. And when your grandchildren speak about this victory, your memorial shall be blotted out of their minds." He turned and went back into his tent, leaving the others alone in their angry embarrassment. Eventually, they wandered away.

Anam held his hands close to the fire. When they were very warm, he placed them on the boy's cheeks and neck. The little one released a breath of air and took another.

"Breathe life into him, Lord. Heal him. You are the God of life and death and, now, I beg you to restore to him that life. Seldom have I seen a desire burn so deep in one so young to avenge an evil, Lord. Love him now because of his devotion and let him be a testimony for you. Oh God, heal this child."

"Marissa, is that you?" Reka mumbled.

"Speak on," Anam encouraged.

"I'm looking for my sister," he answered, still not awake.

"Have you seen her?" Anam asked.

"Oh, if anyone saw her, they would remember. Her skin is unblemished and as gentle as dew drops. I love to watch her eyes twinkle in the sunlight. She has such a charm to her voice and her hair is so beautiful. I love her so much, but I am afraid. I cannot find her." He was trembling with fear.

"She is safe."

Reka smiled and relaxed.

"You know," Anam continued, "as fair as your sister is, there is one fairer." Reka was quiet. "Do you understand God?" The boy remained silent. "Reka, can you hear me?" He smiled. "God loves you and wants to heal your wounds." Suddenly, Reka became very relaxed and it was obvious to Anam he was completely asleep. Anam tucked him in well with a heavy blanket to keep the cold off and then huddled near the fire. Soon, he was also sleeping. In the morning, they would return home.

Nearly all of those who had arrived three days before had now completely packed their belongings and prepared to depart. The crowd would be leaving with as much fanfare as they had arrived. Only the Calodians, the ones who always dwelt on the seacoasts, would remain with Lamarr and his nomads. These and a few others who claimed no allegiance to anyone.

Lamarr had managed to get all the leaders to agree to come together one last time before they headed home.

"It is with a very heavy heart I bid you all farewell. I am at least pleased we have been able to come together in peace for these few days. Hopefully, having laid aside our differences and hostility and uncooperativeness, even this will come of good and show the world, especially Lusack, we are not squabbling children. Perhaps, Amelian shall think better the next time he sends his bullies to us and demands payment. But, despite all that, the Calodians are still at war with Lusack. Tomorrow, we shall either be free on earth or free in heaven. But still, I have an emptiness about me that I have been deserted."

There was suddenly a stir among some of the people who were standing away from the ring of leaders. All eyes were aimed in the direction of the activity, wondering what could be causing this interruption. Finally, the crowd parted, allowing Anam and Reka, hand in hand, to pass through. The people waited for Anam's rebuke.

"Good morning, warriors. You are nearly set free." Anam locked his eyes onto Lamarr, expecting some words of explanation. Many gazed at Reka who still bore the wounds dealt by the men of Lusack. "This brave soul with no words of encouragement, no vision, no prophesy, declared war against Lusack and attacked Amelian's army alone. Despite his wounds and knowing he caused no damage in the enemy camp, he still achieved some victory. His victory was over his own flesh and mind. He loved his sister and could not see fit to allow these cruel barbarians the freedom to take advantage over him. He decided not to accept defeat. Reka is heaven bound. It is clear that many of you do not find yourselves so worthy."

Reka looked up at Anam. "I am so very tired. May I sit down?"

He walked toward Lamarr who stared at the boy in amazement. "He can speak. The boy's tongue has been loosed," he yelled with joy. None of the outsiders understood his great excitement at this happening. Lamarr nearly threw his arms around Reka in jubilation, but stopped short when he realized the extent of the boy's injuries. Some healing had taken place over the last two days or the Calodians might not have even recognized him. Lamarr looked at Anam for explanation as others of the village began gathering to see this spectacle. Thereafter followed a thorough discussion of what had happened to the boy and the events leading up to this meeting of the leaders.

"I do not understand," Reka stated looking at Lamarr. Lamarr began to explain about some of the visions and dreams but Reka cut him off. "I don't mean those things. I mean I don't understand their fear. I went nearly to that ugly man's bedside, was treated bad by a dozen men and I survived. Perhaps, the children should lead this war," he finally added sarcastically.

One of the leaders stepped forward. "I am prepared to fight with my people." One by one, every man there relented and all agreed to renew their pledge to follow the Calodians into battle.

"Then, tomorrow will be the beginning of the end for Amelian," said Lamarr. "Let us go down to the river and complete the last step of our vow to God."

It was nearly a full day's march to the place where Lusack had encamped. They marched out in the morning and then tarried the following morning before launching their attack. If the allies had reconsidered the odds, they would surely have fled. But God blinded them to the odds. Lusack had nearly ten thousand trained fighters. They represented hardened criminals and refugees from different countries. They each came armed with a variety of swords, spears, javelins and hatchets. There were over a thousand expert archers. They also included nearly fifteen-hundred on horseback. Against an army like Chiam's of Marsa, they would be quite hopeless. Against Lasapulis, they would have been evenly matched. However, against this uncommon gathering of pathetic rabble calling themselves an army, they were as solid as rock.

The allies represented about two dozen different groups of people. After having left their family members behind and after the desertion of a few due to the dispute, they numbered almost a thousand. They had five-hundred horses, however, most were mere workhorses and many would not even carry a man. They had two-hundred men bearing swords. That many again bearing other hand-held implements of war. Most of this weaponry was in sad shape as they had been dragged out of heirloom closets or were merely for show. They also had four-hundred archers, many of whom were excellent, but not like the warriors following Amelian. The rest of the allies carried clubs and sticks. Besides all this, physically, the men of Lusack were half again the size of the allies. If Amelian had considered this new enemy, he would have saved Lamarr the trouble and laughed himself to death.

The allies completely surrounded the enemy camp which was located on an unfortified piece of flatland. Most of Lusack's soldiers had tents. The horses were located at the very center of the encampment. The operation was very well planned. The attack came during the darkest time of the predawn. The overconfident enemy had posted only a handful of sleeping guards and these were finished off quickly. The rest of Amelian's highly-trained soldiers were still sleeping off the previous night's drunkenness, which for many had only just ended. Torches were lit and the first squadron began their dash toward the goal, the horses. Most of the tents were set ablaze as they made their mad dash. The frightened, drunken soldiers who scurried out of the blaze were no match for the next mob who came through bearing clubs and staves. Naturally, as the battle progressed the allies began accumulating a menagerie of weapons. Within minutes, Lamarr and his band had rescued the horses from their fiery ring. Lusack had been wise enough to leave a very wide path through which the horsemen could enter and leave the camp without disturbing the others. The horses eagerly shot through the avenue to freedom. As soon as word spread that the horses were free, the allies mysteriously disappeared into the darkness, out of sight but not out of reach. As the camp blazed, it clearly illuminated the insane activity of men dashing about in an attempt to find safety. One by one, they were easily picked off by the archers who had now encircled Lusack. The activity continued, slowly tapering off until daylight. The allies waited, mostly in awed silence, for further signs of activity.

Eventually, Lamarr gave the order to search the camp and take survivors. Cautiously at first, but then with increased zeal as they realized the devastation, they searched the camp. There were no survivors. A few terrified men had obviously taken their own lives. It was clear, however, Amelian had not committed suicide. His body was found near his tent. A pole had pegged him to the ground and his head had been chopped off and cast aside. There was no devotion to him when the tide had turned against them. Lamarr first gave an order to leave the area, but then relented, allowing his army to plunder everything from the camp which might be useful. Soon, the looting done, they left the camp and reorganized a short distance away.

Then they began to take a toll of their own losses. Many of their men had been injured, some severely. However, all would heal. Not a man was missing. As each new revelation came upon them, it became increasingly clear to whom the victory truly belonged.

The last command before they began to disperse was for prayer.

"Dear and mighty Lord. Oh, Lord, we weep and we shake for joy and for fear at the mightiness of the power that you have displayed. None of us are righteous enough to accept any praise. We have done nothing. Forever, people will remember this day you took a handful of derelicts and waving your hand before them, smote this powerful army in the wink of an eye. No man can explain it. Thank you, Lord."

Lamarr finished his prayer, but the prayer time went on for most of the day as each man tore himself apart before God and repented of his life. When at last it was clear they should depart, Lamarr spoke to the other leaders and they headed to their many homes. The Calodians, still full of zeal, rode most of the night to return home.

Chapter 3
Death

It was raining. It had been raining for several days. The few times the sun had appeared were but brief respites from the weather. When it wasn't raining, the sky usually remained overcast, seemingly in an effort to dispel any joy.

Anam sat quietly in a chair, staring blankly at the wall opposite him. He was tired and bored. Life had settled into a routine and become drudgery. For nearly a year, he and the Rasomites had been content to remain in the more than adequate quarters provided by Chiam. They traveled often back to Lasapulis to aid that city in its spiritual growth, and when they were home, received guests almost daily from throughout the region. He was very pleased with what had been accomplished, but everyone was beginning to realize it was time to go.

Many of the women and young people had married and moved away and this was good as they were therefore able to evangelize everywhere. Zoana, Crazon, and, of course, Paluqua continued on as though they would be with him always. The diversity of their gifts and their great love for one another was always a source of joy for him. However, they also were becoming much too homebound. Seldom did they evangelize, but were more content to preach and teach. This was good as they helped their flocks grow closer to God, but Anam knew they were called to travel the world and preach the light of God.

Anam could see Togorasom growing also. He would often find a place to sit and pray and would scarcely move for many days. Often, he would go to his apartment in the evening, supposedly to sleep, and emerge the following morning tired and weeping as he had been up all night praying for a particular situation.

The bad weather had dampened everyone's activities, but it had also given many a chance to reflect and determine what needed to be done next.

"Reveal to us your purpose, Father," Anam spoke aloud. "Help us, Lord. Tell us the way to go. You know your people are like driftwood to be cast about in an angry sea and, thereafter, to calm the storm but, lately, we have found ourselves settled in the sand of contentment. That's not your desire. Tell us clearly what you want us to do."

Anam felt the light touch of his wife's hand on his shoulder and she said, "When your purpose is revealed, Father, make us strong enough not to be angry or too lazy to obey. But let us follow you at the appointed time and fulfill your will."

She sat on the floor by him and rested her cheek on his bare leg. Anam toyed with her hair as they stared into each other's eyes.

"I love you so much," he said.

"You are a good husband. Do you believe when God speaks we will be ready to obey?"

He thought for a moment and said, "I know who will obey, but I know there are many who shall remain behind and that is fine. They also have a work to do."

"Then you believe that what has happened concerning the marriages and departures is a good thing?"

"Yes," he nodded emphatically, "as I've said before. It is as though we are gardeners and we are moving across the countryside spreading new and beautiful seed. Perhaps, some of the seed will not produce abundantly, but it is altogether a good thing."

"Tell me again of the remnant of our nation," she said with a smile, "for I love to hear it."

"It has been nearly five years since we departed the mountains of Pitakae and went in search of a home. God told us he would tell us when we had found a home, but he never said we would all settle in the same place. Instead, we have made the whole world our home. And everywhere we have visited, the spirit of God has dwelt there. I wonder if the progeny of the Rasomites shall ever end."

"And," she reminded him, "God has put his seal on every one of them and cares for everyone that we care for. It is a miracle."

"Perhaps tomorrow, the rain shall cease and we'll know where to go."

Paluqua took a deep breath and sighed. "I wonder what kind of packing we shall need to do," she said mockingly.

Many of the Rasomites had been given gifts of clothing and other valuables by the people they had led. However, they all realized when it was time to leave, they would return to their traditional way of dressing and traveling. God would provide everything needed.

They heard a noise at the door and Zoana entered the room. Her cloak was dripping wet and Paluqua ran to her side, helping her remove it.

"It is so cold out there," Zoana commented.

"Colder even than the winter before the fall of Rodan when we lived in the mountains of Pitakae?" Anam asked.

"No," she answered without even considering, "there shall never be another winter quite that cold."

"Still," said Paluqua as she draped the cloak over a chair, "you're cold. Let me fix some tea. Yes?"

Zoana nodded. "That would be nice." Paluqua left the room. Zoana stood with her back to the fire for several minutes. Her eyes were closed as she felt both the warmth of the fireplace and good friends. "Oh, by the way," she said, suddenly opening her eyes. "Remember Oruni, the young boy who has been tagging around after me?"

Anam nodded and she continued.

"He has had so many problems with his father, who is so adamant against his faith and has hindered Oruni's development. Yesterday, he came to me and said he could no longer talk to his father about anything. He was in tears. We spoke until very late and he finally said he desired to be filled with the Holy Ghost."

"Praise the Lord!" said Anam as his whole face seemed to light up.

"Wait. There's much more." She sat cross-legged on the carpet. "He opened up instantly and spoke in tongues. He admitted he was still afraid of his father but, after we prayed, he said he would try one more time. This morning, he came running into my apartment in tears again. But they were tears of joy. When he got home, as it was so late, both his parents were still up and his father was extremely angry. His mother even needed to restrain him. Early this morning, Oruni woke up and his father was sitting at the end of Oruni's bed, full of grief. They talked for a long time about problems and things on both their hearts. When they were finished, Oruni asked his father if he could pray for him. He said that Oruni had a lot of funny ideas, but that, yes, he should always pray for him and to give him time so that he could become as wise as his twelve-year-old son. Then, they hugged each other for a long time and when his dad left, he said, 'Oruni, I love you'. Oruni told me his father had never said that before. He was so excited, though he went back to sleep, he only slept for a few minutes. When he arose, he thought perhaps it was all a dream, but his father was so nice to him. He asked for permission to come see me and his father suggested that I come over soon to eat and talk. Oh, Anam, there is so much work left here despite all that has been accomplished."

"I am so pleased that Oruni's prayers, and yours, have been fulfilled. Zoana..."

She put her hand up and he waited. "Anam, who will continue the work after we leave?"

"The same one who has done all the work so far, the Holy Ghost. He lives here now. He is not merely a visitor. The church in Lasapulis has grown phenomenally, as has the church here in Marsa and throughout the region. They no longer require us. It is nearly time for our rest to be over."

"I know," she said a bit sadly. "We'll be leaving many friends behind us right in the middle of things."

"You should have been training teachers."

"But I have," she said defensively.

"Fine. So, if we leave tomorrow, who's in charge?"

Zoana's mouth fell open as she tried to think of a response.

"Let me ask you," he went on sternly. "We will probably be leaving here very soon. When we leave, do you want to remain behind?'"

Nervously, she shook her head and stuttered, "No...no. I mean, I'm not sure."

"Very soon, we will be moving on. You need to talk to God about this and you need to quickly choose leaders. Perhaps you should go see Togorasom."

Zoana was standing quietly, looking out the rain-streaked window when Paluqua finally reentered the room with a tray of cups and hot tea and cringed when she immediately realized there was a situation going on. She cast her eyes back and forth several times between the two until Zoana finally turned and looked at Anam. She was nearly in tears.

"My precious sister," said Anam as he got up. They held each other very tight and he looked her again in the eye. "Regardless of what you decide to do, I shall completely support you because I know you shall do what you think is best." Her sobbing was too strong for her to answer.

After a few moments, she looked over at Paluqua who quickly put down her tray and they all embraced. Finally, the three sat down and sipped at their tea, until Anam suggested she tell Paluqua about Oruni. Immediately, the room was again filled with joy as Zoana recounted what had happened and Paluqua excitedly took it all in.

Slergotu was a foreigner. He was born in the mountains not far from where the Calodians spent their winters. As a teenager, he had roamed the mountains and desert alone. He had even lived in Lasapulis for a time but could not stand the spiritual darkness present at that time. He had moved to Marsa.

All his life, he had lived with an empty feeling inside of him but also had always had a feeling of anticipation. He had been searching for something, but did not really know what it was. He would go through long periods of loneliness and weep a great deal. The day the first messengers returned from Lasapulis with word of the treaty, he had been encouraged. He had become excited at their words of miracles and strange people from far away. When the first Rasomites arrived in Marsa, he knew he was very close to finding what he had been seeking all his life.

Though he had been befriended by all these people, Zoana considered him to be her star pupil.

Slergotu wiped the tears from his eyes. He never felt lonely these days but wept often, though now for a purpose. He looked across the room where fifteen young boys and girls sat cross-legged on the floor awaiting him to lead them in prayer so they could begin. It had taken many tears and prayers to draw every one of these misfits into his home. When they had first arrived, each had a tale of misery to tell. Their backgrounds included poverty, theft, and beatings. Angelique had been sexually abused by both her parents. Claire had been deeply involved in the occult and had even participated in human sacrifice. Aaron had been a pickpocket and burglar until one of his intended victims had beaten him and blinded him in one eye. Each had shared a tale of misery.

Slergotu opened with a prayer of encouragement. He knew a lot of healing was still needed among these young people. He prayed for inner healing. He also realized, despite their faithfulness in attendance, many were still half-hearted in their obedience. He prayed for trust. He knew none of them, including himself, had abundant finances. He prayed for them to be thankful for what they did have. He finally prayed for spiritual guidance.

"Marti!" A young girl near the front of the room picked up her head and looked at her teacher. "You said you had something to share."

"Yes sir!" she responded enthusiastically.

"Go ahead."

"I had a dream. There was a grove of trees spaced close together and a horrible wind came. Many bushes and other objects were cast about and destroyed but the grove of trees abided unharmed. They protected each other and their roots were wound about each other and grew deep into the earth. Finally, the wind stopped."

He leaned forward and stared into the young girl's eyes. "Do you know what this means?"

"We are the grove of trees and must protect each other when the fierce wind, the devil, comes. We must have our roots tightly bound together and buried deep into the earth, which is God."

"Spoken wisely, child. Now, Marti, consider this question."

"Yes, sir!"

"In what ways have you today sought to bind yourself more closely with this fellowship? You needn't answer, only consider the question."

Marti sat in silence as she remembered the vicious argument that had taken place between her and the other girls only a few moments before coming in and sharing this dream.

"The power of God," Slergotu said as he looked about the room, "is of only very limited value when it is restricted to shared insights. His true power is released not so much by what we say as by how we act. He wants to be your God all of the time. What is a way we can show he is our God?"

One of the girls spoke up. "By sharing and helping persons less fortunate then ourselves."

"That is excellent, Mabi. In what ways?"

She considered for a moment. "We can watch little ones so

that a harried mother could have a few moments of peace."

"You are excused, Mabi. Go and do so."

The young girl arose to leave the room eager to please her teacher. As she reached the outer door, a familiar face met her.

"Zoana!" she exclaimed as she threw her arms around the woman.

"Oh, Mabi. I'm so happy to see you," she said as she held her close. "And where are you off to?"

"Teacher has sent me off on an errand. Actually, I'm going to watch some young children."

"And whose children could that be?"

"I don't know," Mabi said as she shrugged her shoulders, "but I'd best be off."

Mabi's answer confused Zoana, but she merely shook her head as the girl disappeared through the doorway. Zoana entered the room where Slergotu sat with his class. When she came in, he had his eyes closed as he meditated upon a point he desired to make. She quietly slipped into Mabi's place near the back.

"Our God is a god who accepts our repentance, but true repentance means to turn ourselves over to God and to be cleansed of sin and then perform acts toward those we have abused to strengthen our relationship toward them and theirs toward God." As he opened his eyes and looked around the room, his gaze fell on Zoana to whom he directed his next statement. "For we cannot serve God as we ought. We can love him and worship him and obey him but we cannot make him greater. The only way we can truly serve God is to serve man. We serve man by spreading the truth of God's love and that God is alive and by helping relieve people from their suffering."

"But," asked Andreas, "what is true suffering? Let me explain. I know a family, a large family. Several of their children are injured or handicapped. They are poor, as the father cannot work. I attempted to be generous to them and offer them money, but instead of accepting my money, they invited me to dinner. It was a simple meal, but these people seemed satisfied. After eating, they played on their instruments and danced. I had a wonderful evening, and it was I who offered the gift in the beginning."

"Then," asked Slergotu, "what is suffering?"

"I'm baffled," admitted Andreas.

"We all suffer," Slergotu stated. "If we are alive, we suffer.

The world has no perfect solutions and all its solutions are paid with a price. Even if we are close to God, we suffer. But he has offered healing and an eternal life with no suffering. If you want to relieve someone's suffering, do things which reveal to them the promise in your life to bring them close to God."

"This family seems so happy," Andreas said thoughtfully, "but I got no indication they knew God."

"They probably are happy, but you can give them eternal joy, even if it causes some dissension or confusion in this life." He looked at Zoana and smiled. "For any of you who are not familiar with my teacher and good friend, this is Zoana. Welcome. If there is anything that any of us can help you with, we will be pleased to do so."

Zoana stood up and responded quietly. "No, Slergotu, I believe you've already helped me. Thank you." She turned to go, but when he called her name she looked back.

"Thank you for the confidence you've impressed upon me. I shall never forget you and your departure will be a sad day for me."

"I'll never forget you either, my friend. I must go now, but I will see you later."

Zoana stepped outside the door with a heavy heart. It seemed she would spend her whole life saying goodbye and starting over. She walked a few paces along the deserted back street and suddenly collapsed to her knees amid a flood of tears.

"Oh God," she said aloud. "My heart aches for having to constantly say goodbye to your people. I want to be a vessel chosen to spread your good word, but in a sense, I am very selfish. I want it all. I want to travel the world with your truth, but I want to keep all those I love close to me. I know I can't have it both ways. I know I could stay right here in Marsa and do a very good work for you. I know that's not what you want of me. I have a mission. But it breaks my heart to spend my whole life leaving my friends. What shall become of me?"

And then she knew when she felt the presence of that voice inside of her. "My dear child, I love you so much and though it hurts me to see you suffer, it pleases me to know you have such a tender heart. You can have it all. Can't you see that one day you shall all be gathered together in my kingdom? There will be no goodbyes. If you love me, and I know you do, and if you love those chosen to be my people, then you must fulfill that ministry I have set before you. You need only say goodbye until my kingdom comes. Zoana, fill my kingdom."

"Of course," she thought, "how short-sighted of me. I'll see all of these people again. How silly of me. Thank you, Lord, for showing me this."

She stood up and took a moment to compose herself before she went off to continue her rounds. It had been so dark and dreary all morning, but now the sky was beginning to clear up and the sun occasionally broke through. It would take a lot of sunshine, however, to dry up these muddy back streets. Overcoming the desire to return to the relative neatness of the main streets, she instead headed down a very narrow side street, which was barely wide enough for a handcart to maneuver along. By the time she arrived at her destination, her legs were caked with mud up to her knees.

Approaching the dilapidated picket fence, she peered into the darkened windows with regret at not being able to visit her friend, Orphar. Just as she prepared to turn to leave, she heard her name being called from inside the house. As she pushed the little wooden gate open, the front door of the house bolted open and a teenage girl dashed out.

"Melanie!" Zoana called out. "I'm so glad to see you." By the time she had finished her sentence, the red-haired, freckle-faced girl had collided with her and thrown her arms around her.

"Oh, Zoana," the girl moaned. "I'm so pleased that you're here. Orphar so hoped you would come by."

"Why is the house so darkened? Is everything all right?"

Melanie took a deep breath and stepped back, pushing her long hair over her shoulders. "No, things aren't quite right. Orphar is very depressed. She's become ill and has taken to bed."

"Then why wasn't I called?" she asked as she headed into the house.

"I don't believe she wanted to be seen like this. You see, she has always been quite sullen and lonely, until you and the others straightened her up. This is like the old days."

"Melanie!" came a voice from the back of the house. "Who's here?"

"Please, go see her," the girl asked. "I know it will do her good."

As Zoana entered the darkened bedroom, the elderly lady sat

up in bed. "Oh Zoana, my dear friend, I wanted to see you," she rasped. "But I didn't want you to see me ill like this."

"Why is it so dark in here?" Zoana asked sarcastically.

"Uh…why…I don't know."

Zoana opened the curtains and let what light was available in. It was still quite cloudy out, but this provided some light. "That's much better." She turned back to the bed. "Why didn't you call me or one of the others?"

"Well…I…uh…didn't want to be a pain. I felt I'd get better if I rested for a few days." Her voice had improved considerably.

Orphar was a slight lady in her eighties. What remained of her thin hair clung in a sweaty bundle to her head. She sat there with her lower chin trembling as though she'd been caught, which she had.

"Orphar, my precious sister," Zoana said as she sat next to her and took her hands. "You are so valuable to the church here. They need you, but we all know the strength of youth is gone. You do need your rest. We understand. But you don't have to pretend to be sick and sit here in loneliness to justify it."

"It's hard for an old woman, Zoana. Sometimes I feel so alone and like no one cares. I know people do but it's hard for me."

"Is it hard for you to let them love you?" Zoana whispered.

"You always seem to go right to the point." She chuckled and became sullen again. "Yes, it's hard for me. I feel like I should reciprocate, and sometimes, I'm just not up to it."

"You mean the doing of deeds? Yes, that's important, but it's only a part of love. There's much you can do."

"What can an old woman do who can hardly get about?"

"You know," said Zoana looking longingly out the window. "I believe God created each of us the way we are with an ability to do something very valuable for him. Some with strong bodies can perform his physical work, some with nimble fingers and a keen eye can create beauty, some with a quick wit or great wisdom to make decisions. But sometimes, it's to the weakest vessels he has given the greatest ministry." Orphar was very attentive. "I believe everyone filled with the spirit is called to pray, but I believe some are fortunate enough not to have a lot of distractions and can lead a mighty prayer life. They can save multitudes and break through barriers man cannot in his own strength. And even if, God forbid, not one of those prayers were answered because the evil one came and destroyed, I think God is pleased anyway. And as a person develops an abundant prayer life and learns the will of God, their prayers will get answered."

"Zoana," Orphar was crying, "teach me to pray."

"God is a good God and a good Father. He will give us so much if we simply ask for it and have faith. But, we don't want to be like spoiled children, we should yearn to please him. His greatest desire is for all people to come to know him and accept his saving grace. First, when we speak to him, we should remind ourselves of his great magnificence. Then, we should admit our own sins and limitations and ask for help. It is vital we wait for his response as we intercede for others."

"Can we pray for Melanie and her boyfriend, Beor? He's such a rough guy and not good for her at all in his present shape. I'm so angry that she won't even listen to me. I'd also like to pray for the man who runs the market. He's nice to talk to, but I know him personally. Everything is money."

"I've been waiting for you," the boy said as Zoana entered his tiny room. She sat on the edge of his cot. The adornments for the room consisted of the small bed upon which she sat, a candlestick in a brass holder and a clay water pot and cup. The room was small; however, this is what Togorasom had insisted on.

She sat for several minutes just staring into his eyes. Her mind wandered to the many incidents proving his prophetic abilities. When he prayed, things happened. His total commitment to God did not vary from day to day. It was difficult for even her to imagine so much devotion from a boy so young. She had to look him up and down as he sat there cross-legged, to remember he was not some old man seasoned in wisdom, but only a young boy God needed.

"I felt a need to see some old friends to help reassure my faith," she commented, feeling foolish after saying it. "I mean…"

"I understand," he said and smiled. "It's a good thing to see the reality of our faith mature. You've done so much and worked so hard for these people. One day, they shall thank you."

"I don't do it for the thanks. I do it because I must."

"Has the weather improved?" he asked, looking at her dry clothes.

"I thought you among all people would know something like that." She smiled at her dry attempt at humor.

He snapped his gaze to the floor, dejectedly. Zoana felt awful at being misinterpreted, but before she could speak he said, "I'm only a little boy." He looked back at her. She could see all the child now in his face and the realization struck her that it must be terribly difficult for him to maintain such spiritual commitment in a young mind. Most boys his age would be playing ball or tag or teasing other children.

"I'm sorry, I didn't mean to hurt," she said. "It's hard…"

He grinned and shook his head. "It's fine, Zoana. I understand and forgive you. It is hard, isn't it, always trying to read each other's minds and trying to find the right thing to say. God has a special place for you in his kingdom. I pray when that day comes, I am found worthy to be even your servant."

Zoana laughed. "Togorasom, the sweet Lord, I am sure, has a far better task awaiting you than to be my servant."

He looked as he was about to cry. She shifted quickly to the floor on her knees beside his bed and embraced him.

"I love you so much," she said.

"I love you, too. It's so hard," he said quietly. "There's so much to do and though we work hard, we make so little progress."

She nodded her head. "But he rejoices whenever we lead one a step closer to home."

He looked her in the face. He seemed so grief stricken. "I weep for the multitude which are lost. Sometimes, I become so upset I would like to slap people in the face to make them listen. They kick against God and others stare at us dumbly. I get so frustrated." Suddenly, he grew very calm. "And then one day, I see what looks like great hope shining from a person's life and I glorify God. And the next day, it's as though nothing had happened."

"But many are saved," she said encouragingly.

"Praise God. If only one person had been saved through our travels, I believe I would have done everything exactly the same."

"Togorasom," she said and kissed him on the cheek, "you are a perplexity. Sometimes you're like a very wise old man and again like a frightened little boy."

"Zoana, do you ever get lonely?"

"Sometimes I get very lonely," she admitted.

"I get so lonely I can hardly stand it. Please, don't tell anyone. I think people are afraid of me. I'm not like anyone else. I get confused."

She looked at him in amazement. "I never knew. You have a very unique gift from God. Your life is a gift. I believe people hold you in great awe and some are jealous."

"I always want to be used by God, but a prophet is nothing to be jealous of. In fact, it's quite terrible."

The woman and boy sat on the floor of his room embracing in silence for a long time. He finally asked her why she had come.

"I wanted to ask you to pray for me to be strong when it comes time for us to leave. I've grown so close to people here. It seems as though we no more than get to know people and we are moving on."

He closed his eyes. "Are you quite certain that, when we are called to leave, God wants you to go?"

His statement took her by surprise. She hadn't seriously considered remaining behind. Despite her ties with people met along the way, the Rasomites were her family. She would feel deserted if they left without her, though others had already made known their intentions to remain behind.

"When we call upon the Lord for direction," he said, "we leave the direction to him. If you want the strength to do what you have already decided to do, he can give you that as well. However, these are quite different prayers." He opened his eyes and gazed into hers. "Do you want to know God's will or do you want the strength to fulfill your convictions? If you want to know God's will, he can also, afterward, give you strength. But if you merely want strength then you must be willing to accept the consequences." He smiled and became a bit less serious. "Do not worry though, Zoana. You are a woman of God and you are living in God's will. He will be pleased with whatever you decide to do." She sat quietly looking him in the face. "I'm sorry," he said, "if all I have managed to do is confuse you more. Sometimes we can be so absolutely convinced we are in God's will and be heading in the complete opposite direction. But, if a person is truly led by God, it won't take long before they realize they made a mistake. How should I pray?"

She nervously shuffled about for a few seconds. "Of course, pray that I truly seek God's will and do what he wants. One can never be truly happy living outside of God's will." She hesitated. "I assume, of course, that you will be going?"

"Yes, I'll be going. I knew that from before we ever came here. God has a plan for me. I guess I'm young enough that I'm not aware of all the inducements the world has to offer so it's easy, I think, for me to follow his call."

"A lot of folks feel young people are very rebellious and they must need some age and maturity before they become obedient."

"Mind you, this is not always the case," he said. "It depends upon who is being rebellious against whom." She furrowed her brow as she tried to understand what he meant. "A lot of young people are rebellious to a lot of older people who are set in their ways and living outside the will of God. What right does a person have to accuse another of rebelliousness when he is the one who is actually rebelling against God? Let me illustrate. When I first arrived in Lasapulis, the King's desire was to destroy me. He knew I was a rebel and opposed to his way. It was only later, after he had learned God's will in his life, that he befriended me. But I understood that and dealt with it. How can a person learn God's will except another person teach him to listen? Of any father who says his child is rebellious, I would ask him if the child has been taught to seek God's will and know what needs to be done. If that father has not listened to his child and taught that child to listen, then that child is really not a rebel but confused and the parents are to blame. However," he said as he settled down, "if that father has been diligent to teach God's love and the child rebels against both parent and God, then the child bears the blame of deciding to be damned."

Zoana sat silent and amazed, gazing at the boy. Finally, she spoke up. "I hope someday you have many children, for they should do well."

He shook his head nervously. "Bringing a child into the world is too grave a responsibility for me to contemplate at this time. Parents need to consider that the labor truly is not over after the baby is born. This is when the work begins. They have made a decision to bring a soul into the world that can very easily fall prey to Satan. It's too much for me to think about right now."

When Zoana reemerged to the outdoors, the sky again was nearly overcast with a thin, light grey blanket of clouds and a light drizzle was falling. She stopped to adjust the hood on her cloak before going out, and an elderly lady, face set in grimness, passed by.

"Will this foul weather ever let up?" the woman asked, shaking her head. "I'm sick of it."

Before Zoana could respond, the woman shuffled on.

"May I help you?" Zoana called out, but received no response. She said a short prayer for the lady's disposition and prepared to leave.

The old woman turned back and made a comment. "I suppose it's always like this at this time of year. It could be much worse. Have a nice day just the same, dearie." So saying, she turned and walked away.

"Even in the little things," thought Zoana. "He even answers the little prayers." She slowly walked down the empty street, unsure of what to do next. She thought of half a dozen devoted students of hers she could visit whose company she enjoyed, but they would all be busy this time of day, fulfilling their own ministries. She had taught them well and so had run herself out of a job. It was becoming quite clear she was no longer needed here and this thought both pleased and depressed her.

Suddenly she caught the familiar figure of Crazon heading her way.

It was quite clear she had been walking a long time in the rain. Her wrap draped from her shoulders as a sodden weight. It was so soaked through that its heaviness seemed to permeate Crazon's attitude and act as a heavy burden. Crazon walked slowly with her head down and her hands in her pockets. Sensing someone was watching her, she looked up at Zoana, who was still several paces away, and gazed expressionless as though she were staring at a stranger. For a moment, Zoana did not know how to react toward this usually joyful woman. Then Crazon's face contorted as though she were preparing to cry, but she regained her self-control before the weeping came. Zoana rushed to her and embraced her.

"Oh, Zoana," she moaned, "I just can't go on. My spirit has been destroyed. My peace has left me."

"Shh," Zoana encouraged her, "and have strength for God is still in you. Whatever could have happened?"

"Very little. And that has caused my anguish. How hard we have tried. We pray. We witness. We teach. It all falls on deaf ears. I can't stand it anymore."

"No, my sister," Zoana corrected her, "many have indeed fallen, but we have done great good in this place."

"No, you have done good. My fruit is like a rotten heap. I have done nothing."

"Crazon, how can you say that? You teach the King's house. From all about, people come and pass by the rest of us seeking your prayer. And your prayers get answered."

"Where is the benefit of all I've done?"

"This isn't like you. Even I owe my spiritual growth to you. So many times I've stumbled, and so many times your helping hand was there."

"Zoana, I feel like my life is a lie. I feel so empty. I see how hard I've worked and how little progress I've made."

"I feel we've made great progress. I agree we leave this place far short of perfection, but where would it be if we had never arrived? We can begin from the first day. The entire region would still be torn to pieces with war and bloodshed. We did that. God did it, and we were his ministers. Can you deny the region is at peace?"

Crazon nodded. "The region is at peace."

"Will you admit you have made any progress with the King's household?"

"They are doing well."

"Do you love me?"

"Everything you say is true and yet I feel so spiritually weak."

"I asked you if you love me," Zoana repeated, "because I want you to listen to me. Do you love me?"

Crazon took a deep breath. "Of course, I love you. You know I love you."

"I often feel weak. It is the enemy. If he can convince you of your weakness and that you fight a senseless battle, perhaps you will give up and he can more easily snatch away a few more souls. Believe me, if King Chiam's household denied their faith, God forbid, the Devil would cause great damage. When I feel weak, I sometimes think it best to go off on my own and try to sort things out and regain my strength." Crazon nodded her head. "That's usually the worst mistake I could make. I wind up running myself into the ground. I find it best to find someone to pray with and talk with. Someone I can trust and who is honest with me. Someone who can reaffirm me. Someone..."

Crazon was shaking her head. "That's enough. I'm beginning to snap out of it. I wished I had run into you earlier."

Zoana laughed. "No. I wouldn't have helped much. I was

confused and depressed and too disillusioned." Crazon looked surprised. "However, I came here and talked with Togorasom, and even though I'm still confused, I'm no longer depressed or disillusioned. I know God will work it all out." Crazon suddenly sneezed. "But the least I could have done is to get you to come in out of the rain. You need to change into warm, dry clothes."

Later, in Zoana's apartment, Crazon sat on the carpet by the fireplace sipping tea. Zoana had lain down on the floor beside her and, after hours of chatting, had fallen to sleep. Though her friend's words were true and her companionship warm, Crazon still felt an emptiness inside that said she had fallen far short of what God had expected. She felt her successes were obvious and praiseworthy, but no one knew of her failures. There were times when God had said, "Go!" and she had not. She remembered the times when she had pretended to pray or promised to pray and she had not. There was an endless series of good deeds she had not performed. There were times when others had encouraged her to participate and she had not. There were times when she knew she had duties to perform but had gone along with the group because she felt it was expected. She sometimes felt as if her life was out of control. She actually shivered at the thought of the unsaved souls because she had not spoken up or acted quickly enough.

The heat of the fire felt wonderful on her face. It pleased her that Zoana had brought her in and encouraged her. She also knew she would continue in her work with the royal family until it was time to leave or she was presented with a weightier issue. Still, there was an empty feeling of her ineptitude and shortcomings. Unexpectedly, she began to weep.

"Oh, God," she whispered, so as not to disturb her friend, "help me. I've learned to be so loving and patient with others and yet so angry at myself. You and I both know how hard your servant has worked to share the light. And how many failures I've met. I love you for every time we've softened a hard heart and brought someone closer to you. So much good has been done and yet I feel so incomplete. What's the matter with me? Why, Lord? Why do I feel so down? How can I get my emotions out of this slump and get back to work?"

She paused in her prayer and looked out the window. It was

dark now. From her position she could not tell if the rain had stopped. It would please everyone if the weather let up a bit.

"Lord," she continued, still gazing out the window, "give me the strength to keep going. Make me more able to follow my convictions. Make me more obedient. Break my heart, if you need to. I know I am not perfect. Of course, that is my goal. If I need to think of my failures to remain humble, so be it. But please, Lord, don't let that be an excuse for me to fail or give up. Let that be an excuse to try harder and to more earnestly follow your will. I know the way of this world and this foolish mind is to find my own way. But the path is easier following you. And even if it doesn't seem easier to us, it is more pleasing to you. I also know, Lord, that hereafter you shall remember all and shall remind us. Thank you, Lord, for listening to me." She looked down at Zoana. "And thank you for allowing me to be part of your family."

She lay down by Zoana and soon fell asleep.

Ernie shook himself back awake. He placed the palm of his hand gently on his forehead wondering if his headache was from lack of sleep or if he was falling prey to the same bug that had struck Darophil. Ernie had set up camp in the kitchen so as not to disturb the rest of the household. With the curtains over the doorway and the windows drawn, the wood burning oven made the room very warm. He sat on an old wool rug with a bowl of nuts and beaker of water beside him. Darophil had come to him in the middle of the night burning up with a fever. He had given him a cool sponge bath and a cup of warm chamomile tea, hoping its soothing qualities would at least allow the four-year-old to get some sleep. Now the boy lay sprawled out on the carpet with his head on Ernie's lap. He was sleeping, but not soundly. However, his temperature had returned to normal. Ernie didn't know what else to do now but encourage him to sleep and himself to pray. He had been praying a great deal.

His concerns were basically the same as everyone else's, though he hadn't been praying for himself. He knew as long as Anam and Paluqua needed help with the children, he would be wherever they were. That was his job. He prayed for the others whose lives seemed more complicated than his. There always seemed to be so much going on, and although he was often overlooked, he never resented it as he hadn't the time for most of it anyway. Sometimes he would feel rundown and begin to wonder if he was doing anything that really mattered. Paluqua was a great encourager. Though she was often out building God's kingdom too, they were usually a team. Paluqua was also considered to be, in most ways, in charge next after Anam. Fortunately, the Rasomites did not need a mother very often, but they did need someone to talk to. And they drank a lot of tea and ate a lot of soup. Paluqua had virtually every blend of tea imaginable and, as Ernie had become a great tea-drinker as well, this pleased him beyond measure.

He adjusted the blanket over the boy and leaned against the wall with his eyes closed.

"Oh, God," he said quietly, "bless these beautiful people that have devoted their whole lives to serving you and saving souls. Again I plead with you, Lord, to show these friends exactly what you would have them do. I know it's not easy trying to help other people when we have to be continually moving on. I think some of them will have their hearts broke no matter which way they decide to go. I know I'm content and I thank you for that." He could have fallen to sleep at that point, but he opened his eyes and glanced down at the boy.

Darophil's eyes were wide opened and looking at Ernie.

They smiled and stared at each other for a few moments before Darophil said, "I love you, Ernie." Then he closed his little eyes and went back to sleep.

Ernie stifled the lump forming in his throat and then he fell to sleep as well.

It seemed like only a moment of rest but he actually slept soundly for over an hour. When he opened his eyes, he first realized it was beginning to become light outside. Then he realized the fire had gone out. Darophil was gone and, upon inspection, was found sleeping soundly in his own bed. Since everything seemed fine in the children's rooms, he went back to the kitchen to clean up. There came a timid tap at the door.

Expecting it to be one of the Rasomite women, he only casually peeked out the window before opening the door. It was a woman, however, upon greeting her he did not recognize her, though he dimly recalled meeting this woman before. He put his finger to his lips to indicate his wish for her to speak quietly and invited her in.

She stepped in and noiselessly closed the door behind her. Ernie invited her into the kitchen where they could speak more freely. Once in the kitchen, she pulled the hood down from her cape and tassels of beautiful red hair tumbled over her neck.

"Oh, I'm beginning to remember," he said. "The princess from Lasapulis..."

"Daedena," she said with a warm smile. "And you are Ernie. Is that correct? Anam's right hand man."

Though Daedena stated it as a fact and not as a compliment, he took it so and it took a moment for him to continue the conversation. It was at this point he realized his visitor was damp and had obviously been traveling overnight.

"Why on earth," he asked her, "is a woman of your prestige traveling in such a manner. I hope nothing is wrong."

"Absolutely nothing is wrong," she reassured him. "I entertained Zoana and Crazon at my house recently because I knew they were leaving. I just couldn't stand the idea of them being only a few hours away and not seeing them again."

"A few hours from Lasapulis!" he said surprised. "You have flown, haven't you Madame?" It usually was a two-day trip.

"Let's say I know the shortcuts." She took a deep breath. "But it is nice to be in a warm house again and dry off."

"Oh, I'm sorry," he apologized. "This thing has gone out." He indicated the oven. "Let me get it going again. It won't take a minute. I'm sure Paluqua will want you to stay for breakfast."

In a few minutes, the room was again cozy and warm. Ernie went out and led the horse around the house, leaving it with a trough full of fresh water and a bucket of oats. When he returned, Daedena had hung her cape near the heat and squatted herself on the floor as there was no furniture in the little room.

Ernie began to prepare breakfast. This morning would be pancakes. As he went about his duties, they talked about all the fine things going on in Lasapulis. In the midst of their conversation, Paluqua walked in.

"Well, praise the Lord!" she exclaimed. "I thought I heard voices, but I never expected to have you for a visitor this morning. I'm so glad to see you again."

Daedena got up and gave Paluqua a hug, explaining the reason behind her unexpected visit.

Paluqua finally cut her off and addressed herself to Ernie.

"Were you up last night with Darophil?"

"Yes, ma'am," he said as he continued cooking.

"Why didn't you wake me up?" she asked sternly.

"For what reason, ma'am? So the whole household could be miserable? I think I'm capable of getting a little boy to go back to sleep. How is he now?"

"He's fine, but…"

"Then why the need to get everyone up, when the reason I brought him out here was so everyone else could sleep?"

She couldn't answer that question. "Can't get good help," she said to Daedena. "I'm sorry," she said to Ernie. "I appreciate your concern."

Daedena pointed to him. "If you ever decide to get rid of him, send him my way." She gave Ernie a wink and he continued his cooking.

Paluqua and Daedena stood in the kitchen for several minutes talking about the still growing church in Lasapulis. Not only was the old hall always full, many had started church groups in their homes and other places around town. Her sister-in-law, Omitu, was now carrying a baby, which gave the King immense pleasure. Daedena's son was getting stronger every day. Madaro usually took him everywhere he went, especially when visiting. He was glad to let her go for a few days to visit her friends and regretted he could not go as well.

Oranea and Bonifa walked into the room with their little eyes still closed and surrounded Paluqua, each clutching a hand.

"My Lord," said Daedena, "they certainly have sprung up since I saw them last. They certainly do grow fast. And how's the baby?"

Paluqua laughed. "The baby is probably waking up her father."

She was shortly proved wrong when Comeana nearly ran into the room. Ernie put down his cooking utensils and swooped her up, giving her a batch of kisses. Paluqua excused herself to see what was keeping Anam and Darophil, leaving Ernie and Daedena to set the table and finish the preparations.

"I wish I'd known we were going to have a guest," Ernie apologized. "I would have prepared a regular banquet."

"This is better because it makes me feel like one of the family. Thank you for so graciously allowing me to be a part of this."

"I've done nothing beyond what I would do for any friendly stranger under the same circumstances. Thank you for being part of our family."

Paluqua returned. "I'm worried about those two. Darophil seems okay, just tired. But Anam has an awfully high fever and is bathed in perspiration. He wanted to talk to Togorasom this morning about leaving."

"Let's agree in prayer," said Daedena, taking the hands of Ernie and Paluqua as she prayed for Anam's health.

When she was finished, Paluqua continued. "He says he's fine and just needs to sleep. You know how he gets."

Ernie laughed. "He wants a nursemaid to wait on him when he's feeling fine, but when he's under the weather, he's well enough to take care of himself. Just the same, I believe we should get all of us fed and then get you all out of the house. You can go find Crazon and Zoana. I'll try to get some sleep and be around in case they need any help."

"Now I don't want you getting sick, too," cautioned Paluqua.

"That's why I need to get some sleep. They'll be no trouble. Let's eat."

"I am convinced it is the boy. If we can destroy him, we can tear them to pieces."

"No, I still disagree. It is the man, Anam, we are after."

Rotal adjusted his cap and spat on the ground. He was dressed in simple street-cleaner clothes. He fit his role well as he had neither cleaned nor shaven for several days.

"Shecktel, damn you!" he barked at his sidekick. "I have argued with you over this for months. They revere that boy. They think he is someone special. I have watched them coming and going for weeks. Anam may act as a commander, but the boy is the key. I think they revere him like a god. When he is gone, we can expose them."

"We can't risk taking a chance. Suppose you are wrong?" challenged Shecktel.

"I am convinced I am right. I think it's pretty obvious. Besides, Anam is too well protected. He is nearly always surrounded by these chattering women. We could not get in. The boy is often alone. I have watched. He would be an easier catch."

"The poison?"

Rotal patted his bosom. "All I have to do is sneak into his

apartment and pour it into his drink. No color. No taste. After he dies, we can show they are not what they say."

Shecktel looked toward Togorasom's apartment. "I've waited a long time for this day. I think maybe you are right. Besides, it was his fault Martin was killed."

Rotal looked very thoughtful for a moment. "We had a good thing going before he arrived and ruined it all. It irritates me to no end they did it so easily."

"And everybody sold out," Shecktel snapped back, "or died. I want back what we had. My father trained me in the arts and now it is gone. Lasapulis was ours and these Rasomites have stolen it."

"I still don't understand how the King could have had Martin slain. We tried so hard to serve him. How could he have been tricked so easily?"

Shecktel looked back at Rotal. "Can we get this done today?" he asked. "I don't want to drag it out any longer."

"It'll be today. There's still one thing left to cover."

"Which is?" Shecktel asked.

Rotal pulled the metal cylinder out of his pocket which contained the poison and gazed at it in the palm of his hand. "We need a recourse in case something goes wrong."

"I shall strangle him with my bare hands," growled Shecktel gritting his teeth. "I'll smother him with his pillow. I'll beat him to death."

"I detect," smiled Rotal, "you are sufficiently angry, but...I don't know." He shook his head. "A small part of me is still unsure. I'm simply afraid something will go wrong."

"The only thing that will go wrong is you are losing your nerve."

"Oh, shut up!" snapped Rotal. "I'm not losing my nerve. I simply don't want to screw this up. We'll only have one chance. Something could go wrong."

"If you're afraid, I'll go in!" snapped Shecktel back.

"I am not afraid at all. I'm merely not as foolish as you are. Suppose he doesn't drink it. We may be interrupted in the midst of it. He may vomit it up. We need an alternative. I've got to think about this a bit."

He turned and began pushing his broom again. Shecktel gazed down the street towards the entrance of Togorasom's apartment. The earliness of the day was on his mind. It seemed this would be the best time of the day. No one was about and waiting any longer would decrease their chances. The boy was probably sleeping and would soon wake up and reach for his water glass.

"Will you stop your gawking," Rotal grumbled. "Who knows if we're being spied upon."

"We need to move now," replied Shecktel soberly. He slowly turned his head back toward his partner. "I feel it inside of me. In a few moments, I am sure, it will be too late."

The seriousness of Shecktel's comment struck Rotal as requiring immediate action. He nodded his head, passed over his broom and walked back down the street. He kept his head down in an effort to conceal his identity and also from the fear he was beginning to feel. It was almost as though there were a spiritual aura about the premises. Nonetheless, he entered the building without being noticed and found Togorasom's room easily. He had been there once before when the building was empty to plan his evil deed.

Rotal peered into the room. Togorasom sat cross-legged, eyes closed, with his head back looking as though he were in some sort of a trance. His assassin slowly opened the tube, crept into the room and emptied its contents into the goblet of water sitting on the floor next to the unflinching prayer warrior. It all seemed so amazingly simple. Rotal turned to leave and Togorasom spoke.

"Your return is most welcome, enemy of God. Why have you covenanted with Satan to do this thing?"

Rotal froze as terror crept over him. He didn't know what to do.

"Sit down!" Togorasom ordered.

Outside, the minutes ticked by. Shecktel was becoming nervous.

"What is that fool doing?" he mumbled.

A well-dressed man passed Shecktel and commented on how clean that one slab of sidewalk appeared. He was gone from view before Shecktel realized he had been furiously sweeping the same piece of pavement over and over. He angrily threw his broom to the ground and glared in the direction Rotal had gone nearly an hour before. Something had obviously gone wrong with the plan. Rotal must have been caught. He then remembered what had happened to Martin and suddenly became aware his own life was in danger. Quickly snatching up their cleaning tools, he left the area.

Rotal stumbled from the building and sat on the steps. His mind was swimming. He slid on his buttocks along the stairway and leaned his head on the guardrail as he sank deeper and deeper into his subconscious.

It was a beautiful morning. The sun had completely cleared the horizon, and even this early, most of the main streets were fairly dried up. The air was warm and there was not a cloud in the sky. By the time Paluqua and Daedena had left with the three children, the streets were already getting busy. It simply seemed like a good day to get out.

"It's so lovely this morning!" exclaimed Daedena. "I knew coming here would be a good idea. The horrible weather was the only concern I had."

"It is nice today," agreed Paluqua. She had a little boy's hand in each of hers. Daedena carried Comeana. Paluqua looked tense.

"What's wrong, dear?" asked Daedena.

She shook her head. "I don't know. I just have a very bad feeling about something. I can't think of what it could be."

They were going to Zoana's apartment after having followed Ernie's advice to leave him to rest and play nursemaid to Anam and Darophil. Everyone they met was in high spirits, but a feeling of dread was coming over Paluqua. After a great deal of meandering from one shop to another and stopping to chat many times, she could contain herself no more.

"Daedena, I have to return home. Something awful has happened. If you want to, I urge you to go to Zoana's, but I must go back."

Daedena was concerned and confused. However, she handed Comeana over to her friend and, after embracing her, she went on. Paluqua turned, walked a few paces, and burst into tears. After getting her emotions under control, she gathered her children together and headed home.

Zoana and Crazon had slept soundly in front of the fireplace and were awake early. After eating, they decided to go out into the sunshine as well. But before their departure, they began to feel the same unexplainable grief Paluqua was feeling.

"I think I need to go see Anam and see if something is up," suggested Crazon.

"No," said Zoana, "we need to go see Togorasom. Something has happened to Togorasom."

They departed immediately, walking at first but soon breaking into a run. Upon reaching Togorasom's apartment, it was instantly apparent that their concern was justified. A large crowd had gathered at the entrance and with the shocked and dismayed expressions the people bore, the unknown dismay the women were feeling began to become understood. The crowd parted in respect to allow them to enter. They were met at the entrance by one of King Chiam's officers.

"Oh." He shook his head sadly. "How awful and how unexpected."

"What has happened?" demanded Zoana.

"The boy, Togorasom, is dead. He appears to have died in his sleep as there is no evidence of foul play. One of the cleaning people discovered him."

Zoana and Crazon pushed their way passed him and went to Togorasom's room. He was being attended by a doctor.

"Oh, thank God you're here," the doctor said, moving to one side. "You're much better at this than I am. Unfortunately, we are all too late."

Zoana reached down and placed the palm of her hand on the boy's cold and lifeless cheek. Immediately, both women began praying.

It had been nearly two weeks since Togorasom's death. At first, there was a general attitude he must have been murdered, for it seemed someone as wise as he could not have allowed himself to merely expire. As the days wore on, though, it became more and more evident that there was no one else involved. This must be simply part of God's plan. The entire city was now pervaded with a deep sense of depression. The boy had been unknown to most of the people, as he lived in seclusion most of the time, but everyone sensed the feeling of loss among the Rasomites. Finally, Anam had reluctantly consented to his burial in the King's own sepulcher.

The crazy man, Rotal, had been arrested in an unrelated incident. Since his encounter with Togorasom, his mind had snapped. He had lost his ability to speak and, instead, babbled meaninglessly to everyone he came in contact with.

Shecktel hid himself. He kept a very low image, and when he was out, he scurried about the city like a rat. Inside, he felt supreme joy at what was going on around him. The one public appearance he did make was to shuffle passed the body of Togorasom with the rest of the people when his corpse was put out for a viewing. Part of him wanted to burst out into the open and announce to all the world what they had so easily done. What kept him back was the terror of what had happened to Martin and his cronies, and now to Rotal. He had seen Rotal only once and that was enough. The man had spasms of jumping, he slobbered and acted like a wild animal. Shecktel figured that if he knew what had happened to Rotal, he could avoid the same fate himself. If he could not figure it out, he knew he had best avoid Rotal.

It had also bothered him that many from Lasapulis had come to pray, comfort and watch. He had laid particularly low those days when the crowd was present for fear of being recognized. Now, nearly all had returned home and his ducking and dodging had subsided.

"How earnestly we think we understand what God is trying to say, and in a moment, our dreams and hopes seem to go up in smoke." Anam sat in his apartment and allowed his bleary-eyed gaze to wander about the room and fall upon those gathered who continued to support each other. The ones closest to the dead prophet; Paluqua, Crazon, Zoana, Ernie and the children were included. Daedena had decided to remain behind until she was certain there was nothing else she could do.

"What is needed now," spoke Zoana softly, "is to raise up our spirits and continue our work. Togorasom is in a better place than us. We need to keep going for his honor. I say this and I am about to again burst into tears. It seems so unfair."

"Did you realize," said Paluqua as she gazed upward thoughtfully, "despite many having left us, this is the only death we are aware of since Mebiktu went to his savior back in the desert?"

"I have thought of that," commented Anam. "In another way, we have been very blessed. Before Mebiktu died, there was hardly a day when the lives of the Rasomites were spared."

"Anam?" asked Daedena abruptly and received his attention. "How did Togorasom die?"

He looked bewildered. "I do not know, my lady. I have diligently petitioned God concerning this and have been answered with silence. We have all sought God on this." Everyone nodded in agreement.

"Is there not," she asked, "a covenant of protection by God over your people that if one of you is slain, God's wrath will destroy that person?"

"There is," he answered, "and that is one clue we have that there was no foul play. There were no other deaths in the city after this incident that seemed at all related to it. Though, it still beats contrary in my heart. Something is not right. It is beginning to seem like a moot point as we have bantered this around for two weeks. I believe it is an empty issue until God leads us or reveals it to us. We all need to diligently continue calling upon the Lord."

It had started raining again. It was a gentler and warmer rain than what had fallen previously. Before, the rain had kept people in and farmers from their spring planting. Now, the crops were in and this rain would encourage new growth.

Daedena walked the streets. In every face she looked upon and in every situation that arose, the burning in her heart to find the truth of the boy's death continued. However, there were no answers. The Rasomites were rebuilding their ministries from the neglect they had suffered. They were very busy.

Every day she would go to the tomb where Togorasom had been placed in expectation of something. Occasionally, there were other visitors, but none so devoted as her. Doubt was also growing. The longer the length of time since his death, the less the people truly expected a solution.

One day, while praying, she fell to sleep in front of the tomb's entrance under an eave out of the rain.

"Daedena!"

She was alert.

Togorasom sat on the little stone bench opposite her. "Do not be alarmed, only listen. You must find the man, Rotal, and bring him here. He has lost his mind, and I need to restore him. Will you do that?"

"Of course, I will do whatever you ask." She spoke to an empty space. The image of Togorasom was gone.

For a minute, she sat there and wondered if the image was real or merely a dream. Slowly, she came to the realization that it didn't matter. This was a piece of the puzzle they had been looking for. She prayed for God's wisdom and strength and then hurried off to see King Chiam's warden. She felt led of the Spirit of God to the warden. It also made sense that he might have word of a man who had recently lost his mind. He would help her find this man, Rotal.

"I cannot do it, my lady. You do not know what you are asking."

"I know what I am asking," Daedena insisted. "On the day Togorasom died, this man was found wandering about. He was charged with insanity due to his peculiar and uncontrollable ways, and a short time later, he was locked up in your prison. I believe there is a relationship between the crazy man and Togorasom's death. I need him."

The chief warden buried his face in the papers on his desk and Daedena detected he was shivering. He finally sat up and again nervously reiterated the man's activities leading to his arrest. Shop windows were smashed, innocent people pummeled, the arresting guard had been bitten and his arm was swollen like from a dog bite. The crazy man could not speak or respond in any intelligible way. The only way they had found to subdue him was to beat him like an unruly dog and place him in chains. Even some of the Rasomites had attempted to pray over him to no avail.

"I dare not allow you near him, madam. Did you give a name?"

"I have reason to believe his name is Rotal."

"How did you learn his name? No one knows anything about this…this man."

Daedena pursed her lips and thought for a moment. "I cannot tell you how I learned of his name. I ask you to trust me," she begged in desperation.

"I do trust you," he answered patiently, "but you must trust me as well. I have enough faith in you to know you would not make this unusual request without reason. However, I cannot release him. I would be committing a crime."

"May I, at least, see him?" she asked hopefully.

"I suppose there is no problem with your seeing him. He is secure. Come with me."

They passed a guard and entered a doorway leading into a long corridor of prison cells. All of the cells were empty and clean, displaying the power again of the Rasomites' word. They entered a doorway at the far end of the corridor which led them down a flight of stairs. At the bottom of the stairs was a solitary prison cell. Seated at the far end of the cell on a wooden bench bolted to the floor sat a figure secured by four shackles, one to each arm and leg. His back was towards them. The man was nearly naked, wearing only a few rags. His hair hung together in clumps of sweaty, frothy tassels. The skin on his back that was exposed was raw and bleeding where he continuously dug at himself.

The warden leaned to Daedena's ear and whispered. "We can do nothing for him. He is so uncontrollable. We can scarcely feed and water him. I wish something would put this poor man out of his misery."

"Perhaps I can help," she whispered. "Rotal!" she called out.

The crazy man sat upright in his seat.

"Amazing," whispered the warden. "He'd respond to nothing from us."

"Rotal!" she called again.

He turned and stared at her. His gaze tore right into her heart. For a moment, he looked like a sad puppy who no one understood. Then, he changed. He gritted his teeth and began growling and then roaring. He kept snapping at his chains, which were securely bolted to the floor.

"We must leave, immediately!" ordered the warden.

They turned and ran back up the stairway. Rotal's howling could be heard until the warden closed the door securely on his office again. The warden gave instructions to the guard to go watch Rotal but not to abuse him.

They sat back down in their seats, nervously shaking. Finally, the warden spoke up angrily.

"Now do you understand!" he yelled at her. "I cannot possibly allow this animal out of these walls to go with you. I insist you leave here and do not come back. I am sorry for my anger, but I have to think of my prisoner and the security of the people. Now go!" He pointed at the exit.

Daedena slowly rose from her seat and backed towards the door. "I will leave for now. However, I will return. I will be taking Rotal with me."

As Daedena walked along the streets she continued to replay in her mind Rotal's violent outburst, but she concentrated on the man. His face was so ugly. His lips were bleeding. He had a scraggly, dirty beard. His eyes revealed the obvious demon possession that was upon him. She knew that kind of terror as she had experienced it herself. However, in her mind she began working on his appearance. She trimmed his beard, washed and brushed his hair, tended his bleeding lips and the face of a real man began to emerge. She prayed silently to her God to help her. Suddenly, the name and the face made sense and were known. She never knew the young astrologers in Lasapulis very well but would see them in passing in the old days, and her husband would make mention of them. Both she and her brother thought the astrologers were an annoyance.

All of the astrologers had died, been converted or disappeared within the first couple of days of the renaissance of Lasapulis. No one gave much thought to them after that. It had been a long time of peace.

Daedena knew then she did not have the power to bring Togorasom back, but she did have the clue to unlock the mystery of his death and to restore Rotal to his senses. Only she didn't know how to get him into that graveyard.

Anam had called an emergency meeting of all the Rasomites as well as many guests in King Chiam's courtyard. It was the only area large enough to seat everyone.

"My beautiful sisters and brothers. Our hearts are broken. However, it has been nearly three weeks since Togorasom left us to go home. Many still carry too heavy a burden. A burden the Lord does not want you to carry. What has happened has happened. We cannot change the past. I have called all of us together to pray for healing and unity and an answer. I believe, though we cannot change the past, we deserve to know what has happened. I believe with all of us united in prayer we can receive an answer."

They began to clasp each other's hands until the entire congregation had formed a chain. Then, their voices began to raise toward heaven, speaking in the Rasomite tongue and in many other tongues and in unknown tongues. It was upon this circumstance that Daedena, the only one who had not been informed of the meeting, entered.

She stood passively in the back for a minute until she realized, because of their prayer, her arrival would remain unnoticed. She began moving forward, ducking and dodging the warriors, in search of her close friends. She felt a tug at her sleeve and a young man pointed through the crowd toward where Zoana, Paluqua and Crazon were huddled. As she approached them, they quietly reached out and brought her into their circle. Zoana huddled her close.

"Zoana!" called Daedena over the din, "what is going on?"

"At Anam's suggestion, we all decided to come together and pray for an end to this dismay that keeps us bound."

"Oh, sweet Lord," she said, shocked, "I must talk to these people."

The noise was deafening. Daedena and Zoana could scarcely hear each other. However, as if on an unspoken command, the volume of the prayers began to tone down. Anam was up on the podium.

"I believe someone has a word of encouragement," he said over the murmuring.

Nervously, Daedena joined him. "I have something to share, Anam. But the information I have to share has suddenly made me so nervous I can hardly think."

He raised his right hand toward the people. "Please, everyone hold your tongue. Let us all give her our attention. Go ahead, Daedena," he said quietly. "Take your time."

She closed her eyes for a few moments to gather her thoughts.

"Each day," she began, "I have gone to Togorasom's tomb. I have no special ministry here or family to occupy my time, so I have spent nearly all of my time contemplating this situation and seeking diligently for an answer as many of you have." As she spoke her nerves and volume improved.

"A short time ago, I sat on one of the little stone benches at the entrance of the burial site. I know not if I saw in fact or in a dream, but it matters not. Today, Togorasom spoke to me." There was an excited commotion among the congregation until Anam had restored order. "I know it was him because he gave me a man's name and I have found the man. The Holy Spirit led me to King Chiam's warden and he has the man in solitary." She glanced over to where Chiam sat with his wife. "He is the only occupant at this time. He is the crazy man who was arrested for attacking people." Chiam nodded his head as he was aware of this prisoner.

"The man's name is Rotal. I now understand it was not merely a coincidence or for pleasure I came to this place. I know the man. He was one of the astrologers who went into hiding during the changes in Lasapulis. I doubt if anyone in Marsa would know him."

"Chiam. Anam." She spoke to the two men. "I need your help. I have promised Togorasom I would bring Rotal to him for healing. The man, Rotal, is completely uncontrollable. I am unable to fulfill his request without your help."

"Are you of the conviction," Chiam asked her, "that this man, Rotal, is responsible for Togorasom's death?"

"I do not know, sir. If he is responsible, Togorasom has forgiven him."

Anger filled Chiam's voice. "Togorasom is dead! We placed his body in my own family tomb and sealed the entrance. If this man is guilty of this death, he must be tried and suffer the consequences."

Daedena became angry and retorted. "I would love to hear you question the accused and give him a fair trial." She turned to Anam. "Anam, are you not of the conviction that God has put a curse of death upon anyone who should raise his arm to take a Rasomite's life?"

"That is correct," he answered.

"Therefore, I reason only one of two possibilities can be. Either Rotal is innocent of the death of Togorasom. Or Togorasom is not dead at all. If Rotal were guilty, the Lord would have already struck him down. If Togorasom were dead, he could not have spoken with me. Either that or I am as crazy as Rotal is."

She waited a moment and looked at Chiam. "Sir, I petition you to respond to my request and give Togorasom the opportunity to heal Rotal. I am convinced this is what the almighty God desires as well."

Chiam looked down at his hands clasped in his lap. A few moments later, he looked at Daedena with tears in his eyes. "All of my sons are dead. I loved that young boy as though he were a son of my own. Every time I was in his presence, he would offer me a word of knowledge or encouragement. I have deeply longed to know why he died, and I have gone nearly mad in my desire to gain vengeance. Perhaps it is my warlike spirit and a part of me has grown weary of peace. If Anam will support you in fulfilling this desire that I cannot understand, I shall not stand in your way. Do as you will."

He huffed and puffed as he arose and worked his way through the crowd. His wife followed a few paces behind.

A throng of people had followed them to the prison and to the cemetery. Rotal had docilely followed Daedena. The chains that bound him between Anam and Zoana, he had accepted with little notice. All of the followers had been given strict orders to stay several paces behind and remain alert while they led this madman through the streets. Upon their arrival, Anam had securely locked the chains to the bench of the sepulcher. He and Zoana had retreated to join the others. Daedena remained behind for a time to ensure Rotal was calm before she retreated.

Due to the mounds of dirt placed around the sepulcher, it was impossible to see any activity. The crowd waited in anticipation to see what miracle would happen. When they had arrived, it was still early in the afternoon, but the day kept moving forward and turned into evening. The people were beginning to wander away. Many wanted to investigate to see if anything had happened to Rotal.

"God will give us the answer," Anam had told them. "Rotal is in no worse place now than he would be locked in prison. If his voice is set free, he can easily call out to us. However, I fully expect a greater miracle and an answer from God."

To the question of how long he would wait for the answer, Daedena had responded. "I am quite satisfied to wait until evening or morning or as long as it takes. God is not a faithless God that he would make his servants wait forever."

So the sky got darker and the crowd got smaller.

With early morning, as their eyes became very heavy with sleep, the vigilant stragglers lifted up their heads toward the sepulcher. The newly risen sun stabbed at their eyes as they gazed in eager anticipation. There was a common sense among them that it was time.

Suddenly, man and boy emerged from among the mounds. With the sun glaring from behind them, it was not possible to make out details. It was clear by the way they walked and spoke with each other they were in good health.

The observers did not know how to react, and the man and boy were within ten paces when a reaction beyond shock passed over all of them. The two were mobbed by the faithful watchers.

Dozens of questions were shot at both of them, especially at Togorasom. Finally, he sat upon a row marker and raised his arms to silence the shouts of joy.

"I have been at God's footstool for these last several days. My death was all in his plan. This one," he pointed at Daedena, "was very faithful. The Lord showed me many things which caused me great joy. One thing though made me sad. When I considered the vast multitudes in the earth, his kingdom was not a crowded place. There is so much work that needs to be done. The call of the world screams loud in one's ears. The evil one rules here and his shouts of triumph are heard everywhere. The call of God, however, is like a whisper in a noisy room. It is heard in the heart before it can be known in the mind. It is our task to stand in the gap between destruction and salvation. We are to allow the people in the world to spiritually trod upon us and use us as a pathway to God. All of you were faithful. You lamented my departure as I would no longer be part of your ministries and, then, you went back to work. God loves every one of you and extends his thankfulness to you for your work.

"This one," he extended his hand to Rotal, "unknowingly fulfilled God's purpose in what he did. Now, he has seen the light. He knows the darkness in which he lived before. It is time for someone to take him and have him clothed and fed. There is much more he needs to know."

Rotal was still dirty and bleeding. His clothes were still tatters. However, without hesitation, Daedena arose and took him by the hand. "He shall stay with me. Our faith in God has increased for both of us due to the things which have happened here. He can go home now and show what great things God has done."

"Who can tell," said Rotal, "but perhaps someday I will be found worthy to again work for the King. Shecktel, with whom I concocted this evil, needs to be brought to truth and justice. Otherwise, he may decide to lash out again. I will be praying for him until he also is made correct. Let me make a warning. The days of correction are coming to an end. Mankind must begin to praise God before it is too late. It is our duty in this ugly world of sin to shed a little light and perhaps a few will put down their old ways and begin to obey God. No one, having lived that life, would ever want to fall into the hands of God. The God of love wants to mold us. The God of revenge will crush us."

Chapter 4
Layta

During this time, there was a great division among the Rasomites. Many had formed relationships or gotten married during their time in Marsa or had become attached to families there. Also, many had moved away to cities in the surrounding region. However, not one had lost either their faith or their life, except for the prophet Mebiktu, since they had begun their pilgrimage.

Finally, God had called upon Anam and stirred him up to leave the finery and easy living in and around Marsa.

"Where shall we go?" Paluqua began mentally checking off in her head things she would need to take. It was not so easy to travel with small children as it had been to only be responsible for herself.

"The Lord has not shown me everything yet. He has shown me we need to discern who is called to go and who will continue the work here."

"Do we need to organize a meeting?" It would take several days to get all of the people organized to depart. There would need to be a lot of prayer, discussion and packing.

"I am going now to discuss this with Togorasom. You go talk to Zoana and Crazon and have the word spread quickly. We leave tomorrow." She was stunned, but tried not to show it. "We will pack and dress as Rasomites pack and dress. We take our weapons and tools, the clothes on our backs, and a week's rations." Paluqua smiled and nodded her head. Suddenly, Anam pulled her close to him and looked into her deep, brown eyes. "Do not fret, Paluqua. I love you. We need nothing at all, save God. Has he let us down yet? Have there been days we have had less than those things I have mentioned? The babies who survived the winter in the mountains had far less and also less to look forward to than our children. Our children will rule kingdoms."

"You are so amazing. I truly must love you, because what

another woman would call blindness I call faith. You are correct. All we need is faith in God. I want to kiss you now but there is too much that needs to be done, so I should hurry." She pushed him away teasingly, but he held on.

"You are a wonderful wife to show this faith to follow me. I know you believe there is a lot to do. All I need is to pray with Togorasom, so I have more time."

When he kissed her, it lasted only for a couple of seconds but it seemed, to her, to last so much longer. "I love you," he whispered in her ear.

When they finally backed away from each other, it was knowing their errands would not take that long. They would do what needed to be done and hurry home to complete this unfinished business.

"Surely we cannot leave as soon as tomorrow." Zoana stood, hands on her hips, staring at Paluqua who had just delivered the message. "There is simply too much to do. There is packing…"

"We need nothing," Paluqua countered.

"I think we need to pray," she said almost indignantly.

"Zoana," Paluqua pleaded with her, "when did you ever stop praying? I believe the truth is that you shall miss your friends. I can understand that. But you have known this day would come. Would tomorrow or next month make a difference? They can handle it. You have trained your teachers well. I am very proud of you. However, do you feel they may not be ready?"

Zoana answered with the sound of resignation in her voice. "They are ready."

"Do we need extensive preparations for us to leave?"

Zoana admitted they did not. "I have prayed. I have talked with my people. They are ready. I just feel unsure about myself. I don't know what the future holds. These times have been so free with us and our spiritual life so unrestricted."

Paluqua held her as the tears began to come. "The times were not good when we arrived here. There would have been an awful war. So many unnecessary deaths. Who can tell what awaits us out there. Probably more turbulence. Definitely more starting over. But Zoana, regardless of what is met out there, I want to meet it with you."

Zoana looked at Paluqua in shock. "But of course, I'm going with you. Like it or not, that's my destiny."

Suddenly, Crazon bolted through the door. "Hi," she said meekly and out of breath. She then realized their serious expressions. "Did I miss something? What's going on?"

Zoana explained. "We leave in the morning. Anam's orders."

Crazon's mouth fell open in disbelief. "That's not possible. There's simply too much to do on such short notice. I have the palace and royal family to be concerned over."

Zoana and Paluqua gave each other a knowing smile as they prepared to counter her arguments.

"How have you liked the room?" Anam looked at the furnishings in Togorasom's new apartment. It was still furnished quite simply as according to the boy's instructions. He had a small, single-size wooden bed with a feather mattress. Alongside of this stood a serving table upon which had been placed two oil lamps and a serving tray of tea. Facing the bed was a wooden armchair with a feather cushion, upon which Anam was sitting as he sipped his tea.

"The other place really bothered me," Togorasom answered looking intently at Anam. "It was strange." His eyes darted around nervously. "I couldn't sleep there again. It was like..." he hesitated. "It was like someone had been murdered there, but I couldn't really identify that person as myself. It was even strange going in there. Have you ever had a bad dream once and then, later, you start having the same dream again?" He shivered. "The place gave me the creeps. I'm glad the King allowed me to stay here." He laughed. "He said I could have any room in the palace, including his own. I asked for servant's quarters. This is more than I needed." He leaned back on the bed and rested his head against the wall. "And now it's time to leave."

Anam had not yet announced the reason for his visit.

Togorasom continued. "It's quite interesting, in fact. My spirit and a part of my mind vividly recall everything that took place as I related to the Lord and his angels. So much happened and was said and I can reveal so little. However, my flesh and another part of my mind are deeply disturbed. Like I said, I could not remain in that room. I was afraid. I know nothing would happen to me there. God is in charge. Now, whenever I do anything, I feel this power greater than myself come upon me and I realize how imperfect and bumbling we really are. Imagine your spirit set free and being ministered to by angels and then going back into your physical body. If I learned nothing else there about this world, I learned that the spirit and the flesh are at war with each other. I also learned the physical world we live in is the dwelling place also of a spiritual battlefield. They are, right now, battling for our souls."

"We need to talk. Do you understand the reason for my visit?"

"It is time." Togorasom sat up. "I know that we leave tomorrow. We shall travel with the wind at our backs."

"Then we shall go north. Every day the warm winds come in from the south."

The boy laughed. "Are you in charge of the winds, as well?"

"Then, perhaps we shall go south. Who can tell? Let's pray."

They sat in silence for nearly an hour. Even though no words passed their lips, the prayers were similar. They first prayed for God to direct and preside over their travels. They prayed that each of their people would be properly motivated by God as to their going or staying. They recalled many individuals and situations they had encountered and prayed over each of them.

"So many unsaved souls," Togorasom muttered. "Your servants have worked diligently. The fruit, however, is yours." He hesitated. "Oh, Lord!" he nearly wailed. "Why, so often, does our message fall on deaf ears? Why, if they cannot believe what we say, cannot they believe the glorious things that have been done? To those who have the eyes of the Holy Spirit, it all seems so clear. The blessing. The grace. The miracles. But those who are still deeply into the world can see nothing. They call grace maturity and miracles are a coincidence. Open their eyes, my God."

He went on for some time and began to describe instances of the Holy Spirit's work that was shown to those who did not understand. Anam listened to his voice and realized how deeply the boy felt for every one of them.

Finally, both sat quietly and stared into empty space for a time.

"Have you eaten today?" Anam asked suspiciously, knowing the boy had what many considered to be poor eating habits.

"They brought breakfast early this morning." Togorasom was still not completely alert.

"I see," Anam replied, "but did you eat?"

The boy smiled and looked at Anam. "I had crackers with jam, raisins, cold milk and goat cheese. It was excellent. Did you eat?" he asked humorously.

"I had an excellent breakfast. I have a feeling Chiam will throw a big going away party when he finds out our plans. I urge you to get out and get in with the people. You're still a mystery to many. You should accept their generosity at least within the bounds of what you are capable of."

Togorasom sipped at his very cold tea. "I will mix together with the people. I will accept their generosity as long as I don't get entangled." He seemed resigned to the situation.

"I know it's not easy for you." Anam stood up. "Those things we do not do often, never come easily for any of us. These people have been very generous to us in their hospitality. If we avoid them now, their feelings will be hurt and, possibly, our witness weakened." He backed toward the doorway. "I've got to go now. There are things to do. Any messages?"

"Ummm. Keep me in your prayers?" He stood up. "When you get together with Paluqua, tell her I love her as well."

Anam blushed and looked away. "I guess I'll be going now." When he was out of sight, Togorasom realized he could not hear Anam's footsteps as he walked down the hallway. The sandals he had become so used to were gone.

"Do you ever miss home?" Orphar asked Paluqua as she walked along with the Rasomite woman.

"It is a hard question, which I have considered often." She looked off into the distance. "We have never known a real home. We lived in fear before the defeat of Rodan. It would be hard to miss that. I think what I truly miss is the home we never had. Perhaps, someday..."

"You need to get that man of yours to settle down," the elderly lady suggested.

"He will, at God's time. Suppose we had settled down before we arrived here? Your life would be so much different."

Orphar swallowed the lump in her throat. "Oh my word, I hadn't even considered that. I am desperately going to miss you and the others. I don't know what shall become of us."

"Orphar. Love God. There are only two ways to go. There is

only one path to God. Don't ever give up." Their gazes locked. "Do you ever want to go back?"

"Sometimes, it's hard. I feel that old loneliness and depression trying to drag me down. Sometimes, I give up. I just have a real good cry. Then I go back to God and start over. But, they don't give me much time to feel sorry for myself. Did you know I lost all three of my boys and my husband in the wars?"

"I had heard."

"I think, if only they had known God, but I can't rest on that. There's too much happening. The old ladies coming over to pray almost every day. The wedding coming up. Beor will be moving in with us. My gosh, I've never seen a young man with so many questions. And he's become so helpful."

Paluqua and Orphar had settled into a small table in a quiet corner. There was not much quietness to be found. As soon as Chiam discovered Anam's plans, he quickly organized a festival.

Crazon discovered Paluqua and Orphar in their hiding place. "This was really nice of him. I wondered how in the world could even a king feed a whole city. The whole city has turned out with its own food offerings. There is a lot and to spare. But we must be careful. We have a long trip ahead of us in the morning."

"Have you seen Anam?" Paluqua stood up and looked around. It would be almost impossible to pick anyone out of this crowd. The streets were packed with every person in the city. The weather was lovely. Shopkeepers and vendors were giving away free food. In the morning, it would be all so different as they headed out of town.

"I believe," she said as she sat back down, "that wherever you find the children of God, there shall be someone nearby trying to feed them."

Zoana was approaching the table, but before she was able to say anything, she heard her name being called from the crowd. As she turned, a young boy could be seen leading a man by the hand towards them.

"Oruni. I am so glad to see you. I prayed I would see you today. And I'm pleased to see your father also."

The man clumsily extended his hand. "I just wanted to say thank you for all that you've done. Because of you, my family has been made whole again. The change that has taken place in us is truly wonderful. I finally realized my problem. I have always lived in fear that the little I have, my wife and son, would somehow be taken away from me. I would become agitated at any outside disturbance. It took an outsider to reveal to me that I was driving my most precious things away. I'll be truly sorry when you and your friends leave, but your effects will be with us forever. Thank you."

Even though the man spoke calmly and politely, a tear began to form and it was difficult for him to speak at the end.

The Rasomite women there would receive appreciation from many such as him that day. As if on cue, Orphar took Zoana's hand which was resting on the table in front of her.

"The Lord has done a mighty work on us through your hands." She buried her face in her free hand to control her emotion. When she continued, her voice was very strained. "Thank you. I know you think God will continue his work here through us and he shall. But, it just won't be the same. You are very special people. I know you say we are very special people also, but it still won't be the same."

Zoana clutched Orphar's hand and, spontaneously, the little group formed a prayer circle holding hands with each other. "Oh, my Lord," Orphar continued, "thank you for the unity that has been formed here. You know our hearts at times may grow faint, but the fire that has been kindled here shall never go out. Even though we must part, Father, we shall always be bound together in our hearts until that day we can all live together under your roof."

Zoana followed her with a similar prayer. Then each said a short prayer of thanksgiving. When they were done, they realized a group of well-wishers had gathered around them. Not many hugs were exchanged before the tears began to flow freely.

"You seem to be quite nervous this evening, Chiam. Is it our departure that wears you down?" Anam took another sip of wine. He was half sitting, half leaning against the arm of the chair that would have been occupied by Chiam's wife, but she was busy scurrying about, directing servants.

Chiam slouched back into his massive seat. "I do not wish you to go. However, that is not my major concern. I have accepted the inevitability of your departure. These times have been grand. I pray history remembers who to properly give the credit to. I have seen all my friends and family slaughtered or mutilated in war. I think I can accept just about anything at this point. It's just that I had a gift planned and now it appears something has gone wrong with its delivery."

Anam put his hand on Chiam's shoulder. "My friend, your hospitality tonight and for the last two years have exceeded our need. Like I've said, we could not be encumbered by any gifts at this time. I appreciate the thought, however. While I'm on this subject, you do understand our feelings on the disposition of all the property we leave behind?"

Chiam brightened. "A wonderful gesture. Yes, we understand. Very soon, when all the items are gathered together, we shall have an auction, the proceeds of which shall go to feed the poor outside the city limits." He laughed. "I also understand the implications. You shall force us to continue your ministry. Very wise." He took a deep breath. "I did have a special gift. I cannot explain it, but I suppose, I must resign myself to its lack."

"Your generosity is still appreciated."

"You do know," Chiam said as he raised an eyebrow, "if you had given me more notice, we would have had a much larger sendoff. We could have invited dignitaries from all over the region."

Anam laughed. "Chiam, it was not my decision to leave tomorrow. The Lord made that decision. We have said most of our farewells. Perhaps that is the very reason he called us out so quickly. To avoid all of that. There are a few of us who probably would have been quite satisfied to sneak out in the middle of the night."

"By the way," the King interrupted, "just where is Togorasom? I haven't seen him all evening."

Anam shook his head. "I told him this morning that I expected him to participate in the activities tonight. I would not be surprised at all if he has hidden himself away somewhere."

A smile crossed Chiam's lips. "How can a person be so calm in the midst of angels and before God himself, and yet, be so frightened of harmless people?"

"He's not always off by himself. There have been times."

"The only times I have seen Togorasom out and enjoying himself are those times when he is in charge. People go to him for help. He is so afraid someone might try to do something nice for him. There is also beauty in being able to receive a gift. This is growth in the Lord." He stopped and thought about what he'd said. "Pretty good, huh?" he remarked.

"We shall turn you into an evangelist yet. Would you like me to find the boy?"

Chiam nodded. "I would like to spend some time with him on this his last evening here."

A servant girl came before the two men and bowed. She offered them choices from her tray of cheese. Chiam took a generous portion of each of several types. Anam politely waved her away.

Anam stood in the doorway of Togorasom's room glowering down at the boy who was sitting on the edge of his bed. Anam's face was displaying a great deal of anger, however, his mind was thoroughly under control as he fished for the correct words to begin. Togorasom looked down at the floor with a guilty expression on his face. The puffiness of his eyes showed he had been crying. The boy broke the silence.

"I... I can't go," he stammered.

"Why?" Anam asked without changing the expression on his face.

"I don't know." He looked up. "I simply can't."

"Why are you so afraid?" Anam asked him patiently. "They love you. They're not going to harm you."

Tears began to trickle slowly from the boy's eyes again. "I know all that. I don't know what's come over me. I just feel so afraid to be around people."

"You've always been a loner. I suppose prophets are like that." He smiled slightly. "However, it's gotten so much worse since your experience. I would think that you would seek these outlets. Perhaps the Lord is preparing you for another step closer to him. I don't know. But right now, I want you to come with me. All you need to do is speak briefly to King Chiam and eat a bit of their food. After that, it's up to you. I would prefer you to mingle with these good people so that they know you love them."

"I do love them."

"Then go tell them. Most of them are just common folk who want to say goodbye." He extended his hand.

Togorasom slowly got up and reluctantly headed with Anam back outside to the party.

"I feel foolish," he admitted.

"You've done nothing to feel foolish over and, if you have, it can be corrected. It's a wise man who is able to face and overcome his enemies."

"I have no enemies!" the boy insisted.

"You are your worst enemy. That is our principle battle all through life. Those who contend against us are not as deadly as that which contends within us. For within us are the enemies of hatred, apathy, laziness, cowardice, pride, deceitfulness and much more. We spend our entire lives trying to slay these enemies or making excuses for them."

"Let's pray before we go out there," Togorasom insisted.

They stopped in the doorway and Anam fell to his knees, embracing Togorasom. They both said a short prayer asking for strength and guidance.

"Thank you," Togorasom said as Anam got up. "I am able to face my enemies."

They stood in the doorway for a few moments and surveyed the commotion. The streets and yards were packed with friends and fellow travelers. People had carried their own indoor furniture outside for adequate seating. They had emptied their own shelves to provide food for all. No one went hungry that day. Despite the roar of the talking, there were also many silently praying with each other or embracing.

"I wish," Togorasom said looking up at Anam, "that it could always be like this. Why do people wait until someone is leaving to tell them they care? Why are they so reluctant to share their property and their time?"

"To a certain extent, you are correct in your observation. It should always be like this. However, to a lesser extent, you are wrong. You have prayed earnestly for this outpouring of love, as we all have. These same activities are happening most of the time behind closed doors. You need to get out more often so you can see your prayers are being answered."

A smile crossed Togorasom's face. He was pleased with what he saw and glad that Anam had encouraged him.

They were easily assimilated into the crowd. Several people had never met Togorasom but stopped to speak with Anam. He corrected all of them before they went on their way and introduced the boy. Eventually, they made their way back to Chiam.

"Togorasom, my young friend," he said as he arose and headed for the boy. "I'm so pleased that you came out." He folded both of his enormous hands over the boy's.

"It seems as if the entire city has turned out." He nodded his head in the direction of the crowd without taking his eyes from the King.

"These people are very grateful." He looked at Anam. "Why shouldn't they be glad? The prisons and hospitals are empty. Families are together. Everyone has a decent home and food to eat. The wars are over. There is peace in the land and available for every heart. Why shouldn't they be glad?"

Togorasom admitted. "They should be glad." The King released his hold on him and put a hand on his shoulder.

"I thank you, son. You have done well. I know others had their ministries. Our home will never be the same with Crazon's departure. However, you were the one, I feel, who contributed the most. And yet, you are still a mystery. That's because you perform in areas I don't even understand. If you ever have any doubt in yourself," he raised his arms toward the crowd, "here is your testimony."

Several people had stopped their activities and were listening to the conversation.

"However, don't forget, your majesty, that this is also your testimony as well," Anam said as he approached the other two. As he reached them, Chiam gave him a short hug which was very uncharacteristic of him. "From now on, it's up to you. You can do as well as you decide to. You must leave your costly life behind and let God do the work."

"When it's all over," Togorasom added, "everything which is not of God will vanish away. We should be seeking to acquire many things which are of God."

"I am convinced that nothing of this world that we greatly love will be of any value in our next life," said Anam.

"I have learned a lot from you." The King turned and walked back to his seat. He paused for a moment before sitting down and then finished. "I have learned that war does not come from what one feels is his rightful territory. God does not look on the outward man and how he appears or even so much on what he does. God looks at the inner man to discover his motives. Some day, I'd like to walk away from this throne. All the pomp and ritual used to be such a joy, but now it has become stifling."

Anam leaned towards him. "You just said it. He is not against the pomp and ritual. If it is a burden, you are the one who can do something about it. God is looking at the inner man. If your station were suddenly swept away and you lost everything, would you still love God? How would it affect you?"

Before he could answer, the crowd parted and Crazon and Chiam's wife passed through.

"The two most beautiful women in the world," Chiam said quietly. "She doesn't nag me, she encourages me. She's kind and understanding and always a good help. My wife is also very good." He chuckled at his little play on everyone's thoughts. "I'm going to miss you most of all." He stood silently for a moment.

"Chiam," Anam called his attention, "it's fine. Everyone is doing it."

When he looked back at Crazon, there were tears in his eyes. "For two years, I've called you names like child and daughter. I was wrong. I should have called you sister or, perhaps, even mother." He suddenly burst into tears, and she ran into his arms. "I wish I had done the right things," he said to her quietly.

"That's a good sign." Crazon dried her eyes with her sleeve, though it made no difference. "God told me this a few days ago when I felt the same way. Keep trying to do the right thing, but don't ever become so satisfied and contented with your deeds that you become stagnant. He wants us to grow. He wants us to be brave enough to do new things and continue to improve on the old. Sometimes, he cuts us off from what we've been doing. We've done enough. He wants us to do something else. As long as you keep doing the right things and desiring to do more, God will be pleased. Always be willing to forgive and to ask forgiveness. Continue to be generous to strangers for, who knows, perhaps one day the Lord himself shall come knocking on your door."

"Pray for us," he told her, "especially those of us in the palace."

"I shall."

The party went on far into the evening. Eventually, Anam knew he had to break things up, so he first gathered his people together. There would be a lot of traveling in the morning.

"When there is light enough to travel, we leave. Togorasom will direct us at first. We have all been in prayer these last few weeks. We know where the Lord wants us. If you are leaving with us in the morning, be in front of the palace before sunrise. We are Rasomites, so I should not need to tell you how to travel. King Chiam's good stewards are preparing food for us to travel with. You need your tools and weapons. I see little need for much else but the clothes on our backs. God's rest." He spoke briefly to a few people and departed with Paluqua. Chiam and a few others promised to send them off in the morning. With the exception of a few servants who remained to begin cleaning up the mess, in a few minutes, everyone had gone off to sleep.

Long before sunrise, Anam had already returned to the palace to ensure that the departure plans were complete. He was pleased to see Chiam's servants had carefully packed nuts, dried fruit, grain and cheese in several hundreds of small paper packages and then bound these in larger leather packages for carrying. Satisfied that he could be of no further use to those workers, he went looking for Togorasom.

He finally found him in the kitchen helping to prepare breakfast.

"Good morning, Anam!" the boy called out cheerfully when he saw him. "This shall be quite a meal." Togorasom waved his arm in the direction of the other workers. "Biscuits, honey and hot bread, eggs, pancakes, cheese." He shook his head. "So much more. We have a long trip. We shall need a good meal. Praise the Lord for hospitality. Is the sun up yet?"

Anam took a deep breath. Togorasom never ceased to amaze him. "No, the sun is not up yet. How long have you been up?"

"Not that long, actually. Just a few hours. These poor generous souls have been up all night."

Over a dozen men and women were engaged in various aspects of preparing the morning feast. Though they were still quite busy, it was obvious from the expressions on their faces that they needed some rest. Anam was offered a cup of tea and led to a seat by one young woman who assured him things were well taken care of. Still groggy, Anam sat and enjoyed his warm drink.

Togorasom came over to him drinking a cup of water. "In a

few minutes, they will start carrying breakfast out front. How did you sleep?"

Anam nodded his head and then, after considering, shook his head. "It wasn't long enough. I hope we have the energy to travel today."

"I believe our goal today should be to get out of here. If we can get organized enough to leave town in an orderly fashion, I think we should conserve our energy until our boundless health returns." Anam smiled at his reference to their physical well-being. "We have been spoiled, you know. This apartment living and traipsing around the country on horseback is not really conducive to what may be expected of us in the future."

Anam heard and understood but still was not totally awake. He sat with his head firmly resting in his hand. "I'm glad you are so clear-headed this morning. I need about ten hours more sleep."

"Don't worry." The boy laughed. "I'm sure in the next few days, you shall get ten hours of sleep."

Anam's head sank lower into his hand.

"Have you seen anyone else that will be leaving with us today?" Togorasom sat back as if considering his own question.

"No one," Anam admitted, "except my soundly sleeping wife. How I envy her." As Togorasom arose, he affectionately slapped Anam's arm. "I'll be fine," the man assured him.

"Oh, I understand. You had to get up early so you could be in charge and organize things."

Anam managed to laugh. "Do you think we should be outside?"

Togorasom hesitated and looked at the servants again. "Yes. I see no need of us staying in here any longer. These people are nearly done, and I want to eat my breakfast while it's still hot."

They waved farewell to the servants and headed for the street.

The sun was just beginning to show its light when they exited the palace. Anam was shocked and dismayed at what he saw. He counted them. He counted them again. Seventeen women. With the exception of his own, there were no children. He looked at Togorasom.

He had known exactly who would be there. "What had you expected?" The boy displayed some sadness in his voice. "Count those who are not here. Most of them are married or intending to get married. Many have even moved away. Name one you expected to find here who is missing. They had a choice to serve God here with their new families or to leave and to serve God with us. They all love the Lord, but not everyone is called to go out."

"I know all this," Anam responded as he slumped onto a bench, "but I never expected it to be like this. I suppose as I prayed for each of them to make a decision, I never presupposed what their decision would be."

"Let me ask you a question. Are there always plenty of fish to eat?"

"I don't understand."

"Each fish lays hundreds of eggs, but only a few of these actually mature and go out. And they continue the cycle. There will always be plenty of fish. Out of the wombs of these women shall spring kingdoms."

Anam glanced at him. Togorasom nodded, indicating the truthfulness of what he had said and looked back at the women. He went and joined them and Anam followed.

As they approached, Paluqua turned and, noticing her husband, handed Comeana to one of the other women. She gave him an affectionate hug.

"Do you see how many of the saints have turned out to do God's work?"

"I had thought to see many more."

"Does the Lord work in numbers? Do you recall how many attacked the city of Rodan?"

Anam smiled. "One. And a handful of people to watch." He looked the women over with satisfaction as he suddenly realized they had all left behind their fashionable garments they had been accumulating and returned to their much more basic dress. They each carried their small satchel of personal items and their weapons. These few who had come out were obviously prepared to follow his word. He took Paluqua's hand and she embraced him.

"I had thought King Chiam would have been here by now." He said as she ran her hand across his chest.

"It's still a little early. We still have time."

"Ah look!" Togorasom announced cheerfully. "Breakfast is served."

Half a dozen servants paraded through the doorway wheeling carts laden with a feast.

"Don't be hesitant," Anam advised. "We have some time, but I don't want to tarry unnecessarily."

Togorasom was first and began to load down his platter. "I don't want much, just some of this delicious hot bread with apple jelly." He smeared it on heavily. "Some scrambled eggs, cold milk, hot tea." He tried to juggle both cups and his platter. "Yes, some fried potatoes," he told the lady dishing up. He glanced around as though looking for another set of arms. "I'm sorry," he told one of the men, "I'll have to come back."

"I've never seen him eat like this in my life." Paluqua was still holding Anam.

"I'm hungry," he told Anam as he passed by.

"I can see that. Eat hearty," he added, doubting the boy's capacity to consume it all.

Very soon, everyone had settled into the surrounding benches and tables and were busy with their last meal. It was then Chiam appeared on the scene. He proudly stood over them with his hands on his hips, pleased his offer of food was accepted so gratefully.

"Better dig in, sir, while the eggs are hot." Togorasom took a break from his devouring.

"I'll eat later, but thank you."

"I would be pleased to share this meal with you, sir." Togorasom stood up, indicating he was waiting on the King. "There is a great deal of food left over. The cooks have worked hard most of the night with this meal and with the packing."

Realizing Togorasom's sincerity, the King changed his mind. "Well, I guess I'd better have a bite then. It would be a shame to see this go to waste." He proceeded to laden down a platter with all it would hold. He sat at the table opposite Anam and Togorasom.

"I just cannot say often enough how dearly you shall be missed. I shall wear myself out with saying goodbye. It cannot be said enough."

"We shall also miss you, sir." Togorasom finished his milk. "We have a mighty work before us. We are prepared. However, we will miss the comfort that we had here and your wonderful hospitality." He paused to ensure he had the King's attention. "You are more than a King. You are a child of God. So often when one has possessions, he has no desire to share. You have shared abundantly. God knows your heart."

"God does know my heart. He breaks it a little more each day but not more than I can bear. That is why I can so easily share with you. You know the will of God and you are harmless. You bear no ill will at all." He spoke up so all could hear. "You say I have given you so much. I have given you nothing at all. Lodging and food? You take the least of my lodging and eat little." He looked at the remains on Togorasom's plate. "Usually," he added. "But what have you given me? Peace. Security. Prosperity. The love of my people. You've healed my kingdom of a dozen plagues. And you've shown me how to reach God. I have given you nothing."

There was suddenly a commotion from inside the palace. Four excited guards escorted one weary-looking man in ragged clothes out into the open. He carried a goatskin flask around his neck. He approached the King, who arose to meet him, and prostrated himself on the ground. The King offered him a hand and helped him up. The man showed fear for being in the presence of a King.

"You need feel no fear, young man," Chiam reassured him. "If you come in peace, you are among friends. What is your message?"

"I come with a gift from the Mountains of Pitakae."

Everyone gasped. The King was overjoyed. By this time, everyone had gathered around so they would miss nothing. With as much ceremony as he was able to offer, the man removed the goatskin from around his neck and handed it to the King.

"Here is my message. The three men whom you sent some time ago to retrieve this valuable prize fell among thieves upon their return. I am a trader from the region of Aris-Akana, and I and my partners were fortunate enough to find those poor men and bring them into my own home where I left them to renew their health. I expect soon they will return here. However, they mightily pressed upon us that we should hurry and bring this to you. The Rasomites are very much respected in my house, and I would have done anything to perform a service for them. I have traveled night and day with little rest or food to arrive here on time. I understand I was only a moment early."

Everyone stood in silence for a moment. Chiam laid his valuable gift on the bench and moved aside from where he had been sitting. Then, he aided the weary traveler into his own seat and urged him to eat from his plate. The man was stunned at the offer, but as the King continued to encourage him to eat and he was famished, he began to gorge himself. Chiam picked up the goatskin and a sly smile crossed his lips.

"Three months ago, I realized you would be leaving. I knew it was fruitless for me to try to make you stay. I began to ask myself what I could possibly offer these people which would be appreciated as well as acceptable. I knew that no sort of material possession would mean enough. I sent three of my most trusted servants to your home in the Mountains of Pitakae." He hoisted the goatskin. By this time, everyone knew what its contents were. "I have here a few precious goblets of the water from the springs in those mountains. This is my gift to you."

Anam approached Chiam and prepared to speak. Tears were flowing from his eyes. It was too hard for him to form the words. Chiam embraced him. It was several minutes before the two men separated.

With tears still flowing, Anam expressed his pleasure. "I am almost speechless at this gift. On the one hand, it is among the simplest of all things you could offer. On the other hand, nothing can surpass its magnitude. It was in those mountains that we found life. This water gave us life. I have something I would like you to do."

"Name it. It is yours."

"Would you take a handful of this water and anoint each of us who are prepared now to go out and proclaim God's truth?"

Without a moment's hesitation, Chiam poured a small handful of the water in his hand and allowed it to dribble from Anam's forehead. In a few minutes all of the Rasomites, including Ernie and the children, had been so anointed. All of the water was gone.

"God has just impressed something on my heart." Togorasom gathered everyone's attention. "Whenever anyone accepts God and is filled with the Holy Spirit or is desirous to be filled, let him be anointed with water as a public testimony. Let him not wipe away the water but rather leave it be until it dries and that will be his testimony. Let the water be a physical sign that God has come into his life and washed him inside and set his mind free. It will at once please God by this act of humility and build another's faith. Let all those who love the Lord do so." He spoke this last to the man who had delivered the water.

"As I go on my route home," he answered, "I shall spread the word. But how shall they believe me and have this not become a matter of division?"

"This is something each new believer will have to deal with God about. Our task is to spread the word and obey God, not to judge."

It became silent for a few moments and Anam finally spoke up. "It's time. We need to be going." As he spoke, the servants began handing out the food parcels to them. It all went quickly and in a few minutes, the last handshakes and hugs were exchanged. They headed out of town.

When they reached the main intersection near the edge of town, Anam asked Togorasom which way they would go.

"North!"

So Anam headed north into the mountains. Besides Ernie, the Calamite from Foramen, these are the Rasomites who accompanied him. Zabikta and Maftu, his counselors when they began in the Mountains of Pitakae. Shulea, who had aided Zeda and Anna on their raid of Rodan. Sholemazar, the cousin of Anna who had died in her sins in the Mountains of Pitakae. Macosena, who had rescued Sarare and Suya. Also Coralena, Shadi, Bufaskada, Buscis, Elea, Didyadim, Ambacudadi, Bulshadi and Umfuwadea who had been with him from the beginning. Also Crazon, Zoana and, his wife, Paluqua, who were the three over the Shamra. Then were his triplet sons, Bonifa, Oranea, and Darophil who were four years old when they left Marsa. His daughter, Comeana, and she was two years old when they left Marsa. And the prophet, Togorasom, and he was ten years old when he left Marsa. So altogether there were twenty-four souls who left Marsa.

The early summer sky was beautiful. There was not a cloud to be seen so the stars, whose counting was beyond number, and the full moon shone brightly. Anam lay on the grass and contemplated the activities of the day and the majesty before him now. It had been nerve-wracking. All four of the children behaved miserably. The heat and the long walk were too much for them. He had carried Comeana all the way and had finally had to take turns with each of the boys, as well. Even for a man of his physical strength it had worn him down to carry his own items and all of his family's food for a week and the children. They had traveled all day, with many breaks, and had gone a mere ten miles. He had walked that far often in the past just for the joy of walking. Tonight he was sore.

No one else fared much better. Fortunately, his main complainers had been the children. However, everyone moaned over their aches and pains. They certainly had grown soft. Their strength would return. He also wondered about their deftness in handling their weapons. He was certain that area would also be weak. As their spiritual and emotional strength had improved, their physical strength and agility had deteriorated. It would all come back with practice.

He marveled at the intricacy of the universe. He knew each of these stars represented a sun. He wondered if any also had a planet such as his. Was this the only one? How marvelous it seemed that the same God who could create innumerable suns could also create a living, breathing man that loved Him.

Without realizing it he had passed out and woke up several hours later. The moon was now resting on the horizon and the pattern of stars before him had changed. All of nature seemed so intricate and in perfect order. He sat up.

In the half-light he could see clearly everyone else was still resting. He was especially pleased that the children had slept soundly. Assured that all was well he lay back down and soon was sound asleep once more.

Anam felt the gentle sting of the sun on his face. At first he tried to ignore it. It would be so nice to sleep on. However, the dawn and the sound of quiet chatter reaching his ears finally won over and he sat up.

He was starved. Paluqua saw he was awake and walked over to him. They only exchanged a few words and she handed him breakfast; a bowl of oatmeal and a handful of nuts. He remembered the feasts of Marsa and thought for a moment what Chiam would probably be eating this morning: he and the others that had been left behind. His wife returned with a cup of hot tea.

"What is the plan for today?" she asked him.

He looked her full in the face. Her eyes revealed how tired she still was. Placing his breakfast on the bare earth beside him and hastily casting the nuts into the bowl, he held her cheeks in his palms and kissed her. Then she lay on the ground next to him as he ate his meal.

"Today's plan is to walk. We are not in a race so there need be no rush. Slowly our strength will return and we will be able to bear more. We will continue to head north as far as the road takes us.

Have the children ate yet?"

"The baby was up for a while. I fed her and she went back to sleep. The boys are still sleeping soundly."

"There's no rush to leave. I don't want to loiter all day, but I'm in no hurry. About ten miles from here, the road meets the river. Perhaps that will be the goal for today. There is a small village there. That is as far on this route as I have traveled. It also marks the line of Chiam's domain so we will be entering new and, I believe, unexplored territory."

"Will we be able to survive on this sparse, bland diet?" she asked, gazing at his cereal.

"We shall thrive," he assured her as he began eating again. "We lived in the mountains one winter on a diet of tree bark." She suddenly burst out into laughter. "It is early summer. All of nature is alive with a banquet. We shall have plenty to eat for several months. Didn't I say not to worry about clothing or food because God shall supply all our needs?"

"We also need time to work with our weapons. I'm afraid we have grown very rusty." She took out her knife and ran her finger over the blade. "Sharp enough to spread butter, but not to cut the bread."

"Once our strength is back and we are back in harmony with nature we will take a break from traveling and spend time honing our skills."

"Anam." She waited before she spoke about a tender subject.

"What's on your mind, dear?" he asked.

"Do you ever think of Zeda or, for that matter, Aurora?"

He didn't know what to say.

"I'm sorry," she said bowing her head. "It's none of my business."

"I have been very remiss." He closed his eyes and tried to think of what to say next. "There are so many things on my mind I don't share. I need to share everything with you. Will you forgive me?"

She looked up and smiled at him. "Of course, I forgive you. And you are right. There are many things I don't know about you. I'm sorry for the way I approached this topic. I didn't handle it well at all."

"Don't be concerned about that. There are things we should have discussed long ago. I think, since we reached Marsa, we have been so involved in everyone else's problems, we haven't had time to worry about our own. If you will give me some time this morning to pray and to think, I will have a lot to share with you as we walk today. It will make the time go more quickly and it will be good for us."

"The time is yours." She glided toward him like a leopard. "Talking about ourselves is very important to me. Thank you." She kissed him, stood up and walked away, glancing back at him several times.

"I don't remember at the time how I felt. It all happened so quickly." Anam was explaining to Paluqua what had happened when Aurora was killed. "I know I had a feeling of fear as I knew any second the guards would pounce on me. However, it wasn't really my need for self-defense that prompted me to kill her." He stopped talking for a moment as he considered the fact he really had killed his wife. "I know that the Lord set up the whole thing. Even in fear or hatred I could never have planned it the way it all happened."

They were walking along the narrow dirt road toward the village of Layta. They had relaxed that morning. Prayed. They had mentally prepared themselves for the walk. It was as far as they had walked the previous day, but they knew it would be easier.

"Things certainly did go very quickly that day," Paluqua reminisced. "I believe we were all swept up in a storm. We certainly were no more than vessels. It was only one day from when Aurora died until..."

"The worst moment of my life."

"If this is too painful..."

"No. I mean, it is painful." He stumbled over the words. He glanced around for his children. The boys laughed and entertained themselves with Ernie. Comeana was being passed to Crazon by one of the other women. For at least today he and Paluqua would not be burdened with the children and the children loved the extra attention they were receiving. He took Paluqua's hand.

"I need to talk," he said. "I love you. You are so wonderful. You're a good mother. Obedient to God. A wonderful wife. One of the best things you are is that you are not Zeda. Zeda was Zeda. You are yourself. You've never tried to fill the gap of emptiness that losing her created. There was nobody like her and there's nobody like you. Without trying to fill the emptiness, an emptiness made worse because of my own foolish disobedience, you have been even more esteemed by me.

"Did I ever tell you she told me on the day we were married that she felt that day she would be a blessing to me. I brushed aside her comment. She had to die so that I could see how deaf I could be. Then, she had to come back from the grave to tell me it was time to get out of the mountains. The same message Mebiktu needled me with. I am so often so slow to obey."

"Obedience is hard," she said emphatically. "Especially when it's obedience as a matter of faith. We want to do the right thing. We want to obey God. Sometimes, when we believe we are obeying God, even when we have suddenly changed a course of action, what we are actually following is still our inner self. We are wise enough to know that. So when the spirit gives us a course to follow, we wonder if it is really from God or is it still ourselves. Sometimes, we make the wrong choice and don't obey.

"There was not much time to react when you thought you felt the spirit speak and we were suddenly under attack. God moved those walls out of the way. We thought he moved them aside so we could go in, when really he moved them aside to see if we would listen."

"We?" he asked her.

"Yes, we. We are a team. We will prevail or fail all together. Let's not let any one of us get so prideful and believe they are on their own. God will deal with us separately and as a people. He will judge each of us separately. One of the things he will judge each of us on is how effectively we worked as a team.

"When we mess things up, whether alone or together, we need to ask God to forgive us and repent. He will forgive. He has told us we must forgive everyone for their sins. To withhold our forgiveness from someone who is truly sorry is a sin. That includes forgiveness of ourselves when we are truly sorry. He has told us to lay down all of our burdens and he will gladly pick them up and carry them for us.

"I saw the man I was going to marry chopped to death before my eyes. I praise God I passed out before I had to go on any longer."

"But Paluqua, that wasn't your fault. You weren't guilty. I agree. It was awful. I saw many die. I was there when the last of all our men were slaughtered. But that wasn't my fault."

"Are you certain?" They both had raised their voices considerably. "What were your prayers when Garasom handed all of our weapons over to Atrocene? Were you concerned over that or were you more concerned your wife was still apparently held captive? Were you praying for her and for yourself and your hopes for a happy life together or were you praying for our leaders?

"Was it your fault Anna died? When she began sneaking off to Rodan did you even realize she was gone or were you more concerned over your own loss and your guilt?

"Did you ever question why the Lord told us there would be times that he would not be with us? Did you suppose he would be so busy that he wouldn't find the time for us? Or could it be that though he would never leave us, there would be times that we would leave him? What were you thinking when you decided to chase after that witch outside Foramen? Were you guided by God that day? But he forgave you for everything. Every sin that was ever laid up against you has been cast away forever.

"We have all sinned and fallen away from him. We have all fought battles in our own strength, and sometimes we have lost. Still, we have to learn to repent and let it go."

Tears were rolling down Paluqua's cheeks. She was nearly in a rage. She had never harped at him like this. He was baffled. Then her whole composure changed to gentleness. There were still tears in her eyes.

"Anam, lay it down. As our leader, you have to make a lot of tough decisions. You do very well. One of your best decisions was to surround yourself with people that love you. When you hurt, we all hurt. Every one of us has been hurt. We've been hurt really bad. What does it matter if your hurt is not just like my hurt? God still loves you. Lay it down."

He was almost ready to break into tears as well but he closed his eyes as they walked and finally relaxed.

"I didn't ask you to compose yourself," she said sternly. "I asked you forgive yourself."

He winced at the comment as the truth really hurt. She suddenly stopped and raised one arm to get everyone's attention.

"We've been walking for quite a while and I believe it's time to take a break." She indicated a small grove of trees. "This place here looks just lovely." That's all it took to get the boys off the path.

They scampered into the ankle-high grass to the shade and gave themselves over completely to the coolness.

"You come with me," Paluqua instructed Anam. She glanced over at Zoana and Crazon and motioned to them to follow. Ernie quickly took Comeana from Crazon and she joined the others.

The three warriors led Anam to a place a little apart from the rest of the group. They relaxed and stretched their tired muscles for a couple of minutes and then moved upon Anam and laid hands upon him. Crazon and Zoana had heard the angry outburst that finalized the conversation but were not completely aware of what had taken place. After a few moments of silence, Paluqua quietly led out in prayer.

"Lord, we know that you want us to learn from the past, but we know you don't want us to be laden down with our past failures. We have all failed. We have all come far short of perfection. Some of us continue to be weak in certain areas. Some of us allow you to show your strength during those times. Some have resigned themselves to walking about with unhealed and unneeded burdens. It may be a misguided sense of pride or of humility. Both pride and humility are virtues, but self-centered pride and false humility are sins. Sometimes the line between virtue and sin can be so thin we don't even see it.

"Lord, this man is a mighty tower in your kingdom. A giant oak tree under whose shade we all can come for sustenance, but we know he is not perfect.

"Zeda was so great a warrior for you. No one can compare. She was a trusted friend for me and a great inspiration. When we lost that battle, my faith was broken. But when you had the victory, even over my tears, my spirit soared. I too was indignant when I found you had spoken to this man. And as I watched him the next few days, I continued to wonder if you could really use him. But he obeyed you, Lord. If he hadn't listened that time we surely would have starved to death in the mountains. But he did obey you. Oh Lord, thank you for continuing to have faith in him. Because of him perhaps the face of the whole world shall be changed. Imagine the darkness if we had not moved. Imagine the hopelessness. If the lesson to be learned from this is to go when you say so, he has learned well. Because from that time when you have told him to go, he has obeyed.

"So now we come to this, Lord. He has learned his lesson. He has repented. You have forgiven him. He has to forgive himself!" she called out emphatically. "I ask you right now to release him!" She spoke more loudly. "The burden he has for this woman's death is no longer reasonable. He needs to let it go. He needs to lay it down at your feet. Dear God, I love him so much, it drives me crazy to see him so burdened. Give him that strength, Lord. Give him the strength to be weak. Oh, Lord, what will it profit him to continue to hold on to it?"

Anam opened his eyes just as Paluqua did. "Let it go, please," she begged.

"I... I have," he stuttered. "I feel so peaceful. I understand now that it was all a part of his plan."

The three women exchanged knowing looks of pleasure. They sat silently for several minutes. Zoana finally spoke up and asked him how far they intended to walk.

He shook his head, wondering why she would change the conversation. "I really don't know. It's all up to the Lord. Why do you ask?"

"Well," she continued, "it seems to me if we can make this much progress in barely one day of traveling, how much shall we be set free of and how close will we draw to one another if this becomes a considerable trip?"

The question wasn't answered, but the prospects excited all four of them. They all took a long draught of water and soon after headed on their way.

The road they traveled on was of dirt and there were many deep gorges and large boulders which had appeared during the spring thaw and flooding. Traveling on foot was fairly easy, on horseback would have been difficult, by wagon would have been impossible. Along the side of the road was a gully which had been created when the road was made. However, in certain places, it had worn down to a deep chasm because of the constant flooding in the spring. Also the gully had often diverted and cut across the road digging a ditch two or three feet deep in some places.

It was still early summer, so the new grass along the side of the road was only about a foot tall in most places. Beneath the new grass was a bed of decaying matter from previous years. It seemed a little odd that they had passed no other travelers or seen any major animals in two days of traveling. The area was very alive, however, with a variety of birds and burrowing animals. They stopped at one point and watched a family of groundhogs who had laid claim to a small clearing and dug several holes.

Beyond the roadway in many places was a thick forest on both sides. Deep and dark and quite uninviting. When the sun was high in the sky, however, they opted for the cool forest floor to lounge and eat their lunch. The children needed a nap so they decided on an extended break.

Four of the women: Coralena, Bulshadi, Umfuwadea and Macosena came to Anam and asked that they might wander off alone for a time. They also suggested they might find fresh water.

Once away from the road, the forest changed from tall, closely-grown trees to shorter trees crowded about with shrubs and bushes. A few places were impassable, but they managed to find a deer trail and follow that for about a mile. After traveling along the hot, obstructed road for so long it was a pleasure to walk along the cool pathway. The only interruptions were an occasional tree root. They reached a point where the path had ascended up to a peak and descended rapidly to a meadow below.

What a wonderful sight. There the women saw a herd of about two dozen deer. Included were five young fawns and their mothers, all led by one huge fourteen-point buck. Most of the females looked up at the intruders and, ignoring them, went back to their browsing. However, the buck was less receptive to having visitors. He stared down at each of the women, snorting and digging up earth all the while. He finally showed some acceptance of their presence by making a show of eating, all the while keeping an eye on them as if to call their bluff.

The women had sat down on the edge of the small field and spoke only in subdued whispers. They merely wanted to watch.

Finally, deciding that this situation was too agitating, the buck gazed back in their direction and, snorting a few more times, led his tribe out of the clearing.

"Thank you, Lord," breathed Macosena quietly. The others also quietly expressed their satisfaction. Macosena stood up and stretched. "Well, water or no water, we've gained from this and I think we should be getting back."

"Perhaps," Bulshadi spoke up and pointed off in the distance where the trees once again began to slope downhill, "the river is there."

"We all know we did not come out here to get water,"

Coralena said. "We have plenty enough water to last to Layta."

Therefore, they all agreed it was time to retrace their steps so the group would not have to wait for them. In a few minutes they had rejoined their friends and delighted them with their experience. Soon, they were all on the road once more.

They reached an area where it was obvious people had been working to clear the obstructions from the road. There were no large stones, and the few boulders that had rolled into the road had been dragged away by horses. Even though there were still areas where the road had been washed out, it would have been possible to get through with a horse-drawn cart, though with difficulty.

Not much later, they saw the first signs of their destination, which appeared as wisps of smoke above the treetops.

The main industry of Layta was fishing. It was hard work but very dependable. Its ideal location on the curve of the river created a natural catch basin where the villagers could lay their traps and nets. The fish were always plentiful, and they needed to restrain themselves from overharvesting beyond their needs and beyond their ability to transport the fish downriver and then overland to Marsa. They would return a few days later laden down with fresh supplies and paddle their way upriver until they reached home.

The children of the village were the first to see the visitors. By the time the Rasomites passed the first of the little huts, the streets were already beginning to fill up with a welcoming committee.

Foremost among these people were Sami and his wife, Reba. They were an elderly couple, and it was Sami and his sons who had first camped alongside the river on fishing trips. Eventually, they had opted to remain on the banks year-round and eliminate the traveling. He had not realized his early retirement would turn into an enterprise. Most of the villagers had either married into the family or were his descendants.

Anam had been there on one previous occasion and spent a few days enjoying both the break from Marsa and the hard work involved. Sami didn't travel anymore, but whenever one of his offspring were in Marsa they would always spend some time with Anam or the women. Several of the women had also visited here.

"Anam, my friend," called out Sami when he was close enough to see clearly. "I'm so glad you have come." Sami ambled his still strong, but slow-moving eighty-year-old frame over to his friend as Anam handed both Comeana and Oranea over to eager hands among the villagers. Sami first clenched Anam's outstretched hand and then gave him a bear hug.

Except for his slow-moving walk and gray hair, Sami could have passed himself for being a man sixty years younger. He was a tall man with bulging muscles and probably could have, if he took him by surprise, downed Anam.

"Sami," Anam said with joy. "I'm so pleased God led us this way."

Sami continued. "We knew you would soon be leaving Marsa and prayed you would be coming this way. We expected you would go the other route as there is so much more activity and the traveling is easier that way. We should have known you wouldn't base your decision on comfort. Despite our lack of faith, we have made some preparations for you. We have cleared out the meeting house and lain blankets and cushions for you. There is plenty of room there and also the best kitchen in the village. There is always more than enough to eat here. I know you won't eat much fish, but we still have abundance.

Anam changed the subject. "We noticed the last few miles that the road had been cleared and some repairs done."

"We're doing that. When fishing is slow, we send a crew out with a team of horses to work. It goes very slow, however. Our hope is to get it cleared so we can use that route as well as the river. Sometimes the river moves too quickly to allow any upriver travel so we get trapped in Marsa."

The rest of the Rasomites had begun to mingle with old friends and several introductions were made. The people of Layta were mostly younger families. They dressed scantily as they spent most of their time working in or along the river.

"Have you asked Chiam for help in clearing the road?" Anam asked. "He has people there who specialize in such work. It is their responsibility as well."

"I know. I know." He shrugged. "I just thought it would be much easier going than it's been." He shook his head. "But, it's really going slow. Perhaps we should just leave it alone. We don't need this place too easy to reach." He called Reba over and suggested she take Paluqua and the children inside. "They surely need to be fed and bathed."

Reba was as slender as her husband but only stood about five feet tall. She also still had a youthful appearance and easily hefted

Comeana and took Oranea by the hand. Anam watched as his family was led away. He realized that most of the other women had already linked up with the families and gone with them. Togorasom stood alone, and Anam waved to him to join him and Sami.

Sami gave them a quick tour of their sleeping area, then they went down to the river shore. Except for half a dozen small fishing boats neatly hanging from a rack, there was very little sign that the beach was inhabited. The river raged nearby, but they stood on the beach that had been cut where the river turned almost at a right angle. The bay was poised on the inside of the curve and one could safely walk, waist deep, several hundred feet out. The water on the opposite bank also crept quite slowly. However, a channel in the middle prevented easy access to the other bank as the river moved quite quickly there.

The bay was surrounded by fir and pine trees. On the opposite bank was a different view of deciduous trees and the snow-capped mountains beyond. Anam and Togorasom stood side by side for several minutes escaping into the panorama. It was so different from the city.

Sami sat behind them on the sand. It was a familiar situation for him with city-bound visitors. He could tell they were grateful for his hospitality. It was good to discover that there was so much more to life than Marsa. Finally, Anam looked back at Sami who was busily making a small reed basket, as his hands were usually busy.

"I know, Anam, I still love it. Why do you suppose I have stayed here all these years? As far as I am concerned, only heaven can be better. It should be an easy transition. As long as you want to stay, you are our guests."

"I wish we could stay," he answered by way of apology. "One night, perhaps two. I feel driven to keep moving. We've been bogged down for too long. But, if we didn't have a mission, the river rapids could not even pull me away from here. This is incredible."

"We needed this, we really did." Togorasom sat down on the clean sand. "If you don't mind, I'd like to sit here a while."

Sami stood up. "You stay as long as you want. I need to get back to the family."

Sami and Anam climbed back up the bank and disappeared into the overgrowth that separated the bay from the village.

"Thank you Lord," he said quietly as the two men slowly walked away. "Your mystery and beauty are beyond description. To the worker you also grant a time for peace and rest and I appreciate that. God, make me a worthy vessel. Forgive me for my sins and for when I fall short of the mark. Bless our family who remained behind in Marsa that they may do good and prosper. Accept their sacrifice, Lord. Bless Anam's and Paluqua's children. They are so young to be able to understand your ways and to know what is going on around them. But, teach them for they are not so much younger than I was when you first began to guide me. Consider Crazon…"

Anam and Sami arrived at the meeting house which would be their home. It was a warm day outside, but the mostly stone structure was quite cool. Sami fetched a bucket of water from the inside well and poured them both a drink of cool water.

"Will he be all right?" Sami asked of Togorasom.

Anam sat down on the floor among the blankets. The entire floor of the main room was thick with cushions, furs and blankets. Sami sat facing him.

"Togorasom will be fine for hours," he said as he rolled his eyes indicating there was nothing anyone could do about it anyway. "He'll pray for everyone he can possibly think of and then he may start over. After a while, we'll have to go out to get him to eat and come inside."

"He's a very odd child."

Anam nodded. "Odd? Yes, I'm sure. A child? I suppose he's a child. He cannot be labeled. There is no one like him. We each have our special ministries, but the Lord is really doing something different with Togorasom."

"He's a fanatic?"

"Oh yes, he's a fanatic. But he's still only a young boy. Perhaps that is why it's so easy for God to teach him. He's young and meek, but also bold. He's not set in old-fashioned ways like we are."

Sami got up. "I'd like to stay and talk, but there's a great meal being prepared and I should be involved in that. Feel free to relax or go out and visit or whatever."

"Thank you, Sami. I need to be alone for a bit, but I'll join you soon."

"No, I don't miss city living," Reba said with a smile. "Lord knows I don't miss that." She continued to slice and chop the potatoes as she answered Paluqua's questions. She was preparing a favorite family soup, however, to feed so many required four other women in addition to herself and Paluqua.

"We do get into town once or twice a year for a couple of weeks," replied one of the younger women. "It's a nice change, but this is home." The other ladies all nodded in agreement.

"We all envy you that God has called you out," Reba said. "However, we are all very satisfied to stay here. It's very secure. We don't have a great deal, but all we have we worked for and the Lord gave it to us. Would you like to stay forever in town?"

Paluqua laughed. "Oh, no. I loved Marsa, but I think we overstayed ourselves. We've grown so soft. It will take a lot of work to get us physically back to where we were."

"But you were doing God's work," another woman said. "Look at the change all over this area. And what would have become of us if you had decided not to stay in Marsa?"

Reba smiled again. She had such a genuine and disarming smile. Despite her age, she still had a full set of healthy, sparkling teeth. "We can only thank God that they did. We had a good life, but it was through their ministry we received a meaning for our lives. It's such a shame that they can't stay longer here. But, I know, they have a work to do."

This seemed to cut off the conversation concerning the differences between the Rasomites and the people of Layta. They concentrated on their food preparation and what would be needed to feed the visitors. It was the wrong end of the growing season to adequately provide meals for a crowd of vegetarians. However, they brought forth quite an abundance of stored items; potatoes, cabbage, carrots, onions, dried beans, and canned tomatoes. They also had apples for applesauce and fresh strawberries and rhubarb for pie. Also, much wine. Other groups were baking massive amounts of fresh bread and biscuits. By late afternoon, everything was prepared and the meal was ready.

While the last items were brought out and placed on the tables, the children of Layta had prepared a show for the Rasomites which the little ones performed. One of the older children explained the activity as it went along. One of the boys dressed in a grey robe was the main character. First, he was attacked by a black rain cloud, portrayed by a child in a black cloth bag. The boy became confused and ran around as if lost. Then two young girls came and began to tease him and call him names. He slumped down on the ground and looked very depressed. Finally, two other boys came and pretended to beat him. He lay down on the ground and beat one fist on the ground in frustration. Then an older teenaged boy came and helped him up. He put a white robe over the grey one and finally hoisted him up on his shoulders. The other five children came back and tried to torment him again. But all they could do was to pull at his feet. He had a great, big smile now that he was safe.

Sami was setting next to Anam and whispered. "Are you enjoying the show?"

Anam nodded. One of the women handed him a mug of wine. He took a great swig of the beverage and then realized the star of the show was approaching. The boy was only five years old. He stood proudly before Anam with his smile still intact. "Anam, thank you." Anam gave him a quizzical look. "The children and I would like to thank you for giving each of us a white robe." Anam looked slightly embarrassed. The boy went on. "In the story I played the part of myself. My friend, Sean," he indicated the boy that had picked him up, "played your part. Thank you for lifting us up."

Anam looked at Sami. "You should be very proud. You have wonderful children here."

Sami nodded. "He's my great grandson."

"Sami," laughed Anam, "most of the little ones in Layta are your great grandchildren."

They partied until late into the evening. Most everyone had finally gone off to bed. A few had apparently opted to sleep where they partied. Togorasom, who was used to lack of sleep had a small circle of followers eagerly engaged in conversation. For all his great wisdom he spoke seldom and only to guide the conversation by making a point or asking a leading question. Finally, the last of them nodded off to sleep and he sat alone. The embers had burned down to a black-crimson aura.

"Thank you, Lord, that these people are free of the stranglehold of idle busyness. That their lives have meaning and that they have not vainly devoted their lives to striving for something of no value. There is also a great innocence here and that is so clean and fresh. Thank you also that they were here to minister to us. Place a hedge of protection around them and teach them to seek after you." He lowered his head and fell to sleep almost immediately.

Activity in Layta was not very evident the following morning. The babies, as usual, were the first up. They were quickly fed and returned to bed.

There was no more activity among the Rasomites than anywhere else. A few of the women arose and went out to spend a quiet morning with friends.

At noontime, most were beginning to prepare breakfast. Togorasom slept on the ground next to the stump of wood he had used for a seat the night before. Someone had compassionately covered him with a blanket and placed a pillow under his head. He slept soundly on until mid-afternoon despite the increasing amount of activity going on around him. When he finally arose he was still quite drowsy. He wandered around and exchanged greetings with a few people until he finally stopped in the shade of a grove of trees not many feet from where he had spent the night. He lay down on the ground, and soon once again was soundly sleeping.

The timing of the Rasomites arrival could not have been any better. If they had arrived any earlier in the season the people of Layta would have been involved in either spring fishing or planting. A later arrival and summer planting and the early summer fishing season would have been occupying all their time. At this time some modest weeding of the Laytan fields was the main enterprise. This was their traditional period of relaxation as in a couple of weeks they would, once again, become very busy.

"How long will you stay with us, Anam?" Sami asked as he fidgeted with the straps on his sandals.

"Tomorrow we must leave. We cannot allow ourselves to get bogged down again."

Sami looked very depressed. "I knew you could not stay long, but I had hoped you would be able to remain longer than a couple of nights."

"I need to apologize for our haste, my friend. The time we spent in Marsa was wonderful. The word of God has been spread far and wide. However, we became very soft while there. Our physical strength and weapon-bearing agility has really dried up. We need to travel so we can have an opportunity to train."

"Have you noticed our weakness and laziness?" Sami asked sarcastically. "This could be a wonderful opportunity for you. There will soon be a lot of work to do. There nearly always is. You would be out of harms' way and have a chance to regain your health and strength. We are known everywhere for our good health. It is due to our lifestyle and diet. We can also defend our village from attack, even though we are not mighty warriors. You would have abundant opportunity to train. We would not impede you."

Anam sat quietly as Sami watched him in the belief that Anam was considering his offer. Actually, Anam had already made up his mind but did not want to hurt his host's feelings. "I'm sorry, Sami. I really feel the Lord calling us to continue on." This was true, but also, deep in his heart he had another reason for not staying. He felt bad that Sami looked so dejected. However, he was very apprehensive of staying any longer. Leaving so many of his loved ones behind in Marsa was a great motivator to never settle down again until he knew he was where God wanted him. He feared staying too long in Layta would either result in more losses or divisions when it came time to leave.

Even while he and Sami talked, most of the Rasomites were having a wonderful time refreshing old friendships and making new ones. The Laytan men were taking turns escorting their guests on boat rides up and down the coast. Also, in between trips, the swimming was wonderful. Many of them had not been near a major body of water since they had left the coast where they were raised. In that place of fear, frolicking on the beach was not such a pastime as hiding from enemies. Therefore, only a few knew how to swim and most of those had learned in these same waters on previous visits.

Miscal had not grown up in Layta but had spent his childhood in Marsa as the son of a shopkeeper. He had always been in trouble because of his mischievousness and his nervous way of doing things. He had been wise enough not to run completely afoul of the law but had always pushed his luck. Finally, when he was sixteen, his family could stand it no longer and threatened to throw him out of the house. One of Sami's sons had heard of the boy and taken the chance of bringing him to Layta. Miscal had been worked like a slave, but he had also been loved and encouraged.

He had lived in Layta for five years and had become the best steersman in the village. There was nothing concerning the operation of any of the fishing boats or canoes that he could not handle in an expert manner. That is why, when he proposed taking Zoana for a ride down the rapids, Sami had encouraged it. "You'll remember it as one of the most exciting experiences of your life," he promised.

They had left early in the morning, before most were up, since it would be a four or five-hour climb into the hills before they could begin their trip.

They had talked only intermittently during the sometime treacherous climb with the canoe. Mostly, Miscal talked about his adventures and abilities, but Zoana encouraged him to open up. Finally, near the top, they settled down for a small meal before their trip back. Miscal had become very quiet.

"Is something wrong, Miscal? You seemed so cheerful during the walk and now, I don't know, so sullen."

Miscal shook his head and gazed off into the fluttering leaves beyond her. Zoana had closed her eyes and bowed her head to silently pray for Miscal and the upcoming wild ride. Except for the leather thong and brassiere, his eyes wandered over every inch of her exposed flesh. He mentally removed the little she was wearing. The peaceful look on her face only added to his desire.

She suddenly looked up and surprised him. "What is wrong?" she pleaded. Miscal was speechless, but his nervousness completely betrayed what was on his mind. "I think," she said, standing up over him, "it's time to be going. You need to concentrate on getting us out of here."

Miscal took a deep breath. "Zoana, I have never seen a woman as beautiful as you. If you were my woman, we would live life to the fullest. One adventure after another. It would be wonderful."

"Miscal!" she yelled at him; the birds hopping in the branches over their heads took flight. "Snap out of it! I am not an adventurer. I am God's messenger."

He felt rebuked but tried one more time. "I could do that!" he said excitedly. "I can learn to do anything." He thumped his fist against his bare chest. "Just let me come with you and give me a chance."

"I told you we need to go. I'm getting angry."

He stood up so he could face her. "I thought you were a great woman of God. Doesn't God even give a man a chance to prove himself?"

His face was set like stone, but her gaze tried to cut through him. "Your desire right now has nothing to do with God." She turned and started in the direction of the river.

He grabbed her arm and snapped, "I wasn't finished!"

The suddenness of Zoana's reaction surprised even her. Despite his hold, she swung the back of her hand against his chin. He landed flat on his back. If she had swung much harder she would have broken bones and teeth. Even still, he gaped at her with amazement of her great strength. She extended the same hand and helped him up.

"Are you going to be all right?" she asked with concern. He nodded. "I have no intention to hurt you, but if you can't get your desires under control, I shall. Have I made myself quite clear?"

He nodded as he stretched his neck about trying to free himself from its little kinks. "Zoana," he said almost in tears. "I'm really sorry this happened. I... I can't make excuses. Please, don't let anyone know."

She looked at him sympathetically. "I have to tell Anam. You probably wouldn't understand that. I won't tell any of your people if you've really gotten yourself under control. However, I would expect you to tell them. Are you ready to go?"

He looked down in shame. "I'm ready," he said quietly.

A few minutes later they had found the path to the stream Miscal had used many times before and carefully mounted the canoe with Miscal at the back end. To steer the canoe, he used two short, narrow paddles with niches for his arms and hand holds, making them more of an extension of his body. Zoana sat near the middle at the front end of the canoe. Her purpose was merely for balance and to enjoy the ride as she had rarely ridden on the water before and never in waters like this.

The point at which they entered the stream was fairly calm for a mile or so and then suddenly careened over the mountainside into rapids that lasted to the bottom ten miles away. It would be a wild ride but she trusted completely in Miscal's skill and experience. He had traveled every bit of water for miles around and this particular stream dozens of times.

The sun was high overhead as they left the riverbank. Despite the skin-searing heat, they felt quite comfortable as they were already drenched with cold mountain water.

Zoana nervously glanced back at Miscal several times as they headed out, but he seemed completely preoccupied with steering the canoe. She said another prayer and decided to enjoy the ride.

Once Miscal had maneuvered the craft away from the bank, the river began to take control of it. He knew where every dangerous rock and twist would appear and exactly how to react. He silently slipped the paddle from his right arm and propped it in its nook on the side of the canoe. Never taking his eyes from Zoana's torso, he carefully slid forward in the canoe. He knew a place only a few feet ahead where a broad stone lay just beneath the surface. He could guide the canoe along that stone and leave the boat perched in the middle of the stream for hours.

Zoana kept her eyes riveted to the water directly ahead. A couple hundred feet beyond the stream suddenly seemed to disappear as it leaped over the mountainside. Suddenly, Miscal latched onto her waist. She swung back with her right hand without looking and missed, but he grabbed hold of her arm. He didn't let go.

"Back on the shore you may have been in charge," she heard him say. "However, out here is my kingdom, and I'm in charge. I know you can't get out of here." She could feel the boat begin to speed up and had no idea what he thought he was going to accomplish out here. As if to answer her, he continued, "I'm going to put up the canoe out here and you'll do whatever you're told. I may only get this advantage once in my life, but I intend to take you right here. Then again, who knows, you may enjoy the spirit of the adventure and demand more."

She could see the canoe begin to turn sideways and was certain in a few feet they would be into the rapids. She felt his arm begin to move up from her waist and reach for her breast as he pulled her towards him. Fear gripped her. Her brain could not function well. She sensed him rise from his position and move towards her. Suddenly, the ironlike fist of her free hand met his chin. The boat lurched forward as he flew into the water, and the front end of it violently struck the broad stone.

Zoana glanced over her shoulder long enough to see Miscal's lifeless body float by, face down, and topple into the rapids. But she lost her attention of him quickly as the boat glided away from the rock and leaped into the rapids, tail-end first. Terrified, she hoped for a miracle but her thoughts were cut short when the canoe flew headlong into a pile of rocks, casting her into the stream and onto her back.

As she was jolted overboard, her left leg desperately clutched the side of the canoe. She could see the craft was poised only inches from the bank. Nearly reaching a sitting position, she lost her grip as the canoe suddenly rocked violently.

Zoana bounced and struck her head against the rocks, then began drifting down the stream like a sodden ragdoll. Unable to swim or fight against the torrent, she allowed herself to move along. A large projectile-shaped boulder loomed before her, and with one last burst of strength, she reached for and clung to it. It was a good thing she did as the stream quickly took another downturn and descended like a waterfall.

The roost upon which she now sat was poised over the cascade like a great arm. From here she was safe, but it was impossible for her to escape. Both shores now loomed far away. She was able to climb the object and was out of the water except below her knees.

With the small amount of power left in her, she clutched to her pedestal and sobbed herself to sleep, hoping help would soon be on its way.

She heard the peeping sound of a gull and opened her eyes. She couldn't have dozed long as the sun appeared to be in the same place. It was not possible to release her hold from the perch for she would tumble into the rapids. There was a long gash on her right arm which had stopped bleeding. Her right cheek still felt warm and damp, so she pressed her face against her arm to discover that it was swollen and bleeding. That was from the concussion which had nearly knocked her out. There were probably other marks, but she couldn't be certain. Her whole body ached from being slammed about. The sun was her enemy now. She was used to heat, but right now, it seemed unbearable. Her throat was so dry it ached. She felt no humor in being so thirsty while being surrounded by water.

A dozen birds fluttered back and forth in the air above her head and continued their racket. Each shore was perhaps twenty feet from her. The birds made it seem so easy to get from one side to another.

Due to the heat, Zoana found it difficult to keep her eyes open. Again, she was thinking of her rescuers. She calculated when she and Miscal would have been able to return to Layta. Shortly after that time, when they did not arrive, she expected someone to come look for them. Then, she realized she had told no one when they would return or where they were going. Would Sami be able to figure out where the boy would head? Certainly they would send out search parties, but they wouldn't know where to go. Her thinking became very desperate. How long would she be stuck up here? She couldn't hold out for long. Anyone coming up the riverside would not be able to see her very well. She glanced back and forth at the opposite banks. Both seemed too thick in brush for anyone to easily penetrate. They could pass right by her and never realize she was there.

She opened her mouth to call for help, but only a squeaking noise came from her dry throat. Even if she could scream, it would be drowned out by the roar of the river.

Then, another thought struck her. "Oh my God," she whimpered, "I've killed a man. Oh, Lord," she continued, "please forgive me. I was so terrified; I didn't even know what I was doing. I didn't mean to hit him that hard. I just wanted him to stop it. Oh, Lord," she sobbed, "help me. I don't know what to do. I need you to help me."

There was a stirring inside her which made her feel suddenly calm. Despite her situation, the closeness with God right then made her feel as though things would turn out well in the end. She sensed something bump against the rock next to her dangling legs. Her immediate thought was to brush it away, but she strained her neck to look over her shoulder. She was shocked to see the canoe resting a few inches away from her in the water. There was a split in the water, directly behind her perch, where it was calmer than on either side, but this was not an adequate explanation for what was happening.

A voice inside her told her to get in. She glanced at the rapids again. It seemed like certain death to cast herself into that maelstrom. There was no way she could control the craft. It would head downstream too rapidly for her to consider trying to handle it. Also, she was certain the stream was filled with jagged rocks inviting death and an endless number of twists and turns.

Her eyes were wide in disbelief as she slid down the rock and clambered into the canoe. She sat in the bottom of the boat near the middle and made an attempt to hang onto the sides, but only weakly. Her arms and hands were numb from holding the rock. It took only a few seconds for her to get in. All of this activity had an unreal, almost dreamlike, quality. Her mind and body were awed by what was happening and terrified at the thought of entering this splintered canoe that had already taken on some water. However, something deeper in her made her obey. Shutting out the distractions of the rapids and the noise, she went through with it because she knew who was really in charge.

She had no more than sat down when the canoe turned toward the right and careened into the rapids. Any sense of confidence that was felt before dissipated immediately as she forgot her aching muscles and clamped her hands firmly onto the sides of the canoe. All she could see was rocks and white water. The canoe would come so close to crumbling into a pile of rocks and then, as if guided by an invisible oarsman, suddenly turn aside. Many times, the front-end of the canoe would dip into the water and then thrust itself back up, throwing her back and forth. Her view was constantly obstructed as buckets of water were thrown into her face and she dared not release her fearsome grip to wipe it away.

Zoana slunk lower and lower into the tiny craft as though she could somehow get away from the danger by not looking, until she finally lay in the bottom of the canoe on her back.

He whose hand it was guided the canoe needed neither Zoana's eye nor her terror to steer properly. Not only did he know each twist and turn and water current, but he also created them. Zoana tried to calm herself by thinking on these things as she was thrashed about. She thanked God for sparing her life and hearing her prayer. She couldn't remember when she passed out.

She had a sensation of something creeping up on her flesh as she still lay on her back. It took a moment to respond. She felt it crawling and engulfing her legs and torso and slowly moving over her face. Zoana sat bolt upright. The canoe was swiftly sinking into the river. Once again, she was afraid. She didn't understand how, but she had floated into a much larger, slow-moving stream. The nearer shore was met at the water edge by a rock cliff about twenty feet high. The further shore was met by a large, deserted beach. However, it was well over a hundred feet away. She dove into the water, hoping she had enough strength to swim it. She hit the water and realized the river was less than three feet deep at this point. With a sigh of relief, she waded to the shore and sprawled on the sand.

She could still feel the stinging rays of the sun directly overhead, but no longer cared. It seemed amazing that the whole adventure had happened in such a short length of time. A renewed sense of strength slowly filled her mind and limbs, and eventually, she sat up to consider where she could be.

As she'd never been here before, the area was completely unknown to her. However, she knew they had traveled upriver before going into the hills. She headed south taking solace knowing most of the trip before had been the climb.

Togorasom had not slept long during his mid-afternoon nap. A few minutes after laying down, he was up again looking for Anam whom he found talking with Sami. Despite the many hours of sleep he'd gotten, he still looked exhausted.

Anam smiled when he saw the boy. "Did you sleep well?"

"I had a dream." Anam casually nodded for him to continue. "Zoana has survived." They were instantly attentive. "In the first part of my dream, Miscal raped Zoana and then threw her out of the canoe." Both men were wide-eyed. "She was unable to fight against the rapids as Miscal followed her until she struck her head against a rock, lost consciousness and drowned. Miscal prepared to head home with a tale of tragedy. However, in my second dream, she was able to prevent his aggression and it was Miscal who went out of the boat. I have been looking for her, but she is nowhere to be found."

"I thought you were resting," Sami interrupted.

"I have been looking for her in my heart. I believe Miscal is dead, but I cannot find either of them. We need to go after them."

"Of course we do," said Sami as he stood up. "However, I don't believe anyone knows where they went."

Anam leaned forward and stared intently at Togorasom. "Think back, is there anything in the dream you can remember that could give us a lead?"

Togorasom shook his head. "I saw no river or anything else in the dreams except the activity between Zoana and Miscal. The only important thing I know is that it has already happened. I believe Miscal is dead and Zoana is somewhere out there either stranded or trying to return."

Anam nervously slapped the palm of his hand against his bare leg as he quickly tried to determine the best action.

Sami put his hand on Togorasom's shoulder. "Have you ever been exposed to rape?" he asked, hoping to calm him after the exposure in the dream.

Anam winced, awaiting the reply. "I and my father were forced to watch my mother repeatedly raped by a gang of Atrocene soldiers before she and my father were killed and I was released. Only a few days later, another man tried to rape my sister, but we managed to escape. Shortly after that, she was captured and taken to Rodan. I never saw her again."

Sami shook his head. "I... I'm sorry. I never knew. How old was your sister at the time?"

Togorasom shook his head. "I really don't remember exactly. She was younger than I." Sami was even more shocked. "All of my people have drank out of the river of sorrows many times. But, it is not the past I am concerned over. I am only concerned now for my sister, Zoana." Tears were beginning to well up in his eyes.

People had begun to gather around but no one else had heard what Togorasom had said. He began crying uncontrollably and clutched tightly to Sami.

"Where would Miscal have taken her if he wanted to ensure they were completely alone?" Anam asked.

"I just don't know," Sami answered, shaking his head. Suddenly his face brightened. "I think I know where they would go. A place that offers one of the few rapids with navigable falls. Still, it's quite dangerous. I'm sure they would go there."

Zoana had walked and stumbled about a mile along the shore before she again collapsed onto the sand. The strength she thought she had was mostly only her eagerness to get back to Layta and have this disastrous day behind her. She was physically drained. Her body hurt with each movement. She couldn't understand why a woman of her physical ability should be so exhausted. Suddenly, her thoughts turned to Miscal.

"I've killed him," she mumbled under her breath. "Oh, my God!" she called out. "What have I done? I didn't mean to hit him so hard. I was scared and he was acting so stupid. I know I overreacted. Oh, Lord, I pray he somehow survived. But I'm not sure if he could have. Oh, God, I didn't mean to kill him, but I can't change that now. Please, forgive me. There's nothing else I can do right now but to ask you to forgive me. Please, give me the right words and right attitude when I get back to Layta. If I get back to Layta. Oh, God, I hurt so much and I don't really understand why. Help me, Lord."

She lay there for a few minutes, wanting to cry but not actually breaking down. It was an awful feeling of emptiness that crept all over her and deep inside of her. Slowly though, she began to feel another surge of strength and finally sat up and looked towards the water.

Zoana wished with all her heart that Miscal would appear, walk up to her out of the water and sit down beside her. She couldn't understand why he had done that thing he had tried to do. He was so bright and good-looking and had so much going for him. Does everyone have a drawback? Why is it so hard to conquer ourselves and gain self-control? We want to accomplish so much and we can't even control our own actions. These thoughts struck her as she sat gazing at the slowly moving river. Occasionally some object would float by, bobbing up and down in the water. She looked intently at each unknown object until she could verify it was merely a tree branch or some other natural object. How she wished the young man would appear, even dead, so she could at least know his fate. However, she finally figured he had gone by long ago if he had ever appeared. Her hope for finding him now was also an excuse to stay in place and try to get the strength needed for the walk back. She also wondered what would be the reaction to her return and explanation when she reached Layta.

She lost track of the time but finally realized the sun had moved a considerable distance. It was time to go back. The bleeding from her arm and face had stopped and the blood dried. Before departing, she went to the water's edge and washed up. A small amount of blood oozed from her arm, but the sun quickly dried that up. Once in motion again, her head began to throb terribly which required her to stop several times to get it to simmer down.

She walked on, though unsteadily, for over an hour. Occasionally, she would stop to slow the throbbing in her head or take a drink of water. Always, she was scanning the area looking for something familiar. Zoana figured by now it must be mid-afternoon. The sun had dropped considerably in the sky, though it was still very warm. She couldn't understand why no one had come looking. But another part of her mind realized they could not. Why would they? Of course no one knew where they had gone, so how could they begin to know when they should return? The sudden revelation disheartened her. She considered flopping down in the sand and giving up.

Then her eyes strayed back to the other shore and she saw exactly what she had been looking for. A small group of trees which lined the water's edge stood out in stark contrast to the surroundings. Whereas the rest of that area was bathed in various shades of the newness of spring and early summer, these trees seemed to have forgotten. Instead, the branches were mostly bare of foliage except for a few leaves of gold and brown left over from the previous fall. This sight stood against the background of evergreens. She and Miscal had passed under these branches that morning. Layta was only a few hundred yards downriver. However, she would have to ford the river to get there.

Cautiously she entered the stream, hoping she would be able to wade across. She knew the river was not too deep in most places. As she neared the center of the stream and the water began splashing against her cheeks, she realized she would have to swim part of the way. It actually felt good to feel her body gliding underwater through the coolness. She popped back to the surface only long enough to gulp a mouthful of air and go back under. She was not able to fill her lungs with air and was soon back to the surface. She attempted to stand so she could continue wading and was not able to touch bottom. Again she grabbed at air and consumed a great deal of water. Fear quickly took hold as she tried to resume her breast stroke. She knew she was totally inexperienced as a swimmer. For a moment, she considered returning to the shore she'd left, but did not know how to get turned around. In a last frantic effort, she took another gulp of air and water and dove straight down. She discovered the bottom and crawled along it for a few feet. Pushing off from the bottom she blasted through to the surface, took a mouthful of air, and went back under, crawling a few more precious inches. She resurfaced and tried to remain calm. As she quickly glanced around, she knew she had been moving downstream at a much greater pace than she had been moving across. The trees she'd identified earlier were getting further away. She dove under again, but not for long. With great joy she ran aground and stood up in neck-deep water.

She breathed the beautiful air for several moments before she pressed on. Very soon, she sank into the sand on the shore and rolled into a ball, knees under her chest, in a worship or fetal position. She didn't want to move, ever.

She heard the pounding of bare feet against the sand and looked to see from where it came.

"There she is!" called out a young man leading several others toward her.

She was gently led the few feet back along the shore to the village, and as they mounted the small rise above the beach, they were met by several of the Rasomites, first among whom were Paluqua and Crazon.

Upon first seeing their weary friend, they were both shocked as she didn't realize how bad she looked. The laceration she had received had begun to heal but ran the full length of her upper arm. This, however, caused them little concern. However, the place where her face had been slammed into the rocks was a mess. Her cheek was swollen and bloody. Her one eye was swollen partially shut. For a few moments, they didn't know how to react. Old and painful memories began to take shape. The three of them clung together in silence as Crazon and Paluqua allowed their mere presence and the warmth of their bodies to minister to Zoana.

Zoana naturally did not realize any of her friends knew what had happened. The gathering of people continued to grow until Anam and Sami appeared on the scene. She looked into Sami's compassionate and understanding eyes. "I'm sorry," she sobbed. "I've killed him. Please believe me that I didn't mean to do it. I'm sorry."

"I feel so terrible," Sami said. "I wish I'd never sent you out there. Miscal has always acted before he thought, but I never suspected he would make a move on you. Can you ever forgive me? Can you ever forgive us? I feel responsible for the whole thing. We were all so wrapped up in our joy before this happened. Now, I feel like a darkness has settled upon us. Is this how the people of Layta and the Rasomites, whom we love, shall part company?"

"Oh, Sami!" She left her friends and the old man and young woman embraced. "Our God can heal all wounds and sorrows if we will allow it. I will always love you and your people and your beautiful home." She looked back at her friends. "I don't understand how you could have known."

Anam answered and explained the dreams Togorasom had experienced. "I believe that Miscal had planned to kill you, however, God is stronger than that. Even though he couldn't deal with the evil in Miscal's heart, he could change the circumstances and outcome." He took Zoana's hand. "Come on, let us go and tend to these wounds and pray together." Sami took her other hand, and they returned to his house.

The entire time between Togorasom's announcement of his dream and Zoana's return had only been a very few minutes. Most of the villagers, including Reba, knew little or nothing about the attempted rape. Therefore, when they arrived in her kitchen, she was caught totally off guard.

"Oh, my Lord!" she proclaimed, placing her hands on her cheeks. "Now, what has happened?"

Zoana glanced at Sami. She had not yet revealed any of the details of what had transpired. He led her to a comfortable chair and then urged her to explain what had happened as Reba began to clean and dress her wounds.

"It's very hard," she began slowly. "I prayed for him, and I trusted God to minister to him. I understand now why I am still alive. Sometimes, maybe, we have to expect less than what we had desired. I surely had no desire to harm him." Reba told her to continue as she dabbed her face with a sponge of warm, soapy water. Zoana spent a long time explaining everything she could remember from the time they had left that morning until she had nearly drowned only a few hundred yards away. She spoke quietly throughout, except when she spoke about the canoe mysteriously coming to her and being guided to the bottom of the rapids.

When she had finished, Sami suggested they all join hands as he led them in a prayer of unity. Once he had opened the door to prayer, many others also led out in similar prayers which continued on for a couple of hours. They finally had to begin to break up so some could go about fixing the dinner meal.

As they were leaving, Zoana overtook Anam. "I need to talk with you. I still have a problem."

When they had wandered off a bit so they could talk privately, he started the conversation. "Which problem is this?" He pretended to consider his question. "Is it that you don't know how to swim?" She gave him a disgusted scowl. "That certainly would have helped out today." He paused. "Or is your problem men?" She was relieved he had brought it up.

"They never seem to leave me alone. I'm so gullible, I keep getting into trouble. Right now, I don't really ever want to be alone with a man." He frowned and patted himself in a few places. "Oh Anam, you're different. You don't have a problem with women. I feel as you are my brother. I can trust you."

"Maybe you forgot the circumstances that led Paluqua and I together." He took her hand and kissed it. "I'm not the least bit amazed that men are attracted to you." He leaned very close to her face. "Zoana, my sister, you are one of the most beautiful women I ever laid eyes on."

"How can you say that with my face all distorted and these bandages. I feel awful."

"Your wounds will heal. True beauty comes from inside."

"But, Anam, I'm so frustrated. What am I going to do? Everywhere we go, some young person wants to latch on to me and go see the world. It's driving me crazy."

"Just be patient. Serve the Lord and keep praying for his guidance."

"But it's taking so long and, deep inside, it really hurts. I'm really confused."

They were sitting on a bench under a tree. He reached out and embraced her. Then, with her head resting on his chest, she began to weep.

"Almighty Lord. This is your valuable servant, Zoana. Consider her, my God. Her heart and mind are troubled with unwanted desires poured out upon her by young, ardent admirers. She doesn't know what to do. Guide her, Lord. You be the light for her path. If there is to be a special man in her life, show her. If she must continue to wait, teach her to be patient. If she's to be alone, then make her strong enough to bear it. And, once again Lord, thank you for bringing her safely back to us."

He carefully cupped her still hurting chin in the palm of his hand and carefully kissed her on the lips. She was startled but not at all offended.

"Personally," he admitted, "I feel that God would have done a very wasteful thing by creating a female so lovely to spend her life alone. On the other hand, there are no women anywhere to be found with a ministry like yours coupled with such physical strength and agility. There can be only one man in the whole world who God would find worthy to be your mate. If there is such a man, I pray the Lord reveals him to you quickly. The poor man is probably in deep anguish over having to wait so long for you."

She embraced him again. "Oh, thank you, Anam. It would take a man of your strength and gentleness to interest this woman. If there is only one man like that, it seems he is already taken."

"You are so much exactly like Paluqua. You are so much completely different. God has put both of you together and he is also wise enough to fashion a man for you who will exactly meet your needs. However, do not fall into the temptation of creating him in your mind already because then, when God does act, you may miss your opportunity. Do you understand me?"

"Yes. I will allow God to both decide if there is a man and to fashion him, if that is his will."

After receiving assurance from Zoana that she would be fine, Anam got up and slowly walked away. He looked back to see how she was doing and saw her on her knees praying. However, he sensed that very soon the tears would begin to flow again so he hurried off in search of Crazon. He found his wife.

"How's she doing?" she asked as he approached outside Sami's house.

"We talked and I prayed with her. We're waiting on God, and I know she's real tough, but…"

"She's been through an awful lot today. I'll go and be with

her."

"Thank you. I was trying to find Crazon."

"I'll get her on my way." And she was gone.

"Lord, is a woman so incomplete without a man?" He spoke out loud more to himself than to God. He felt very blessed to be married to Paluqua, but on occasion, it hurt to see all these unattached women, and he wondered how they dealt with it. There was no way he could solve their problems except to pray for them and play the brother when he was needed. Somehow, that didn't seem enough, but he knew it was all he could do. He sat on the steps of Sami's house and began praying by name for each of the Rasomites they had left behind. His concern for them didn't diminish merely because they were separated by distance. He could sense people passing him by as they entered and departed the house, but he finally realized someone had sat on the steps near him. He prayed through for a bit longer and finally could not overcome the urge to know who his visitor was.

"We have a tool that when used by the will of God is powerful enough to break down and set up kingdoms. If only they would pray and wait upon God. They can work miracles, but they won't because they are too busy being involved in their own things. The more they pray, the more they would see the need for prayer." Togorasom sat one step lower and at the opposite side of the stairs looking at Anam. His pale, drawn face and squinting eyes revealed he was still very weary.

"I know how important prayer is, Togorasom. However, I am also concerned for you. You are a young boy and need your sleep. I'm always afraid that your fatigued condition will lead you to some sickness. You really do need your rest."

Togorasom rubbed one hand firmly over his face, attempting to squeeze a little life into it. He took a long, deep breath and stood up. "Somehow, God had me intercede in Zoana's life today through those dreams. I don't understand. I've done those things before, but of course, I'm not sleeping soundly. It's hard mental work."

"I appreciate that, but…"

"If I had not done whatever it is I did, Zoana would be dead now. I am as certain of that as I am that we are alive. If I had not interceded for her, she would have died." Tears were beginning to form in his eyes as he turned around and walked away.

Anam sat quiet and alone for several minutes after Togorasom left, considering what had been said. He knew Togorasom had a different and much closer relationship with God than most people ever would. He wondered if the difference was in the boy's attitude or if God had a special calling for him. Perhaps it was special because of both those ingredients. In many ways, Anam envied Togorasom's closeness to the Lord, but in another way, it frightened him. It was an awesome responsibility. Not only did he bear the spiritual load of all the Rasomites, but especially at his young age, it was taking a tremendous toll from his physical well-being. Another thought struck him concerning how Zoana's life had been spared. How many other catastrophes had been changed or averted due to Togorasom's intervention? The boy prayed almost ceaselessly, slept and ate little, and spoke only on occasion. Could his constant prayer be the main or even the only thing which had let the Rasomites be so successful?

It was beginning to get dark. The meal hour had come and gone with no fanfare like Sami had planned. Other events had swept it away. But Anam was becoming hungry. He felt something on his arm and instinctively reached for the wetness. Glancing upward, he felt another drop on his arm and one on his face. He could see no stars and sensed the arrival of a rainstorm. The horizon lit up in the distance, exhibiting the beautiful silhouettes of the forest. He heard the rumble of thunder. Then, silence for a few minutes. Suddenly, lightning struck much closer, followed by an almost immediate crack of power. The sky literally opened to a drenching shower. Too late to seek shelter anywhere else, he scurried into Sami's house.

Reba was still working in the kitchen at cleaning up from the evening meal. It appeared she was the only one home. She looked up from her dishes when Anam walked in and smiled. "Gonna be a big one, sounds like." She had to speak over the roar of the rain.

"Uh, yes. It certainly picked up in a hurry." He felt the nervousness of being alone in the house with her. "I'm sorry. I just didn't want to get stuck in the rain."

"Oh, Anam, that's fine. Sami has already gone off to bed," she said, putting his anxiety to rest. "Can't do much in the rain, but he figures there'll be plenty of work in the morning. You must be hungry." She lifted the lid from the big pot on the stove. "I've got a big batch of onion soup still warm." He looked interested. "Togorasom must have been famished."

"He ate here?" Anam asked as he sat at the table.

"Four or five bowls and a whole loaf of bread," she chuckled.

"I haven't eaten yet, and I am hungry. I would appreciate something while I sit out this storm."

In a few minutes, he had a large bowl of soup, warm bread and honey, and a mug of tea before him. Reba was back to work at the sink. He felt very comfortable and at home here.

Without looking back at him, Reba asked, "What were your parents like, Anam?" Then she nervously looked over her shoulder. "I keep forgetting. These simple questions often provoke painful memories."

"Don't worry," he assured her. "Actually, I have no recollection of my early childhood. As a very small child, I was kept by the priests in a village far from the rest of my people. We supposed it would be safe, but our enemies found us and dealt with us terribly. Only a handful of us escaped. I suppose the only one like a father I had was the priest I lived with all my life after that raid. We finally returned to my homeland about a year before the last great battle there."

"I've heard so much about those days." She wiped her hands on a towel and sat down at the table opposite him. She was silent while he ate for some time. Finally, she spoke up. "I feel so bad." She lowered her head and appeared deep in thought.

"About Miscal?"

She looked up at him. "Yes, Miscal. What a rotten situation. I had, we all had, so much hope for that boy. He was such a hard worker. Skillful. There was nothing about canoes or fishing craft he couldn't figure out. There had been problems with Miscal, however." Anam could see she was desperately holding back her tears at the mention of his name.

"I'm sorry." Anam encouraged her to continue.

"He'd been a rebel since birth, I guess. So stubborn. Always tried to have his own way. Several young girls had their eyes on him, but he never seemed to have a problem with girls. That is, he was a showoff. He flirted with every one of them, but nothing serious. He wanted to be independent. Maybe, he thought a wife would just be someone else to boss him around."

She sat quietly for a minute as Anam waited and sipped at his tea. She continued. "Oh, but he was loved, though. All three of my boys treated him like a son. They were real close, but he never seemed to quite fit in."

She took a deep, tired breath. "I guess none of that matters now." She suddenly burst into tears and started shaking. Anam placed his hands over hers and began praying. In a few minutes when she had regained control, she gave him a weak smile.

"Thank you. You know, several of the men went searching for him but had to turn back when they saw the storm coming. I do hope that something turns up. I just feel so bad, and there's nothing I can do."

"You have done a lot," Anam corrected her. "When he had no home, you gave him a home. You've raised three good men. In every household of Layta, you are highly spoken of. It's not your fault for what has happened. I do not mean to speak poorly of Miscal, but his behavior was formed long before he arrived here. I also feel bad for what happened. Zoana feels terrible. She feels as if she has murdered him. You already know she had no intention that this would turn out like it did."

"Oh, I know that, Anam. I have a great burden for her, as well. She asked for none of this. Whatever can we do?"

"Just keep praying and supporting and loving each other. And hope that God and time will heal."

The pounding of the rain had stopped, though there still were some showers. Anam finally excused himself to go back to his family. He walked slowly through the dampness as he headed toward the lodge building. His heart ached for those who had lost Miscal. He bore him no grudge. That would be pointless. The healing process had already begun.

There was still some light, though the sun had already dipped below the horizon. It appeared as though many had gone to bed as witnessed by the darkened windows. Only a few lamps burned.

Their sleeping quarters were dark except for the miniscule amount of sunlight coming in an opened window. He carefully tiptoed his way around the sleeping women as he strove for his family's area at the far end of the room. He tried to construe in his mind who was present and who was not as he gazed at faces and torsos in the dimness and his eyes adjusted. Elea. Shadi. Shulea. Maftu. Macosena. Umfuwadea. There were two Laytan women also sleeping here which was fine with Anam. There was the noticeable absence of Zoana, Crazon, and Paluqua which made perfectly good sense. Ernie and Anam's four children were all huddled close to each other on a large quilt. Anam assumed the rest of his people were spending the night with friends.

He sat on a heavy blanket near the window and glanced out to see a very bright star.

"Good night, Father." He turned to see Darophil staring at him and extending his arms. The boy crawled across the floor and joined his father and, embracing, they fell to sleep.

Anam awoke before sunrise the next morning. He lay quietly beside his son for several minutes, savoring the new strength and ambition he felt. He considered that today might be the day they would depart, considering everyone else's preparedness. He also did not want to seem too willing to make an early departure and thereby cause hurt among those left behind and damage the plans of everyone. There was still a lot of healing to take place. It would be better to proceed slowly and ask lots of questions.

He glided away from the small sleeping body and went outside. There was a slight breeze about, and a chill was in the air, but he didn't let this affect him. He headed for the riverside where the air was even cooler. Anam sat down facing the water with his back braced against a tree. He thought about yesterday's excitement. He tried to compose in his mind the line of thinking he would use when he finally announced to Sami they were leaving. He remembered the evening conversation with Reba. He began recalling how much he appreciated Paluqua.

"Our lives are filled with so many concerns, Lord," he prayed aloud. "I try so hard to do everything in love, but I am so often weak. Strengthen me, Father. Give me the direction that I need to go and the words I need to say. Then give me the strength to obey. Always teach me to be compassionate. I want to do the right thing because so many are counting on me, Lord. But, the main reason is because you're counting on me. Teach me compassion and patience and knowledge. Teach me to continue to be your servant. Thank you, Lord."

He lay back on the sand and stared up at the stars. A lump formed in his throat as he considered the immensity of the heavens and all that God had created. At the same time, he felt immensely puny for the very same reason. The same God that had created all the universe and the earth and all its people had created him. Then

God had chosen him as a special messenger to these people. He fell into a light sleep.

A few minutes later, he wasn't certain how long, he felt the presence of someone near him. Opening his eyes, he could see the most beautiful woman in the world beside him.

"Paluqua," he took a deep breath. "You are so beautiful."

She lay down and snuggled up next to him. "We finally finished our praying and talking so we came back. I couldn't find you. Ernie was half awake and said you had just left a few minutes before. I hoped I would find you here."

"So you've gotten no sleep?" he inquired seriously.

"No," she yawned. "We were all so full of energy, but I am completely exhausted now."

"Then today you should sleep. I believe tomorrow we will leave."

She nodded her head slightly and fell to sleep.

The only substantial damage that had appeared from the previous evening's storm was in the fields and gardens. The most noticeable problem was that so many of the new shoots had been knocked over or dislodged by the heavy rain. Anam, Togorasom and several of the women went with a group of the Laytan women to inspect and rectify the destruction.

Anam was always impressed to see the layout of their plantings. It consisted of several large fields with the various types of crops intermingled. There were never more than three adjacent rows of the same type of crop. Every hundred feet or so would be a planting of brambles or brush and the entire area was quartered by two rows of trees.

Wanda, one of Sami's daughters-in-law, explained. "There are so many enemies of our crops. During the summer it can get very hot, so the gourds and squash that cover the ground provide a great deal of shade. We always provide a thick carpet of mulch to keep the ground temperature even and contain the moisture, as well as to provide a constant source of nourishment. By providing the cover of the trees and brush we provide a habitat for a variety of different animals that come in and feast on destructive insects.

"Wouldn't it be a lot more organized," he asked, "if the crops were sorted out better?"

"In some ways," she smiled. "The reason the crops are mixed up like this is to guarantee some survival. If a blight or some other destructive thing strikes a certain area, you have the hope that all won't be lost because you have another crop. In the fall, we carefully lay out the following spring's planting system so we are ready. Of course, there's something going on in here all year."

Later, she took him to see the grain fields which were also subdivided. The winter wheat crop had already been taken in and the rest of the plantings were just emerging from the ground.

"The Lord and hard work have been very generous to us here. We have never lost a major crop. Of course, there are bad years for certain things, But, we have always had plenty to eat and plenty to sell. Our being here has also been good for the people of Marsa."

The Rasomites had gone out to help correct the damage, but Wanda explained that the damage was too minimal to be concerned over. Instead, they returned laden down with armfuls of food for lunch and dinner.

Reba was waiting for their return. Already a fire had been kindled and the water pot was beginning to bubble. Anam watched as they began the slicing and cleaning that would lead to the stew later. Sami appeared.

"Did you sleep well, friend?" Anam asked as they exchanged hugs.

"Oh, yes." They sat down, cross legged, facing each other. "I need to talk to you." Anam was attentive. "I want to apologize for putting any pressure on you to stay beyond your plans. We love your presence. We would willingly let you stay here forever. However, I know you have a goal, and I know you will do what the Lord directs, anyway."

"Thank you, Sami. I have felt pressure because your feelings are very important to me. We all feel so at home here. You have made us feel better than guests. You give me an opportunity to tell you we will most likely leave tomorrow. By then, everyone should feel very rested. I have learned there is no good time to leave the house of a friend and move on."

"A couple of years ago, we were all believing we were blessed and living fine. We lacked for nothing. Food was plentiful. Our daily lives were peaceful and productive. About that time, you arrived here. I had discovered we had nothing. We have always strived to be a considerate and hospitable people. However, God has shown us that even if you make all the right moves and have not God, you have nothing. Perhaps the Lord was here all the time directing us, but not knowing, we never gave him the credit. It is to you I pay the praise of showing us what we were missing. I am an old man and, even though I am not willing to die just yet, I am prepared."

"Thank you, Sami. It makes me feel good to know we are so appreciated."

"Do you know where you shall go next?" Anam shook his head. "Let me make a suggestion. As you know, the road ends rather abruptly not far from here. It is possible to go through the forest and into the mountains, even though the travel is difficult. It will be harder still with children. Along the riverbank travel is easier for a day or two. You will reach points, however, that make travel in the mountains difficult or impossible. People from Layta have traveled perhaps a hundred miles from here upriver. They have always given up and returned. Who can tell, perhaps on the other side of the mountains are thriving civilizations just ripe for salvation. Then again, perhaps that is where civilization ends. We will pray for you and hope for your success. Who can tell," he smiled, "you are always welcome to stay here if you have a return trip."

They sat quietly for a few minutes until Anam spoke up. "There is one thing that we lack. Do you remember when I told you about Chiam's gift?"

Sami nodded. "I had waited for you to bring that up again. Reba and I spoke of it. If you would perform the honor, I am certain everyone in Layta would partake."

"It is indeed an honor."

Later that day, the Laytans and Rasomites arranged themselves in two lines. As each of the villagers stepped forward, one of the Rasomites would step forward. They would take up the cup that lay in the wooden bucket and say a short blessing for the one they would anoint, then pour the water over their head. As chance would have it, Anam anointed Sami.

"I've desired this moment since you first arrived here, Anam."

"Do you understand what you are doing?"

"Only insomuch that Togorasom felt the saved should make

this public affirmation of their faith in God and desire to be made clean by his spirit, which the water signifies."

"I believe you understand clearly." They both lowered their heads. "Thank you, Lord, that Sami had this desire. A desire to serve you. A desire to do what is right. Continue to bless him and his family, Lord. Continue to nurture him. Bless not only with the obvious wealth but with that abounding wealth that is locked within a man's heart. Thank you, Lord." And taking the cup, he anointed Sami.

Chapter 5
Orioni

Togorasom lay on the stony earth using his clasped hands as a pillow. The birds soaring overhead had kept his attention for over an hour. How easily they seemed to float on the air currents. They would rotate around for several minutes, often not even flapping their wings. Occasionally, they would lose the current and would make a sudden dip to pick it up again or they would lose interest and disappear into their rocky alcoves above the boy's head. He thought how wonderful it would be to allow his spirit to soar like this. Even bridled by time and distance he was eager to be released, knowing one day he would be released totally again. His thought came back to the problem at hand. Still gazing at the rocks above him, he pondered the impossible climb. The mountainside seemed to escalate into the clouds. Perhaps with the right equipment at the peak of training, Anam and a few of the women could have conquered the height. But he knew it was certainly beyond his ability and far beyond that of Ernie and the little ones. Indeed, it had been difficult to reach this crag where they now lived.

It had been ten days since leaving Layta. The first couple of days were pleasant as they walked carefree along the riverbank. But, then the going became increasingly difficult. They had bedded down on this ledge for three nights. The ledge seemed like the foot of a towering giant. Despite the difficulty they had in reaching this level, it was nothing compared to the wall hovering above them.

Now they were all gone except for himself, Ernie and the children. The day prior several parties had been formed and departed in search of a gap or any means of overcoming this obstacle. Everyone agreed the trip in the opposite direction from Layta would have been easier, but no one doubted they were headed in the right direction. Before nightfall today was their agreed upon time for everyone to return and they would assess all the information that had been gathered.

His thoughts went back to the birds. It was an easy task for them to bypass this obstacle. As he began to pray again for the explorers, the sound of faraway voices reached him. Sitting up, he instantly saw three of the returning travelers ascending the steep path below him.

He stood up. "How did it go?" he called out. At this, Ernie and the children, realizing people were returning, joined him near the edge.

"It didn't go well!" Crazon called back. "We'll talk about it when we get up there."

In a few minutes she, with Buscis and Coralena, appeared over the edge. They were obviously tired from the appearance of their hunched over bodies, squinting eyes and drawn-out faces.

"Mostly," Crazon stated firmly, "we need a break. I feel frustrated because we felt so close." She lay down on the ground and was on the verge of going to sleep when Buscis and Coralena explained. They had walked a ways with the group and then broken off to climb the heights of an old river bed. This levelled off and they spent most of a day entering a canyon. Their hopes were soaring until they suddenly reached a cliff face several hundred feet high. They could go no further and realized the time for returning was getting closer.

"Let us hope," Buscis finished, "the others were more successful." She arose and moved to the shade where she fell asleep.

"You seem so worn out," Ernie told Coralena. "Can I get you anything?"

"Not just yet," she answered. "We are tired. We were so convinced we had a good trail we went all night, so I need to rest as well before the others return."

Togorasom lay back on the ground. The birds were still soaring overhead and continuing to draw his attention when he heard a noise beyond the lip of the cliff. He sat up and a moment later saw Anam's smiling face appear. Anam pulled himself onto the ledge and then offered a hand to Elea and Maftu. Togorasom opened his mouth to ask the obvious question, but Anam lost his smile and shook his head.

Anam looked at the other group which had already returned and were dozing soundly in the shade.

"They had no luck, either," Togorasom said quietly. "They felt near, but in the end, could go no further."

"We thought we also found a streak of luck. We scaled several cliff walls that each brought us to a ledge. Unfortunately," he said looking up, "the last climb brought us to a ledge very much like this. We tried several routes and methods but got nowhere." He revealed a gash on his arm. "I took a real nasty fall. Please, keep praying for the safety of the others."

"I thought you would travel with Paluqua."

"We drew straws to determine the teams." He was quiet for a moment. "I am confident someone will find a way through."

Togorasom nodded. "I agree with you. I don't believe God would lead us here to leave us deserted and frustrated."

By now, Elea and Maftu had already retreated to the shade and were dozing off.

Anam began to describe the climb and how he had fallen. The speech didn't last long as they could hear women's voices far off in the opposite direction from that which the first two groups had returned. Zoana's voice was distinct among the rest. Getting near the edge, Anam and Togorasom soon saw the returnees moving through the brush. It seemed clear from their hung down heads they were also returning empty. Soon they could distinctly see Macosena, Zabikta, and Didyadim with Zoana far in the lead. A few minutes later Zoana clambered quickly over the edge. Anam and Togorasom were nearby awaiting her. She could tell immediately by Anam's sad look no one previous to their return had been fortunate either. Her jaw was set firm, teeth clamped together. The boy took her hand.

"All have not yet returned. There will still, perhaps, be a good word."

Despite her obvious frustration, she spoke. "The other two groups split off from us early. We took a slightly different route when we returned." She gazed up the rock wall. "It seems so impossible, but I know all things are possible for those who believe and wait on the Lord. I'm really frustrated. We just went on and on. We found not even a crack or crevice worthy of looking into. We are also all very tired."

"I know. I believe you," said Anam. By now, the other three women were just arriving. Several hugs and various words of frustration and discouragement were exchanged with the women who had returned earlier. Finally, Anam cut them off. "Listen to us!" he shouted. In all our travels, I have never overheard such negative babble. 'It's impossible', 'We wasted our time', 'Satan has bound us', 'God has forsaken us'. I just can't believe you are all so easily defeated. The faith God has built over these years we have been together, as he answered our every prayer, you are all eager to cast aside because he wants you to wait a couple of days. Perhaps we are not even doing the Lord's will. I don't believe that. I believe he sent us here to test our faith and resolve. This mountain range stretches on for hundreds of miles in both directions. How far have we traveled to get here? Shall we give up? I believe I shall never give up. I'm frustrated as well and now all of your frustrations are laid on my conscience. Are you angry at God? Has God changed? Do you suppose he is talking evil of us now? Is he about to give up on us? Has Satan bound you? Has the Lord ever asked you to do the impossible? He has always shown you the way." He sat down on the ground, closed his eyes, extended his hands and said quietly, "Let us pray."

The Rasomites quickly formed a circle, including the children, and began to raise their voices to God. They began with asking forgiveness. They wept. There were again words of frustration, but they were followed by words of hope and insistence of faith. They asked for assured guidance. Words in heavenly tongues were spoken. The prayer lasted for over an hour. In the end, they all retired back to the shade but continued to share words of encouragement and await the return of the rest of the women.

Paluqua hung by her toes on the tiny foothold, her fingers digging into the granite wall to maintain her balance. Below her Bufaskada, Umfuwadea, and Ambacudadi also clutched the merciless rock. Paluqua looked slowly and carefully about. There seemed nowhere to go. She hovered about seventy feet above the earth, finally deciding this was senseless. The breach was unscalable, at least, by these four. Bufaskada was just below her and to her right.

"Let's retreat," she whispered hoarsely as every bit of her strength was used to maintain her position. The word was passed on and they slowly began to inch their way back down. She reached for the stub of a bush projecting out with one foot, then slide her hand along the rock to find the handhold. As it wasn't where she expected, she craned her neck to look. Her foot slipped from the dead stump. She reached quickly up and latched onto the previous handhold. Only for a moment. With a frantic effort she placed her foot again on the stub. But, what had been a dried out branch before, was now wore down to straw by their continued use. She screamed and fell. Ambacudadi attempted to grab her on the way passed as she had the best position, but the woman was not close enough. Paluqua fell and disappeared into the area below. Terrified, the other three women sped their descent, but it was still slow going. The seconds and minutes slipped by.

Ambacudadi was the first to reach the bottom and spun around in the action of a leopard as if preparing to attack. Her friend was nowhere to be seen. "Paluqua!" she yelled.

A moan was released from an enclave of boulders. Paluqua had fallen on the deep grass and soft earth between three large boulders. Ambacudadi quickly mounted one of the boulders and gazed down into Paluqua's semi-conscious eyes.

"Paluqua, are you all right?" There was no response. By this time, the other two women had arrived. The injured woman lay in a hole just out of reach. It was a miracle she had missed the boulders and landed nestled between them on the soft earth.

Ambacudadi slid down the inside of the hole toward her friend as the other two held onto her legs until her face could touch Paluqua's.

"Paluqua," she said softly, "can you hear me?" Paluqua's eyes were still open. She was breathing normally, but there was no response. "We'll get you out of here somehow." She kissed her on the cheek before telling her two friends to pull her up.

"Lower me down," said Bufaskada. "I'll get a hold on her and then raise her up." In a moment, she was lowered to Paluqua. "I don't know if you can hear me, but I'm going to try and lift you out. Help if you can." She cupped her hands under Paluqua's shoulder blades and gave the order to be pulled up. No words escaped Paluqua's mouth, but her face registered massive pain. Bufaskada carefully released her and rejoined her friends.

The three sat quietly thinking what they could do for several minutes. Finally, they joined their hands and prayed.

"Perhaps," said Umfuwadea, "we can dig around below the boulder somehow and so get her out."

This was attempted. They discovered a small crevice between the boulders and could actually reach in and touch Paluqua's thigh. The next several minutes was spent digging away by hand and then using blunt stones to hack away at the gravel which was packed together. At first the going was easy, but then they hit solid rock which would not give way. Frustrated and nearly in tears, they were forced to give up.

"We've got no other choice," Bufaskada said, "God help us make the right decision. Somehow we have to lift her out."

With renewed determination, they again mounted the boulder and gazed down at their friend. It was much more difficult to see her now. The sun was just beginning to set and Paluqua was buried in the shadows. Bufaskada was again lowered into the depth. Once again, face to face, she could see Paluqua's eyes still open, but still unresponsive.

"I am going to lift you. This may be painful. There is no other way. I love you."

She again slipped her hands under Paluqua's arms and behind her back, clasping her fingers. Then she gave the order to lift her quickly. This time, Paluqua did not respond. She was quickly lifted out like a giant rag doll and a moment later lay on her back on the flat top of the boulder. She was then, swiftly and carefully, transferred to the ground. The women checked her from head to toe and, except for a few minor scrapes and bruises, she appeared unharmed. The three breathed a sigh of relief.

"Let us hope she is merely stunned by the fall," said Umfuwadea. "There may be, however, internal injuries. We cannot move her anymore until we are certain."

"It's nearly dark," said Bufaskada. "there is no way we can get back to the others tonight. It's simply too dangerous. It's at least three hours from here if one moves quickly. Let us stay here and one of us go very early in the morning. Perhaps also, she may improve by then."

Ambacudadi had been inspecting Paluqua for injuries. She looked at the other two nervously. "When I poke or try to move her arms I get a response. However, there is no response when I try to do the same to her legs. I'm really afraid something may have happened to her back."

"There is nothing we can do," said Bufaskada. "Let us leave her be for the night. Come, let us pray."

Shulea was dreaming. She was sure of it.

"When you breathe upon a feather, which way does it go?" a voice asked her.

"I do not understand."

"When God breathes upon his children, which way do they go?"

"They follow him."

Before her a man materialized. But not a mortal man, for, though it was night, his face and other exposed flesh glowed like the sun. She could see the other three women still sleeping. Though the sky above appeared dark, their campsite was bright with light. He wore a helmet of what appeared to be gold. Over his legs was a leather skirt. His feet were shod with sandals. In one hand he carried a large, iron shield and, in the other, a two-edged sword.

"Come, follow me."

"But where are we going?" she asked as she stood up.

"The way is too hard for you. He has sent me to show you the way."

She realized his voice had a metallic sound to it, as though speaking into a metal drum, giving it an other-worldly tone.

"Will you pray with me?" she asked as a means of checking his intentions.

"There is no need for me to pray for we are in constant communion with him. However, you must pray because of the wall between you and him."

"The wall?"

"You know exactly what the wall is."

Shulea was suddenly overcome with grief as she realized he was referring to sin and fell to the ground before him. She lay there quivering until he reached down and helped her up with such a touch of strength and tenderness she had never known. Shivering still, she looked into his face.

"Please, forgive me."

"I am not the one who forgives for you can do me no harm or insult. But he has given me a word for you." He touched his fingertips to her forehead. "Peace, child, be still."

Shulea felt a surge of energy run through her. It was such a feeling of peace she wanted to scream out for joy, but for those sleeping, she controlled herself.

"Who are you?"

"I am your fellow worker. Follow me." He turned and headed up the path, and she obediently went behind.

She could hear the sounds of the animals rustling in the bushes. The path was well-lit by her host. She had a lightness about her that made her feel almost as though she could leap into the air and fly. In an attempt to make this rational, Shulea tried to remember going this way earlier. She could not. Of course, she realized, if this were a dream there was no way she could remember a path that didn't exist. After walking for perhaps ten minutes, they stopped abruptly at the foot of a cliff.

"We have arrived. In the morning, you must remember this place and get the others and bring them here."

"But why here?" she asked, looking back and forth at the wall before them interrupted only by a few clumps of brush at its foot.

He pointed towards a particularly large bush which appeared to almost grow out of the rock. "There," he said.

She turned away from him to look at the bush and realized she had been plunged into darkness. For a moment, terror seized her. She tried to wake up, but realized as her eyes adjusted to the darkness, she was already awake. She wondered if she had walked in her sleep or if the whole thing had been real.

Eventually, she was able again to see the bush he had pointed out. Inspecting it in the dark revealed it was not much different than any other such plant except it had a more gnarled growth caused by its less than ideal place of rooting. With a heavy sigh, Shulea gazed into the darkness, realizing she would not be able to return to the others until morning. Traveling this area in the dark was simply too dangerous. Finding a soft piece of earth to lie down on, she began to think of how she had gotten here and was soon sound asleep once more.

She awoke with a start a couple of hours later. She glanced nervously around until the events of the night came back to her remembrance. It had really happened and not been a dream at all. The path they had taken led up to the point where the gravel and stone began a few hundred feet from her. It would be easy to return.

The sun was not yet over the horizon. It was still quite dark. She looked at the scraggly old bush, attempting to decide why that was chosen by her night-time guide. Standing up, she walked nearer to it. There was nothing at all special about it so she could not figure out why that was chosen as the meeting point. She reached into the brush and placed her hand on the flat stone slab behind. It was very cool. There was a small crevice near the base of the bush, large enough to reach her arm part way in. She expected to find solid rock inside the crack but it seemed empty. Upon digging away at the gravel she accidentally dislodged a large portion of stone. It had been broken up, apparently by the growth of the bush and years of downward pressure. The hole was now about a foot across.

Leaning her face nearer the hole to peer inside was pointless as it was pitch dark. She sat stooped over for a moment deciding her next move when she heard the distinct sound of running water coming from inside the rock.

"Oh, my Lord," she exclaimed. "There absolutely must be an underground cavern here." Immediately, she turned and ran down the path to tell the others.

All had been worried the night before when the last two teams had failed to return. Hopes were high the delay was caused by the discovery of one or more routes through the impasse. More time for exploration might be needed to return with positive information. However, the fear also loomed over them of an accident or something else preventing their return. Early in the morning they all gathered together and prayed again for a good outcome. The decision was made that if the rest of the women had not returned by noon, a search party would be sent as the general location of both groups was known. Until then, they would remain in prayer.

During the morning they took turns sitting in silent, expectant vigil on the ledge overlooking the landscape. Several times they caught a movement in the brush below; however, there was no sign of the women until late in the morning.

When the morning broke, it had been easy to select Ambacudadi as the one to return with the distressing news as she was the fastest runner. The trip was much longer than she or the others had expected, however. It was nearly noon when she wearily approached their temporary home, too weary to even climb up.

Before he saw or heard her, Togorasom sensed her imminent arrival. He was the first to hear her pleas for help and, without explanation, leapt over the ledge and scurried down the steep path. Everyone else followed him.

When they reached her, she was found crouched upon the ground, gasping for breath. She said nothing until Anam arrived.

"It's Paluqua. She's...been injured...in a fall," she said between short breaths.

"Where?" Anam asked.

She pointed in the general direction she had come from. "It took me nearly six hours. I...want to show you, but...I cannot go any further."

"Rest," he told her. "I shall find her."

"Anam, wait!" she stood up. "It would be nearly...impossible. She's nearly thirty miles from here. There is much climbing."

"I will find her," he assured her.

They embraced each other.

"She will be by a great wall. At the foot of this will be three very large, round boulders that seem out of place. We shall pray for you. When I am able, I shall follow."

He turned to the rest. "Zoana! Crazon! You two are in charge here. You know that. When the others return, you decide what to do. Keep us lifted up in prayer." He turned away and dashed off in the direction Ambacudadi had come from.

"I wonder if he should have waited," Zoana commented.

"No," said Togorasom. "this is right. He has lost too much. The Lord will guide him."

Some of the women began to massage Ambacudadi's sore limbs and back. By this time, Ernie had arrived.

"She'll also need water," he said, understanding the situation immediately. "A lot of water. Enough to make her nearly sick. But, what has happened?" He was quickly brought up to date. When they had finished their explanation, he sat on the ground next to Ambacudadi. "When you are able you must take me there. She's had a back injury or a concussion or both. Let's pray she remains motionless or more injury will result."

In Shulea's case, her problem was to convince the others of her adventure the night before and her early morning discovery. Only after being led back to the cavern entrance did their doubt begin to taper off.

"But, Shulea, how can we know if this passageway will actually lead us all the way through?" asked Shadi.

"And," said Sholemazar, "it's black as tar in there. How will we ever see to travel?"

Shulea merely shook her head.

"It really doesn't matter when you consider her words," said Bulshadi. "She was told by the man, obviously a messenger from God, to gather the rest and meet him back here. The Lord won't forsake us. Do we have to know each step before it happens or can we just trust?"

The other two women were humbled and quickly agreed they must all hurry back to join the others. It would take all day to make the trip, so they expected to spend the night and return here the next day.

Anam had easily followed Ambacudadi's trail for over an hour. The further he went, the more difficult it seemed for him to travel her route in reverse. He stopped several times to regain his sense of direction. There were periods, however, he felt he made very good time. Finally, nearly wore out, he lay down on the grass to relax and restore himself.

His mind began to wander to his wife. He loved her with all his heart, but it often seemed so hard to show it. He felt clumsy and sometimes dimwitted around her and these other mighty women of God. It was difficult for him to understand why God would have chosen him for the task of leading these people. Surely there was someone more qualified than he. But, then, he remembered many of the conversations he had shared with each of them. He recalled Zoana's tear-filled moments only a few days before. They all felt weak and empty at times.

Now this accident. He wondered if they were truly obeying God or if this was all an act of stubbornness. If they had been in God's will, why did Paluqua get struck down? Was being his wife some sort of curse?

He sat up with his eyes still closed, wishing there were a more direct route to her. He figured he could not be more than halfway there.

"Dear Lord," he said quietly. "I feel foolish for having run off like I did. But, you know how important she is to me. I need your help. I can't do this alone."

He opened his eyes and was startled to see a young, well-tanned, blond-haired man standing a few paces away staring at him. He wore only a loin cloth and leaned upon a walking stick.

Immediately, Anam wanted to solicit his help. If the man was from this area, perhaps he could direct him to this place with the three boulders.

"Who are you?" Anam asked. He decided to proceed cautiously so as not to scare him away. There was no answer. "Do you live near here?"

Anam leaned forward to stand up, taking his gaze away from the onlooker. Suddenly, he was knocked hard upon the forehead with the walking stick. Leaping to his feet, he saw the assailant fleeing down the hill. Anam tore after him, determined to be less kind when he caught him. However, it was not an easy race. There weren't many men he'd come across who had both the speed and endurance God had given him. However, it appeared the young man's knowledge of the area coupled with Anam's already fatigued state was his great advantage.

Anam hoped that if he couldn't catch him, he could at least stay on his trail and be led to a settlement or village where he might find some help.

They ran on for most of the afternoon. After reaching the bottom of the hill, they crossed a dry creek and headed up the opposite side. The going became more difficult. No matter how fast Anam traveled, his quarry was always far ahead, just short of disappearing entirely. He wanted to stop and rest but eventually the spirit of the chase caught him up and he continued on, doubting he would ever actually catch up.

Many times the younger man would stop and turn to see Anam still plodding along behind. Eventually, Anam figured the man wanted him to follow. If only he would stop and explain things.

Most of the time they were headed upwards. Several times, Anam called after him. Occasionally, he would stop and turn to him, but when Anam tried to approach him, he would turn and run. After one fairly steep climb, Anam burst through the thicket at the top, face to face with the man he'd been seeking. Anam clutched the man's arm, not to harm him, but to verify he would not escape. He had expected the man to be terrified after finally being captured. Instead, he turned his head and raised his free arm to a point slightly higher than they were about a mile away. There stood three great round boulders against a bare cliffside. In awe, Anam slowly released his grip. Glancing back to express his thanks to his guide, he found he was standing alone. The other man was nowhere to be seen.

Anam took a few steps in the direction of the boulders when the full realization of what had happened dawned on him. He fell to his knees and began to weep. He didn't know if his guide was an angel or only a man, but he realized he had been sent by God.

Finally, he sat up. He had gone a long way with no rest or water. Before going any further he took a long draught of water and began the long walk across the shallow gorge which separated him from the end of this day's journey.

It was mid-afternoon by the time the women returned to the others with news of Shulea's discovery. It heartened everyone to finally receive some positive news of an obvious work of God.

"I am very worried, though," Ernie confided to Togorasom as they sat alone in a shaded area together. "If Paluqua has suffered some internal damage, Anam and those women won't know how to deal with it. Let's hope they keep her lifted up in prayer constantly because, if they stop praying and actually try to help her, they'll only worsen the situation."

"My friend, Ernie, they are not stupid," the boy countered.

"I'm not saying anyone is stupid!" he snapped. "I'm only very concerned for someone very important to me. I love her nearly as much as Anam does. I probably know her better than anyone else." He gazed up into the cloudless sky, then closed his eyes. Togorasom saw him tremble slightly and tears begin to flow. The boy had seen these tears before as Ernie was a very compassionate man and often cried when he felt helpless. However, when the old man's mouth fell open and he began bawling so loud several of the women came running to him, Togorasom was unprepared.

He knelt in front of Ernie and held him tight. Then they both started crying. When they stopped, Ernie looked up into Zoana's face.

"When can we leave here?" he asked.

Zoana looked at Crazon and back at Ernie. "The ones who have returned are still very weary. We cannot expect them to travel again so soon. Besides, travel at night is very dangerous."

Ernie raised his hand to stop her. "I cannot bear just sitting here. I have lived in the wilderness most of my life. If I must travel alone to leave now, I shall."

Zoana wasn't certain if she should be stern and order him to remain or if her own love for Paluqua demanded action as well.

"Have you prayed?" she asked.

"You know I have prayed, but you also know I must be there. I'm sorry that I am torn between my allegiance to your leadership and my need to doctor someone I care strongly for."

She leaned against a small tree that stood near her and thought about the situation for a few minutes. Finally, she came over and sat down next to Ernie.

"I'm sorry, I cannot allow you to leave. You are a practical man, so let's be practical. You can't travel alone because you don't even know where you are going. Even if you did, before you were half the way there it would be dark. You would be forced to start over again in the morning. We will leave very early; I swear to you. Ambacudadi will be ready to show us the way. The other women will be ready to travel again, as well. In this way, you will probably arrive there sooner. It breaks my heart to say no."

They embraced. Ernie sullenly nodded his head. "Yes," he admitted, "you are right."

Long before dawn, Ernie and Togorasom were up. They prayed together for a few minutes and began packing their few belongings. As each of the children was aroused, they were quietly fed and laid back to rest. Before sunrise, Ambacudadi approached them.

"I have slept well," she said as she yawned. "I'm still a bit tired, but a long walk will surely revive me. I am ready to leave. At first light, let us depart quickly."

Ernie looked around. Many of the women were still sleeping soundly.

Ambacudadi smiled. "Don't be concerned. When it's time to leave, they shall be ready quickly." She gazed at the faint glow on the horizon. "Actually, the path is very good for quite a ways from here. We could probably start now and make excellent time. It would be light long before we needed to climb."

As if on cue, Zoana and Crazon appeared from out of the half-light. "If we begin getting packed and organized now," Zoana said, "we will be ready to leave here before sunrise. I'm sure everyone is refreshed and ready for the trip."

Crazon turned and clapped her hands over her head several times. "Attention everyone. I realize it's still early, but it's time to get going. We have a lot to do today."

There were no complainants or groans. The women quickly gathered together their few belongings, then helped rouse the children and got them ready to go. In a very few minutes, they struck out with Ambacudadi in the lead, Ernie alongside. As she had said, the traveling was very easy the first hour but became increasingly difficult. An added benefit of departing so early was the coolness of the morning.

Everyone was full of energy and anticipation of getting there early. Long before noon, Ambacudadi pointed off into the distance at the three large, out of place boulders.

The moment the travelers saw their final destination, there was a mad dash across the basin. Ernie, due to his age and fatigue, was the last to arrive on the scene. Besides the sound of panting, weary people there was a scene of despair. In the midst of the throng, Paluqua lay, sallow-faced, barely breathing. A tired, shaken Anam looked blankly into Ernie's face. Bufaskada and Umfuwadea sat at Paluqua's shoulders.

Finally, Bufaskada broke the solemnity. "We have been up all night and not ceased in prayer. She continues to slip further and further away. What more can we do?"

Togorasom shouldered his way to the front of the circle and caught Anam's attention. "Do you believe God has given each of us eternal life?" The man remained silent. "She is no more dead than ever, for he really has given us eternal life."

Anam spoke. "You are my last hope." He paused. "Do you have a miracle?"

"Oh, father, how can you think of that? I am neither anyone's hope nor do I offer miracles."

"I only meant that...that is. I hoped there was something you could do. We have been praying ceaselessly but..." his lips quivered, "we seem to have had no effect."

"Father, do you truly love her?"

"Of course I love her."

"Then," Togorasom said as he got to his knees beside Anam, "you must let her go."

Anam winced. Tears formed in both eyes. "I have told God to have his will."

"Did you mean it from the bottom of your heart? She will be happier before the Father's throne."

"But I don't want her to die."

"Don't you believe she shall live forever?"

Anam looked at his wife. "She's so young and so good. I had hoped to grow old together with her."

"You shall both live forever."

Slowly Anam dropped his head to his knees. His body shook with sadness. Several hands laid upon him, and they began to pray for him.

Togorasom felt Darophil's hand on his shoulder, but it was not gentle. He glanced at the child. Darophil's mouth was gaping, his eyes wide open, staring. Togorasom turned to see.

"Orioni!" he spoke aloud, then covered his mouth.

"It's good you remembered." Perched atop the boulder sat Shulea's angel. His face still glowed with light brighter than the light of the noon day. He wore a white robe and sandals. "I have been called, but you know I have never left you."

"And also the others..." Togorasom began.

The angel sternly shook his head for Togorasom to say no more. He effortlessly slipped off the boulder and dropped to the ground standing by Anam. He sank to his knees and spoke to Anam. "You realize you can keep nothing in this world. The more you desire a thing, the more your heart will ache when it's lost. Do you realize you and Paluqua shall spend eternity in the kingdom?" Anam nodded. "However, your prayer has been answered." He looked at Paluqua whose life was still flowing out of her. "Paluqua, arise!" As signs of life began returning to her, Orioni faded away. Before he vanished, he looked directly at Shulea so she would know it was nearly time to lead them to the underground cavern.

The change in Paluqua was not immediate. She began

breathing more deeply. Her fingers and toes began moving around. Her flesh became darker. She finally opened her eyes and then yawned. No one touched her, but all continued to murmur in prayer and watch in amazement. She looked at Togorasom and said, "it's so beautiful!" He smiled and nodded. She looked at Anam and smiled. "I feel strength returning to my body. It still aches, but I can feel things happening inside me I cannot describe it." She reached for his hand and sat up. "My throat is so dry. I thirst." A vessel of water was handed to her. She drank all of it greedily. "I feel like I am arising from a long sleep. In my sleep I feared I would never rise again, but also I had a peace about it. Then, I was standing before the throne of God. There are things I don't understand. I'm very hungry." She and Anam embraced.

Later, after they had eaten, Shulea and her team led the people toward their discovery. It was about a ten-mile trek and they planned to travel slowly considering the distance they had already traveled that day. Paluqua traveled with ease. It was amazing the amount of healing which had taken place. She commented she even felt better than before the fall. Many eyes kept watching Togorasom. His knowledge of who the angel had been and Paluqua's comment to him reminded them of his visitation before God. He was not like them. He knew the details of many things they could not begin to imagine the existence of. Unfortunately, they all knew he could tell them little or nothing. They had seen him return from the dead and now discovered he had befriended an angel. They were nearly frightened of what else could happen. Togorasom knew the state of their minds, but rather than be concerned over that, he allowed his mind to concentrate on praying for the future.

The route they took was across a barren, rocky area. Little but a few blades of grass ventured to poke through the stone. The sun now was directly overhead so the combination of sun and bare rock caused it to be extremely hot. The hot, unyielding stone also burned the soles of their bare feet. After two hours of crossing the rocky plateau they reached a drop-off that led to a small river bed. Here, they took a long break. Finally, Shulea organized them to depart.

"Across the stream we will have to do some more climbing, but the pathway is present most of the time. We are within thirty minutes of the cave. The area between here and there is rocky, but there is some shade as well."

True enough, the path was steep in several areas but easily accessible. After a couple of miles, it began to slowly descend and soon reached the charred embers of the women's campfire. A few minutes later, they arrived at their destination. Everyone, including the children, wanted to poke their head into the dark hole and listen to the dripping of the water. They agreed the cave must be large as they could hear the reverberating of the water and their echoes. Unfortunately, gaining entrance would be difficult as the small hole was surrounded by unyielding rock. After several attempts to get in, they finally gave up and prepared to spend the night.

It was still hot. There were not enough shaded areas of ground for everyone to comfortably relax. It was nearly all bare, hot stone and gravel. Therefore, the children occupied nearly all of the good space. They were in the bottom of a basin which was several hundred feet across and had almost no life.

Anam gazed back and forth across the basin as did most of the others. "This used to be a lake of some sort," he observed. "But, I wonder why it is so lifeless." All around on the horizon they could see abundant foliage which ended abruptly where the dead lake began its descent. It was inviting to leave their camp and go to the shaded area. However, no one wanted to leave as they were expecting Orioni's return to make known his intentions.

The evening turned into twilight and still nothing happened. They had spent the afternoon praising God for Paluqua's healing and conjecturing what Orioni would do.

As the sun touched the horizon, Anam sought Togorasom's advice. "Would it be wrong to send the women and children away?"

"The day is gone now. They have sat in the hot sun all afternoon. Why did you wait?"

Anam shrugged. "I don't know. The angel told Shulea to bring us here and wait for him. I suppose I expected his return sooner."

"It would not be in the least improper for you to care for the women and children."

So everyone but Anam, Togorasom and Shulea headed for higher ground and comfortable sleeping. This left adequate room for the three remaining to find soft earth and lay down to sleep.

"Dear Lord," Anam prayed quietly as the other two slept, "forgive me. I'm always so impatient. I expect when you say you're going to do something, you will do it very soon. However, I'm learning to wait for you. I know you'll keep all your promises according to your plan and there's always a reason for everything you do. Perhaps your plan now is to teach me patience." He lay quietly for a minute. "Oh, my God, I can never express my appreciation enough for having my wife back. You know how crushed I was and would have been, but your word is true. She would be better to be with you and we can spend eternity together with you. I know that. But now you've given her back and I am stunned at your generosity." He wept quietly until he finally fell to sleep.

He awoke with a start the next morning. For a moment he believed it was still night, but then he could see where the shadow of the cliffside ended in the morning sun. It was quite cool. At his feet, Shulea and Togorasom slept on. He detected someone else and sat up.

Paluqua was sitting a few paces away on a small boulder, watching him. "I love you." She moved her lips without actually speaking so as not to disturb the sleepers. He walked over and sat at her feet resting his still drowsy head on her thigh. "Last night," she said, "I fell to sleep crying because of my love for you and the enormity of what had happened to me. I remember falling. I remember being lifted out of the hole. That's all. I know I was conscious at other times, but it's all blank. There's also other things that happened that I can't really speak of. I stood before God in heaven."

"Ernie says you were in such pain, your mind shut everything off."

"When the angel spoke to me, I could actually feel the bones inside my body moving around. I feel wonderful. I had perfect sleep last night. God is surely the great physician." They sat quietly together for a few minutes until she asked what they would do next.

Anam brightened up. "We shall wait upon Togorasom's guardian angel friend's return."

"But do you suppose he has ever left?"

"He told Togorasom he has never left us. I'm not certain how he meant that. He must have left us at other times. For example, to join Shulea."

"But do you suppose," she asked, "he is confined to the same time and space we are or that, perhaps, he can move much more freely?"

Anam was confused and shook his head indicating he did not know.

"And oh," she continued, "if he were always with us would he be able to go, if need be, to the Lord? Perhaps he is able to leave us for a time and rejoin us and never miss a thing."

Anam sat back and looked at her dumbfounded.

"What if," she suggested as she looked around the empty field, "we were always surrounded by a band of angels. Is that possible, Anam?"

He scratched his head and gazed at the empty, blue sky. "Isn't the air clear this morning?" He took a deep breath. "I feel really refreshed after last night's sleep. Did the other women sleep well? How are the children?"

"I'm not sure," she said placing the palm of her hand on his cheek. "I'll go find out." She got up and slowly walked away. A few paces away, she began to sing out in tongues. He knew it was a song of thankfulness for her new body and spirit and he said a silent prayer as well.

The evening found Paluqua, Crazon and Zoana camped out at the cave entrance. The previous evening's sentinels had joined the body of travelers in the more comfortable resting area outside of the ancient lake bed. Of course, the unspoken question on everyone's heart was the wonder of what would happen and when it would happen. Very little was discussed concerning why Orioni had requested they meet him here. They opted for patience. Unfortunately, the desire for patience did not result in a great deal of sleeping. Long after the children were out and the campfires had dwindled to glowing embers many still lay awake.

To calm the anxious nerves, Ernie played lullabies on his flute far into the night. The only thing it caused to get tired was Ernie's breath. Eventually, he gave up and lay gazing at the star-filled night sky. They spoke but rarely, waiting in silent expectation of a great event. However, most of them finally dozed off and the second night passed uneventfully.

In the morning everyone moved slowly except, naturally, the children. They had slept well and, after their morning cereal and fruit, were prepared for activity.

Darophil went looking for Ernie who had wandered away while the children ate. He found him leaning against a tree stump trying to sleep. Darophil sat by the groggy, old man and Ernie pulled him close.

"Why is everyone so tired this morning, Ernie?"

"Folks didn't get much sleep, Darophil. They were expecting something to happen."

"What?"

"We are still waiting for the angel to return and either guide us or tell us what to do next?"

"Just think, Ernie, a real angel. Has anyone ever seen an angel before?"

"Oh, I'm certain they have." He shook his head around as he tried to stay awake. "Of course, they may not have realized it."

"How would they not know it? People don't glow like candles."

"Yes, but Darophil, I'm sure an angel can look like anything he wants to. They can look just like you and me."

"You mean an angel can look like a little boy?"

"Yes."

"Or like a sleepy, old man with a beard?" Darophil laughed.

Ernie smiled and nodded his head.

"I think I'll let you get some sleep. I won't tell anyone where you are."

"Thanks, Darophil. I love you."

They hugged each other and Darophil trotted away. Soon he found Anam.

"Where were you, son?" Anam scolded. "We've been looking for you!"

"I was just talking…"

"Never mind! Please join the rest as we are going to the cave entrance and wait." He pointed across the barren rock to where the rest of the Rasomites were nearing the cliffside.

"But, father…"

"Go!" he said sternly. "Go quickly. I will join you in a few minutes."

Forgetting that he had meant to speak of Ernie, Darophil desired to quickly be with his family and, so, hurried away. Anam knelt and prayed for the Lord's guidance and soon he also started across. It crossed his mind that he never found out what Darophil had wanted to say. The boy was too young to wander off alone and they rarely had problems like this. Suddenly, he realized there was a commotion at the cave entrance where all had gathered. He hurried to join them.

"...and if you felt forgotten, I must tell you that you are never forgotten. He knows everything about you. You must not trust in your feelings but in your knowledge that he loves you. Even when you hated him, he loved you. When you ever feel forgotten by God, you must pray and wait. Your time and his time are not the same." Orioni stopped and looked quietly at the crowd. "Everyone is prepared. Let us go."

Over the last two days, everyone had attempted to squirm into the tiny opening of the cave. It was large enough for the children to wriggle into but impossible for any of the adults, including Togorasom. Therefore, they could not easily explain what happened next. Orioni motioned for everyone to follow him and easily glided through the entrance. In a few minutes, everyone had joined him.

They landed about five feet below the opening on the solid cavern floor. Anam, being one of the last, handed his children down to Paluqua and other waiting arms. Joining the rest of the Rasomites, he received Comeana and watched the last of the women enter. When the last one hit the floor, he studied the tiny opening again and pondered how they could enter a hole only a foot across. He held his little girl close. Something was wrong, but he could not conjure up in his mind what it could be. It was as though he was aware of a problem but could not decide what the problem was.

The cave was several degrees cooler than outside. Orioni's illumination provided a candlelight of visibility; however, it was not sufficient for discerning anything more than a pace or two from him, even with their keen eyesight. Anam was aware of several human forms mingling together but could recognize no one clearly, except Comeana.

"It's time to leave," Orioni announced. "We have far to go. It would be good to reach our destination in daylight." Suddenly, the illumination provided by their guide increased tremendously. It hurt their eyes to stare too long at him. It was easy now to view this great cavern. Anam gazed over his head and could see the rock walls thirty feet above them but still could not see the ceiling. Before them lay a stream bed and a slowly moving river. Orioni started his trek along the shore of the underground river. It was, at first, not an organized march. People bumped into each other and walls and stumbled over rocks and cracks in the floor in their attempt to survey their temporary abode. In the beginning, also, the children were frightened; however, after a few minutes, they began to love this awesome underground adventure.

However beautiful and amazing their surroundings, something still nagged at Anam as missing or not right.

Ernie snapped awake. The sun was high in the sky, indicating late morning. He sat for a moment savoring the wonderful sleep he had enjoyed. Now he felt he was willing to face whatever challenges the day would offer. He listened to the morning song of the birds. It was very inviting to close his eyes and steal a little more sleep. However, there were responsibilities. He had the job of tending for the children, so he had best be about it. It was nearly lunch time. He picked up his bag, tied it about his waist and slowly forced himself to his feet. It seemed unusually quiet. He hurriedly headed back where they had camped the night before where he expected to see the clan awaiting. The closer he got, the more nervous he became as he expected some sight or sound of his friends.

He was awestruck when he arrived in the vacated clearing. There was no trace of them left behind. They had packed up everything and moved out. In the middle of the clearing he gazed across the ancient lakebed fully expecting to see them gathered at the cliffside. Now he became nervous and confused, wiping his eyes with the palms of his hands hoping to see something to mollify him. Anything. He began running across the basin, praying somehow the hot sun was playing tricks on him.

He literally crashed into the rock wall and fell to his knees by the tiny entrance. Craning his neck into the hole, he saw nothing but darkness. Straining to hear the sound of voices, he heard nothing but the monotonous dripping of water on rock. He sat back, thinking perhaps they were somewhere else. He glanced around, studying the earth he sat on. It was clear a number of people had somehow passed by and gone through the hole. This was impossible. He stuck both his feet into the entryway and was able to force himself almost to his shins inside. Realizing the foolishness of believing someone had gone through, he pulled himself back out. He wrapped his arms around his legs and sat staring at the dark pit, trying to understand how they could leave him. It still made no sense they had gone this way. He turned about and sat with his back against the cliff wall, shaded partially by the bush.

He felt a peace come upon him. He knew it would be fine. Someone would come for him or this would begin to make sense. He sat contented for a few minutes, but then began weeping. He shook with anguish. Holding his breath, he soon had regained control. He felt very deserted and very lonely.

"What have I done that I should be left alone like this, Lord?" he said aloud. "These are my people, and I cannot understand why I have been separated from them. We have worked hard together and now, it seems, you have chosen them, and I am left here empty. I do not understand your ways. However, I know you are the Lord and your ways are best. If I have done wrong because I slept, I am sorry. If you are merely playing a joke on an old man, I do not understand. But I will wait on you."

By this time, Orioni had led the Rasomites far into the mountain. They had been traveling for nearly four hours before Ernie had realized his situation. Orioni turned to Anam.

"Now I must leave you." Anam shuddered to think of being plunged into the darkness. "It is needful that I go." Anam stared at him without comprehension. "Ernie is not with us." Suddenly the blinds that had been placed on Anam and the others were lifted.

"Oh, my God." Anam leaned against the cave wall. "How could we have ever forgotten him? His heart must be broken."

"It is for a cause," Orioni reassured him. "It is to show you that your ways and God's ways are not the same. Now, gather all the people together and I shall soon return."

Anam did as he was told and quickly explained what had happened to Ernie. As Orioni walked away, Anam led them in prayer. "Almighty Lord, our hearts are heavy as we have been shown how our good brother, Ernie, has been deserted. We all know a little of how he feels and we ask that our guardian angel,

Orioni, be able to lead him to us and restore him with us quickly."
By now, they had been plunged into complete darkness. "Be with
us now, Father, as you are also with him. Let us all know we are
never deserted as you are with us always…"

Ernie sat in the little bit of shade which was left with his head
down, praying steadfastly either for knowledge of why he was in
this situation or deliverance from it.

He believed he was alone and, therefore, was startled when a
voice boomed out. "Let us go, Ernie, your prayer has been
answered." Orioni stood before him, and Ernie fell forward in a
prone position as to worship him. "See that you do not do it, my
friend and fellow laborer. There is only one worthy of your
worship. Come, let us go." He slipped through the hole and Ernie
quickly followed him. Once on the cave floor, he also glanced back
up at the entrance and shook his head in confusion. "Let us go, my
friend, your family waits for you."

Ernie was awed by the underworld beauty which surrounded
him. This was increased by Orioni's illumination. They walked at a
leisurely pace and, even so, many times the angel prodded Ernie
along. Also, they took many breaks. Ernie was full of questions and
a desire for conversation, but being in the presence of this divinity
kept him so awed he felt restrained. Therefore, they spoke scarcely
at all, except an occasional word of warning or instruction by
Orioni. Progress was ever so much slower than Orioni's previous
trip had been but finally they heard Anam's voice.

"…we are never deserted as you are with us always." He cut
himself short and all looked at Orioni in shock. "I do not
understand. You were gone but for a moment," he said as the two
approached them. "Is it possible he found his way to us
unassisted?" Anam asked glancing doubtfully at Ernie. But then it
did not matter, Ernie was engulfed in a mob of hugging.

"Do you need to rest?" Orioni asked of Ernie.

"No. No, I feel fine," he answered enthusiastically. "I'd really
like to press on if everyone is ready."

Several gave their assent and they continued their trek along
the creek bed. Anam caught up with Orioni.

"I do not understand how you were able to retrieve Ernie so
quickly and rejoin us. We had expected you to be gone for several

hours."

Orioni gazed into Anam's face as they walked along. "All I can tell you is that your ways and God's ways are not the same. He is God and always has been and always shall be. If you never doubt him," he said looking away, "there is no limit to what he is able to do in your life. Behold, we are coming to the end."

Anam began to sense light coming from in front of them and the temperature of the air increasing slowly. They reached the mouth of the cavern, which was several feet in both height and width. Beyond that was an expansive ledge, which provided an excellent view of their new world. The blue mountains in the far distance were preceded by seemingly an endless forest broken only in a few places by bodies of water.

"These are your instructions," Orioni told Anam loud enough for all to hear. He extended his arm and pointed to a gap in the mountains. "Go that way. You will know when you are there." Everyone gazed off towards the mountains and were almost unaware when Orioni vanished.

They sat down or milled quietly about and stared in the direction of the mountains.

"Isn't the Lord immense, Togorasom?" Anam commented quietly.

"He is totally awesome and there is no understanding his ways."

"Oh, my Lord," Ernie exclaimed looking skyward and gaining everyone's attention. "I was so long in the cavern with Orioni and the sun, look at it, is still in the same position as before. I shall never understand all his ways."

They began to investigate their surroundings. The side of the mountain towered over them and appeared to be as unscalable as it had been on the other side. They found themselves on a very large shelf about a hundred feet above the ground. It would be easily descended by rope when the time came.

"We have entered a new world," said Togorasom. He paused and smiled. "This is our world. I don't believe we shall go back."

"Let the Lord be praised!" called out Anam. "Let everything having breath call upon him and praise his name." His hands shot skyward, eyes closed. "He is our God! He is our redeemer! He is our salvation! Our protector! He lives in the very air we breathe. We thank him for watching over us and protecting us and healing us in body and spirit. You are our all and to whom else can we turn to when in need. We are always in need." He sank to his knees. "I thank you, Father. I thank you for everything. Besides you there is none other. Let everything with breath praise the Lord!"

By now everyone was in prayer so the mountainside seemed to burst forth with the sound of their many voices in praise. Finally, the din receded as they began silent prayer. Paluqua laid her hands on each of Zoana and Crazon and prayed for them. They then prayed for Paluqua's children. After that a great deal of intercessory prayer began. The three women prayed for Anam and Togorasom. Finally, over an hour later, the praying began to cease and Togorasom spoke.

"The Lord has shown me something and told me to reveal it. Let the words of my mouth be engraved on your hearts. Let there be no mistaking we have a great battle before us. But, also rejoice, for he shall win the battle for us. And also rejoice, because our homeland is before us."

Chapter 6
Onoshe

Their supplies were nearly run out. Anam considered the meager handful of grain and nuts that had been offered to him by the women. Further, they could prepare no hot cereal for the children as they normally did. There was nothing to build a fire with on this lofty perch. He always felt awkward feeding his children the last of the rations when everyone else went without. Briefly he recalled the ample supplies they'd had upon leaving Layta. Now this was all that remained. However, he knew it was not a dismal situation, merely one of conjecture. It was like a sign that the old was running out and the new was soon to come. True enough that their supplies were gone, but only because they had opted to spend the night on the ledge. In a few minutes they would descend to the lush earth below. He could imagine the smell of spring berries and herbs that awaited them and the thought of digging in the earth for the winter produce caused a smile to cross his face. Suddenly Ernie swooped the trifle from his hands and began cracking the nuts for the children. Anam spoke a word of thanks to the Lord for offering him sufficient grace.

Far off in the distance, Anam gazed upon the divide between the mountains. He wondered what challenges they would face in this travel. The land before them seemed so peaceful, but there was always something wrong. There were always unseen enemies. They had already been warned.

He did not wonder for long as a few particles of sand seemed to rain onto his forearm from above. This action startled him, but did not immediately alarm him. Then, a terrible thought crossed his mind. He quickly looked to the rocks above him and saw some sort of movement about forty feet up.

"Quickly, everyone, flee into the cave!" he called out. "Get under cover!"

There was no confusion or lack of concern. The entire tribe immediately headed for safety. As Anam ran towards cover he glanced up again as a fairly large boulder appeared on the edge of the upper ledge. He reached safety just as the rock smashed into the ground at his heels. Glancing up again he saw the face of what appeared to be a great ape, but seemed to bear the intelligent expression of a man. A few more large boulders and many small cobblestones were rolled off or thrown off onto what they had thought was a safe haven. Eventually the barrage slowed and finally came to a stop. With Anam's permission, Macosena and Zoana climbed to the upper ledge. "There's no one up here!" Macosena called back down. "Come and look at this."

Anam and several others soon arrived at the scene of the siege. From the appearance of the ledge and study of the footprints left on its sandy surface, they eventually figured out the attacking group consisted of six to eight members. Anam explained what he had seen and a few others verified this knowledge. The rush for cover had taken place so quickly few had even glanced up at the enemy. They reassembled below.

"Well, I guess we've been exposed to our enemy," said Bufaskada.

"Half a dozen apes?" Maftu posed. "I'm not so sure. I think we have a much greater predator seeking us than that. We have to be ready for something considerably more deadly."

"We were all enjoying a serene moment, weren't we?" asked Sholemazar. "Many of us were gazing peacefully into the land before us. Did anyone see these intruders arrive? Or depart? We are sharp. God has pruned us down to the sharpest of the sharp. If we can be caught unaware so easily, we shall easily fall prey to these…these…whatever they are."

"Let's pursue the idea that this is the enemy we were forewarned of," said Anam. "I think they were there," he pointed to the upper ledge, "long before we knew about it. I'm sure they could have caused us some damage, but here we all are without a scratch. I wonder if they meant us harm or merely wanted to scare us away."

"If," said Zoana, "they considered us safe, but intruders, it would make sense if they wanted to scare us away. It also may be they sense the protection of God on us. Unfortunately, or not, there is no clear choice for us but to press on. We cannot go back. I am convinced we are where God wants us to be and that he also desires we quickly move on. Let us try to make peaceful contact with these…er…natives, until we can determine their true intent. We were told to travel toward the mountains. We were told we would have trouble. I think it's time to go."

"You're always a woman of action," Anam said. "You have spoken well. Let's leave immediately."

The descent to ground level was not a sudden drop off, but rather a series of short climbs. This made it possible for everyone, but Comeana, to reach the bottom on their own power, with the use of the ropes. Paluqua insisted on trailing behind to disengage the ropes. In a few minutes the group reassembled at the base of the great cliff. Togorasom took charge.

"My friends, you have all heard this before. However, it needs to be repeated. We are going to face a great many challenges. There will be encounters we simply do not understand. The element of unity must prevail among us. The natives of this land must see us as a unit. They will not be awed by our number. This is fine. We have never outnumbered our foes, rather, our foes have often become our friends. Eventually, God's people will outnumber our enemies because we shall be all that remains. This is like what I need to tell you; we shall all survive this challenge. The Lord has not given immortality in this life. He has given us his righteousness to cause the world to repent. He has given us a space of time to do his work. We must continue to use this time wisely. Our time is not yet, this is his time. We must work while we still have time. During the next few days we have to help one another. We must stay together. I urge you all not to wander off until we know the danger is passed. These creatures are not our main enemy. Our main enemy is invisible. You will understand later."

In the next few minutes they discovered the forest around them had a banquet of food prepared. When all had eaten well, they formed a tight group again and headed in the direction of the mountains. The area was beautiful compared to the starkness that had been on the other side of the ridge. The land was very much alive with an array of trees and flowers. However, they noticed few forms of wild animals. Also, they felt at home with the maple and elm trees, but other trees were new to them. A few chipmunks and squirrels chattered out their warning from above as the group moved through. It would have been a pleasant trip without the pressure of attempting to keep track of an unseen enemy. They walked along a good path for over an hour when one of the women called out. They all tried to force their way to the front to see. Protruding from a tree was a very well-wrought arrow. Anam pulled it out. It had been lodged there for some time as it was well-weathered. Three rows of feathers were on the notched end. The tip was metal.

"Well," said Anam after several minutes of silence, "it appears there is an advanced people here. I cannot believe that those ape-men constructed this thing."

"We've seen no other sign of civilization," said Paluqua. "No fire pits, no built paths, nothing. What can this mean?"

Ernie stepped up to Anam. "It means our wits are being severely tested. I am more nervous now than before."

"As well you should," said Anam. "We have more to fear now than these creatures we encountered earlier. They may not be the threat at all. We need to be aware of everything now that we know people here can fire upon us. If they can construct arrows, they can also build traps and plan attacks."

"Our greatest enemy, however," said Zoana, "is fear. We must move on and we must do so boldly."

They headed out once more. That day they traveled for another six hours, taking only a few short breaks. There were no unusual sightings or findings the rest of the day. Shortly after noon, they came to a wide, slow-moving stream. The ground was soft and dry everywhere so the decision was made to stop for the day and sleep under the branches of a great oak tree, which was fairly isolated from the forest. In the morning they planned to ford the stream.

"Who's there!" Anam sat up quickly from his sleep. It was not dawn yet and the sky was just beginning its entry into an eerie dawn. For a moment, fright gripped him. Their campsite seemed to be besieged by ghosts or some sort of spirits. Then he realized these were the ape-men. They seemingly floated about the area as they moved quickly and were extremely agile. One passed only a few feet from him, but when he attempted to pounce on him, he seemed to disappear. Then, they were gone. Naturally the entire site was an uproar of confusion. He finally realized several of the women were attempting to pin one of their unwelcome visitors down with very little success. Anam joined in.

With Didyadim on one arm, Sholemazar clinging to the creature's back and Shulea futilely trying to gain a hold on both legs at once, Anam approached for what he thought would be an easy victory. As he neared the ape-man, he glanced aside and ordered a rope. Instantly, the ape-man charged, three women in tow, head down, ramming Anam in the face as he turned back toward his opponent. Anam crumbled to the ground, almost losing consciousness. Shulea loosened her grip with the intent of getting a better hold. The ape-man flew out of her grasp and cast the other two women aside. Paying them no more attention, he vanished into the forest.

Paluqua quickly knelt by Anam's side. He clasped onto her with one arm and she helped him to his feet.

"I think I'm fine," he said, shaking his throbbing head from side to side. "That thing is stronger than ten horses." He leaned against a tree. "Two questions. First, I want to know who was on guard duty? How did this happen? Then, I want to know the extent of the damage, not including my half-fractured skull."

Elea approached Anam. "I was on duty," she admitted. "I don't know what happened. One moment, it was totally peaceful. The next, they were all over the place. I was wide awake all of the time. I'm very sorry."

"That's all right," he said. "I should have posted more than one guard, but it's never been needed before."

Zoana came before him. "Except for your injury, no one is hurt. Nothing appears to be missing, but they did some ransacking. If I may conjecture. I don't think they came to pick a fight. Considering their strength and speed they could have done extensive damage. I believe they were either just curious or they are trying to frighten us off.

"I'm sure your right," he said. "Look, I need to sit down." He slid to the ground. "Let's get this mess cleaned up and then, let's pray. And stay alert!"

By the time they had reorganized the camp and gotten their nerves under control the sun was beginning to appear over the horizon. While some formed a protective guard round the others, most of them met under the tree and prayed.

After prayer and eating they crossed the stream, always in the same general direction toward the twin mountains.

"What would they be driving us away from?" Anam asked. "I'm certain they mean us no direct harm for they surely could have accomplished that by now. Are they afraid of allowing us to proceed because of danger to us or because we may later pose a challenge to them?"

Anam walked between Paluqua and Zoana. Suddenly, he stopped. "Listen," he said, "it's very quiet, too quiet." He raised his arm to indicate everyone should stop. A few paces ahead of them was a place where the path widened out into a clearing. "Take cover!" he called out.

Immediately everyone dove into the brush. Arrows were strung and poised. The air seemed charged with tenseness. For several minutes they lay quietly hidden. It was a blessing for them that the area was thick with undergrowth and debris. They were easily buried and out of sight.

The tenseness seemed to disburse. Zoana announced quietly that she would check out the area in one direction. Macosena checked the clearing on the other side. Both women crawled silently away and quickly returned.

"I cannot tell how many," Zoana explained, "but there was definitely someone waiting for us."

Macosena agreed. "From the appearance of all the trampling and broken branches I would say twenty or thirty on my side alone. But that's just a guess. There may have been not so many at all."

"Any identification?" he asked.

They both shook their heads.

"I want to check it out." He took Zoana and three other women and circled the clearing. There had been a lot of traffic, but no apparent signs left of whom their would-be attackers were. Anam concluded there were probably less than a dozen clumsy attackers.

"What's this?" pointed out Umfuwadea. She carefully scooped up a small object from under a bush and brought it to the others. It was a small string of feathers. "It's very much like the ones on the arrow we discovered."

"Our lives could be in danger. Traveling with this large group and the children," Anam said, "is too dangerous. We're setting ourselves up for an ambush from both parties. However, we are moving as quickly as we can." He sat silently pondering for a moment. "Any suggestions?"

"I have a suggestion," said Umfuwadea. "Allow me to follow

them now while the trail is fresh and they will not suspect it." Anam grimaced at the thought of sending her out alone. "I can move quicker than this party who lay in wait for us." Anam started to shake his head. "We are God's people. He sent us here. He gave us a home. I am not quite pleased hiding under a bush up to my armpits in dead leaves waiting to be attacked. Can we safely go on?"

"Perhaps the danger is not as great as we suspect. We have been set up for an ambush three times and not harmed at all," he said. "Perhaps these people mean us no harm at all."

"Well, then it's either dangerous and they must be tracked down, or else, it's safe and we must make contact. The trail grows cold. Eventually, we'll make contact with these people. Why wait?"

By this time several of the women had appeared and been brought up to date.

"Anam," Umfuwadea continued, "I want to follow this easy trail so bad my insides quiver! Please?"

"You are right. Follow, but take one other."

Her eyes quickly passed among the women and came to rest upon Crazon. With no further word the two warriors bounded into the forest in silent pursuit.

It seemed incredible that the path left for them was so easy to follow, which clearly indicated these people had no expectation of being pursued. Either that or the two were being led into another trap. They traveled about a mile and reached a small brook where they paused for a short break. The trail led across the stream where several branches had been broken during the scramble up the opposite bank.

"Is this too easy?" Umfuwadea asked Crazon quietly.

Crazon shook her head in amazement. "Well, they surely never figured we'd be on their trail. They laid such a good ambush. Why such a messy retreat?"

After taking a drink they headed out again. Both women sensed they were moving much faster than their prey. They reached a small clearing.

"They rested here," Crazon suggested. "We must be very close."

"They could have left only moments ago," Umfuwadea agreed. She pointed to the tumbled down grass. "They headed this way." As she dashed out of the clearing back into the woods she felt something about her ankle, but only for a moment. The rope snagged her around the calf as she brought down her knife in its direction. Too late, however, as in a moment she was suspended from a tree by a rope around her right ankle. Her knife lay in the grass. Her quiver had emptied itself.

Looking quickly about to ensure it was safe for her, Crazon leapt toward her friend to hack her down. Umfuwadea called out as she saw a movement in the bushes, but again, too late. Several men grappled with Crazon as she struggled to get free. Umfuwadea could not see the fight from where she was. She heard a noise on the branch above and glanced up to see a smiling-faced, curly-haired man in rags. She saw him only for a moment, though. He brought his hand-ax down on the rope to release her. Then, everything went dark.

She found herself inside a great canvas bag being rolled and pushed about. Outside the bag she made out several male voices, but could not understand them. Moving her hands up and down her body, she ensured nothing was broken. Aches and pains from being strung up and thumped about, but no permanent damage. Her knife was gone; all her arrows had fallen from her quiver. She sat quietly for a moment. The next time somebody tried to handle the bag she brought both fists down hard on his back. There was a moan of agony, some more talking and then silence. After a couple of minutes the bag moved again and she sensed she was floating. Realizing she was suspended from a carry pole of some sort, she decided to save her energy for later on.

Crazon and Umfuwadea suffered in silence and bounced along for an hour until they came to an abrupt halt. There had been a great deal of talking the whole trip, but now everyone became silent until one voice called out. A few moments later the procession moved a few more feet. Then began what was obviously an argument between two men. There was some scuffling and loud yelling until they finally continued moving. A few paces later the bags and carrying poles were set down and the women heard the voice of one of the men who had been arguing before, now speaking. Suddenly, the bags were opened.

Umfuwadea and Crazon had been sitting in darkness for over an hour. Now both women shielded their eyes from the glare of a torch being brandished in their faces. The air stunk and was heavy from the burning fat. For a few moments, all either woman could see was moving forms, but they could make out nothing. They could hear, however, the voice of their captor still speaking.

Still unable to see their opponents, Crazon boldly stepped forward and demanded to know why they had been brought to this place. The room was silent.

Defiantly she spoke again. "You are not aware of the danger you bring upon yourselves by taking the position of our enemy. We are protected by a vow of the most high God! I demand our immediate release!"

After a few more moments of silence, another male voice, kinder but still speaking in another tongue spoke.

Umfuwadea stepped over to Crazon's side. "That was fine, sister, however, I don't think they understood a word of it. We do not know each other's language." Umfuwadea then attempted several greetings in every tongue she could recall, but to no avail.

However, as she spoke, their eyes began to become accustomed to the glare of the torches. They could see two dozen men mostly squatting in a circle around them. Before them was a podium, upon which was a single chair. The voice which had responded to Crazon came from that chair. A few of the men carried staves or spears, but most of them appeared unarmed. The man in the seat stood up and approached them.

"They have been gone over three hours," Anam complained. "What could be keeping them?" He sat with Zoana and Paluqua.

"Perhaps," suggested his wife, "someone needs to trail them."

"Hah! So we can go wandering off one by one?"

"Well then," said Zoana, "we've prayed. I guess we sit and wait. Isn't this area just beautiful and fascinating?"

Anam's hands shot up in frustration. "All right, who will go?"

"I am already prepared," Zoana said quietly. "I can leave immediately."

Anam closed his eyes. "You are most qualified. Go!"

She was gone. Togorasom strolled over a few minutes later after Paluqua had left..

"Zoana is gone?" he asked.

"Yes," said Anam looking up at him. "I sent her to find the other two."

"Then you can afford to spare her?" Anam looked puzzled.

"You have lost her and sent her away so casually? Did you pray first?"

"Well, no," Anam sputtered. "But you said, remember, we shall all survive this challenge."

"I also said we are none of us immortal and we need to stay together. Our real enemy is invisible. You have sent three women into dangerous territory with too little concern. But, do not fear, the Lord is in charge. I commend them into his hands. Zoana, however, shall be defeated and overcome by her enemy. This is all the Lord's doing."

It was as easy for Zoana to follow the trail as it had been for the others before. When she reached the point where the pursuers met the prey, her intuitive mind knew immediately they had been captured. She continued to follow the well-beaten path until she reached the point where the forest came to an end. Staying on their trail she arrived at a place where the party had entered a mountainside. The way was blocked by a heavy wooden door accessible only from the inside. Then, she realized she was not alone. Behind her, moving slowly, were six of the ape-men. She strung her bow and shouted a warning to stay back. Instead, they let loose with a blood-curdling scream and attacked. She released her arrow and it lodged in the chest of the nearest one. There was no time to try again. When the first one hit her she felt as if she were being crushed to death. Their strength was amazing. The creature stared back at her for a moment and opened his mouth to reveal a set of jagged teeth as he prepared to clamp down on her neck. She struggled for a moment, but the creature was far too strong. Suddenly, it began to release its grip. Zoana stared into the hairy face again and saw the tip of an arrow protruding from its forehead. Pushing it from her, she got to her knees and unsheathed her knife. The other four creatures milled about her in a confused and nonthreatening manner when an arrow struck the shoulder of one. It screamed out in pain and began whirling around on the ground. The other three looked at Zoana for a moment, grabbed their wounded companion and ran off.

"Hey!" she heard a voice call out. The wooden entrance was open. A call was made she could not understand, however, she needed no further invitation. When Zoana first stepped inside and the door slid shut with a slam she was in almost total darkness. A moment later a man appeared from around a bend carrying a lantern. The details of his features were not easily discernible as the little light cast them into grotesque shadows. He was much shorter than she. His dark hair fell down over his shoulders. Clothed from his feet up in rags and carrying no weapons, Zoana did not consider him a potent threat but was wary in these confined spaces for any surprise. He led her along the dark entryway and finally into a small room, actually a nook off of the main path. It was lit only by one small torch. He motioned for her to stay and continued on down the hallway they had been traveling.

There were no accommodations or ornaments in the room except for the torch and a large, well-worn woven rug. She moved her eyes around warily ever suspecting some sort of trap, but finally felt a sense of calmness that there was no trick. She sat on the carpet and waited.

She hadn't waited long when flickers of light appeared on the cave wall and she heard the sound of one man's feet on the earthen floor. He was much larger than the first man, taller even than she. He carried a large torch so his features were obvious. Sandy-colored hair cascaded over his broad, bare shoulders. His arms and legs were thick with strength. His otherwise flawless skin had a scar that descended from his right breast almost to his waist. He wore only a tattered pair of shorts; nothing on his feet. After moving the smaller torch to a notch near the entrance and replacing it with the larger torch he turned and faced Zoana.

For a moment she simply stared at him towering over her until she suddenly came to herself and leapt to her feet, extending her right hand. Instead of clasping or shaking hands with her, he gazed at her extended hand for a moment and then gently took it in his.

He spoke a word of greeting which she could not understand. After thinking for a moment he spoke another word of greeting.

Zoana shrugged her shoulders and said, "I'm pleased to meet you." Her eyes went to their still joined hands.

He released her hand and motioned to the carpet where they both sat down. It was then she noticed he was wearing a knife and belt. Remembering his belt, he flung it a few feet away and she responded by doing the same.

The man appeared to be around thirty years old, but looked older due to his fatigue. His beard, the same color as his hair, covered his face, also making him appear older. His eyes appeared gentle and he closed them often to think, which encouraged her to trust him.

They sat silently for a while and stared at each other. Gesturing toward the cave entrance she had come through, he attempted to explain something, but realizing she could not understand, cut it off in mid-sentence.

"Mashua!" he said, thumping the palm of his hand on his chest.

She pointed at herself and said, "Zoana," which evoked a smile from him. "Where are my friends? Do you have the other two women?"

He indicated he couldn't understand. She leaned over towards the dusty floor, drew a small stick figure and pointed at herself. Then, she drew two more like it and looked back at him. He drew the shape of a wine cup and pretended to drink.

"No, I've come to take them home." He didn't understand. She drew a circle around the three figures and pointed towards the entrance.

Mashua looked frightened. Drawing another stick figure, he moved his hand across the other three, removing them. He was afraid of the ape-men. He tried to motion something to her, but she couldn't grasp it. Drawing the three stick figures again and, adding a fourth, he pointed at himself. He drew a circle indicating beams radiating from it to represent the sun. Then erased it, replacing it with the crescent shape of the moon. Zoana knew the others would become impatient if they waited all day and probably would follow them. Even if they didn't, she desired to return to them. Mashua took her hand again and shook his head. He was extremely agitated. Zoana slowly nodded her assent. Holding his hand, she followed him to his feet. Mashua grabbed both the knife belts with his free hand and led her into the cave.

When they reached the main hall, Zoana noticed about two dozen men milling about, but her attention was directed towards the far end of the room where Crazon and Umfuwadea were bound hand and foot and tethered to the wall. She had little time to consider this, however, for she was immediately jumped by two men. One attempted to grab her right hand which she had just released from Mashua. Her fist collided directly into his throat and he reeled backwards, gagging. The other man ran at her from the front to press her against the wall. Instead, she grabbed his wrist, twisted him about backwards and nearly wrenched his arm from its socket. Then she shoved him into the wall.

By this time most of the other men were on their feet and encircled Zoana and Mashua, who had drawn his knife. For a few tense moments he stood poised for their attack. Quickly thereafter he regained control of the mob.

A silver tray and two wooden cups, as well as several pieces of fruit, sat on a small table. Mashua pointed at it with his knife blade and began sputtering a stream of unidentifiable curses at each of the men. He then approached one man who seemed to be the ring leader and cuffed him across the cheek. He arose slowly, amid Mashua's continued verbal assault, and cut the two women free.

Finally, Mashua waved toward the doorway and ordered everyone out until only he and the three women remained. Clearly by his huffing and slamming his fist into his palm he was still angry. Unexpectedly, he approached Zoana and bowed to his knees before her. She helped him back to his feet and they stared at one another's faces for a great length of time. She finally reached out and clenched his hand. Then she directed her attention to her two friends.

"Are you all right?" she asked.

They both nodded nervously. "We're fine," said Crazon. She then explained how they had been captured and what had happened upon their arrival. There had been a constant argument between Mashua and the other man over leadership and how the women should be treated. Mashua had been extremely friendly and tried to communicate with them, but had no luck. The other man had kept up a constant harangue the entire time and was rebuked often. Mashua had just called for drink when a messenger, the guard from the door, arrived and Mashua left with him. Zoana told them about the attack by the ape-men and how Mashua didn't want them to leave, but had promised to escort them back at night.

While they talked, Mashua had called for a young boy to bring two more cups of drink. When Mashua returned, the four of them sat down on the stone platform on which stood Mashua's 'throne', merely an old armchair.

Zoana finally began to look over the hall where they sat. The floor was bare, sandy earth. There were no emblems or festoons nor even furs hanging from the walls. The ceiling was fairly low and could be easily touched from most places. The room measured about fifteen paces each way. The only entrance was the one they had used and stood about five feet tall, requiring people to lower their heads to enter. This entrance circled about back to the main hallway. Positioned near the edges of the room and across the front of the entire podium were about half a dozen torches poked into holes in the floor. A steady supply of air kept them burning bright, but was not strong enough to remove much of the odor. The air was very heavy with the smell of burnt tallow.

For Mashua's part, as Zoana inspected the room, he inspected her. Though Zoana wore little, as always, her physique did not seem to attract his attention. He found her black hair and dark skin intriguing. He watched her face, gazing at the softness of her cheeks and waiting for her to look his way. When she did and their eyes met, she blushed and looked away.

Zoana could not understand the thoughts going through her mind concerning this stranger she knew nothing about. Her eyes looked into the flame of the torch, refusing to look back at him. She wanted to touch him. She wanted to know more about him. She didn't want to leave him. She felt they must find a way to communicate. She looked at Crazon and Umfuwadea, sitting opposite from her by Mashua, hoping for emotional support. She received confused stares.

Mashua laughed as he turned his focus to the floor and nervously ran his fingers through his hair. He gulped down all of his drink and then called for more. Then, realizing no one else was drinking, he put his cup down. Quickly rising to his feet, he turned around toward the women and made a short statement. Taking a deep breath he looked away. After nervously rocking back and forth for a while he looked back at Zoana to speak again. She smiled. Her lips looked so soft and inviting. He looked at the curve of her neck and wanted to place the palm of his hand there.

He ran out of the room.

"Zoana," insisted Crazon. "What's going on? Do you know anything about this man?"

Zoana closed her eyes and bowed her head, as if to pray, and then looked back at Crazon. "No, I know nothing at all about him. I am, in fact, extremely confused over my feelings."

"Let's pray," suggested Umfuwadea, "before he comes back." They formed a circle and she began. "Almighty God, it has been so very long. You have called us warriors, but we have not stopped being women. Continue to guide us in this high calling, but remember we are still weak compared to you. This emotional feeling, this interest, that has begun to develop between these two, Lord, if it is not of you I pray you stop it now. This child of yours, Zoana, help her to always remember her God and her relationship with you ahead of all others. But if whatever it is that seems to be happening, is within your will, Lord, then let it be guided by godliness. Continue to remember and to bless each of us, Lord."

Zoana's eyes began to mist over with tears. "I wish we could speak. I want to talk with him. He seems so strong, don't you think? And, at the same time, compassionate and gentle. I am confused. And I am afraid. You know I'm really foolish when it comes to men. Why do they always seem attracted to me? What did I do?"

Her conversation was cut short with sounds of a scuffle outside the entrance. Crazon's and Umfuwadea's captor strode into the room. His face was set firm. Anger blazed from his eyes. He carried a heavy, wooden staff. He snapped some orders to the throng gathering behind him. Another wooden staff like the first was produced. Then, Mashua was forced into the room. His hands were bound behind his back. They forced him to the floor. Zoana took a step towards them which enraged the man with the staff.

He shouted at her, "Mashua!" and gestured with his hands as though he were breaking a stick. Then he thumped his fist against his chest. "Magnon!" He raised his fist in the air. She took another step toward Mashua and Magnon screamed something at her. Zoana looked at the other two women and back at Magnon.

He yelled his name at her again. She spat on the floor. This shocked him for a moment. Then he ran back to Mashua and kicked him in the chest. Mashua groaned and crumbled into a ball. Zoana flew at Magnon and the crowd yelled their glee as they restrained her.

By now there were about twenty men gathered around as well as three women and a few younger children. They all backed away and encircled the room. Knowing a fight was on they yelled their encouragement. A space was made for Umfuwadea and Crazon, so Magnon and Zoana had the whole floor. The extra staff was tossed to Zoana who was not used to fighting with this type of weapon. She handled it uneasily. It was not much more than a heavily-shellacked walking stick. She tossed it from one hand to the other.

Magnon side-stepped across from her while wielding his staff like a club. Without warning he swung his staff down upon her. Instinctively, she braced her staff in both hands and blocked him.

He swung back, preparing to take another swing, this time from the side. Their staffs clattered together like swords as he continued to wildly swing at her and she successfully stopped him every time. Over and over he tried to beat her down, but she was continually able to counter him and remained untiring.

Then, he surprised her with one well-aimed swing which smashed into her knuckles. She changed hands and quickly clenched her sore fist. Magnon, teeth glaring, shouted at her and swung again. She deftly moved aside. He began to madly smash blows down on her once more, but she was still able to block each one.

Zoana had not swung at him yet, after several minutes of fighting. She had also been the one to continually back off. Her defensive attitude had been planned. The blow to her hand, which still ached, had not been planned, but she intended to use this for her advantage as well. Her opponent was the type with too large an ego. He also was not professional or well-trained in the use of this weapon. His strategy was to merely rain down blows upon her and hope some struck well.

Zoana sank to her knees. Magnon, believing he had a great advantage brought his staff over his head preparing for a heavy blow, exactly as she had expected. The butt of Zoana's staff rammed into his belly. He lost his breath, nearly dropped his staff and tottered back and forth for a moment. One arm covered his injured gut. He moved his staff to his free hand. Zoana swung her staff at his legs and broke it over his knee. Magnon screamed with pain and lowered his free hand to his knee, clutching it. He was now in a position, doubled over, from which he could not fight back.

Zoana used her injured fist and boxed him in the side of the head. He grunted and fell onto his side, unconscious. She immediately leapt to her feet and yelled at those around Mashua to untie him.

Not understanding her words, but knowing what she wanted, they quickly cut him loose. He took charge and ordered Magnon removed from the room. Then he began to berate the people. This yelling lasted for several minutes until he turned back to Zoana. He carefully took her sore hand into his, which by now bothered her not at all, and inspected it.

"It's fine," she said. "It really is." However, she did not let go of him.

During the evening the women had the chance to meet Mashua's people. There were twenty-one young men; an elderly man named Mehi, whom many of the others treated like a father; six women; and a dozen young people ranging in age from Mashua's ten-year old servant to a new born baby about a month old.

They once had all lived in a nearby city of several thousand around which lay several smaller towns and farming communities. When Mashua was a boy, the ape-men had appeared. The life of these ape-men was to kill and destroy. This they had accomplished quickly with Mashua's civilization. In only a few days his people had been decimated and they had to flee into the hills and other hiding places. They were quite certain there were other groups in hiding similar to theirs.

Mashua called his people the Denarites. He called the ape-men, 'Onoshe'. This word was very similar to another Zoana knew which meant 'man with no soul'. However, when she probed Mashua on the origin of the word he could not understand.

During the war between the two peoples many of the Onoshe had also been destroyed. They numbered now only a few hundred. Regardless of their lack of need for so much territory, the Onoshe had no idea of peace. They took what they wanted and destroyed anyone caught unprotected. Mashua would organize a band of men every few days to go out and gather food. Women and children were not allowed out at all except near the entrance where they could be easily guarded.

All of this communication took place between the women and Mashua and a few of his people by the use of hand signals and drawings, lasting far into the night.

In the morning Zoana awoke and inquired of Mashua as to when they could leave. He firmly shook his head indicating they could not leave. Despite her upbraiding of him all during the morning, he continued to insist they could not leave. Zoana knew that Anam would send someone else looking for them and that they would be in danger while traveling away from the group.

After nagging at him for several hours, her anger finally overcame her and she jumped on him from behind. Zoana suspected she was physically stronger than he, for she had found very few men who could best her in a fair fight. She recalled the fight with Magnon the night before and suspected that cave dwelling had made these people soft. She wasn't prepared for Mashua's defense.

With one hand on her neck and the other across her back he flipped her sideways and over his head in a second. He then fell upon her and pinned her to the ground. She found struggling to become free was not possible.

"No!" he shouted at her, one of the few words he had learned. Then he casually got up, brushed himself off and walked away.

Zoana lay on the floor, stunned for several moments before she slowly got up. Next, she decided they must escape.

The women were allowed free access to go wherever they wanted in the cave. They had even been given a tour and were offered an opportunity in the future to help as a guard at the entrance. The entrance was maintained by two guards posted at observation points. One was a natural tunnel which had been cleared away and which snaked around from the entrance and ended just a few feet from it. The tunnel ended with an opening about a foot across offering plenty of room for an archer. This was the spot from which the arrows came that had brought down the ape-men attacking Zoana. The other lookout had been carved into the rock and was located directly above the entrance. This spot also posted an archer, but this man was also given the responsibility of opening and closing the heavy wooden door of the entrance. This door was operated by a thick rope and set of pulleys. When the door needed to be opened all that was needed was to trip a lever. To close it one turned the wheel attached to the pulley and the door was pulled tightly against the opening.

When the three women appeared all at once the guard at the doorway was immediately suspicious. He attempted to motion them to leave. They decided to use the approach of honesty and motioned for him to open the door. He shook his head and scowled at them. As they began to consider a more devious way of escaping, Magnon appeared. They had not seen him since the night before when Zoana had drubbed him. He looked at Zoana with eyes of hate but kept his distance. The guard loosened up when he saw Magnon and explained what the women wanted. After considering this for a while he snapped an order to the guard, obviously telling him to open the door. The guard gazed at him in awe. He repeated the order. Reluctantly, he hit the lock on the pulley and the door slid open. Magnon smiled and waved his hand toward the door.

The women looked doubtfully at each other. Magnon did not flinch.

"Let's go!" Zoana said. They bolted out of the door and heard it fall back into place as they headed out.

"Do you think this is for the best?" Crazon asked Zoana. "Mashua was very concerned about the ape-men."

"He gave us no choice. Yesterday, he promised to escort us, but today it seems it has become too dangerous. I know he is concerned for our safety, but we also have to think of the others. We need to rejoin them. There is no telling how long he would have kept us locked up in that cave. Anam would have taken extreme chances to find us. Besides we all have our knives, bows and arrows. We'll be safe enough."

They stopped for a moment and gazed at the two dead ape-men from Zoana's battle the day before. Then, they nervously headed away to rejoin their group.

"I am not going to send anyone out there!" Anam snapped.

Paluqua and several of the other women were gathered around him. She spoke quietly, but gravely. "There are three women out there who may have been captured or harmed. What do you plan to do?"

"Do you suppose I should send someone else on a rescue mission? Should we be trickled away one by one?"

"But, my husband," she spoke on the verge of tears, "I love them. They are too important to me."

"I understand, Paluqua," he stated firmly, "but everyone here is just as valuable. I cannot send anyone out."

"The Lord has promised to protect us."

"Aye. He has also promised a curse on our enemies. I cannot and will not tempt God by sending anyone else away. His protection is also over these three. If you trust him, and I know you do, have faith that they shall rejoin us. Perhaps he will also ask supreme faith as he asked me only a few days ago concerning the one I love most. He has vowed to protect us, but he has not vowed to make this flesh immortal. There is nothing you can do except pray. Pray for them, but also pray for yourself. I have nothing further to say."

Anam stood up and walked away. Maftu leaned over to Paluqua.

"What will you do?" she whispered.

"I will obey my husband," she said somewhat sadly.

"But, has he ever been wrong before? Is it possible he is wrong now?"

"Yes, but you see, that doesn't matter. Anam's direction from God is to make the best decision possible. My direction is to obey my husband. I must advise him, but I am not accountable for his errors. I am accountable for my own."

Maftu, still eager to depart, looked around at the other women. "And what of us!" she demanded.

"Your direction from God is to obey me!" she stated firmly. "You and the others are to remain here, in prayer, until told otherwise. That is my decision."

"And what if you are wrong?"

Paluqua smiled, took a deep, relaxing breath, and stood up. "Don't you see, Maftu? That isn't your problem. You're only accountable when you disobey God." She followed Anam to where he had walked several paces away and knelt by a fallen tree to pray.

As soon as the women had left the safety of the cave it had been the guard's intention to run and tell Mashua what had happened. During the evening before when the people had become fully aware of both the strength and gentleness of the Rasomites, nearly all had come to enjoy them. The exception had been Magnon and a handful of his followers. They had kept away from the previous evening's fellowship. Magnon, knowing the guard's intentions, had purposefully kept him engaged in conversation for several minutes. Finally, one of the men could bear it no more and attempted to excuse himself. Coming down from his perch, he headed for the main hallway, but Magnon refused to allow him to pass.

Suddenly, Mashua entered and inquired about the women. The guard explained everything. Mashua ran back inside and organized a band to go after them and only a couple of minutes later they left the cave in pursuit of the women.

Two of the men who traveled with Mashua had been with Magnon the day before when Crazon and Umfuwadea were captured, therefore, they knew the route the women would take. They also knew the area much better than the women and could follow shortcuts to head them off. Mashua knew they would take the only route familiar to them back to their people.

The women made good time. Unlike the previous day, there was no need to stop and make decisions. They moved quickly with Zoana in the lead not speaking a word. She hoped to cover the distance within an hour. Her major thought was to avoid the ape-men, of course. She was confused over the need to outdistance Mashua, convinced he would follow. Inside her the desire was still strong to see him. However, she would be a prisoner to no man. If he could not accept her independence, she would have to forget him.

In their rush, they burst through an opening and stopped short. There, only a few paces from them, sat one of the ape-men gnawing on a piece of animal bone. His mouth curled into a snarling position like a rabid dog, but he sat still. They retreated a few feet out of his sight and cocked their bows. Nothing happened.

After a few minutes, Zoana cautiously peered back into the clearing to see the ape-man had departed. This increased their sense of determination as they considered it a sign of God's blessing their escape. They ran on. However, only a few feet further they could see through the brush several of them. They had stumbled into some sort of camp.

"What can we do?" Zoana whispered.

"Dear Lord, help us," said Crazon.

"Let's backtrack," suggested Umfuwadea, "and find another route."

"We must be careful," said Zoana, "as none of us know this area. I only know the route I followed yesterday. It will be easy to get lost."

"God forbid we get lost out here," whispered Umfuwadea.

They heard an awful scream from an ape-man through the brush and several anguished moans. The women retreated a few paces keeping their eyes in all directions. Suddenly the bushes burst open and more than a dozen of the creatures appeared.

Zoana's arrow met the first in the chest. He ran forward a few more feet, stumbled and fell to the ground. He moved slowly, indicating he was still alive, but made no sound. The others stood and nervously watched the women as well, whose arrows were poised for firing.

The women knew in a headlong rush they would be lost. They would have time to fire only once and were greatly outnumbered. The creatures were wise enough to know the danger to each of them.

"If they go for their friend," whispered Zoana to the others, "allow it and don't panic. But, unless they retreat, anything else is to be considered an attack. Don't be afraid."

"We are hopelessly outnumbered, sister," said Umfuwadea. "If they attack, we are lost."

"Two things," Zoana said. "They are obviously also concerned for their lives and, as long as God and I are on the same side, I am never lost." She aimed her arrow at the fallen creature and aimed it back at the others indicating they could retrieve him.

There was some sort of discussion among them until one got on its knees and moved toward his injured friend. He cradled his friend's head in one arm and gripped the arrow. Suddenly, he ripped the lance from his chest causing him to scream in pain. A few moments later the one hoisted his injured comrade up and carried him back through the brush.

There was a noise behind the women. Umfuwadea, who stood behind the other two, spun around instinctively. The other two women stood motionless due to their training. Mashua and his men appeared and quickly tried to analyze the setting. In a moment they all had their bows drawn and were prepared for conflict. Umfuwadea stood up, leaving her bow on the ground, and indicated they should not fire. Her diversion worked as it was too dangerous for the newly arrived archers to fire passed her and into the enemy tribe. In a few seconds the startled Onoshe had vanished again into the brush.

Zoana and Mashua approached each other indignantly. A few paces from each other Mashua stopped and crossed his arms, glaring at Zoana. Not to be subdued, she also halted and stood her ground in the same manner. Mashua reached out and grabbed Zoana by the arm as if to lead her away. She jerked away from him, at the same time, unsheathing her knife. Zoana backed off, nostrils flaring, her gaze sharper than her blade.

Mashua turned and quietly conferred with his followers for a few moments. Looking back at Zoana with a forlorn and resigned expression on his face he nodded his head slightly. He raised his arm in the general direction of the trail back to the Rasomites.

Zoana nearly shook with her desire to go and take his hand. However, she turned, and, with Crazon and Umfuwadea, was back on the path to rejoin her friends.

There was a lot of joy expressed upon their arrival. Everyone gathered around and listened to the three women tell their story. Nothing was said about the intimate feelings Zoana and Mashua had for each other. Umfuwadea and Crazon avoided the subject as they felt Zoana's anger against Mashua had replaced her romantic feelings. Zoana avoided the subject of Mashua completely, believing the Rasomites would continue their travels soon and it would all be forgotten.

That evening Anam came to Zoana. "I have been thinking," he began. "I am considering going to Mashua and asking for his assistance as a guide, possibly even as support for us. We do not know this territory. Do you think he would help us? Perhaps even join us for a time?"

"I...I'm not sure," she said nervously. She thought of subtle ways to dissuade him. "We can't communicate with these people very well. It was so hard for us just to understand each other in a general way."

"The Lord can breach any gap in our speaking. Besides, I know a few tongues the others here do not. Do you think he'd join us?"

"Anam," she said, attempting to look serious, "these people don't seem to know about God. When we tried to bring the Lord into our discussions they were awed. They seem to believe in some general way that God is the creator but don't understand having a personal relationship with him. Should we ally ourselves with unsaved people?"

He shrugged his shoulders and half-smiled. "I don't know. We always have. Look back at all the people we have met. God has always blessed us and blessed these other people through us. I'm just wondering if any of these folks would help us even as a guide."

"You know also about the things which Togorasom has said. That is, there is a greater danger here than the Onoshe. Perhaps, and I don't understand this, he was speaking of these other people."

"I don't know. Togorasom spoke of an invisible enemy, which I do not understand. But, Zoana, what do you suggest? Should we flee from these people? Earlier you and the others said nothing about them that would justify any fear. Besides, if they are to be our enemies, when have we fled from our enemies? We have always gone to face them bravely with God at our side. We have only encountered one enemy, which I can recall, we were not able to conquer."

"What enemy could we not conquer?" she asked, trying to recall.

"You see, I had an enemy I could not conquer. I guess I was just too weak. But, now I have a helper and this enemy has been laid to rest. You cannot live all of your life in defeat, Zoana."

She was instantly defensive. "I am afraid of no foe!" she shouted. "Have not I always been the first to be willing to go alone and face our enemies or regain our friends? I have faced many perils by myself bravely. How can you say I am defeated?"

Anam sat quietly for a moment. "Yesterday, I wept for you because I didn't understand. Togorasom told me that you were defeated, that your enemy had vanquished you." He was quiet again. "Yes, Zoana, you have always been the first to go it alone. But, your time for going it alone is nearly over. I pray that you and Mashua will always be happy."

Zoana was nearly in tears. Anam pulled closer and held her. "How did you know? I said nothing about my feelings?"

"That is what gave it away. When you returned I could not understand what Togorasom meant. I then remembered who your enemy really was. Crazon and Umfuwadea included Mashua in their talk, but you carefully avoided even mentioning him by name. I looked for it in your speech and you said nothing of how you felt for this man. So I knew your feelings must be very deep. Tomorrow, we shall go there."

In the middle of the night, they felt the air suddenly cool. The wind began to stir up. In the distance, lightning lit the horizon. The stars disappeared. The Rasomites curled up tighter in their bags. A few minutes later they could hear the sound of raindrops crashing into the leaves. Finally, it was upon them.

The rain continued in a steady downpour for the rest of the night. It was difficult to determine when day began as the sky was so overcast. There was little activity in the Rasomite camp for most of the day. In the afternoon, the rainstorm slowed to a drizzle.

Anam and Togorasom sat talking.

"I had wanted to go and find these people the women met," Anam explained. "But, now I think it's best we stay another night and dry out some."

Togorasom looked into the sky. "I think not. It will continue like this all day. Tonight it may clear some for a while, but I expect another downpour. I have no interest to sit out in the rain when we can find shelter. In fact, I think it will rain for most of the next several days."

"Then we should go now?"

"I think we should go now."

Anam found Zoana shivering in her bag. "We are preparing to leave. To go find Mashua. Are you okay?"

"No," she whimpered. "I feel terrible. I'm hot and cold all at once. I can't seem to stop shaking. If we are leaving, I must get ready."

"We'll wait just a bit." He stood up and looked around. Paluqua was headed towards him through the drizzle.

She motioned for him to move towards her. "Is Zoana ill?" She seemed worried.

"Well, yes. It's probably the weather."

"I don't think so, though the weather probably is of no help. Crazon and Umfuwadea are also sick. They must have caught something from those people."

"Togorasom has suggested we go to the cave now, instead of waiting for the weather to let up."

"But mightn't we all get sick?"

"Yes, but he wasn't aware of this problem when we talked."

She looked at Anam doubtfully. "I'm not convinced that Togorasom is ever unaware of our health or of the dangers we may face."

"Let us be certain and talk to him before we let anyone else know."

Togorasom was well-mannered but adamant in his desire to go. He agreed that the sickness was caused by contact with this other race, but that it could not be avoided. Eventually, they would contact these people and face these complications anyway. He felt they had best get it over. He told them again it was all part of God's plan.

The three women were brought together and much prayer was offered by everyone. In the end, they seemed somewhat better and agreed they could walk to the cave.

Zoana confronted Anam. "I am willing and able to do this thing. However, I am not pleased that I must crawl back to Mashua in this sickly condition. I had hoped to be able to approach him and make known my feelings and desires. Now, I feel like, I don't know. It's hard to explain."

"Like he may get the upper hand in your relationship?" Anam quipped. Zoana looked disgusted. "Do not worry, my sister. If we are obeying the Lord, and we are, in the end all will be well."

During the first part of the trip, Zoana had a heavy heart. She had no interest in appearing before Mashua sick with fever and pleading for a dry place to sleep. She did not need his pity, which she feared she would receive. However, as they moved on, the sun came out and began to dry things up and revive the forest life. Inside, she also began to feel revived. She remembered in the past how she had usually approached men with an attitude of innocence and been hurt or made to feel foolish. Somehow, Mashua seemed different. While he was strong and bold and able to protect himself, at the same time, he also had great feelings of inadequacy around her. She considered how much Anam and Paluqua loved each other. However strong they were, they were tender toward each other, except when one needed to be corrected. Even then, they were kind. She thought of what it would be like to be with Mashua, to learn about each other. In the midst of her thoughts she heard the voices of Anam's children and suddenly cut her thoughts short. She redirected her thinking to leading the others along the path.

Before they reached the cave it was raining again. It was no problem getting in as the door-keeper was one of Mashua's close friends. As soon as everyone was inside and the door sealed again, he dashed off to find Mashua. The Rasomites meandered along the passageway with Zoana still in the lead. For a while during the trip she had begun to feel her strength return, but now inside the cave, though the air was warm, she began shivering again. She placed her hand on her forehead; it was hot and wet with sweat.

Mashua appeared with several other men trailing him. His grin revealed his pleasure at Zoana's return. As he approached her, she extended her right hand. A wave of dizziness came upon her. She steadied herself against the wall of the passage as Mashua dashed toward her. She passed out in his arms.

Ernie, who was behind Zoana when she fell, let go of the children and assisted Mashua in picking her up and carrying her to one of the sleeping chambers further in. He began to explain what had happened to the three women and why they were motivated to come here, but remembered they had no common language and grew silent.

When Zoana, Crazon and Umfuwadea were comfortable and one of the Denarites was left to care for them, Anam and Paluqua prayed for them with the laying on of hands. Mashua watched all of this closely. When they were finished and leaving the small sleeping area, he approached Anam with his hand out in greeting. Recalling the capture of the women and the fights between them and not knowing what Anam had been told or even Zoana's current feelings, Mashua eyed Anam nervously.

A smile flickered across Anam's face as he took Mashua's hand. "Grend Am!" he said. The word 'Onoshe' was one word from one of the many languages Anam had been taught by the priests as a child. 'Grend Am' came from the same language. Though Anam had never actually used this language he knew a few words. He knew this was a greeting and believed it meant a simple hello.

As soon as Anam spoke, Mashua grew very excited and surprised him with a hug. "Grend Am!" he shouted several times. What Anam didn't know was the word actually meant 'brother' or 'old friend'. Mashua took an instant liking for Anam. Although this was not his native tongue, he knew several words and began reeling them off. Unfortunately, though Anam recognized a few of the words, he did not know most of their meanings.

When Mashua was able to control himself, he led Anam to a quiet corner to attempt conversation. The rest of the Rasomites were led to the main assembly room. This was the only room large enough to contain them all and would be used as their living quarters during their stay. In a few minutes the room had been well -padded with many thick furs, and food and drink were being prepared.

When Anam was settled and made comfortable, he was offered a goblet of water and a small platter of meat, which appeared to be rabbit. When he indicated he would not eat the meat, the servant breathed a sigh of relief and replaced it with a plate of fruit. Mashua had left Anam alone to be attended, but returned a few minutes later with Mehi. This man wore a long, cotton gown with brightly colored designs embroidered into the fabric. He was well-advanced in years, in his eighties, and could not get about without assistance. As they made attempts at conversation, Anam also realized the man was nearly blind. However, his wits were still very sharp. Mashua explained the situation to him, and it was clear he understood.

The three men sat on the floor in a tight circle. The old man patted Mashua on the leg and said, "Ledamm." Anam knew this to be, 'my son'. He then took Anam's hand and repeated the words indicating that Anam was also his son. Instantly, Anam made the relationship and understood what he had said earlier and why Mashua was so pleased. Then the old man patted himself on the chest and said, "Mehi."

Realizing Anam's shallow understanding of this tongue, he began to teach him several words. It was amazing the speed with which they were able to move through the language. Each time Anam began to grasp the meaning of a word, Mehi would add a new word to the string of words Anam knew or he would change the string of words around to begin explaining something else. Even Anam was impressed by how quickly he learned.

They paused several times for breaks. At one time Anam and Mashua went outside the cave. Mashua explained how Zoana had been attacked by the Onoshe upon her arrival. The bodies had finally been removed by their kin during the rain the previous evening. He told Anam that this was typical of the way the Onoshe dealt. They would find small groups or solitary wanderers and kill them. This was how his people had been destroyed. All of his family had been killed, including his parents and three siblings. Anam could see the tears begin to well up as this strong man explained his loss. Finally he had been taken into hiding with several other young people by Mehi. Mehi had been a teacher of culture and language at the school in the main city. Most of these people had been his students.

Too soon, the break was over and they had to return to Mehi. Anam determined to explain their own history.

Soon Anam, Mehi and Mashua were again gathered in their

circle with several onlookers, most of whom could not understand this common language. Tea was served in a beautiful little ceramic teapot and matching cups. It continued to amaze Anam at the contrast between the sordid life these refugees lived and the continual appearance of elegant items which were obviously vestiges of their nearly-forgotten civilization. Though the women were clothed in rags, all wore at least a token of expensive jewelry. Most of the gold and crystal and other fancy items were contained in a separate room and, apparently, only brought out on special occasions. Some of the men wore tattered pieces of clothing from the past, some wore fur and leather made items. Only Mehi wore an outfit with any real grace.

Their language classes had been going on for over four hours now with a few breaks. Anam decided it was time to utilize his training.

"Mehi," he began slowly, searching both for words he knew and which would convey the seriousness of his testimony. "Many years ago your people were many and your knowledge great. You all had nice homes, families and a sense of peacefulness. Then, one day, this was shattered. A strange and wild enemy appeared and crushed your people with no sense of love or compassion. A few of you were able to survive. You may wonder why you were spared while so many you love are gone."

Mehi and Mashua sat and stared at him in silence as he continued to describe wives and fathers and mothers and friends. He told them of their enjoyment of games and in visiting each other. He told them of the independence they felt by raising their own crops and building their homes. He explained the anguish they felt when they saw it destroyed and the sense of weakness they felt by not being able to take it back.

He paused for a moment and Mehi spoke up. "Why do you go on about our great loss? What is the value of seeing my tears again? But, go on."

"I know why you were spared. I believe God is about to return you to your homes. I believe he has sent us to you. But tell me, what do you believe about God?"

"When I was younger, I was a wise man. I pondered on many things. One of those things was to understand God. He is the creator. He created all things. I believe this. He created good and evil and has no sense of justice. He has proved this to me because of what he has done. What do you believe concerning God?"

"He truly is the creator. However, I know nothing comes from God but goodness. There is a devil who takes everything lovely and good and turns it to evil. Someone who knows God will not lose their faith with him when they are given evil. They will continue to love him. Now I must tell you our story." He then began to describe to them the destruction of his people and his story was much like Mehi's story. Anam made it clear, however, they did not blame God for the evil. He finally explained why they had left their original home.

Mehi listened well and believed what he heard. It was clear there was something very different with this race than with what he was familiar.

"God knew his people would be destroyed if he did not protect them. This remnant of his people knew that without his protection they were doomed." Anam drew his statement to a close. "Therefore, he made a special covenant with these people that if they would love and honor him, he would protect those people. He was so serious about his promise that he put a curse on any that would do those people harm. Therefore, many have fallen and many have come to believe."

Mashua's and Mehi's expressions suddenly changed from one of interest to one of fear. They gazed at each other in silence. Mashua began trembling and acting extremely nervous. After a few moments he jumped up and quickly left the room. Mehi looked back at Anam.

"I do not understand," Anam said, shaking his head. "I cannot believe you would consider doing us harm. You've been so kind and we have committed no offense. God does not curse our friends."

The old man attempted to speak but was overcome with trembling. "Anam," he finally said slowly, "we do mean you no harm and perhaps you are correct that your God has led you to us. However, there is something we have kept back. Now, I shall explain."

Mehi sat in silence for several moments. Finally, with tears beginning to form in his eyes, he looked Anam in the face.

"Perhaps you have noticed that our women are few. When the Onoshe came they also brought with them a disease. It affects only the women. The men and young girls are spared, that is, until the females are of age. The symptoms are exactly like those these three who were here before are suffering now. A few survive. Most do not. They live for three or four days and then they die.

"We had hoped you would be spared. If we had been sure of the danger we never would have allowed you in here. However, the disease is probably rampant among the countryside and in the Onoshe anyway. Now that you are here, it is too late. If what you say is true, then the lives of our people are also in danger."

"Do they always die?" Anam asked slowly.

Mehi shook his head and pointed to a young woman standing in the doorway. "As you can see, they do not always die. However, the sickness always comes upon them. In nearly all cases, they are lost. On about the third or fourth day, if they are to live, their health begins to improve. If not, they simply continue to wither away."

"What can be done?"

"Nothing. We have tried many things; drugs, every sort of natural product, even magic."

Anam brightened. "You have not tried prayer? You have not tried to reach out to God?"

"Until today, we did not even know God cared. We felt it was part of the evil placed upon us by God."

Anam excused himself and organized a hasty meeting with Paluqua and Togorasom. They soon understood the 'invisible enemy'.

"Should we get out of this place?" Paluqua asked.

"It is too late," Togorasom said. "Where would you go? You have all been filled with this. Leaving this place now would be the worse choice for, soon, you shall all be sick. You could neither defend yourself from the elements nor from the Onoshe. We would be totally open to attack."

"But, what can we do?" she asked a bit frantically. "We are all standing at death's door."

"Not all," Togorasom said. "You will only be touched by this sickness. The other women will truly suffer."

"I don't understand. Why should I be spared?"

"Because of the healing Orioni brought to you. Do not become alarmed. This sickness will not result in death, but is for the glorification of God. All you can do now is stay in prayer and see what God shall do."

By the following morning most of the women had begun to

experience the first phase of the disease; nausea and dizziness. There was nothing that could be done with them, but to put them to bed and offer them drink. For the most part, food would not stay down. Zoana, Umfuwadea and Crazon were deep in a troubled sleep and bathed in sweat, one of the last phases. In the end, they would lay in a deathlike state, their skin would grow cool and their breathing would be very shallow. At that time they would either begin to improve or their lives would slowly trickle away, which could take several weeks.

The Denarites were extremely helpful in caring for the stricken women. They organized a schedule so that several would be on hand at all times. By that night, everyone of the women were sick, except, as Togorasom had noted, Paluqua. Her strength actually seemed to increase in proportion to the need of the others.

The next morning Anam sought out Mashua. He found him sitting quietly alone.

Mashua stood up as Anam approached him. "If you hate me, I can understand. I have led you to your destruction." Anam tried to speak, but Mashua cut him off. "I know you will say it is God's plan or something like that. But, still, I feel I must bear the blame. I should have warned them the first time. I should not have allowed you in when you came back. Now, we are all helpless. If those women die, your great hope of finding a home is destroyed. I wish there were something I could do." He stopped for a moment. "I can think of nothing I can do, but I will do whatever you ask."

"Will you do whatever I ask?"

"I will do anything. I even offer my life!"

"I have something for you to do. I need you to deny everything you just told me."

"But...Anam...I cannot deny it."

Anam appeared to be angry. "Then you have lied to me. You gave me your word!"

"But...but...Anam... I cannot deny the truth. I am in charge here. Therefore, I am at fault."

"Mashua, you cannot deny any truth because you have not even accepted the truth yet. You gave me your word to do anything I asked. You even offered to die, for no reason at all. If you cannot accept the truth then, perhaps, you are right! These people will die! I will be broken and heavy with sadness, yes." By now Anam was shaking and pointing his finger at Mashua. "But, I will not be destroyed! Even if I die, I will not be destroyed. The Lord has promised to lead me to a new home. But, that is not my great hope. My great hope is that someday I will be with him. Tell me, brother, what hope do you have? To live a few more years before you rot in this cave or the Onoshe tear you apart?" Mashua was slumped against the wall, head down in his hands. He looked up. "You have no hope, Mashua!" Anam turned around and walked away. Just before he disappeared around the corner he looked back at a frightened, gaping man. "But God has something to give you. You only need to reach out and ask for it."

On his return to join Paluqua and the others he came upon Magnon. Except to have seen him in passing during the past two days they had made no effort to communicate. To do so would have been impossible as Mashua and Mehi were the only ones that understood this common language Anam had learned. Besides, Zoana had already explained to him that he was a troublemaker. Anam felt he had much more important issues to deal with than this pest. When Magnon saw him coming along the corridor, he stood up and approached him. Anam was wary but he stopped and offered him his attention.

Magnon uttered a few words that made no sense to Anam. He moved his hands about and tried to symbolize what he meant. Anam shrugged his shoulders, but was still attentive. Magnon finally, with a disgusted look on his face, shook his head and walked away. Anam was left feeling terrible that Magnon's efforts were so fruitless. He said a silent prayer for him as he continued on.

When he entered the assembly hall, where all the women were staying, he was instantly overtaken by the heavy burden of death. Three Denarite men slowly moved between the rows of women wiping the sweat from some with damp cloths, adjusting the coverings over others, occasionally offering a drink of water to one or another who was still conscious. Ernie and Paluqua sat slumped against a wall, she resting her head on his shoulder. They had been up since early morning. The children, Anam knew, were being kept in a separate area.

"Good morning, Anam," said Ernie as Anam approached them. "Mehi was here just now. He spent time with the women for a minute, stared at us even in his blindness, and left. He was weeping. Is there nothing we can do? And, yes, before you ask, we have been praying."

Anam sat down. "Now all I can do is clutch to the word of Togorasom and wait. It has taken me a long time to realize just how much I can trust him. Have you seen him this morning?"

Ernie shook his head, indicating he had not. As if on cue, Togorasom walked into the room. He stood in the doorway for a minute with his eyes closed, obviously praying. He then strode over to where the other three were sitting.

"Good morning!" he nearly yelled at them. His voice cut through the dismal quietness like a quiver full of flying arrows. A smile was on his face. Anam shushed him. "But, Anam, cannot you see the beauty of all this? Very soon God shall display his glory and a new day shall dawn for both Denarite and Rasomite." He had not toned his voice down at all.

The three of them, Paluqua as well, as she was roused, winced at his brashness. "Don't you recall how I said that none of them shall perish? I even told you that from every one of them shall spring forth kingdoms. Did you forget? Oh, I'm sure you remember." Anam tried to wave his head yes and no at once and, instead, ducked his head into his hands. "And how can you doubt him?" he continued looking now at Paluqua. "Only a very few days ago the Lord took your broken body and refit it better than before." He chuckled. "If he can do that, can't he heal a little fever?"

Paluqua acted apologetic. "I'm just tired, Togorasom. I've been up most of the night helping to care for them."

"But why? The Denarites are doing fine. You should allow them the chance to help. We are their guests. Besides, in a few days the women will be up and running around and you'll be sleeping in a corner somewhere."

Paluqua looked around the room. A few of the women were still stirring a bit, but most of them were totally unconscious.

Togorasom took a deep breath and stood up. "Why do you continue to doubt." He walked slowly back out of the room.

A few moments later, Mashua entered the room and approached Anam. As he passed near Zoana he stopped, took her hand, and looked on her face for several minutes. He finally brought her near-lifeless hand to his lips and then carefully lay it back alongside her. Arising, he scanned the dark and dismal situation. Finally, he continued moving toward Anam.

"I cannot understand how you can see any hope in a place like this." His eyes were moist and it was difficult for him to speak. "I have seen death take them too many times before and we always hoped. Our hope had nothing to do with their survival. Why do you believe your hope is of more value than mine?"

"Because our hope," Anam explained, "does not hinge on their survival. We have already been given eternal life. Our hope is in the one who controls their lives."

"I do not understand. You have indicated they will not die. Is this only a symbol that they will live somewhere beyond this life?"

"More than that. Togorasom has said they will all survive."

With that revelation, Mashua looked even more doubtful. "You have faith in the words of a mere child? Is he your messenger from God?"

Anam smiled. "Togorasom has been with God."

Mashua started to turn away. "Each time you say something to make these things more clearly known, I am more deeply confused." Then he noticed Paluqua intently watching him. "This, I suppose, is your woman. Why is she not ill like all the others?" Anam opened his mouth to speak. "Never mind!" Mashua cut him off. "I am certain your explanation would more thoroughly confuse me. I am confused enough for now. Anyway, the reason I came here is to offer an invitation. We are organizing a hunting party. I am aware of your concern over meat so I will not ask that you even help slay animals. However, there is a place we go for herbs. Unless we come upon some fowl or other we shall forego that this time. Some of our men cannot go as they are tired." He indicated those still attending the sick. "We would appreciate your help."

"Of course we will go with you. You have been very generous in bringing us in, feeding us, and caring for us. It is a small thing for us to help."

Mashua gripped Anam's hand and left. He sat down next to Paluqua again.

"What is it, husband?" she asked so he would interpret.

Anam explained all that had been discussed to her and Ernie, ending with the invitation. "You must get your things together quickly so we can be prepared to leave." It was normal for Anam to want to include his wife in his plans, especially in this little adventure.

"That would probably not be the best wisdom, Anam," she said. He looked at her for explanation. "These people don't allow their women out on such things. The plan today is to go gather some food and you will all need to be protected from the Onoshe. My presence would simply cause undo alarm and detract from the purpose." Anam shook his head and began to counter. "No dear," she continued, "I have already decided. When these people grow more accustomed to us I will go." She yawned and stretched her arms. "Besides, I am very tired and need some rest. I am so weary I would just be a burden. Also, I want to stay here and await the fulfillment of Togorasom's promises."

"All right," admitted Anam. "I am defeated." He turned to Ernie to speak.

"Of course I am going," he said quickly. "I want to show these people some of my cooking skills and there are things I need for that. I have my knife. As soon as I get my sack, I am ready to go."

The rain finally had stopped. The ground was still wet. One needed caution in walking or he'd find himself in a mud hole. However, Mashua knew the path so he led most of the time and the group stayed fairly dry. The group consisted of Mashua in the lead, followed by Anam and Ernie, four other men and Magnon at the end. They all were aware with the weather clearing the Onoshe would also be roving for food as well so everyone was alert. Mashua had instructed them that as long as they stayed together and paid attention they should be fine. The Onoshe normally only attacked small groups or individuals. Everyone was equipped with a bow and quiver of arrows as well as a hand ax which could be used for close in defense and harvesting. All of the Denarites carried a broad sword. Everyone also packed two large leather bags for carrying the harvest back to the cave.

Mashua and Anam spoke quietly to each other.

"I do not understand," Mashua said, "how so strong and normally healthy a race of people can survive on a diet of so little. This is, we believe, what normally kills our women from this plague. Once they can no longer eat, they soon starve. However, your women do not appear sickly. It's as if they were in a deep sleep except for those still in turmoil. You eat no meat, only cheese or milk on occasion, and survive often on a handful of beans and nuts."

Anam explained, "the body seems very adaptable. If it

normally lives on a scanty diet it does quite well. When we have plenty, that is, when we eat like normal people, we become heavy and sluggish. God has blessed us with good health so we seldom fall prey to the normal problems you may have. As far as meat, the Lord has told us this is not for us. We don't eat meat so we can show a difference between us and everyone else. He has also shown us that animals are our little brothers. Because of the way our society is, we must make use of their products for things such as the feathers on our arrows and the leather bags. We do eat a piece of fish on occasion and, rarely, some fowl."

"If we ate as you eat, would we become like you?"

"Did God tell you this? We live like we do because our Lord has said so. When we disobey, we bring problems upon ourselves. Usually when we follow a course of action, it comes after much prayer. Don't attempt to live someone else's covenant with God."

"What is a covenant?"

"It is a word from God that if you will obey him, he will keep his promises to you."

As Mashua and Anam continued their conversation and their trek over the rugged ground, Ernie began to lag behind. His age and lack of sleep the previous night were taking their toll. This caused the rest of the group to fall back as well. Magnon, still in the rear, urged Ernie to move along more quickly, but he still could not keep up. They finally reached a point where they were so far behind Magnon did not dare call out to Mashua for fear of the Onoshe being alerted. He instructed one of the other men to run ahead to Anam and Mashua and he did so. By this time, the other two were at least a hundred paces ahead. Once the group was reunited, Anam cautioned Ernie that it was of the utmost of importance for the group to stay close as they were in dangerous territory. When they left for the last leg of the trip, Anam put Ernie between himself and Mashua and so they finished the final mile of the trip out.

The field they reached was quite bountiful. They filled their bags with potatoes, radishes, and carrots left from the previous fall as well as several green leafy plants. This had been, according to Mashua, a cultivated area once long ago. It was now mostly grown up in weeds, but there was still plenty for them to carry.

By the time Ernie had filled his second bag, he was exhausted. Mashua, through Anam, informed him that they would take a break before making the return trip. Ernie propped himself up by a tree and instantly fell into a deep sleep as Anam and Mashua continued their discussion and the other five men played a dice game and took turns standing guard. The nap, however, was cut short when Ernie, suspecting something, snapped awake. For a few moments he could not understand why he had woken up, then he spotted a movement in the branches of a tree near him. Three Onoshe all sat on one lower branch, partially camouflaged by the leaves. They were no more than twenty feet from him. Though they appeared harmless, like great monkeys only interested in watching his actions, he knew how they had attacked Zoana, and he knew their brutal history. The rest of his group were behind him and he did not know how to signal to them his predicament. Then an idea struck him. Reaching into the inside of his shirt to a little cloth pocket he carefully slid out his favorite weapon. He'd never used it in a circumstance like this, however. Carefully positioning his fingers upon the instrument he began to blow a sweet melody. The rest of the men, considering this to be normal activity, enjoyed the music but paid no attention to Ernie's distress. The Onoshe were enraptured by the beautiful sounds they heard.

This continued for several minutes until Anam announced they must return and quickly approached Ernie. Ernie looked up at Anam and then, nervously, pointed to the overhanging branch. It was barren. As soon as Anam had started to move around, the Onoshe had retreated into the denseness of the upper branches. Anam looked where his friend indicated, but seeing nothing, offered his hand to help him up.

Ernie quickly gathered his harvest together, strung it over his back, and headed out, requiring the others to run to catch up with him. It wasn't until they were out of the field and onto the path when Ernie related his story to Anam. Soon everyone was informed of the incident. When it came time for a break, Ernie suggested they continue traveling until they were safely back home.

However, during the return trip, Mashua suggested to Anam a side trip as he wanted to show him something special. They reached the foot of a cliff about a hundred feet tall. It was not a direct ascent for there was a path of sorts which weaved back and forth and arrived at the top. Ernie protested he simply did not have the energy to mount this challenge and still make the trip home. So Anam and Mashua made the climb, leaving the others at the bottom to relax and guard the food.

For these stout men the traveling was fairly easy, and in a few minutes, Mashua showed Anam a majestic view of the valley. Mashua stood by silently watching Anam's mouth agape as he tried to take it all in. His eyes started at the point where they had first arrived, the great rock wall which separated this valley from the rest of the world. It began far out of sight and weaved around the valley to end at the twin mountains Orioni had pointed out. It was an imposing sight to behold. The mountains now loomed somewhat closer than they had appeared from his vantage point a few days before.

Now Anam could see at the hollow between the two mountains a great city, apparently deserted. He was eager to explore that empty city. Beyond the city he could see a thin blue line which indicated the sea. He had not seen the sea for several years. It would be a delight to bathe in its waters, to watch the sun set over it. He could nearly see Paluqua and himself walking hand-in-hand on the sea shore with the sea gulls clearing the way for them. As if able to read his mind, Mashua spoke up. "As a child I used to run and play on the sea shore with my friends. My parent's home was near the water. I also watched our trading ships come and go. We sold grain for near the city were vast fields of oat and wheat. Our main partners were the Isles of Aboti, which mainly consist of three islands a few days' journey across the water. We all hope that they are safe, of course. I've never been to the islands but had hoped to go there. Now, I cannot even dare go to the city."

"What is the name of the city?"

"It is called 'Ifintim', which means 'Last Chance' or 'Last Hope'. It was named by our ancient relatives who fled here to escape the wars of some distant land that I know very little about. You see, Anam, we called it Last Chance and now even that has passed. We would be better off somewhere fighting a war than here living in a stinking cave afraid for our lives of a bunch of demons."

Anam considered the similarity of the histories of the Denarites and the Rasomites as he continued to gaze across the valley and listen to his friend.

"Have you ever tried to return to Ifintim?" he asked.

"Never. There were a few who were like renegades and left us, some to go to Ifintim. However, we never heard of them again. Even Magnon holds so great an anger in his heart that he has threatened to leave. But, he is not a fool. We have always reasoned with him and changed his mind."

"Once you mentioned Magnon as your brother. Is he a blood relative?"

"Anyone related to me has long since died. I call him my brother as we are close and always contending for leadership, but he has too much anger to be a good leader and most of the people know it. We call Mehi our father as we respect him and I have no other to call father." Mashua stood up. "We need to get back to the others. It is not fair of us to stay here too long."

"I agree," replied Anam. He pointed off across the valley to Ifintim. "Do you see near the shore a nice house with trees in the yard? Listen, I hear a dog barking and children laughing." Mashua looked toward the city. "Oh, look, I see a young man and woman sitting on a blanket under the tree. They are holding hands and smiling at each other. But, they've been interrupted. A young boy has pounced upon the man's back, insisting he play with him. And there are plots of flowers all over the yard. The young woman has just picked up her baby to feed it. And now the man and little boy are hugging one another. How beautiful. Oh, did you hear the boy? He said, 'daddy, I love you'. Now they are walking back to see the woman and baby." Anam leaned over farther, pretending to see better. Mashua, a little confused, did the same. "Why, Mashua, that young man is you. He seems so happy."

Anam stood up a moment later, heading back down the path. Mashua stood, as though riveted to the earth, staring toward the city. After a few paces, Anam looked back and politely called him, but he still did not respond, so he left him alone.

Anam lay quietly cuddling with Paluqua, staring into the near-darkness. They had been given private quarters, and though the space was cramped, they had no need for extra space. The only light filtered from a lone torch a few paces down the hallway. Now he was completely awake. Paluqua, who still felt obligated to spend most of the day and night with her bedridden sisters, was in a deep sleep. He carefully slid away from her and left the room.

It was very quiet throughout the cave. When it was this quiet one could hear a conversation anywhere, except far away at the entrance. He stole into the main assembly room. The three Denarite men who were on duty were sound asleep as was to be expected. There was nothing more they could do with the women as now they were all in a deep coma. He continued along the hallway toward the entrance.

This was the only place that was well-lit and showed any sign of life. The two men on guard duty spoke with him briefly in the few words Mashua had taught them. Anam indicated he could not get to sleep.

"When is morning?" he asked. He received no response beyond their shrugging of shoulders. "The sun. When is morning?"

One of the men drew a line in the sand and then a circle a little below the line, indicating it was nearly dawn. Anam thanked them and they returned to their posts. He sat down on the rocks, having an expectation of things about to happen. A few minutes later, Magnon entered. He was glad to see Anam up and they shook hands. Magnon sat on the ground near Anam's feet and lowered his head. He sat this way for a long time, and Anam wasn't sure if he were dozing, thinking, praying, or all three. Magnon finally looked up at Anam. The deep furrows in his forehead indicated he had important things to say to Anam but couldn't find the words. In frustration, he dropped his face towards the ground again. Anam slid off his seat and sat next to him. They sat this way, facing each other for a couple of minutes. Anam gently placed a hand on Magnon's shoulder.

"Almighty God, who created all language and all men, make it possible now for myself and this other child of yours to speak. Lord, you sent us here to lead this people to you. Help me, I beg you."

Magnon looked at Anam again. He thumped his palm against his bare chest. "I...Magnon." Anam nodded. They stared into each other's eyes for a moment and then Magnon again began to feel defeated.

Just then they heard the sound of someone shuffling along the hallway. Whoever it was proceeded with great difficulty. Mehi entered the room, hobbling and feeling his way along the rocks.

"Mehi!" Magnon leaped up and assisted the old man to join Anam and himself.

When they were all comfortable, Mehi reached over and felt of Anam's arm and face. This was the only way he could 'see'.

"I thought I would find you here," he said. "I was not sleeping well and so I was prompted to come down here. Mashua told me about what happened today with your friend and the Onoshe. He also told me about what you said about Ifintim. Why did you tell him these things?"

"Well," Anam began slowly, "it seems he has given up hope. I think you have all given up hope. God has encouraged me to help restore your hope."

"Do you believe we can ever go to Ifintim again?"

"I believe we shall all go to Ifintim in a few days. I believe your people and my people shall live there together." He spoke slowly so he would be certain Mehi understood him. "I believe your men shall marry our women and we shall become one people and this great valley will be a beacon for people everywhere to learn about God."

Mehi nodded. "I think you are right, young man." He spoke to Magnon for a minute, then turned back to Anam. "He says he could not sleep either and has some questions."

"I know. We were bound apart because we have no common language. I prayed for the Lord to help us find a way to speak. That's when you arrived. I believe God sent you here."

"He must have. It has been a long time since I have tried to walk that far unaided. God, I guess, can even use an old fool who isn't even certain God is there. I have some questions as well."

Magnon spoke to Mehi, who turned back to Anam. "He wants to know why you want to stay in this awful valley."

"Tell him God sent us here."

Mehi relayed the information which seemed to shock Magnon. Anam continued. "Ask him if he believes me."

"I have asked and he does believe you."

"Then why does he seem so surprised?"

The other two spoke for some time and finally Mehi looked back at Anam. "Hmm, let me try this. Since Magnon was a child he has hoped to get the Onoshe out of here and take back our land. We all have, but he has always had greater hope and been more desperate than us. Without even truly believing in a god, he has prayed to him to send someone to free this land. He believes that the gods, or your God, has answered his prayer."

"But, it appears, most of our people are dying. What does he think about that?"

They spoke again. Mehi reported. "He says no one in the

history of our time here, except for our enemies, has come across the mountains dividing us from the rest of the world. The only way in is by water. He is amazed. It is a miracle. Hmm. He says that before you came here he believed you would come, though no one else here did. He also says that no one believes these women will survive. He believes."

Magnon spoke again to the old man.

"He is very sorry for the evil he performed towards your women before. He could not contain his anger because, well…he would like to kill Mashua. He hopes he can do better for you in the future."

"I accept his apology, but he will also have to apologize to Zoana and the others."

"But, my friend, they are near death. How can he do that?"

"That's what you believe, Mehi. But, he and I do not."

Mehi told Magnon what Anam had said and he eagerly nodded his head.

"Ask him," said Anam, "if he is ready to believe in God." Mehi reported that he was ready. Anam had never led anyone like this with such a language problem. He had always had some sort of direct communication with the other person and had never needed an intermediary. "Mehi, tell Magnon to bow his head, close his eyes and repeat after me." Anam continued in short statements as Mehi interpreted and Magnon followed.

"God, our creator. I have come to you this morning to seek peace. I know you are present and listening. I have reached the time in my life when I need you. Show me you are truly my father and accept me as your son. Forgive me for those times when I have turned against you. Blot out all of my sins, Father. Let me be a body you can use for your purposes. Be the Lord of my life. Thank you."

They sat quietly for a few minutes as Anam and Magnon continued to pray. Finally, Anam opened his eyes and watched the other man.

Mehi spoke. "I see no difference in him. I know I felt nothing. But the words were awkward to speak."

"Awkward?"

"I felt uncomfortable saying words I didn't truly believe."

"But the words are true," replied Anam. "Perhaps it was conviction."

A flash of anger covered Mehi's face, but he quickly recovered. Magnon looked up at both of them. He smiled. He closed his eyes again for a moment and then spoke to Mehi.

Mehi reported to Anam. "He says there is a God. He has felt his presence. God is healing him of his anger and impatience." Then he spoke for himself. "I cannot understand how he felt anything. I said the same words he did and nothing happened to me."

"You did not believe the words spoken, Mehi. You told me so. If you profess words of love to a woman when you truly do not love her, do you suppose after mouthing the words you will become devoted to her?" Mehi shook his head. "They are mere words. We spoke them in two different tongues. There is nothing magical about the choice of words. The true work is done in the hearts of those who believe and is proven by the way they act. Tell Magnon he is my brother now and a true son of God and someday he will be with me before the throne of God in heaven."

When they were finished the three men stood up and Anam gave Magnon a brotherly hug. Magnon began to weep. Mehi simply shook his head and slowly walked away. When Magnon offered to help him, Mehi pushed him away and snapped some remark at him. Magnon stepped back and sadly watched the old man leave. Anam approached Magnon. Reaching up into the air with one hand he appeared to grasp something and then hold it tightly with both hands. Magnon knew Anam meant to say to hold on tightly to this that God had given him and not to be persuaded by others to go back.

The next two days crawled by. To those Rasomites who were still conscious, the others who were in deep sleep seemed to have the opportunity as there was nothing to do anyway. Anam thought it would be well if everyone began to learn this language as a common tongue. However, Mehi was actually angry over the changes taking place in Magnon. No one had ever enjoyed his constant battle with Mashua, which often erupted into physical harm as well. Now, however, the once devious and meddling man had turned peaceful and contemplative, spending most of his time alone with his new-found relationship with God. Magnon's trouble-making had previously been one of the few activities of interest to the otherwise boring existence of the Denarites.

Also, despite the help offered by the Rasomites to assist, not only with the sick women but with other common tasks among the cave dwellers, they were quickly wearing out their welcome. The subject was not approached directly, but Mashua and Mehi both made a point that supplies were quickly being consumed. Anam's explanation that four vegetarians and their children could not be responsible for this depletion fell on deaf ears.

As Mehi was not currently interested in uniting these people with a common language, Anam began training his three willing pupils as well as his children. They learned much more slowly than Anam had learned, as they had no previous knowledge of the language, and Anam was simply not as good a language instructor as Mehi.

Everyone began settling into a peaceful, though uncomfortable, existence with the Rasomites seldom leaving the assembly room and the Denarites rarely coming in. As the women were very deep into coma now, they were completely unable to eat and could only be forced to consume meager supplies of water. There was nothing the Denarites felt they could do, so they left them alone. The other four kept quite busy moving among the women and helping as they could; offering water, keeping their sleeping areas padded and, occasionally, bathing them.

Anam's people continued to wait on a full recovery for everyone. The Denarites waited as well, dubious that any would survive as they had all passed the time when recovery would start, if recovery was to happen.

Except for Magnon. He did not desire to upset the fragile community between the two races, but he wanted to show that his faith was in line with the Rasomites. He came and attempted to visit for a few minutes two or three times a day. His visits always began with handshakes and ended with hugs. Though only a minimum of words were expressed, they all appreciated his attempts.

On the third morning after Magnon's salvation, Anam noticed that Mashua and several of the other men were missing. He went to see Mehi.

"Good morning, father!" he said as he entered. Mehi lifted his head from where he sat slumped against the wall but made no other response. "Did you sleep well?" Anam stood in the doorway, awaiting an invitation. The old man merely shook his head from side to side. "I didn't mean to intrude, but I was curious as to where all the men have gone?"

"After food," he mumbled.

"We would have helped. I didn't realize supplies were so low again so soon."

Mehi mumbled something Anam could not understand.

"What was that?" he asked.

"I said they have gone hunting!"

"Oh, I see. There seems to be very little game in this valley. Is that because of the Onoshe?"

Mehi nodded. "They are mostly flesh-eating. They can run nearly as fast as a deer and will eat anything from bugs to human bones. I still say they are a curse from your God." They were both quiet for a moment. "Yes, I believe they are a curse from your God. The God you say is so wonderful. That sort of puts you and these demons on the same side, doesn't it?"

"I'm not here this morning to argue with you. You are wiser than to believe these things."

"These creatures have destroyed everything that I have ever loved. They have robbed me of my life. Once I was a teacher of culture and art. These are concepts these young people know little of."

"Why did you stop teaching them?"

"Because, well, these are things which have passed away. Why teach something to only build up false hopes?"

"You believe that your race will end in this cave?"

"I don't want to believe that." Tears were forming in the old man's eyes.

"Then whether or not it could ever come true, do not accept it. You know, I also come from a doomed and dying race. But, I would not accept it. Against the odds, I wanted the remnant of our people to not only survive, but to thrive."

"But, God has blessed you."

"Yes, he has. I have faced death many times and felt the pit of depression, but I have never completely given up hope. And now I have brought that hope to you. If you can't accept that from me, accept it from your own wayward son, Magnon. His torch of hope has been relit, but it seems, you not only desire hopelessness, you also want to surround yourself with hopeless people. If a stranger with a promising story cannot convince you, then go to your own people. If you want to know why this man believes in restoration, it's because he has nothing else to hope for." With that, Anam left.

Sweat covered Mashua, but it wasn't heat or labor which were causing him problems. All the men felt it. They were afraid. There had been no sightings of Onoshe or of any game. The area's lifelessness was a perfect indication of their enemy's presence. There were only four men accompanying Mashua and, though they were only a mile or so from home, it seemed too great an expanse to cover in a hurry.

"Let us return," one of the men suggested to Mashua. "There is no game. I would rather eat the Rasomite's stew again than stay here any longer."

Mashua nodded. "We'll try again another day. Let us go back."

The enemy moved quickly. The attack came when they had least expected it; in an open meadow. The Onoshe appeared from the forest on three sides of the small group, blocking their path of retreat. Already, at least twenty had appeared and were moving cautiously toward them. The Denarites had remained motionless for a few seconds, hoping that this was merely a threatening gesture as often happened. When Mashua gave the order to fire, everyone responded quickly. Due, however, to the distance and the nervousness of the archers, their accuracy was terrible in the first round. One of the attackers was wounded in the arm, the rest of the arrows flew clear. The second round was much better; all five arrows were true. It was too late, though. The attackers were upon them.

The Denarites could not communicate due to the howling of the Onoshe. When the Onoshe were too close to fire upon, a great surge of power came upon the Denarites and they produced their swords. In a few moments they had made a circle with their backs toward each other and brandished their weapons formidably. The Onoshe were impressed and backed off a few paces, but were still prepared to fight. The Denarites began producing their own threatening noises and casting insults, but the Onoshe paid them no mind.

Suddenly, one attacked. Though he moved quickly, the swordsman was quicker. In a moment, the ape-man's head rolled to the ground. This action produced a great deal of howling and yelping from the attackers. They backed off more.

"Cover me," said one of Mashua's men. He and one of the others backed into the circle and lay down their swords. They began to fire arrows into the pack. They did well. One after another of the Onoshe fell to the ground. The numbers were becoming more favorable. Soon the death toll had reached ten. Two others had fled with severe wounds. The confidence among the Denarites was soaring. They had never engaged in such an overwhelming battle with this level of success. The flight of their enemies was expected.

However, they did not run. Suddenly, the Denarites were engulfed. The swords crashed down again and again. The two men in the middle, who supposed they were safe, reacted too slowly. While the other three were distracted, they were snatched from the circle and were killed instantly. The stench of human blood in the air called the rest of the pack from the battle to join the feast.

Mashua's desire was to dive into the mob with his sword and hack away at them until he also collapsed. But he knew it was too late to save his friends. The three survivors fled.

Retreat was easy, while their enemies were distracted with their devouring. Mashua and the other two men ran and stumbled back to the cave. Exhausted, their bodies collapsed on the floor of the entryway area. The door slammed shut behind them as they were surrounded by help.

One of the men had been wounded quite severely on his arm by his own sword when they were swarmed during the Onoshe's last effort. The men washed it out several times and wound it with a bit of cloth. The blood quickly soaked up the cloth and began to gush down his arm. They lay him on the floor and elevated his injured arm to slow the bleeding. However, they didn't know what else to do as there were no medical supplies available. The man began to drift off into sleep due to the loss of blood. It was then Togorasom arrived.

Saying nothing, he went to the side of the injured man and sat. Togorasom bowed his head for a moment and prayed. Everyone backed away from this scene to see what would happen next. The boy placed the palms of his hands on the man's cheeks to keep his attention and spoke to him in the Rasomite tongue. The man understood a miracle was about to take place, but could not understand the boy's words.

Togorasom placed his right hand directly over the blood-drenched piece of cloth that still ran rampant with blood. He looked the man in the eye and said, "Maka Ta!" which in the Denarite tongue means, "Be Healed!" This he said loud enough for all to hear. Then, he smiled at the man, stood up, wiped the blood from his hand on his own clothes and departed.

The blood had stopped flowing. Mashua was first at his side and tore the cloth from his arm. At first, all that could be seen was blood, so it appeared nothing much had happened beyond the stoppage of blood. More clean water was poured over the wound to rinse away the blood. The gash in the man's arm was gone. Besides the residue of blood, there was no trace the man had ever been hurt. A great fear and silence came upon everyone there.

"Magnon!" a voice called out from the darkness. "Magnon, wake up!" He sat up from where he slept and nervously looked around. The room he slept in was not a large room. It was occupied by six men and these sleeping men covered most of the floor. A small torch near the doorway lit the room and he could see no one else was stirring.

"Quickly, follow me!" came a clearly audible voice from seemingly nowhere as he still could not detect where it was coming from. It seemed it came from inside his head, but it sounded so clear. He arose and crept slowly and quietly into the hallway. Here it was much darker, and he paused both so his eyes could adjust to the dark and also to receive another instruction from his late night visitor. "Come on!" Not knowing where to go, he picked his way through the hallway toward the front. This seemed more and more as a dream.

When he reached the front he was, for a moment, alarmed that the entrance sat wide open and there were no guards present. Feeling the more that this must be a dream he shrugged off his fear. "This way." The voice seemed to come from outside the open door. He reached for one of the two large torches, but heard the voice again. "That you will not need. Only follow me." Trained to be fearful outside, especially after yesterday's attack, his body actually quivered as he left the cave.

A few paces outside the doorway, he stopped. He felt foolish and afraid, wanting greatly to run back inside. "Who is there?" he called out. He thought he heard a noise further ahead so he moved forward. The sound was merely the rustle of leaves in the breeze. Now out in the open he shivered because of the cool, damp breeze which had come up. "Is anyone there?" he called out again.

He heard a creaking sound from behind him and whirled about just as the doorway slammed shut. "No! No!" he called out. "I am outside! Don't lock me out!" He looked at the window above the doorway and saw no one. He hurried to the other opening and it too was vacant. "Help me! I need to get back in!" he yelled only inches from the window. There was no response.

Gathering his wits and reconsidering his situation, he became certain this could not be a dream. In a moment, he felt mentally stronger, though still concerned. None of this made any sense, but it was too realistic to be a dream. He sat on the ground by the entrance and huddled into a ball against the cold. "Yes, Lord," he suddenly said quietly, "this is something. I don't know what. I'll do whatever you say." Sitting with his chin pressed against his bare chest and his eyes closed, shivering, he was suddenly bathed in warmth. Opening his eyes and seeing he was covered with light, he glanced up.

Before him stood what appeared to be a man. He wore a gold breastplate, a leather skirt and sandals. His flesh glowed like the sun, and it was from him the light and warmth came. Magnon was speechless.

"Do not be afraid!" the being commanded.

"But who…what are you?" Magnon was finally able to stutter.

"I am a guide. I have been sent to lead you where the Lord wants you to be."

"I don't understand. Who are you?"

"My name is Orioni. I am your brother. Come, let us go!" The angel turned and headed away. Both from curiosity and obedience, as well as a desire to share in his warmth, Magnon followed.

In the morning, when Mashua arose, he went looking for Magnon with the idea that they should inventory their present food stores and determine if another hunt should be organized. No one, of course, knew where he was. Mashua, supposing finally he had gone outside went first to the front and, after receiving assurances that the door had not been opened recently, went looking for the two men that had been on duty the night before. They were sleeping, but on being aroused, assured him they had not seen Magnon since the evening before and that no one had gone out during the night, nor had the door even been opened.

By this time Mashua was becoming increasingly frustrated. Everyone in the cave, including the Rasomites, had searched the entire premises. It seemed as if to many, Magnon had vanished into the air. He queried Mehi who was as amazed as anyone else and had no answers. However, he did suggest to Mashua that the boy, Togorasom, be spoken to.

"What's the good of that?" Mashua snapped, increasingly belligerent.

"I don't know," said the old man slowly. "It just seems to me that he is a very wise young man. Besides, you saw for yourself what he did for Ahohiel's injury."

"Hmmp. Performing magic on someone's cut arm and helping me find my vagabond brother are not quite the same."

"Anyway, it would do no harm."

"Or good. Besides, he knows Magnon is missing. If he knows his whereabouts, he could just offer the information."

"Then go away!" Mehi snapped.

"What?" Mashua was taken aback.

"You asked me for my advice. I've got no idea where Magnon has gone, but I gave you my advice. If I had told you to do something difficult, you would have eagerly obeyed. But, since you hate this boy, you refuse."

"I don't hate Togorasom," he replied dumbly.

"Well then, go talk to him."

He found Togorasom with the other Rasomites in the assembly room. He approached Anam.

"I know I asked earlier," he said apologetically, "but do you have any idea where Magnon could be?"

"I'm sorry, Mashua, we seem to have looked everywhere and come up with nothing. I'm sure he'll turn up and this will make sense when he does."

Mashua nodded and turned away. Then he turned back and looked at Togorasom. "Do you suppose he would know?"

Anam asked Togorasom if he had any more information concerning Magnon.

"Ask Mashua why he would like to know."

Anam repeated the question.

"Well, because...I need to find him. I don't understand where he could be." Mashua was frustrated at the question.

Anam interpreted and passed back Togorasom's response with a smile. "He wants to know if you are certain where you are."

Mashua began to become angry. "I knew if I came in here and asked you for help, all I would receive would be stupid answers."

"Let's play for real, Mashua," said Anam. "You have shown me you could care less about Magnon, especially now that he has found salvation." He then took a very serious tone. "Have you done something with Magnon? Have you slain him or driven him away and now you are only making a show of concern? He was here last night and prayed with us. You showed no interest in him then. Many times the last couple of days, he has tried to talk to you, but you always push him away and treat him rudely. What have you done?"

Mashua could not believe his ears at Anam's accusation. "No! No, I have done nothing. I am only concerned and amazed at where he could be. I have not seen him since last night." He began to back away towards the doorway, but as he moved back, he approached the place where Zoana lay. He looked down upon her for a moment. "Zoana." He spoke in his own language to her and then, sadly, turned and walked from the room.

Anam explained what he had accused Mashua of. Then he added that he didn't truly believe Mashua had brought any harm upon Magnon but only wanted him to focus on how he had treated him. "I am sure that Magnon's safe, somewhere, and will return to us."

But, Magnon did not return that night. The following morning Mashua again spoke to Mehi about his concerns.

"I am afraid that somehow Magnon left the cave. Perhaps the men were lying and fell to sleep. I don't know. Perhaps they aided his escape for how could the door get closed? I don't know. But, if he has gone out there, his life is in grave danger."

"Mashua, you are worrying about something you cannot fix. One man alone outside could very easily hide from the Onoshe for quite a long time. You know, you have done so yourself."

Mashua was a little relieved. "This is true, what you say."

"However," Mehi continued, "If the Onoshe found him, he

would be totally defenseless. They would kill him instantly." Now Mashua grew alarmed again. "But, in the first place, why does that concern you? You hated him. You never approved of his ideas. You have said many times in the heat of anger you would like to kill him."

"But father, you are unfair. These were words, as you said, spoken in anger. How can I be held in account of them? Magnon himself was always angry and spoke the same words of me."

"That is true. But, you know, in the last few days many times he tried to speak kindly to you. You were always harsh with him. But, what does that matter to you? He is gone now. I was trying to tell you before you stopped me, whether he lives or whether he dies, he is out of your control."

"Then what should I do?"

"I told you what to do! I sent you to the boy. You treated him rudely as well and said he was stupid. Why do you ask for my advice? You want no one's advice! You want someone to make you feel important. But, you want to make everyone else feel terrible. You are a strong man. You are a wise leader. You have done many great things. There! Do you feel important? I hope you feel wonderful. Your father is nearly dead of old age. Your brother is probably dead and fulfills the needs of some ape-man's belly. The woman you claimed to have loved is on the verge of death. Your people are nearly perished. Soon, perhaps, you'll be the only one left. Then, you can be truly great and important. You and your pride can keep each other company."

"How can you be so cruel? These things are not my fault."

Mehi settled back against the wall and relaxed. "I know, Mashua. These things are not your fault. But, that is the difference between a man and a great leader." He grew silent.

"I don't understand."

"My son, another trait of a leader is that he must admit there are things he does not understand. But, let me explain this. A leader is willing to accept the blame for things which are not his fault. He also is willing to admit there are things he does not understand and will accept the help from those who do. Now, please go away and let me rest a bit."

"Yes, father. Only one last question. Why have your feelings seemed to have changed these last few days?"

Mehi chuckled slightly. "You still are so blind." He grew silent and seemed to be sleeping so Mashua stood up. "Have you seen none of the things which have taken place around here? It begins to seem so clear. Also, my heart is broken over how I have treated my son. But, something else has happened." A smile had crossed his face. "Anam has renewed an old hope inside of me. He has promised to take me home to Ifintim."

The sound of snoring convinced Mashua the meeting was over, but, rather than departing, he sat and watched Mehi and mulled over those things he had said for a long time.

Anam was dozing in the mid-day, something he rarely did. Ernie and Paluqua were working with the cooks to prepare dinner. Togorasom was in Anam's private room, as it provided one of the few secluded areas he could pray in solitude. Anam woke up when Mashua entered the room. Mashua looked to be emotionally destroyed.

"Mashua why are you so troubled?"

He slowly walked towards Anam and sat down, staring off into space. Anam allowed him the silence for some time and, finally, repeated his question. The two men continued to sit in silence until, at last, Mashua took a deep breath and looked at Anam.

"I am finally beginning to understand something. There are a few things in this life that we will never figure out. We just have to believe that God is in charge and do what we can." Anam nodded to encourage him. "If one believes in God and an afterlife, this life becomes quite meaningless except as a testing place to prepare us to face God." He smiled. "I have been asking this dumb question about what I have to do to believe in God and there really is no answer. I just need to choose to believe in God. This leaves me with the problem of what to do next, after I believe." He shook his head as if he was even confusing himself. "The answer is that I must make another choice. I must choose to keep believing him." He grew silent and then a little agitated. "But, Anam, this is at once impossible to comprehend and very simple. What should I do?" He gazed earnestly into Anam's eyes. "Can you tell me what to do?"

Anam nodded and put a hand on Mashua's shoulder. "Yes, I can, my friend. Are you ready?" Mashua nodded. "The time has come for you to choose. You must answer your own question." For a moment Mashua again began to look sad and depressed. "Are you going to continue to trust yourself or are you ready to trust God?"

"But, Anam, how can I trust that which I cannot even see?"

"Mashua, I cannot convince you of what to do. You have seen our faith in God. You have seen God's power demonstrated. You have heard his promises. You have been given a choice. When are you going to stop gathering information and do something? If you cannot believe him for his promises here and later on, at least believe him for the miracles you have seen with your own eyes. Believe him for what he has done in other peoples' lives. Ask Ahohiel how he feels. He has no answers, but that's fine, because once he saw, he had no questions."

"Ahohiel is a believer?"

Anam laughed. "Mashua, you're missing the whole thing. Not only does Ahohiel believe, but he's been telling everyone. No one understands, they just give God the credit. How could he not believe? He saw with his own eyes and felt with his own body what happened."

Mashua stood up, ensured Anam he would return, and left the room. He was back a few minutes later.

"I have spoken with Ahohiel."

"Still gathering information?" Spoke Anam as Mashua sat down by him. "Still trying to understand?"

He sat silent a bit longer. "But, how can I know for certain? How can I know for sure these things are true?"

Anam shook his head. "You cannot. You have already seen more than many believers will ever see. This has not convinced you. Most come to God only with the expectation of divine love and guidance and a hope in a future life free from this world. They neither see nor expect miracles to happen or prophecies to unfold. However, your heart is too hard. You are confusing me, Mashua. It almost seems the more the Lord shows you, the more frustrated and less convinced you become. Why do you play this game with God? Every moment you waste is one more thing to cause you shame and a need to repent when you decide. And, God forbid, you turn your back on him now, the greater shame you must carry and the greater condemnation you shall receive in the afterlife. What are you trying to do?"

"I must be certain!" he said firmly.

"You cannot be certain. You simply must decide."

Mashua actually began shaking due to his great frustration. "How can I decide until I am certain?" he said angrily.

"I have said again and again, you cannot ever be certain. I am certain, but only because of my faith. I could be terribly misguided. If this is what you wait for, you shall die and go to Hell. There's nothing else I can do. I cannot serve God to you like one serving tea."

"But what if you are wrong? What if, as you suggest, you are misguided?"

"Then I die a fool. I have wasted myself on an empty cause, but even then I have done no great damage. I have been able to relieve this place of a little suffering. My bones become dust and my flesh food for the birds. It is over. Now let me ask you. What if you are wrong? Which of us shall suffer the greater?"

Mashua opened his mouth to speak and suddenly seemed to realize the choices he was being offered. He sat for a moment with his mouth opened.

Anam reached out and lay a hand on his shoulder. "Father, there is no more I can do for now. I commend his spirit over to you. I ask you to deal with him, Lord. Thank you."

Mashua prepared to speak. "I'm sorry, my friend," said Anam. He shook his head. "No more. Not now. You know everything you need to know. If you have anything else to say I urge you to take your words directly to God and talk with him. And do not fear, he is anxious. Yes, he is excited to talk with you."

"But Anam," Mashua replied nervously, "I do not know how to talk to him. I do not even know how to begin. And, if I do, how will I know when he answers?"

"Mashua, you know how to talk with him," said Anam sternly, "because I have shown you. Besides, if you can talk to me, you can talk to him. Also," he smiled, "you will know when he answers. Now, I'm sorry, we'll be eating in a few minutes and I want to take care of these women before that. I also want a few moments of quiet. Will you respect that?"

Mashua nodded and stood up. "I believe I know what things I must do. And, yes, the time has come when I must face them alone." He turned and walked towards the door, stopped, and turned back. "One last bit of help, please. When you have your quiet time with God, pray for me." Anam nodded. "And," he continued, "keep praying." And he left.

Anam sat quietly for a minute, arose, and began to wander about the assembly room, slowly moving between the sleeping Rasomite women. As he moved about he offered a few drops of water to one, an extra blanket or bit of padding to another. At one point, he stopped. Despite his own and sixteen others' presence in the room, there was an awesome silence as still as death. A great burden was coming from inside of him which he could not understand. He knelt down and attempted prayer but even this action seemed empty and directionless. A sort of fear crept over him as he groped in his heart for the cause of his burden. He looked about the room and fearfully wondered if his concern was for these women, but it did not seem so. He heard the sound of footsteps and muffled voices coming down the hall.

Paluqua and Ernie entered the room, both were in good spirits. As soon, though, as they detected Anam's anguished appearance, they also grew concerned. Paluqua knelt by his side.

"What is it, husband? Why do you seem so troubled?"

He shook his head. "I do not know. I cannot understand. I just feel something awful inside."

She glanced about the room. "Where is Mashua? I thought he was with you."

"He was. We talked. I told him he needed to get alone with God."

"We came after you to let you know it is time to eat."

"Thank you, but what does this all mean?"

"We came here last to give you more time. We have not seen Mashua."

The three stood silently thinking, and suddenly it dawned on Anam what must have happened. He bolted from the room and ran to the front. The guards were in place and looked peaceful. Both were devouring huge bowls of Ernie's special stew.

"Where is Mashua?" Anam demanded.

They glanced nervously at each other and shrugged their shoulders. The guard at the side window was sitting away from his post in the path of the entryway. He was, therefore, closer to Anam. He attempted to sneak back to his protective hole, but Anam's arm reached out and snatched him by the arm, casting him to the floor and spilling his precious meal everywhere.

"Where is Mashua?" he repeated loudly. The man could not move as his attacker sat on him with his huge hand nearly crushing the terrified man's head. The man waved his free arm toward the door.

"Mashua...he go." he sputtered.

Anam leapt to his feet and ordered them to open the door. By now a crowd had begun to gather. Paluqua held Anam's arm.

"Anam, listen to me." she said hysterically. "Don't do this. He was wrong to go, but don't you also be wrong. Don't go out there." He stared into her eyes, breathing deeply. "Please, don't go out there," she said more quietly. "You can accomplish more right here."

Mashua asked himself aloud why he had come outside. "What do you expect to accomplish? The best you can hope for is to hide out for a day or two and go back. This is the most foolish thing you've ever done. Do you expect to find Magnon? You fool, he surely is already dead." His chastisement against himself went on either vocally or in his mind for several hours as he walked.

It began to grow dark. He was well-armed as he carried a small cutting knife, a large carver, his broadsword, a bow and quiver full of arrows so full he would have to dump it in order to extract one shaft. He felt it was still suicide as he would never have time to defend himself if he were attacked by any great number.

When he thought, however, of his last battle, he felt great pleasure. It had never gone so well as on that day. The Onoshe deaths had come so easily as they had employed a tactic which had never been attempted before.

This futile aggression of his now, he felt, would all be worth it if he could only take one of them with him. He shuddered, however, when he remembered seeing his two comrades destroyed and listening to their terrifying screams as they were ripped apart. He ached to wipe out the Onoshe once and forever.

He had made a small fire. His enemy was afraid of fire. He had arrayed his weapons about him so he could easily grab one when needed. He covered himself with a dark blanket so he would not be an easily seen target. Despite the cool breeze, he made camp in an open field so he could not easily be surprised. But now, the surrounding darkness seemed lit up with their eyes merely waiting for him to drift off to sleep. Chills, not caused by the weather, crept over his flesh. He moved so close to the fire, he nearly scorched his flesh and covering.

But it had been a hard day. His body was weary from walking aimlessly. His eyes were heavy. Though he kept shaking off slumber, it finally caught him up and he drifted off to sleep.

He didn't know how long he'd been sleeping. Something ran across his leg. Instantly he was alert and reached for his sword. A hairy arm wrapped about his chest. His sword was gone. Quickly glancing at the ground, he could see all his weapons were gone. In the dim light, he could see their disgusting bodies encircling him. His assailant's ugly face stared into his, teeth glaring. He attempted to push the creature back, but it would not move. The hand moved from his chest to his throat. He screamed.

He was awake. It had merely been a dream. His weapons were still strewn about him. The fire was completely dead. He was sitting in an open field, clutching the blanket around his neck. The sun was just breaking over the horizon. He had slept late and was well-rested, except for the nightmare.

In his great haste to depart, he had spent the time ensuring that he was well-armed, but in his attempt to conceal his departure, he had overlooked packing any food. He had traveled a great distance the night before and not thought much of food. Now though, he was famished. Scanning the surrounding area for any form of sustenance turned up nothing at first. The area was quite lifeless, and all he could see were rocks and grass and a few bushes.

He thought to himself that, if God were so majestic, it would be an easy thing for him to supply a simple breakfast. He arose and, carrying his broadsword with him for protection, wandered towards the bushes to see if they would offer anything. As he approached them, he saw a movement in the base of its branches. He dashed forward to find a small rabbit with its legs caught in the trunks of the bush. Its life ended quickly. He had not seen a rabbit for a long time. Then, he realized, the bushes themselves were loaded with gooseberries.

After the meat had been prepared and roasted on his rekindled fire, he went back to the bushes for dessert. The berries were delicious and so in abundance he could not eat them all. The meal was an unexpected surprise and revived his spirits to go on.

Just before noon he reached a small stream and stopped to quench his thirst. As the water level was far below that of the bank, he would have to descend the steep incline first. The best tactic seemed to be to remove his gear and leave it lying on the upper bank rather than risking its loss in the water. Though it was not an ideal solution to the problem, after carefully searching the horizon for any signs of life, he followed through. Arriving at the stream's edge, he first took a long draught of water and then proceeded to fill his water skin. His eyes caught a movement in the little pool, but supposed it to be a fish. Suddenly he felt a pain like a knife pierce his arm. Dropping back against the river bank and losing his water skin, he dragged with him a three-foot-long black water snake still earnestly clutching his arm. His knife slashed through the midsection of the snake, cutting it in half. A moment later the head of the creature released its vise-like grip and fell lifelessly to the ground.

He stared transfixed at the wound. Blood, venom and pus trickled down his arm. He could not remember what to do as his mind was paralyzed with fear. He wiped away some of the gore with his other hand. Then, he remembered his weapons were lying at the top of the bank, so he thought it best to attempt reaching them. He could only use his good arm, but even with that, after climbing a few feet, he stumbled back to the bottom. Realizing his helpless state and loss of self-control, he immediately settled down.

Removing the cord from his now-empty sheath, he managed to tie it about his arm and so cut off the spread of venom. Then he saw his knife lying near the water by his feet. Shimmying back to the water's edge, he cleaned his knife off in the stream and then gashed his arm over each of the two points the snake had penetrated. Much as a child sucks its mother, he began sucking the wound on his arm and spitting the fluid out. This he continued for several minutes until he felt he should quit. He stood up. For a moment, everything reeled around him and then he blacked out.

He opened his eyes. He felt groggy and unable to move, but except for the still stabbing pain in his arm, he seemed fine. His arm was covered with dried blood, which indicated he'd been out for some time. The cord he'd attempted to use to tie off the wound hung loosely about his arm, so he discarded it.

Then he began to wonder about his predicament. He had seen very few snakes in his life and never had known anyone to be bitten. Yet, when it had happened, he felt assurance he had done all the right things as best he could. No one had ever told him what to do and, if they had ever tried, he would have scoffed at them. He could not tell where this knowledge had come from.

He felt of his arm. It felt as hard as a tree limb and was at once numb and throbbing with pain. As he thought about getting up and moving on, he passed out again.

When he woke up, it was beginning to get dark. For a moment, he thought of how he must get a fire burning and get his pack with his blanket. However, he still could not move. He considered that he was at least out of the wind and that, so far, he'd been safe, except for this snake bite. He looked at his wound. The pain was nearly gone, but it was still swollen a great deal. Having become thoroughly rested, he could no longer sleep. He did, however, doze off occasionally as he gazed at the stream, until it became dark.

At some point he finally fell asleep once more. He woke up, startled, in the middle of the night. There were noises of many feet shuffling along the ground above him. He heard the chattering and grunts of the Onoshe. There seemed to be many of them. Then, he could see them in the half-light of the moon, descending the bank and crossing the stream only a few paces from where he lay.

"Oh, dear God," he murmured, "save me."

It was inconceivable that so many should pass right by him and pay him no mind. He counted them until he could count no further. At least a hundred of them proceeded single file towards the mountains. But, for some strange reason, a calmness came upon him and he was no longer afraid. It was several minutes before the last of them retreated over the bank.

Mashua had never seen so many of them at one time. He wondered at its meaning. Could they be organizing for some massive attack? The Denarites always knew that if enough were to attack at one time the two guards at the cave could not defeat them all. The old wooden door could be beat down with not a great deal of effort, as it had weakened through the years. But, they were not headed in that direction. Why hadn't they noticed him? The Onoshe had a keen sense of smell and good eyesight. They were not bright at all. If they had seen his weapons and pack, they probably would not suspect a man close by.

Finally, when it had been quiet for a long time, he decided to chance climbing back up the bank. There was still a little swelling and numbness to his arm, but he could use it. Then, with less effort than expected, he bounded up the bank.

As he suspected, they had found his stuff. The empty food bag was ripped apart, the blanket torn into shreds, all his weapons, save the knife he carried, were gone. He slumped to the ground.

The sky was just beginning to show the first signs of morning; the sun had not yet appeared. The air was cold, colder than by the riverbank, and he wished he had his blanket. He was still tired so he lay down on the bare earth, hoping to get a little more sleep. And he shivered. Eventually, the air warmed up and he was able to think of something besides the cold once more. He started the reverie of why he had been so stupid as to come out here. He got up and walked around, head hung down, wondering if he should head for home.

Suddenly he looked up and grew petrified with fear. Standing before him were three Onoshe. They didn't appear belligerent, but he knew from experience they could not be trusted. They simply stood and stared at him. Carefully, he drew the only weapon he had, figuring if they attacked, he might be able to harm one of them and scare them off. Otherwise, he was no challenge to them at all. They watched him with great interest. He backed away a few feet, they followed, keeping the same five pace span between them and he. He heard a noise behind him and spun around. There stood Magnon.

"Hello, brother," he said. "Don't be afraid. They will not harm you."

"M...Magnon! Oh, I am so glad to see you." He glanced back at the Onoshe. "But what of these? How can you say they will not harm me? These creatures are deadly."

"God has bound them for now. So, they will not harm you."

They embraced. Mashua's eyes were moist with a combination of joy, awe and fear. Magnon waved his hands in the air and yelled at the ape-men to leave. The three turned and slowly walked away, crossing the streambed.

"I guess you probably know," said Mashua. "I'm really confused. What is happening?"

They sat on the ground facing each other. Mashua began to study Magnon more closely. He looked much younger because the lines of anger on his face had disappeared. He moved and talked with much more grace than before when he was used to snapping out a response and was always on the verge of verbally or physically striking out.

"Where can I begin?" Magnon mused. "I'll tell you as much as I can for I must hurry. I was led out here by an angel, a servant of God, as I am. He has given me a great task, but the God who calls us to serve always gives us the strength and ability to do his will."

"But what has he asked you to do?"

"I am tasked with rounding up the Onoshe and leading them out of this valley."

"How? How can you do something like that? They are worse than wild tigers and they are our bitter enemies. Worst of all, they have a thirst for our blood. How can you do this?"

Magnon shook his head. "Actually, in a way, I cannot. It is he that lives inside me that is doing it. I am only a vessel who tries to be obedient."

Mashua looked off in the direction the three Onoshe had gone and then back at Magnon. "Is there actually any hope for these creatures?"

Magnon smiled. "Probably not. I don't know. They seem to have no more knowledge of God than a pack of dogs."

"I have seen though that they bury their dead. Doesn't that show some hope?"

He shook his head. "It seems they bury their dead with their belongings for two reasons. First, because they begin to stink and their carcass calls vermin and also because they really do not understand death. They believe these people to be sleeping, so they give them their stuff and cover them up. They even bury the living when they become sickly. It seems to have nothing to do with an afterlife."

"After you have them out of here, then, you will come back?"

"As you know, Mashua, my greatest desire has always been to destroy these creatures and return to Ifintim. Now, it seems, I will be living alone with them and never see my beloved city again."

"But why? What's the good of that? What do you hope to accomplish?"

Magnon shrugged his shoulders. "I do not know, my brother. All I know is that God has sent me to them. Perhaps my job is to merely keep them from causing trouble. My time draws short. I must leave, but there is one more thing we must do. The woman you love is going to die." Mashua tried to protest. "Please, let me finish. She will die. My mission to free this land of the Onoshe and for the Rasomites to find a home will be destroyed. Our people will rot in a cave and, in a couple of generations, we will die out. Your stubbornness is the key. I can understand because I was stubborn as well. Give yourself fully to God. You are the natural leader of the Denarites and, at Anam's side, you two are predestined to rule this beautiful homeland of ours. Eventually, this kingdom will be renowned throughout the world and forever into the future as far as God allows a future to happen. And also, perhaps, my Lord will be kind enough to allow me to return someday. If that happens, I would like to see his plan unfolding. Please, don't hinder God any longer. He has led you out here. He fed you with the rabbit and the berries when you were hungry. He protected and healed you when the viper bit you. He also calmed your fear when the Onoshe came through last night."

"How did you know these things?" Mashua was amazed.

"God has revealed these things to me. Are you prepared now to decide, or do you still need more information?"

"I am ready."

They bowed their heads together and Mashua prayed. "Almighty God. Yes, I have been stubborn and indecisive. You have continued to show yourself to me and help me, and I have not given you the credit. Please, forgive me. I have also learned how weak and pitiful I am. I cannot save lives. I cannot even take care of myself. So, Lord, what little bit I have, I give to you. If it be your will, let these things my brother, Magnon, has said, come to pass. Also, Father, allow him to forgive me for what I have done to him. Please, Lord, let these things be and accept me into your kingdom."

He felt a sense of relief as though he had been doing a difficult chore and now the work was finally done. He looked up at Magnon. Tears filled Magnon's eyes.

"I do forgive you, my brother. I also will never forget you coming to this place, though you did it in your own strength, because you thought my life was in danger. You risked your own life for mine. I must go, and you must go as well. Too bad, our travels lie in the opposite directions. But, always remember, in a far greater sense, they lie in the same direction and we will, if not in this world, then in the world to come, be together."

They stood up.

"It's time to go," he continued. He looked over Mashua's

shoulder and Mashua turned about. His heart skipped a beat when he saw nearly fifty of the Onoshe assembled, waiting for Magnon. "Your weapons have been taken back to the place where the beaten path ends near the cave."

"But, it's so far," Mashua said. "How could it be done so quickly?"

"They are so fast and so silent. They move like the wind."

They gave each other one last hug and then a handshake. Magnon joined his flock. Mashua cringed, still unused to these creatures, when he saw his brother touch them. They moved towards the bank. Just before disappearing over the edge, Magnon turned back and waved. Then, he was gone.

Mashua stared blankly for a minute and then started crying. After a few minutes, he resigned himself to the loss of his brother and turned towards home.

It was late at night when he reached the cave. As Magnon had told him, his broadsword and other weapons had been deposited in plain view near the entrance. For a moment, he stood and stared at the entrance. Then, bracing himself for the unexpected, he proceeded. It seemed strange to him to be on the outside and not fearful any longer of the Onoshe. Though he had often been out and seen no signs of them, this day it was different. He knew they were gone.

He approached the entrance and casually called out if anyone were around. For a moment, there was no answer. This too was odd as the guards were always quick to respond to returnees and seldom even needed to be notified. He called out again and the door slid open.

Idiptu, a friend of his, dashed through the opening and Mashua knew immediately something exciting was going on inside. His friend grabbed his hand. "Come quickly. It's so wonderful. The women are waking up. All of them together. I've never seen anything like it."

As they hurried along the corridor, they passed Macosena and Didyadim. The women still looked very tired and hungry, but when Mashua actually saw them moving around, he grew even more excited. Just as he came near the entrance of the assembly hall, she appeared.

For a brief moment, they stood and faced each other. Then they embraced, Zoana's lips pressing against one of his broad shoulders. He cupped the palm of his hand under her chin and looked at her again. Her eyes were moist with tears as their lips met and they became unaware of anything else around them.

Epilogue
Ifintim

Mashua stared out across the desolate beach strewn with wreckage and debris that the Onoshe had dumped. Stooping down, he re-laced his sandals. His hopes of dashing through the sand like when he was a child would be perilous and foolish. Stroking his beard he looked up and down the beach for some sign of hope, wondering why he had so anxiously waited for eighteen years to return here.

However, as disturbing as the scene before him appeared, it looked better than the dismal scene of the city behind him. Every street displayed the rot and filth left by years of neglect and Onoshe misuse. A few buildings were gone; having burned uncontrollably to the ground. The ape□men had occupied several, tearing down walls and shelves, defecating on floors and smashing windows. Oddly enough, his parent's home was largely intact, but for the stifling Onoshe aroma that permeated every room. Their house was sandstone and cobblestone and it would be easy, after hauling trash outside for a bonfire, to wash down most of the interior and clean it up.

On a brighter side, finding food would not be a problem. The grain fields, gardens and orchards, though suffering greatly from neglect, still appeared to be more than bountiful enough to support his small group. He had heard of sightings of fish in the bay. Soon, they would begin some organized harvesting and storage.

Life still seemed so unfair. Stifling a lump in his throat, he could feel the tears of his father as he embraced him so long ago when he had been entrusted to Mehi and sent into the hill country. The rest of his family had already perished. By that time, nearly everyone had been lost. A few had escaped by sea, the vast majority staying behind in a stubborn refusal to surrender their land. They had no way of knowing the battle would be lost.

A sarcastic laugh escaped his lips. The Onoshe were gone, so the Denarites had won in the end. However, what an empty victory it seemed. Suddenly he was overcome with hopelessness and fell to his knees. His body shook with uncontrollable sobbing. Then he felt a gentle hand on his shoulder and looked up at the woman he loved.

"This is fine, my darling. You must cry and you are among people who will understand your tears and weep with you."

"God was so kind for sending you to me. Thank you."

"Shall we pray?" Zoana offered.

"I don't know," he responded with a sense of numbness. "It seems we pray at every street corner for our great loss. Eventually, it becomes foolish and just grinds us down. I'm not denying the sadness, though we still have much to be thankful for." He stood up.

"What shall we do?" she asked, taking his hand in hers.

"Well, I suppose we ought to find some of the others. I'm sure everyone is just roaming around finding things to be depressed about. On the other hand, I like being alone with you for a change."

She smiled and pulled him closer. "We do have a lot to be thankful for. You have no less and much more than you had a few weeks ago. It will just be hard trying to get through the memories." He nodded as she continued. "I would be pleased to stay alone with you, but I think we should go back and find the others."

He let out a long sigh. "We need to find a place to stay the night. Somewhere that doesn't stink. Tomorrow we can start organizing a clean up. I want to move back into my parent's home. You'll love it, once it's cleaned up. I just want everything to be nice for you and everything is... well..."

"I know. Everything seems really messed up. There's just one thing I need and that's for you to love me."

He lowered his head and then looked back at her. He started to laugh, and then, the tears began flowing again. She held him close and felt his beard against her lips.

"Loving you will be the easy part," he whispered.

"There's lots more, even better than this one," Oranea whined as he gazed longingly at the crown Bonifa had snatched away from him.

"I don't care! I want this one!" his brother yelled.

"No, you go and get your own!" Oranea shrieked as he pounced onto Bonifa's back.

Bonifa had shoved the crown into the lacy, oversized, silk shirt he had found and put on. As the two boys rolled across the marble floor the crown fell out and clattered across the room. Oranea dove for it with Bonifa on top of him, smashing Oranea's chin into the floor.

Darophil dashed into the room. "What are you two doing this time?"

Bonifa grabbed the crown from Oranea again. Oranea held his hand over his mouth, trying to quell the pain from striking the floor. "Keep the stupid thing," he cried out as he ran from the room with tears in his eyes.

"What did you do this time?" Darophil demanded.

"None of your business!" Bonifa snapped back. "Oh, great," he said, holding the crown out and inspecting it. "That idiot bent it all up. Now I don't want it." He cast it away and it clanged across the floor.

Then Darophil noticed an open trunk with five gold colored crowns and a space where one was missing. "You shouldn't mess with this stuff without asking."

"Oh, shut up!" Bonifa climbed up on a stool, extracted another crown, and placing it on his tiny head, strode out of the room.

Darophil pulled the heavy wooden lid over the case, covering its contents. Then he realized there was no way to secure it. He shook his head and left the room. Outside he found Bonifa sitting on an old stone bench with the oversized crown still on his head, slipping from side to side as he moved. He held a stick in his hand which he waved about as though making orders, though he didn't actually speak. Darophil approached him.

"Where's Oranea?" he asked.

"I don't know." Bonifa said and went back to his play.

"Well, we are supposed to stay together. Where's Ernie?"

"Will you leave me alone!" Bonifa snapped.

"Father told us to all stay with Ernie. Is Oranea hurt?"

"Who cares," he mumbled.

"Get up and help me find our brother!"

"I'm going to hurt you if you don't go away."

They proceeded to have a staring contest until Darophil broke the silence.

"I said we need to find Oranea."

"Why don't you find him and bring him back? Why do you need me?"

"I said get up!" Darophil demanded.

Darophil glanced away and Bonifa took advantage of the moment, lashing out with his stick. Without looking back, Darophil grabbed the stick before it struck him, removed it from his brother's grasp and slapped Bonifa across the face with it. Bonifa shrieked with pain. Darophil broke the stick in two.

"Now get up and help me look!"

They found Oranea at the front of the house sitting on a bench similar to the one in back. Ernie, who had been with them when they entered the mansion, seemed to have vanished. After some discussion they decided to walk back down the street they had come up and attempt to find Ernie, not realizing he was still in the house.

Anam, carrying Comeana, walked astride Mehi, assisting the older man. Paluqua walked on the opposite side. They moved along a massive marble and slate covered area encircling a neglected garden. Around this were several doorways leading into classrooms. The wall was decorated with huge oil paintings, which were positioned between each classroom doorway. Though the paintings had faded over the years, some of the general artwork was still noticeable and superb.

"Sometimes," Mehi explained, stopping occasionally due to a deep, hacking cough, "in the evening I would just walk around this hallway. If it were nice out I might sit in the garden. Then, I would go back to my classroom. I had a little apartment across the way, but I seldom used it. I usually slept on a mat right here in my room."

Though he could not see, he suddenly turned into a doorway and led the others into a classroom. They could see there had once been about thirty desks arranged in rows before Mehi's larger desk near the opposite end of the room. Many shelves of books had completely lined most of the walls of the room. Now, only a few of the desks remained. Some were thrown into one corner, broken and scattered. Most had been thrown through broken windows along with nearly all of the books. The bookshelves had all been pulled down. Oddly, Mehi's desk and chair had been undisturbed. Anam helped him into the chair.

"I can remember where just about everything was and can see it in my mind," he said. "Is the room in good shape?"

Anam glanced around the room, shook his head and prepared to speak.

Paluqua cut him off. "Oh, it's a little messy and some of the windows are broken, but it can be cleaned up as good as new."

Mehi smiled. "Thank you, young lady. And thank you for bringing me here. I never wanted to believe I would come back. It seemed so impossible. The longer I waited, the more I could not believe. You have shown me the impossible." He started coughing again and Anam knelt down beside him, put Comeana down, and held him until he stopped.

"Anyway," he continued, "you have made an old man very happy, but that's not important. You have been the instrument God used to give this people a new hope. Ifintim. Last Hope. Last Chance." He sat silent for a minute and stifled another coughing jag.

"Remind Mashua and the others that when our people first arrived here there were only about a hundred of them. There were no homes. No crops. It was just one shipload of scared people wanting to survive and they had lost everything." He winced from the pain the pressure in his lungs caused. "The first year or two many died from marauding wolves and from exposure to the weather. They, of course, did not give up. Tell him to never give up. And tell him to serve your God and my God." A smile crossed his lips and he grew silent.

Anam leaned over to him. Looking at Paluqua, Anam merely nodded his head as a tear formed in his eye.

The Denarites took the death of Mehi hard. It seemed, though, God wanted them to face all of their past at once. Anam told everyone, when they had gathered together, Mehi's last words of encouragement.

"Let's pray," Togorasom called out. "We have much to mourn over, much to be thankful for, and much to be concerned about. Let's pray over these things in pairs or small groups."

They had gathered together in the mansion Ernie and the

boys had earlier explored. It was one of the largest homes in that part of the city near the beach and it had been left largely unmolested by the Onoshe. It seemed the Onoshe had some sort of respect for splendor. The huge marble dance floor adjoining the garden was large enough for everyone to have ample sleeping space. A fire blazed in the great hearth.

As people came together and prayed for one another, Ernie made his way to Anam.

"I wanted to show you this," he said pulling a piece of paper from his sleeve. "I found it tacked to the wall in the office on the other side of the house." They looked at it together. "It seems to be some sort of letter, but I can't read it."

Anam nodded and suggested Mashua could read it. Looking around he saw Mashua sitting on the steps near him clutching both of Zoana's hands and speaking quietly with her.

"Mashua," said Anam as he approached him. "Let me interrupt. Ernie here has found a letter and it appears to have been written quite recently. I was wondering if you could read it." He handed him the letter.

Mashua looked it over for a minute and looked back at Anam. "It's written in the Denarite dialect they use in the Isles. It's quite interesting and it's dated less than two years ago. Let me read it."

To anyone who may have landed here or survived,

We live in great fear and wonder if we will be able to defend ourselves well enough to return to our ship, The Farragon. The ape☐men are lurking everywhere, though they do not come into this house. This is our fourth and last visit and they continue to use the same successful tactics. After allowing us to believe we have driven them out, they proceed to pick us off one by one.

Our purposes in returning were two-fold. Our glorious mission was to come and see if there were any survivors or if conditions had improved. Obviously, neither of these conditions were met, though there does seem to be a slightly smaller number of the ape-men. Our more greedy cause of return was to pillage and plunder any valuables that could be salvaged. We have found a few items, however, we have lost so many men now we are only eager to be away from this demonic place.

Life in the Isles is not much more satisfactory than here. Evil tyrants of our own nation have taken advantage of their own people. Our island, being separated from the others, thus far has been spared due to our number and superior fighting force. However, most of our neighbors have been enslaved by Coracus and his band.

To all this I say, "Damn the Onoshe and damn Coracus!"

We will attempt to flee here and return home. I am certain our support is much needed.

> Signed respectfully,
> John Dunley
> Captain of the Farragon

"Well," commented Anam, "at least John would be pleased to see the Onoshe gone from here and a handful of survivors. Unfortunately, the good captain might have made our next journey a bit less exciting by telling us from which island he sailed."

"This is very true," said Mashua. "So, what's next."

Anam shrugged. "When I found out we were home I thought we could settle down and relax. However, it seems to me the Isles are ripe for the presence of God."

"Will you name the place that does not need God?" said Mashua. "When you do, we should sail there immediately. You know you shall never truly settle down, and as long as we are joined together by God, we shall also be with you."

About the Author

Larry loves to read and his reading is wide-spread. His favorite fiction writers are Ray Bradbury, Robert Howard and Nicholas Sparks. However, his constant companion is the Bible, which is also his greatest inspiration. He received his Graduate of Theology degree from the Full Gospel College in Coatesville, Pennsylvania. He retired from the United States Air Force having served during the war in Vietnam and the Persian Gulf Conflict. He currently lives in Bentonville, Arkansas with his wife, Yvonne.

Acknowledgements

The book would not have happened except for the encouragement of my wife, Yvonne. She has been an encouragement and an inspiration from the beginning. When I was filled with doubt, she spoke as if the publishing of this book had already happened.

This book would not have been published if not for the actions of my publisher, Selina Ahnert. Her proofreading, knowledge and suggestions made it happen.

Throughout my life it's been the input and encouragement and occasional rescue from a variety of people, mostly female. The list would be very long indeed for all who have made a positive impact on my life. I am thankful for every one of them.